BECAUSE OF THE LOCKWOODS

Persephone Book N° 110
Published by Persephone Books Ltd 2014

Reprinted 2021

First published by John Murray in 1949

© The Estate of Dorothy Whipple

Preface © Harriet Evans

Endpapers taken from 'Chesnut',
a screen-printed cotton designed by Mary Bryan
for Edinburgh Weavers in 1949 © V & A Images

Typeset in ITC Baskerville by
Keystroke, Wolverhampton

Printed and bound in Germany by
GGP Media GmbH, Poessneck

9781910263006

Persephone Books Ltd
59 Lamb's Conduit Street
London WC1N 3NB
020 7242 9292

www.persephonebooks.co.uk

BECAUSE OF THE LOCKWOODS

by

DOROTHY WHIPPLE

with a new preface by

HARRIET EVANS

PERSEPHONE BOOKS
LONDON

FOR CEDRIC AND PHILIP

PREFACE

The lawyer chose and lit a cigar. Hunter's cigars were always good, he remembered. Before closing the cabinet, Mr Lockwood took his own case from his pocket and packed it to capacity. He wished he could have got more in. He was about to do a good deal of work for Hunter's widow for nothing. Why shouldn't he recoup himself a little from Hunter's cigars?

If, like me, you are one of the thousands of readers who discovered Dorothy Whipple through Persephone's reissues, you know well that feeling of resigned bewilderment suffusing the sigh of satisfaction you utter after finishing one of her novels. Why isn't she better known? Why has she been so neglected, when every time someone picks her up for the first time they almost always become a fan? (I would love to see research of this kind carried out: which authors have the highest read-another-one rate. I think she would lead the pack.) Why is she not acclaimed more widely, when so many of her less talented contemporaries are still in print? In one way it is rather nice, being in such an exclusive club: you know when you meet a fellow Whipple fan that you have met a new friend, and are guaranteed a wholly enjoyable conversation, albeit one overlaid with the aforementioned resigned bewilderment. Georgette Heyer fans were in just such a position ten years ago. Not now. Now they are jubilant, cocky, even (I am one of them. These are happy days for those of us who seriously considered calling their daughters Venetia or Sophy).

Flippancy aside, the case does need to be made for Dorothy Whipple's entry into the pantheon of great British novelists of the twentieth century. Not just because she can so deftly spin a cocoon of a story around you, swiftly rendering you transfixed (the art of which is severely, crucially underestimated by reviewers and readers alike) but because she wrote books quite unlike any others, for all their seeming 'ordinariness'. One might say the time is long overdue for a Barbara Pym-style rehabilitation. In a famous *Times Literary Supplement* article of 1977, Pym – by then out of favour for over a decade, her novels rejected by her long-time publisher as dated and unfashionable – was nominated by both Lord David Cecil and Philip Larkin as the most underrated writer of the twentieth century, the only living author to be so singled out. The effect on her career was immediate: *A Quartet in Autumn,* which had languished without a publisher for years, was swiftly acquired and subsequently shortlisted for the Booker Prize. Now, with her work being reissued, Pym has achieved that rare (and much-deserved) triple: literary acclaim, longevity, popular success.

I am as ambitious for Dorothy Whipple. Her scope is larger, her own ambition grander, the results hugely satisfying, often thrilling, and there is something about her clear, elegant prose which is the sweetest balm to a reader's mind, frazzled after a long day. For me, she is more substantial a writer than someone like Pym or Elizabeth Taylor (both of whose novels I nevertheless adore) in not merely that aforementioned ambition, but in her control of material and characters, her eye for detail and most importantly, the mirror she holds up to twentieth-century England showing good and bad, light and dark and, crucially, the lives of normal people, where she makes the ordinary extraordinary. To me, it seems obvious. However, as we shall see, the obstacles in Dorothy Whipple's way are not inconsiderable.

Before I was a full-time novelist I worked in publishing as an editor of what is curiously known nowadays as commercial women's fiction. Perhaps the most important part of my job was to create a specific vision for each one of my authors, a bespoke package that would sum up the prospect of the book on the crowded shelf for the hovering consumer. Often – all too often – it was fiendishly difficult to accomplish. I think about this process often when considering the Whipple question because, depressing though the idea is, it obviously played some part in the decline in her fortunes since her death.

Firstly, titles, which are so important in the overpublished fiction market. Dorothy Whipple suffers because the titles of her novels, while more than serviceable, are not especially memorable. You may cluck and say it doesn't matter, and I wish it didn't. But *Love in a Cold Climate*, *Excellent Women*, *Brideshead Revisited,* each one published in the era in which she wrote, are all instantly memorable because of their titles. (*How Green Was My Valley*, *The Stars Look Down*, *Gone with the Wind* are all sweeping sagas of varying grit, also blessed with intriguing titles.) *Someone at a Distance*, often said to be her best book, doesn't have a title which reflects the sheer rage and anguish and emotion you will feel at the disintegration of the North family. And with my commercial hat still on, I wonder if the name Whipple doesn't help the cause (with apologies to current Whipples). Her maiden name was Stirrup, not especially transporting either. But 'Dorothy Whipple' doesn't match the books she writes. It's faintly drab, slightly silly. It shouldn't matter, but again, subconsciously, there is a good deal of the snob in the British reader. Daphne du Maurier is, for these purposes, a good name. A name that matches the books you're reading, a name of mystery, exotic, rather grand.

Added to which, the worlds about which Whipple wrote so perceptively and engagingly were always firmly rooted in her own life and interests and surroundings, and so we arrive at what is for me the central issue. The world of literary London, for want of a better expression, is today perhaps more sexist and snobbish (especially geographically snobbish), almost unbelievably, than it was when she was writing (the aforementioned idea of 'commercial women's fiction' didn't exist as a genre then, of course. It was Fiction, or Non-Fiction). When you read *Random Commentary*, Dorothy Whipple's fascinating compilation of notebooks which is a kind of diary, writer's aide-memoire, and private journal to air grievances, you are initially surprised and then heartened by the ease with which she was accepted into the highest intellectual circles of the Thirties: firstly by her publishers at John Murray, then by the likes of JB Priestley (who showed her true kindness, writing encouraging letters, talking to her at parties when she knew no one), and HG Wells and finally, she was rapturously reviewed by, amongst others, Hugh Walpole. In the first half of the twentieth century, despite the horrors of two world wars, there was an appetite for the depiction of solid, normal lives one doesn't see now. It is a great shame, because I think it is something readers want. Look at the intensely moving reaction to the death of Sue Townsend and the warmth with which the Adrian Mole diaries are remembered for their depiction of an ordinary lower-middle class family in middle England, despite Adrian's pretensions to grandeur. Look at one of the most acclaimed British love stories of the twentieth century: Laura and Alec in *Brief Encounter* are not glittering socialites, they are deeply normal. It is the mundanity of their lives – the train, the smut in the eye, the Boots lending library visits – which makes their affair so very romantic and poignant.

Dorothy Whipple is at the centre of that tradition, but the cultural tide of opinion is, these days, against her. Yet her novels are about nothing if not normal people. The most glamorous, one could say, are the Marwoods and their crumbling home in *The Priory,* and even they fall far short of *Downton Abbey* standards. Her plots contain no Russian spies or world-weary London beauties, yet can be summed up with such simple, yet intriguing, brevity you know you must be in safe hands. A husband betrays his family for a younger woman. A blackguard defrauds an innocent man. An ambitious young woman fights for an independent career. A rich family patronises and defrauds a poor one: these are everyday occurrences yet, as we all know, there is nothing so extraordinary as real life. Depressingly, such topics are thought of today (in an age where boys wear any clothes and colour and girls are given tutus and pink sequins from the earliest age and where Jane Austen is seen as a 'girls' author') as 'women's fiction'. I suspect that is also why Whipple has been disregarded by the literary mainstream: we still live in a sexist world and, in addition, one where interest in and appreciation of writing from the North of England is undervalued. And she had no similar contemporaries to share the burden: Barbara Pym was anointed by men (and went to Oxford). Dodie Smith escaped the North and became a glamorous girl-about-town playwright in London, living it up in Marylebone and California and playing with the boys (Huxley, Isherwood et al). Du Maurier was a law unto herself. Dorothy Sayers dressed like a man, behaved like a man, and wrote detective fiction. Elizabeth Taylor and Elizabeth Jane Howard, both authors of traditionally Home Counties stories about the upper-middle class, were both accepted into that world but patronised by it (Howard's death in early 2014, by contrast to Townsend's, seemed to be an excuse for newspapers and even *The Bookseller* to run through a potted biography of her husbands, not a bibliography of her work).

Because of the Lockwoods is, as with every one of Dorothy Whipple's novels, a pleasure to read. She is, when one breaks it down, an intensely moral writer – we long for the pompous, the dishonest and cruel to be cut down, and for the plucky, the hardworking, the passionate, to be raised up. But it is one of her greatest strengths that morality never appears to drive the plot: always character. She never preaches, merely lets us think she is observing and conveying information. We, the readers, are the ones who whip ourselves into a fever of partisan outrage as the story progresses; she appears cool and distant (the real *Someone at a Distance*, perhaps). There is something about the clarity of expression and calm curiosity of Whipple's prose which is hugely pleasing. She never employs excess to drive her point home but uses each word carefully and simply: her description of the secret spot outside the prying, small-minded French town where her heroine Thea meets Jacques, a local French boy, is beautiful in its economy: 'To the left, through the trees, the river slid, full and silent.'

Then there is the readability factor: perhaps that is what mostly damages her reputation, the fact that she is so damned unputdownable. The thinking is the same as it has been for years: shouldn't real literature be *hard* to read? The treatment of the Hunter family by the affluent Lockwoods in *Because of the Lockwoods* rouses one to rage and a deep sense of hopelessness. You are desperate to read on, to know that good, as personified by the heroine, Thea, and her family will prevail; that the world is not as dark as Whipple shows us it can be so often.

This curious mix of rage at injustice and pulsing, engrossing storytelling is rooted in Whipple's deep sense of right and wrong, yet Whipple the novelist has learnt, as we have seen, to separate herself from it. But it is interesting to note that it permeates *The Other Day*, the autobiography of her early life. A good example would be when, as a young girl, she understands from her mother that she and her siblings may have the rest of the day off school when they lose a tooth. That evening young Dorothy works at her latest loose tooth until it comes out, then rushes downstairs. 'Look! I pulled it out myself,' she tells her mother. Yet, despite Dorothy's cajoling, her mother says she's a big girl now and therefore must go to school the next day.

'She left me. I stood among the sheets, betrayed, and by my mother. Father was always doing that sort of thing, but mother – no! it was dreadful.'

The emotion in this paragraph is so touching. Of hot anger and girlish stupidity and also real drive towards something else!

'By and by I dried my eyes on the sheet and went to school. There was nothing else to be done. But I think a little iron entered into my soul.'

All over a tooth, but she had been promised a day off. Writing all those years later, the injustice is still keenly felt. Yet in her novels, she never betrays herself. She leads us down the path, but we take the place of young Dorothy; the grown-up Dorothy is in control now.

Because of the Lockwoods was Whipple's penultimate novel, published in 1949. Just after the publication of *Greenbanks* years earlier in 1932, she had written in her journal:

Home again, thinking about a novel – my fourth.
I don't know whether to write one called They Knew

Mr Knight or one about a young girl in France and England. They Knew Mr. Knight attracts me because the title sums up exactly what and why all is going to happen to this family, but the youth and character of the girl in the other idea attract me too. I wonder which I shall do in the end? No longer do I dash into a novel light-heartedly. I know now what a long hard labour it is.

Greenbanks and *High Wages* had been great successes for her, especially the former, which had topped the bestseller lists, and sold around the world, and she was becoming more certain of her powers as a novelist. But at that time she elected to write *They Knew Mr Knight*, not returning to 'the youth and character of the girl in the other idea' until after the Second World War. The result, *Because of the Lockwoods*, is one of my favourite of her novels. The story is deceptively simple: the entanglement of two families in a northern town called Aldworth. One, the Lockwoods, wealthy and powerful, in a position to patronise and help the second family, the poor Hunters, who have been left fatherless with a weak, ineffectual mother.

The Lockwoods are the kind of family everyone knows, which is why they're so deliciously enjoyable to read about: the ones who have money, throw opulent parties, who are sleek and overfed and utterly confident of their place in the world. They genuinely do believe they're better than everyone else. The twins, Bee and Muriel, are delicious first-class monsters: Whipple shows that their father's pride in and love for his children is not, as he and others would suppose, something that makes him a 'good man', but instead into someone self-centred, maniacally egotistic even. He embodies the idea, clearly so abhorrent to Whipple (though which many might recognise in some parents today) that his family simply must come before anyone else's, that their world is the only one that matters.

Though the thudding heart of the story draws the reader inexorably along, hoping for the meek to conquer the strong, it is a surprising book in many ways, not least for its subversive portrayal of family – the children are often the adults, the parents the untrustworthy, unwise ones, and Whipple makes it clear that what we call today the nuclear family is not the answer to happiness. In many ways, in its use of France as a place that offers an alternative prism through which to view human behaviour, and the mirror it holds up to the English mid-twentieth century family, it adumbrates Whipple's next, and final novel, *Someone At A Distance*, about the destruction by one person of an ordinary marriage. *Someone At A Distance*, the first of Dorothy Whipple's novels to be reissued by Persephone Books, is an extraordinary read, showing her at the height of her powers, in masterly control of her material, the anger that sometimes seeped through about the case for right and wrong, hidden so completely that we are utterly in thrall to the story of the normal, happy North family and the awful Louise Lanier.

Thus it is interesting to consider whether, when writing *Because of the Lockwoods*, Whipple may have, consciously or not, been laying out the groundwork for *Someone at a Distance*, her last, and perhaps greatest, novel. I have a soft spot for the Lockwoods, the Hunters, and their story. To me *Because of the Lockwoods*, while not perfect, is truly memorable for the remarkable character of Thea, who may be my favourite of all of Dorothy Whipple's heroines. She is a unique young woman: passionate, angry, quick to take offence, bitterly sensitive to the unhappiness brought upon her mother by Mr Lockwood's begrudging handling of Mrs Hunter's financial affairs, his casual cruelty and disinterest which grinds the family down over the years after their father's early death. She demands a proper education for herself at the start of the novel. She alone sees clearly that Mr Lockwood is dishonest, that he does not do his best by them. And it is Thea who, in a wonderfully honest depiction of female sexuality, is unashamed of her feelings when, having contrived to get herself sent to France with the Lockwoods for a year, she is caught kissing Jacques, a local boy. France, and the town of Villeneuve, is beautifully conveyed, and wrought absolutely into the symbol of small-town repression and hypocrisy. Thea is gloriously, angrily unrepentant when challenged by the furious Madame La Directrice: '"I've done nothing wrong," said Thea. To have to say it at all galled her beyond bearing.'

What may be most satisfying about the book is how the climax is reached as a result of character. For what at first seem like insignificant actions taken over tiny things grow over time: it is the butterfly effect, flapping gently at first and then hard and fast through the story so that by the end good truly has triumphed. Both small-town, small-minded prejudices and the Lockwoods are banished, and the Hunters, if they choose to, will emerge triumphant. I am not entirely sure the final scene is the most successful conclusion to one of Dorothy Whipple's novels, but the journey there has been so – in the word constantly used by Whipple fans to describe her books – satisfying, that I can forgive her.

When I read Dorothy Whipple I think often of my granny, a kind, funny woman from Kendal in Lancashire, who trained as a nurse in Manchester, and who along with my granddad, an erudite, quietly-spoken Methodist minister from Crewe, seemed to think only of others, of quiet, respectable, living, of family and of keeping that which is important close by. She was not worthy, or disapproving of anyone: she simply tried to enjoy the life she had been given, and be a good person. I think she was one of the women Whipple wrote for: the silent millions who formed the backbone of this country in the last century. As Sir John Murray wrote to Dorothy Whipple, after reading *They Were Sisters:*

'You have a wonderful power of taking quite ordinary people in quite unromantic surroundings, in their normal ways of life and making them live and press themselves on your readers' minds in a way that really grips.'

But it is more than that: it is twentieth-century British fiction at its very best. See you on the barricades.

Harriet Evans
London, 2014

BECAUSE OF THE LOCKWOODS

CHAPTER ONE

I

Mrs Lockwood decided to invite Mrs Hunter and her children to Oakfield for New Year's Eve. It would be one way of getting the food eaten up. There was always so much of it during Christmas week, thought Mrs Lockwood with a sense of repletion. In spite of the large appetites of the household – herself, her husband, the three girls and the maids – the larder would be littered with the wrecks of turkey and chicken, with great dishes of trifle, a spoonful out here, a spoonful out there, with broken jellies and rather damaged bon-bons. They must be eaten up by somebody, and by whom better than the Hunters, who certainly never saw such things elsewhere, since Oakfield was the only house of its kind they went to nowadays?

How a widow, if poor, falls out, thought Mrs Lockwood with a shudder. She devoutly hoped she herself would never be a widow. Life without William was unthinkable. Though of course, William being a lawyer, and knowing everything there was to know about the disposition of money, would never leave her and the girls in the dreadful state in which Mrs Hunter found herself when her husband died, and in which she had remained, poor thing, ever since.

But they should all come to Oakfield on New Year's Eve, thought Mrs Lockwood benevolently. The children should take sweets home and perhaps she could hunt up a blouse for Mrs Hunter. The blue silk probably; she'd really had all the wear she could get out of it. Yes, Mrs Hunter could have that. They must all come and enjoy themselves.

Besides, the twins wanted to give a performance, and, fond mother though she was, Mrs Lockwood hesitated to inflict such on anybody but the Hunters.

The twelve-year-old twins, Bee and Muriel, wanted to emulate their friend, Angela Harvey. When Angela gave plays in the music room at Firbank Hall, she wouldn't allow the twins to appear with her; they simply couldn't act, she said. So Bee and Muriel determined to give a concert of their own. Not a play like Angela's, but a mixed performance where they could show all they could do.

So their mother decided to have the maids in and ask old Nanny and her husband. These, together with the Hunters, would make up quite an audience and one that could be counted on to show appreciation of practically anything.

The drawing room at Oakfield was made ready. Small, hard chairs, brought in from other parts of the house, were ranged in rows. The twins insisted on seating their audience on small, hard chairs to make it more like a real concert. But in the forefront of these they placed two armchairs for their parents. For as with the parents on this occasion, the children's pleasure came first and the guests' a bad second, so their parents' pleasure and comfort came first with the twins. To them, their parents were the Royalty attending a command performance, and the guests were just to fill the chairs. To the Lockwood family, the guests hardly mattered and yet were a necessity.

The Hunters came from the cold night outside into this warm, flower-scented room, the widow and her children, Molly at thirteen, Martin twelve and Thea nearing ten years of age. As a family, they had rather a forlorn air; they gave the impression of clustering together for safety. Fate, by removing the father seven years before, had left them defenceless.

At the moment they seemed bemused by the impact of so much light, warmth and magnificence all at once, and in contrast to their pale looks, wondering grey eyes and diffident advance, the Lockwood children appeared bouncingly self-confident and highly coloured. Their hair was bright gold, their cheeks were pink, their muslin frocks snowy white as they flashed about the drawing room seating their audience.

The twins, programme importantly in hand, seated the Hunters, the maids, their old nurse and her husband, but they couldn't make their little sister Clare sit anywhere.

'Clare, sit down. Sit down, Clare. You're spoiling everything,' they cried, pursuing her.

But Clare, on the point of being caught, evaded them by calling out: 'Mummy and Daddy are coming. They're coming!'

The twins rushed to the piano to strike up the triumphal duet and Mr and Mrs Lockwood, smiling indulgently, advanced to their places. Muriel shot a delighted glance over her shoulder to see them playing their parts so well and in consequence missed a bar, for which Bee dug her in the ribs with her elbow.

The duet continued. Under the piano stool, the narrow crossed soles of Muriel's new dancing-pumps showed like two sponge-finger biscuits. It was Bee who attended to the pedals. The twins were bossy girls, but Bee was even bossier than Muriel and as such had secured the pedals.

Mrs Lockwood, without turning fully round, inclined backwards and said graciously, but with a touch of stateliness: 'Are you all right there?'

Mrs Hunter bent eagerly forward.

'Quite, thank you,' she said. 'We're very comfortable.'

'Sssh,' hissed Bee loudly from the piano.

Mrs Hunter put her finger to her lip to chide it for this interruption and exchanged smiles with Mrs Lockwood, who then turned smilingly to the front again.

From this time forward, Mrs Hunter, looking somehow like a delicate plant drooping from lack of support, gave unremitting attention, wholly unmerited, to the twins' performance. She gave it from a mixture of courtesy, simplicity and a wish to repay her hosts and benefactors, the Lockwoods.

It was so nice of Mrs Lockwood to allow them to share this intimate family party. When Mrs Lockwood said that the Hunters were the only ones she wanted to invite for this evening, Mrs Hunter believed her and felt a glow of gratitude.

And it was so good for the children to see how life, in their mother's opinion, should be lived. If it were not for these invitations to Oakfield, the children would form their opinion of the world as seen from Byron Place and that, their mother considered, would have been a calamity. She looked upon invitations to Oakfield not only as a pleasure, but as a form of education for the children, and she innocently comported herself, when there, in such a way as to assure their continuance. She beamed upon the performing twins now because she knew it would please Mrs Lockwood, and she hoped, if he noticed it, it would also please Mr Lockwood. If there was any way to placate Mr Lockwood, she knew it must be through his family.

When Richard Hunter died, William Lockwood had unwillingly taken upon himself the rôle of adviser to the widow. The fact that he had secretly profited, in one comparatively trifling matter, from so doing, did not incline him to suffer her more gladly. At the beginning he had laid himself out to do what he could for her. But he considered he had worked off his debt to her long ago and did not trouble now to hide his opinion that Mrs Hunter and her children were an unmitigated nuisance.

II

Neither Richard Hunter nor his wife were native to Aldworth. After taking Architecture at Cambridge, Richard came to the town as junior partner to a friend of his father, a Mr Dixon. When old Mr Dixon died, Richard continued the practice. On a visit to Sussex, he fell in love with the daughter of a doctor. When he brought his Constance to see where she was going to live, she was horrified by the ugliness of the first northern manufacturing town she had ever seen, and was only reconciled to the idea of having to live in it by the sight of the house Richard proposed to buy for them on The Heights, the pleasantest district in Aldworth.

'You might be miles from any town here,' he said, as they stood in the empty drawing room of Hill House. 'And look at that noble country!' He swept his arm at the fells and plains below, rolling without interruption thirty miles to the sea. 'You can't deny that it's superb, darling.'

She agreed that it was superb and kept it to herself that she would have preferred a more comfortable outlook. Something more sheltered and sheltering. Her innate timidity needed protection, even from Nature. But so long as he was there, she thought, taking his arm and smiling up at him, everything would be all right. And the house was charming.

'But isn't it extraordinary,' she marvelled again, 'that The Heights should be owned by one of Father's old patients? I do think it's odd that Sir Thomas should own land in this part of the country.'

It was difficult to get a footing on The Heights. Old Sir Thomas Broadbent, although he lived in London and never came near Aldworth, was singularly averse to selling land. There were many covetable building plots, fields, or little woods, dotted about The Heights that people would have paid almost anything for; but old Sir Thomas was adamant. The only hope of getting a house was for someone to die, and Richard Hunter counted it a piece of luck that the tenant of Hill House should die just at the moment most convenient to Richard Hunter, if not to the tenant himself.

Richard had come into a matter of ten thousand pounds at his father's death, and he used part of this money to buy Hill House and to furnish it lavishly in an attempt to make up to Constance by beauty at home for the ugliness she shrank from in the town. There they settled and there, across the paddock, which William Lockwood had tried in vain to buy from old Sir Thomas, stood Oakfield, where the Lockwood children were making their appearance in the world at approximately the same times as the Hunter children.

This fact and the proximity of their houses drew Mrs Hunter and Mrs Lockwood together. Mrs Lockwood was a bustling young matron who went about a good deal, but Mrs Hunter was wholly taken up with her husband and children and her garden. Mrs Lockwood was her only friend, though even she was not an intimate one.

When he bought Hill House, Richard Hunter was a successful architect with every prospect of making a good income. But the First World War upset his plans. He was refused for the Army because of an old injury to his back; and for the four years of war he kicked his heels in what amounted almost to idleness. Building was at a standstill. Not only had he no work, but he had to live on his capital, and it was with relief and energy that he turned, when peace came, to make up for lost time.

But within a year of the end of the war, he was dead. He died suddenly of appendicitis.

In his will, scrawled in his last moments, he left 'everything' to his wife. But everything proved to be almost nothing. He died possessed of no more than the house, his life insurance policy and a few shares.

Constance Hunter was not the sort of woman who stiffened to meet the blows of fate. She was crushed by the loss of her husband and bewildered by the responsibilities thrust upon her. Richard was dead. He was gone; and now they told her that everything that had so far made up her life must go too: the house, security, all the plans for the children, everything.

It was while she was trying to sort out her husband's private papers one afternoon that Mrs Lockwood called. At the sight of the widow's helplessness and the tears blistering bills, receipts and share certificates, she was moved to make the offer that had such far-reaching effects on the lives of both families.

'Don't try to deal with those papers,' she said. 'Let me get William to see to them for you. Without charge, you know. Just as a friend. Leave them to William.'

'It's the children,' said Mrs Hunter incoherently. 'I don't know how I'm going to manage for the children.'

'I'm sure William will act as guardian,' comforted Mrs Lockwood. 'Unofficially, of course, since you have been appointed their guardian. But he'll help you.'

'But he's always so busy,' wept Mrs Hunter.

'I know,' said Mrs Lockwood. 'But he'll do it if I ask him. I know he will. Now, let's put these papers away, and you come and sit down with me.'

She swept the papers into the odd little bag from which they had been taken.

'I'll get William to come round and straighten everything out for you,' she promised.

III

It was one thing to make promises on William's behalf and quite another to get him to keep them. He didn't want to undertake Mrs Hunter's affairs. He didn't want to do anything that did not advance his own. William Lockwood had laid his strong, hairy hands to life and meant to wring from it the best of everything for his wife, his girls and himself. He meant to get to the top of his profession, make a lot of money quickly and live in style and comfort. He had therefore no time for unprofitable work.

'You shouldn't run me into these things,' he said testily, as if Effie made a habit of it, which she did not. She was as concerned to advance the Lockwood family as he was. But she had been moved by Mrs Hunter's distress.

'If you only knew,' William went on. 'It takes me all my time to make the money for us to live as we do. Even with my practice. We spend an awful lot. Oh, it's all right,' he said, seeing apprehension flash into her pretty, plump face. 'I expect to spend a lot of money. It pays in the end. But time is money to me and I don't want to waste any of it on Mrs Hunter. Besides, she's such a vague, fluttering creature I've no patience with her.'

'Oh, William, I'm so sorry for her,' said Effie. 'She looked so helpless going through those papers and there were so few of them. I couldn't help thinking you'd finish them off in about five minutes.'

William laughed shortly at her ignorance. If it had been simply a matter of obtaining probate and winding up a trifling estate he wouldn't have minded, he said. But Effie seemed to have saddled him with the children, and if he once showed willing, goodness knew what wouldn't be piled upon him. He'd be committed to years of niggling, unprofitable trouble.

'But if you've promised, I suppose I'll have to do it,' he said grudgingly. 'It would look bad if it got about that I'd refused.'

On the other hand, he reflected, scraping his dark chin with his hand, it would look good if he did help her. He knew he had the reputation of being a hard man. They said in the town that no one ever got the better of William Lockwood. When litigants found that he was to be against them, they often preferred to give up and settle out of court. William decided that it wouldn't do any harm to show himself doing something for nothing for a change.

'All right,' he said, 'I'll go and see her.'

Effie kissed him. She wouldn't have liked to go back to the sad house and tell the widow that William could do nothing for her.

'It's very good of you, dear,' she said. 'And you must just see to it that you don't spend any more time on her than you can help.'

'Trust me,' said William tersely.

'Yes,' said Effie soothingly and putting coffee and brandy beside him on his desk – he often worked in the library after dinner – she rustled out to telephone to Mrs Hunter that William, although it meant a great deal of trouble for so busy a man, would undertake her affairs.

Mrs Hunter thanked her with fervour. This telephone conversation put the relations of the two friends on their new footing. From this time forward Mrs Hunter was unceasingly grateful and Mrs Lockwood conscious that so she ought to be.

CHAPTER TWO

I

'I shall have to see Mrs Hunter this morning before I go to the office, blast it,' said William Lockwood. 'I haven't a minute on any other day this week.'

'Oh, dear,' said Effie with self-reproach, handing him his hat. The twins – the children always came down from the nursery to see him off – were ready with his briefcase.

'Why is Daddy cross, Mummy?' asked Bee.

'Because he has to do a lot of work for Mrs Hunter, darling, and it's a great nuisance for him.'

'It is,' said William with emphasis.

'See, Clare wants to kiss you,' said Effie, taking the baby from Nanny's arms and holding her up. She knew Clare would soothe him. William's face cleared at once.

'Goodbye, pet,' he said. 'Goodbye, Daddy's girl.'

'Kiss us, Daddy,' clamoured the twins.

'Yes, yes, I'm coming to you,' said William, bending indulgently.

They clung to his neck and had to be detached by Nannie.

'Don't choke your father, Miss Bee,' she admonished.
'That will do,' said William. 'I'm off. Goodbye.'
'Goodbye!' they chorused. 'Goodbye, Daddy.'

As he skirted the paddock on his way to Hill House, the lawyer ran over his connections with Richard Hunter. He hadn't had much to do with him, they hadn't had much in common. But their wives were friendly, their children played together, they had lived side by side. Some months before, William Lockwood had lent Richard Hunter three hundred pounds. Mr Lockwood lent money; he was that kind of lawyer. He thought, at the time, that Hunter wanted to have a flutter on the Stock Exchange and was grimly amused, since Hunter was obviously not cut out for that sort of thing.

When he borrowed the money Richard Hunter had given a promissory note, but he repaid the loan surprisingly quickly. He walked across the paddock one night after dinner, as much in a hurry to repay as he had been to borrow. Since the promissory note was at the office, William Lockwood had made out a receipt. It was characteristic of the dead man that he had not troubled to secure the return of the promissory note later, and William Lockwood had not troubled to let him have it. Why should he? It was Hunter's concern, not his. The promissory note was still in his office.

Mr Lockwood reached Hill House, rang and was conducted by a maid to the drawing room. The morning sunlight lay over the pale gold carpet, the gold brocade curtains, the black and gold furniture – genuine Louis XIV, according to Effie. All this, he supposed, would have to go and it wouldn't be easy to sell. It wasn't in Aldworth taste.

The door opened and the widow came in. Mr Lockwood kept his tenderer feelings strictly for home use. He hadn't any to spare for outside. Besides, he was used to bereavement. He saw a lot of other people's grief. So the change in Mrs Hunter's once flower-like face did not move him. After one sharp glance he avoided looking at her, and he increased the usual brusqueness of his manner so that she shouldn't begin to cry or otherwise waste his precious time.

'Good morning,' he said. 'I understand that my wife has engaged for me to see your husband's papers.'

'It's so very good of you, Mr Lockwood,' began the widow, tears flooding her blue eyes.

'Now I think we'll agree to cut all that out, Mrs Hunter,' he interrupted. 'As you know, I'm a busy man. I have very little time this morning, and I would like, please, to see your husband's papers as quickly as possible.'

'I'll fetch them,' she said. 'They're all together in an old bag that belonged to my father, who was a doctor, you know. There were never many papers and this old bag just kept them together. I'll fetch it. In the meantime, will you have a cigarette? Or perhaps a cigar? Do you smoke cigars in the morning?'

'I smoke cigars any time,' he said.

She opened the small ebony cabinet standing on the massive table and went out of the room.

The lawyer chose and lit a cigar. Hunter's cigars were always good, he remembered. Before closing the cabinet, Mr Lockwood took his own case from his pocket and packed it to capacity. He wished he could have got more in. He was about to do a good deal of work for Hunter's widow for nothing. Why shouldn't he recoup himself a little from Hunter's cigars? He walked about the room, smoking. But not peaceably. He wanted to be off, to get to his own office. He was restive and fretted, as always when hindered.

William Lockwood had an air of importance. Already, at forty-three, he had an incipient paunch – Effie fed him too well – but he was tall and carried his weight with dignity. He had black hair, a full aggressive lower lip, and his cheeks and eyes were shot with thread-like red veins.

He stopped in his perambulations of the Hunter drawing-room to look from the windows at his own house below, and even as he looked, his children appeared in the drive on their way out for their morning walk; Clare in her pram waving the ring with bells he had bought for her only yesterday, the twins running sturdily alongside. They made such a pretty picture that tears came to his eyes.

When people noticed how Mr Lockwood's eyes watered at the sight of his children, they said that it proved that he couldn't be half so hard a man as he was made out to be.

The children disappeared, and their father's eyes fell to the paddock below.

'If only I could get hold of that paddock,' he thought, his face sharpening again. 'The children could have a pony. They'd love it, bless them. Damn it, if I won't write to old Broadbent again. Or even go up to see him.'

Mrs Hunter came back into the room.

'I'm so sorry to have kept you, Mr Lockwood,' she said. 'But I was called to the telephone.'

She carried an old-fashioned little bag, with stiff sides and a handle at the top. He took it from her with impatience and put it on the table. The cigar jutting from his mouth, he plunged his hands into the bag and brought out bundles and rolls of papers, passbooks, miscellaneous scraps. It was evident that Richard Hunter had not been a methodical man. Mr Lockwood held the bag upside down over the table and slapped the sides to make sure that everything was out. A loose flap of lining hung down, but nothing else emerged. He thrust the lining back into place and examined the interior.

'Nothing else there. You're sure there are no more papers anywhere?'

'None in the house. There may be a few at the bank.'

'I'll go through these here,' he said, sitting down at the table.

'Shall I go through them with you?' she asked timidly.

'No, thank you.'

'It's so good of you, Mr Lockwood. I wish I were of more help to you.'

'I don't need help. Just leave it to me, will you?'

Seeming almost to wring her hands at the thought of being such a nuisance to him, she went out of the room and closed the door.

Mr Lockwood gave the papers a preliminary shuffle. Nothing of any value here, apparently. He looked at his watch and swore under his breath. Half-past ten and he wasn't out of sight of his own house yet. He sighed and turned to the papers in earnest.

In the room the French clock ticked delicately, the curtains moved gently at the windows.

He picked papers up, put them down, made notes.

Suddenly, taking a small plan from within a roll of paper, his face sprang into life and interest. He put down his cigar and with both hands spread the plan flat on the table.

'Good Lord!' he breathed.

He snatched up the roll that had enclosed the plan and spread that out. It was an agreement for the purchase of the paddock. Richard Hunter had got the paddock he himself had failed to buy.

He sat back in his chair, his teeth on his lip. Richard Hunter had got the paddock. He forgot Hunter was dead. He thought of him as a living man who had got the better of him. To get that paddock . . . How on earth had he done it?

He took up the agreement again and examined the date. So Richard Hunter had not only bought the paddock, he had bought it with the money he himself had lent him. Never, said William Lockwood, had he been so sold in his life. That he should have been made to provide the money for another man to buy the piece of land he would have given anything for! He positively tittered with chagrin and astonishment. How on earth did Hunter persuade old Broadbent to part with it?

He got up and went to the window to look down on the coveted plot. There it lay, yellow with buttercups, laced with cow-parsley, giving no sign that it had slid from the possession of one man to another.

'I'll be damned!' said William Lockwood, and strode to the bell.

The commotion of his feelings communicated itself to the

wires. The widow came hurrying. She appeared in the doorway, looking startled.

'Is there something wrong, Mr Lockwood?'

From this time on, poor Mrs Hunter was always to feel that something must be wrong. Something else must have given way, or gone wrong somewhere, something she didn't know about, or had overlooked, or had unwittingly brought about. Richard's support removed, life was henceforward to be like this: an insecure, anxious, quicksand affair.

William Lockwood left the bell and walked towards her. His chin sunk, he said accusingly:

'I didn't know your husband had bought the paddock, Mrs Hunter.'

'Didn't you?' she said, her lids fluttering. 'Well, no, we didn't tell anyone. We thought there might be some unpleasantness about it. So many people tried to get it, you know. Richard didn't want to say anything until he was ready to take it in with the garden. He had some wonderful plans for it.'

'And may I ask how your husband succeeded where so many others had failed?' said Mr Lockwood.

'Oh, Sir Thomas once lived near us, you know. He was my father's patient,' said Mrs Hunter. 'So when Richard asked to buy the land, he let him have it. But he asked him to take it over as quietly as possible so that he shouldn't be inundated with letters from other people all wanting to buy land, you see.'

'I see,' said the lawyer grimly. 'Very well, that's all for the moment,' he said, dismissing her.

He sat down at the table and helped himself to another cigar. Lighting it with care, he pondered the situation.

It was obvious now that the house would have to be sold. The paddock would presumably be sold with it. The fact that the paddock belonged to the owner added considerably to the value of the house.

Stroking his jaw, William Lockwood said to himself that he must get hold of the paddock before the house came into the market and certainly before anybody could get the idea that it had at any time formed part of the property. Richard Hunter's un-neighbourly secretiveness might be made to serve William Lockwood's purpose very nicely.

The French clock struck eleven, but he was no longer concerned about the passage of time.

How could he get the paddock? How could he establish his prior claim? Because he certainly had a prior claim. It had been bought with his money, hadn't it? The damned nuisance was that Richard Hunter had paid it back.

He was thoughtful, turning over every possibility and impossibility.

It struck him suddenly that he hadn't come across the receipt he had given Hunter that night after dinner. An idea began to form in his mind, an idea that prompted him to rise to his feet and go urgently through the papers again. There was no receipt there. He went to the fireplace and rang the bell. Mrs Hunter again appeared, again startled.

'You're sure all your husband's papers are here?' he asked sternly, as if she were guilty of keeping something from him.

'They're all there. He never kept any anywhere else.'

'Nothing in his pocket-book or his pockets?'

'There were a few things in his pockets,' she said, her eyes filling. 'I'll fetch them.'

She suffered in bringing his things out, the things he had touched so lately with his long clever hands, and would never touch again. She came back with the pathetic collection and laid them on the table. The lawyer ran his thick fingers through the pocketbook and moved them about among the other objects. Nothing there.

'I can't do any more for the moment,' he said, 'I must go to his office and the bank. I'll take the Will and these papers with me.'

'Will you carry them in this bag?' she asked.

He glanced at it with disparagement. 'No, thank you. My case will take them.'

'I'll come back this afternoon,' he said, making for the door.

She followed him with protestations of gratitude.

II

In the afternoon, he returned to the drawing room. He had made an exhaustive search. There was no receipt. He would take the risk of its turning up later; if it did, he was confident of being able to deal with it. Of course, there was the entry in Hunter's passbook, but who was going to bother about that? Not the new manager at the bank. It was a piece of luck Hadfield had just left. Now Hadfield might – but even that was unlikely – he might possibly have wondered why and how the widow came to let him have the paddock. Though he probably didn't know Hunter had ever acquired it. Hadfield was William Lockwood's friend;

he would have said something. Anyway, Hadfield was gone, and the new man had his hands too full to bother about the small account of a widow whose affairs had been taken over by the family friend and lawyer. And Hunter's papers were all in his keeping; no one else would have access to them.

There was an element of risk, of course, but he pooh-poohed it. Sitting at the table in the sunshine, he calmly, even pleasurably, entertained all aspects of risk as they suggested themselves, and as calmly dismissed them. For one thing, no one would ever suspect or credit him with having taken such a risk at all. Also he was confident of being able to deal with any situation that might arise.

In the meantime, he meant to have the paddock.

He rose and rang for Mrs Hunter.

'Are you aware, Mrs Hunter,' he said, when she had hurried in, 'that some months ago your husband borrowed from me the sum of three hundred pounds?'

A flush stained Mrs Hunter's startled face.

'Oh, I had no idea Richard had ever borrowed money,' she said distressfully.

'There's nothing in that,' said the lawyer. 'We all borrow money at times.'

'But three hundred pounds!' she said. 'I'm so very sorry he owed you so much. It must have worried him. I must repay you at once, Mr Lockwood.'

'You'd find it difficult to repay me in actual cash,' he said, pacing the room. 'I don't expect it. What I suggest is this. Your husband used the money he borrowed from me to buy the paddock. He knew I wanted it myself. I think it is only fair that

I should now take possession of the paddock in discharge of the debt. Do you agree?'

Mrs Hunter's flush deepened. The pain of parting with everything that had made up her life with Richard was beginning. The paddock was the first to go.

'Yes, take it,' she said. 'And I hope your children will have as much pleasure from it as we hoped ours would,' she finished huskily.

'I have no doubt they will,' said the lawyer. 'Well, now, Mrs Hunter,' he continued briskly, 'I suggest that we say nothing about this transaction. No doubt you prefer that no one should know your husband borrowed money from me, and I, on my part, would like to acquire the paddock as quietly as possible. If I can achieve it as secretly as your husband did, I shall think myself very fortunate,' he said with irony.

'I can act for you in this matter as well as for myself, which is very convenient,' he said, as indeed it was. 'And in return I will surrender this promissory note. Your husband gave it to me when he borrowed the money.'

He brought the paper from his pocket-book and extended it between his fingers.

'A promissory note?' said Mrs Hunter.

'Read it,' he said.

She took the slip of paper and read:

I promise to pay William Lockwood, or order, on demand, the sum of three hundred pounds for value received

and there at the foot was her husband's characteristic signature: Richard Hunter.

Mrs Hunter raised her eyes in a bewildered way to Mr Lockwood's face.

'Then you haven't seen anything like this before?' he said, taking the paper from her and bestowing it carefully in his pocketbook.

'Never. Do you think he borrowed money from anyone else?'

'There's no evidence that he did. Unless there are papers I haven't seen.'

'There are no more papers in the house.'

'Well, there are none at his office and only the deeds at the bank, so you may safely conclude that he borrowed from no one but me.'

He smiled. It was a smile of satisfaction, but Mrs Hunter misinterpreted it and tried to smile back in gratitude. He was so kind to take the paddock instead of making her pay three hundred pounds, so kind, when she was in such straits, to make it easy for her to repay him in this way. From this time forwards, Mrs Hunter harboured the conviction that Mr Lockwood, in spite of his manner, was at heart a kind man.

'I'll take possession of these papers now,' he said, tapping his brief-case. 'I suppose you don't want the old passbooks?'

She shook her head.

'And you understand that I shall take possession of the paddock, and receipt this promissory note, which I shall hand over to you? That is, I shall put it with your papers. Your husband's debt to me will then be discharged. You clearly understand that, don't you?'

'I understand,' she said.

'Far better not to pay over any money,' he thought, going away. 'It would only rouse comment and enquiry.'

'I'll make it up to her,' he thought. 'I'll give her something else some time. When I can spare it. Or I'll do something for her somehow. She shan't be the loser by it.'

He felt a comfortable contempt for Mrs Hunter. It had all been so simple. And what he had done really made no difference to her. The paddock was no good to her now, except that it increased the value of the house. And that was where he could make it up to her, probably. Get a good price for the house. Push it up. He must try to do that.

But it was unthinkable that a new neighbour should get hold of, and keep for ever, that paddock. Damn it all, if he didn't get it now, he never would.

He hurried, jubilantly, to look at it. He beamed over the hedge on the buttercups and cow-parsley with the eyes of an owner. Then he hurried home to tell Effie.

He told her as much as he thought fit and kept back the rest. No need for his wife to know exactly how he got the benefits he did get for her and the children.

'William, doesn't it just show?' said Effie with feeling. 'I mean about bread upon the waters. When you went out this morning to do a kindness for poor Mrs Hunter, you never dreamt you'd come back with the paddock, did you, dear?'

III

The acquisition of the paddock fresh upon him, William Lockwood genuinely meant to work off his secret debt to Mrs

Hunter. Everybody, prompted by Effie, said how good he was to her. He undertook the sale of Hill House and its contents. He moved her to the ugly little house in Byron Place where she had been ever since. After much discussion with her, he arranged to buy, with the small amount of capital available, a limited annuity to bring her in one hundred and fifty pounds a year for fifteen years. At the end of that time, he pointed out, her children must be earning their own living and hers.

Having done all this, having given up a great deal of his time, he felt he had pretty nearly wiped out his debt. He felt he'd done about enough for Mrs Hunter. But Mrs Hunter, unaware of the arrangements Mr Lockwood had made with his conscience and having been encouraged to go to him for advice and enlightenment during the first months of her widowhood, continued to go to him. If, on closer acquaintance, Mr Lockwood's temper was more in evidence than his kindness of heart, she was unshakeably convinced that the kindness was there. She was sure he would always do his best for them all. This unfortunate conviction supported her through the most trying interviews and enabled her, though she came away crushed and often tearful, to go back for his advice as soon as there was something else she didn't understand, which was often.

And not only had she to go to him for advice, she had to keep going to ask if he couldn't possibly agree to her getting a little more money from somewhere. She couldn't manage, she told him.

'You must manage, Mrs Hunter,' he said sternly. 'Other people manage on far less. I don't suppose any other householder in the street you live in has so much as a hundred and fifty a year coming in. You must manage and you must *not* keep on bothering me,' he said.

On these visits Mrs Hunter always took one of the children for support, and since Molly and Martin were at school, it usually had to be Thea. Thea didn't like going at all. As soon as she turned the corner of Havelock Street and came into sight of the narrow house, like something in an old book, where Mr Lockwood had his office, her feet began to drag. But her mother gently urged her up the stairs behind the man who came out of a back office to conduct them. They went into Mr Lockwood's room and Thea could always tell he wasn't pleased to see them.

Oppressed by the large blood-coloured mahogany surfaces, the dark red and blue carpet, all the books and black boxes, she sat on the edge of a cold leather chair, unable to understand what her mother and Mr Lockwood were talking about. Except that she heard and dreaded the rising note of anger in Mr Lockwood's voice.

When her mother put her handkerchief to her eyes, which she usually did before long, Thea slid from the chair and went to stand protectively beside her. She stared stormily at Mr Lockwood without making any impression upon him, and by and by, her mother took her hand and they went unhappily home.

After these visits, the small pleasures of the Hunter children were still further curtailed, at least for a time. There was no cake for tea, there were no Saturday pennies, no twopenny story books in which they all delighted.

It was small wonder that they came to associate the name and sight of Mr Lockwood with trouble. Especially Thea.

CHAPTER THREE

But in his own home Mr Lockwood was a different man. On the night of the party, though he did not take much notice of the guests, he showed himself a fond father, listening attentively and leading the applause, calling out: 'Very fine performance, Bee. Good girl, Muriel. You're doing very well both of you.'

He exchanged amused, indulgent glances with his wife as they sat together in the armchairs in front, with the Hunters symbolically behind.

But to the Hunter children, the concert seemed interminable. Their behaviour, however, was equal to the occasion. They sighed quietly and shuffled carefully, only casting up their eyes to their mother from time to time as if to ask how long yet. Their mother made sweet, cautionary smiles at them and in spite of pins and needles in their legs, they sank back to endure – for her sake.

The Hunter children had rather an old-fashioned air. The girls' dresses were made by their mother – not a skilful needlewoman – and Martin's supposedly short trousers were usually too long. Their appearance moved the Lockwood twins to scorn and giggles and Mrs Lockwood to exasperation. Mrs Hunter, she often said, had really no idea. She felt she herself, in Mrs Hunter's place, would have managed so much better. In fact, Mrs Lockwood talked as if having to manage on very little money was a most inspiring situation and one in which she almost wished herself, so that she could show what she could do.

All the same, there was something about the Hunters, in spite of their clothes, that Mrs Lockwood defined reluctantly to herself as 'distinction'. Why they should have it, where it came from and how it persisted in their circumstances, she couldn't think. Obscurely, it annoyed her. It made her wish, somehow, to keep them out of the way. She didn't quite want them to be noticed; especially not by her friends, Sir Robert and Lady Harvey.

The concert went on and on. The twins played the piano, danced, sang and recited. But Clare could not be persuaded to do anything. She only laughed and shook her head and sat in an armchair in a corner, with her feet on the seat and her knees under her chin. Martin Hunter, who had glimpsed crackers on the supper-table, hoped he would get something in his that he could give her, she was so pretty; a ruby heart, a Jap doll or something she would like.

'Clare, I wish you'd do that little dance you did the other day for Mother,' said Mrs Lockwood persuasively.

But Clare only shook her curls and laughed.

'Come and sit on my knee then, pet,' said her father, holding out his arms.

She ran at him, her head down like a little bull, and was

gathered up, her fair hair spread like floss silk against his jacket. Her child's face was pure and clear in contrast to his own, coarsened by time, yet almost transfigured by the look of love and pride he bent upon her. She amused herself by trying to hang her bangle on his nose and all the company smiled.

Except Thea Hunter. The twins were applauded, Clare was loved and petted, but she was unnoticed. Nobody tried to catch or kiss her, nobody said she was clever or pretty. She didn't like her dress; it was of bulky brown velveteen. She wanted a white dress with frills and a blue sash, like Clare's.

Fingering the velveteen, Thea hung her head. She was ashamed, not only of her dress, but of the drab, unimportant appearance presented by the Hunters in the Lockwood drawing room. Dimly, she felt the Hunters ought not to put up with their obscurity. She wished they would look prouder, be prouder. Prouder than the Lockwoods. Shame, envy, resentment warred in her childish breast, but no one knew. All that the company noticed, if they noticed anything, was a pale, quiet little girl with rather lank, though curling, dark hair and long-lashed grey eyes. She had a reluctant smile that gave great charm to her face; but tonight, at the concert, the smile was not in evidence.

At last the concert was over. Mrs Lockwood led the way to the dining room and immediately tedium was forgotten by the Hunter children.

The table glittered with silver and bright jellies, all the brighter for being broken up by Cook and put into glasses. Gold and crimson crackers were arranged like games of noughts and crosses. The lemonade had cherries floating in it.

The eyes of the Hunter children went to their mother in rapture and she smiled back at them.

It was a buffet supper. There were so many fragments to be eaten up that it was the only way to serve it. But it was all very pleasant. Mr Lockwood stood aloof and masculine on the hearth with a sandwich and a glass of whisky. Mrs Lockwood and Mrs Hunter sat in armchairs drinking tea and having things brought to them by one maid, while another attended to the wants of the twins who stood at the table with Molly and Thea Hunter.

The twins gave their instructions.

'I'll have that, Alice.'

'Give me the one with the two cherries on.'

'I said bags me that, that's mine.'

Whenever the maid handed a plate of cakes, the twins unerringly took the biggest.

Martin and Clare sat in a corner, absorbed in food, conversation and each other. From time to time they made a tour of inspection round the table, took what they wanted and returned to the corner.

Thea had had enough of the twins for the time being. She turned her back on them and, a piece of cake in one hand, traced with a finger of the other the pattern in the damask of a napkin, one of a pile folded beside her. She bent closer and discovered a pattern of chrysanthemum petals in the white stuff. Like the real ones in the middle of the table, only curlier. This discovery interested her. With one of those fierce urges that overtake children, she wanted to know if the napkins matched the flowers on purpose. She went to stand at her mother's knee, her question on her lips. But her mother put out a detaining hand. Mrs Lockwood was speaking; Thea mustn't interrupt. Thea waited for Mrs Lockwood to pause, but she didn't. Mrs Lockwood rarely paused. She usually did the talking, and Mrs Hunter listened.

Suddenly Bee called out: 'Time for the crackers!' and Thea bounded to get hers. She put her hand to a scarlet and gold monster, but Bee snatched it away. 'Here – that's for Mummy. It's got a crown on. You can have that one.' She thrust a substitute into Thea's hand and ran with the other to her mother.

'Thank you, darling,' said Mrs Lockwood. 'They're so sweet. They always look after me first,' she said to Mrs Hunter.

Thea, pulling her cracker with Molly and finding a paper bonnet inside, marvelled at the twins. They must have gone over everything. They knew which cakes had two cherries on, which cracker had a crown, which was the best of everything, and since there was so much, the twins must be kept very busy, she thought.

The carpet was strewn with tinsel and bright paper. No one could eat any more. But the ladies still sat on in the armchairs; Mr Lockwood still stood before the fire with a final glass of whisky. Martin and Clare were darting about the room in a game of tig.

'Have you got anything new?' Thea asked the twins.

Whenever she came to Oakfield, the twins had something new. As she grew and dreamed progressively of the things she wanted, she found, when she came to Oakfield, that the Lockwoods had usually got them. They had everything she wanted and couldn't have. They had bedrooms to themselves. Each had a gilt desk with a rose painted on the lid and a gilt chair to sit on while writing; and they never wrote a line if they could help it. They had a toy theatre and they couldn't make up plays. They had all the Children's Annuals and they didn't like reading.

'Anything new?' said Bee, tossing her hair. 'Loads of things. It's been Christmas, hasn't it, silly? You can come and look if you like.'

It was Mr Lockwood who brought the party to an end. Mrs Hunter was under the impression that they had been invited to see the New Year in. The children had been to bed in the afternoon so that they should be able to stay up. So she made no move to go. But Mr Lockwood looked at his watch.

'Effie,' he said. 'It's time our youngsters were in bed. They've had late nights all this week. We've all had late nights,' he said pointedly.

Mrs Hunter rose hurriedly.

'Children, we must go.'

Martin turned an astonished face upon her. Hot, dishevelled and even – though how he had managed it in that house was a mystery – dirty, he was just going to burst out that it was nowhere near twelve o'clock, it was only *a quarter to ten*, when a look from his mother quelled him. He realised that it was as much a shock to her as to him to be told that the party must end. So when Clare darted at him to tig him again, he smiled and shook his head. 'No go,' he said, with curious maturity. 'It's over,' and went to the cloakroom to put his coat on.

Molly and Thea were taken upstairs to the twins' bedrooms. By this time, fires were burning in the grates, the sheets were turned down over pink silk eiderdowns, the gilt desks shone softly, the roses blooming on the lids.

Having shown Thea to her outdoor things, Muriel joined her twin in the next room with Molly. Thea sat on the floor by the fire and slowly put her shoes on. Warmth, comfort, beauty had a curious effect on her. They made her almost sleepy. A feeling of solace and ease came over her and she, who had frowned or stared most of the evening, smiled. If this room were hers, she played. If the desk . . .

'Thea,' said her mother on her way from her hostess's bedroom, 'you're being a long time, dear. The others have gone down.'

Thea got up from the floor. She struggled into her coat; the velveteen dress clung and would not allow her coat-sleeves to pass without a great deal of shrugging and tugging. When the coat was on, she felt bunched up and uncomfortable. She pushed her straggling curls under her hat and felt nothing was right.

On the landing, large and square like a room, she lingered again. Firelight showed through the open bedroom doors. It was peaceful, warm and comfortable.

'Thea,' said her mother from the foot of the stairs as she appeared, 'will you please hurry? You're keeping everybody waiting.'

Mr and Mrs Lockwood watched Thea with irritation. There must be something wrong with her, they thought. What a contrast to Clare, who at the same age was so lovely and so lively!

'You haven't even put on your gloves yet,' said Mrs Hunter reproachfully.

'Well, good night,' said Mr Lockwood, suddenly finishing with them.

He walked off to the drawing room and Mrs Hunter had to say good night to his back.

'Goodbye, Mrs Lockwood,' she said. 'And thank you so much. It has been so enjoyable. The twins are wonderful.'

The twins smirked. They didn't consider Mrs Hunter important, but any compliment would do.

'We might have a party like this next New Year's Eve,' said Mrs Lockwood graciously. 'In fact,' she said, accompanying the Hunters a little way across the hall, 'we might have a party every New Year's Eve, unless there is something else on. It would be interesting to see what progress the children make from year to year in their music and dancing and so on, wouldn't it?'

'It would be delightful,' said Mrs Hunter, to whom it did not occur to be anything but grateful for the privilege of thus marking the passage of time.

'Good night, then,' said Mrs Lockwood, wheeling with her daughters, who were clinging about her.

'Good night, and a Happy New Year again,' said Mrs Hunter.

'Thank you, the same to you,' called Mrs Lockwood over her shoulder.

The maid who had been standing by the glass door dividing the hall from the porch now opened it. The Hunters passed through, but before opening the outer door, the maid carefully closed the glass one, lest any breath of cold air should visit the Lockwood family.

Waiting to be let out, Thea looked back. The Lockwoods were just disappearing into the drawing room. The hall, warm and softly carpeted, was empty; the tinsel and the tiny lights glittering on the Christmas tree at the foot of the stairs.

'Thea, can't you see Alice holding the door for you?' said her mother from outside. 'Where are your wits tonight?'

That was the trouble. Thea was using them.

There was a lamp halfway down the drive that should have been turned on from the porch. The maid was supposed to wait there to turn it off again. But Alice had had enough of waiting about for the Hunters to go. The time that kid had kept her, crawling down the stairs, putting her gloves on and hanging about in the porch as if tomorrow would do! Alice wasn't going to stand about seeing the Hunters off any longer. She knew exactly where the Hunters stood in her mistress's estimation. She not only didn't put the drive light on, she switched the porch light off, and hurried back to the kitchen where the others were still sitting over supper.

Going down the drive the Hunters kept close together. After the warm house, the night felt more than ever cold and dark and they had a depressing sense of having been turned out too soon, of having been suddenly tired of. So nobody said much.

When they turned out of the gates, they saw the stream of New Year revellers in the main road at the foot of the hill, singing, shouting, laughing, their faces tossing white under the arc lights.

'Dear me,' murmured Mrs Hunter, drawing Molly's arm within hers, taking Thea's hand and instructing Martin to keep close.

Hugging the wall, they proceeded. The surging stream of life flowed in the roadway. Lighted trams clanged through the crowds. Mrs Hunter thought it was terrible. Terrible, she kept saying, hurrying under the wall with her children. She felt she didn't know how she would get them home.

But they reached Byron Place without mishap and left the happy crowds behind.

Byron Place was a quiet, short street, closed at one end. Someone had once called it a blind alley, which seemed a dreadful name to Thea, as if Byron Place couldn't see anything. And it couldn't, she thought; only itself. The houses, all alike, each with a bay window beside the front door and two flat windows above, stared at one another over small sooty front gardens and iron railings across a paved street.

When the Hunters reached the gate of Number Twenty-one, Mrs Hunter took the key from her bag and gave it into Martin's hand. To Martin it was an excitement to open the front door; to Mrs Hunter no longer anything of the kind. To open the door, to her, was to take up the burden of the house again, of bringing up the children alone, of making ends meet. She sighed as they went in.

The house was cold; a faint smell of gas and soot met them in the passage. The breath of Byron Place was nothing like the flower-scented breath of Oakfield.

Yawning, the Hunters took off their shoes in the kitchen and went up to their cold rooms to bed.

CHAPTER FOUR

I

Mrs Hunter, uprooted on marriage from the south, had not, as they say of a plant, moved well. After fourteen years, she was as far as ever from acclimatising herself to mills, smuts, rough speech and the rain. Life in the industrial north was too grim for her. From the first she had felt alien. Only her handsome young husband could reconcile her to Aldworth, and when he was dead nothing could do it. She remained, but subconsciously she was always waiting to go home. Where that home was, she didn't know; but it wasn't here, not where she was.

She stayed in Aldworth because of Mr Lockwood. Where else would she find anyone to advise her? Who else could place the children in the world when the time came? Life, even with Mr Lockwood's help, was difficult enough; without it, Mrs Hunter felt it would be impossible. So, sighing, she stayed.

Mrs Hunter imagined she was doing the best for her children by refusing to be assimilated into the life of Byron Place. In the neighbourhood the Hunters remained apart. The widow and her children were seen passing up the street, going into the house, closing the door. The faces of the children reappeared at the windows, watching the games of other children in which they were not allowed to join. Playing in the street was out of the question, Mrs Hunter considered.

Tired though she was when she had finished the housework, she took her children for walks, consciously getting them away from the district. She took them past Hill House where they used to live, past Oakfield, and past Firbank Hall, pointing out the beauty of the gardens there, the fountain, the stone urns that had come from Italy a long time ago. On summer evenings, she would sit in the dank little dining room, looking out on to the backyard where an ash-sapling grew beside the dustbin.

'When we were at Hill House,' she would say, 'the roses . . .'

And the children listened and thought how dreadful everything was in Byron Place and how wonderful everything must have been at Hill House.

'The paddock, where the Lockwoods keep their pony now, was ours then, you know.'

'Had we a pony, Mother?'

'No, but you were going to have one . . .'

She never got used to being a widow. She often sighed as she went about the house; though she was careful to smile quickly if one of the children noticed. She stared out of windows for a long time, and when she turned away, her eyes were wet.

As a family, the Hunters were isolated. There were no relations left on either side. So there was no one to break in and counteract the influence of Mrs Hunter; and to this influence it was Thea who was the longest subject. She was the youngest by three years and Molly and Martin went to school long before she did. She was left at home with Mrs Hunter's sadness, headaches and general helplessness; but her reaction was a feeling that she must always help her mother and never, if she could prevent it, allow anything to hurt her.

She followed her mother about the house, scrambling up the stairs behind her, scrambling down every time Mrs Hunter went for something she had forgotten, which was often. Thea crawled under furniture to rub floors with a duster, emerging backwards, the seat of her brief knickers fully exposed, saying incessantly: 'Am I helping you, Mother?'

'Indeed you are, dear,' said Mrs Hunter, and Thea felt a glow of love and usefulness.

One of Mrs Hunter's recurrent problems was the provision of a pudding. 'I simply can't think of a pudding,' she said every morning, and went anxiously through the cookery books in search of one. Though she couldn't read, Thea went through the cookery books, too. The result was that they usually decided on rice again.

When, as they went about the house, a knock came at the door, Mrs Hunter stood still where she was, on the landing or the stairs, and listened. Thea, holding her mother's skirt, listened, too, and heard the faint creeping noises of the house, the drip of the tap, the tick of the clock. The knock came again.

'Who is it, Mother?' she whispered.

'Ssh . . .'

When at last they went to the door, it was often only the

groceries left on the step. But Thea, looking out, was not convinced it was the groceries. She felt someone had been and gone, someone they would never see again.

In her anxious daily round, Mrs Hunter suffered a good deal from headaches, for which she took powders prescribed long ago by her father and made up nowadays by Mr Bowen, the chemist in Wells Road nearby.

When her mother had to lie down with a headache, Thea knelt on a chair beside the bed, cooling first one hand and then the other on the bedpost and pressing it to her mother's brow. Mrs Hunter lay with closed eyes and Thea looked at her with love and pity, saying in a whisper from time to time: 'Am I making you better, Mother?'

But quite often, in the middle of the morning or the afternoon, on her way to or from somewhere else, Mrs Lockwood called and Mrs Hunter cheered up at once. She discarded what she was doing, she made tea and carried it into the front room, and there the matrons sat, with Thea between them, or rubbing round the furniture like a little cat, her eyes on Mrs Lockwood.

The front room was furnished with things no one had wanted to buy at the sale of Hill House. The gold brocade sofa, now in a holland cover, stood across the bay window. The black and gold table was here, its splendour shrouded in a worn chenille cloth. Its ornate brass feet showed beneath, so the table looked somehow like an operatic grandee disguised in an old cloak for nefarious purposes. The carpet was turned under to fit the floor, the curtains were cut down to fit the windows. The walls were covered with chalk drawings by Richard Hunter, mostly of Greek temples. There were shelves of books, odd chairs, occasional tables. The room looked so much like a collection of job lots that one almost looked for the sale-tickets. And there Mrs Hunter sat, serving tea to Mrs Lockwood, with Thea taking everything in.

Although the matrons had been friends for years, they addressed each other as 'Mrs'. When Thea asked later why they didn't use their Christian names, Mrs Hunter said: 'We were never on those terms, dear,' and Mrs Hunter and Mrs Lockwood they remained to the end.

Mrs Lockwood did practically all the talking. She talked about her girls, about the nice things people said of them, the clothes she was getting for them, the parties they gave and went to. When she wasn't talking about her daughters or her husband or her house or her friend, Lady Harvey, she talked about her figure, her hair, her feet or something else of hers.

'Of course I have a very small foot,' she would say, extending it for inspection. Thea inspected it. It was small and puffy; it was like a marshmallow. But Mrs Lockwood was pleased with it. She always spoke of it in the singular: 'My foot is very difficult to fit,' she would say. 'But as Mr Shaw said to me the other day: "Well, madam, if you will have such an expensive foot, you know. . ."'

Whereupon Mrs Lockwood laughed delightedly about her foot and Mrs Hunter obligingly laughed with her, though Thea couldn't see anything really funny about it.

She gathered, though, that Mrs Lockwood was a very important person.

'Mr Baker said to me in the shop: "Well, Mrs Lockwood, I wouldn't dream of doing it for anybody else," he said, "but seeing that it's you," he said . . .' reported Mrs Lockwood.

'And Miss Barnes just laid her hand on my arm,' said Mrs Lockwood with feeling, 'and said: "Of course, you know what we all think of *you*, Mrs Lockwood."'

Thea considered her gravely, wondering why everybody should be so fond of her.

Mrs Lockwood had a way of making everything that happened to herself and her family sound important and somehow different from anything that happened to the Hunters.

Mrs Paton's school, for instance, where the twins went with the Harvey children. According to Mrs Lockwood, all the pupils were wonderful and Miss Paton simply doted on the twins.

To go to Miss Paton's school was to be stamped with social eligibility, because Miss Paton was very particular whom she took. Admission to Miss Paton's was regulated on the opposite principle of admission to heaven. It is said to be hard for the rich to enter the kingdom of heaven, but with Miss Paton it was the other way round: only the rich were admitted to her school. Yet little of their wealth could have come her way or she would not have ended up in a Home for Decayed Gentlewomen.

Those days, however, were as yet far off. Miss Paton was running her school and Mrs Lockwood was continually making it sound such a wonderful place that Thea clamoured to be allowed to go to it. She didn't want to go to the little school, conducted in an attic, that Molly went to. She wanted to go to Miss Paton's, and when Thea wanted anything, she wanted fiercely. She dreamt about it, she put it in her prayers. When she went out with her mother, she begged to be taken past Miss Paton's, and as she walked slowly past the old dark house turned into a school by Miss Paton when her parents died, she thought how lovely it must be inside, with the children singing and dancing and having fun all the time.

'Please let me go to Miss Paton's school, Mother,' she begged incessantly. 'Please.'

'Well, dear, we must see what Mr Lockwood says,' her mother would say. 'I'm afraid it will be too expensive for us.'

'Oh, no, Mother, no!'

'Well, dear, we must see what Mr Lockwood says.'

But when the time came, Mr Lockwood said she must go to the High School. Molly was taken from the attic and sent to the High School too. Mr Lockwood was on the Board of Governors and got the Hunter children admitted at reduced fees, which was surely commendable. But Thea bore him a grudge for it; she wanted to go to Miss Paton's.

II

In those days, everybody went to church on Sunday morning. The most important people in the town, including the Lockwoods, went to the Parish Church, and since that had been the church they went to before Richard Hunter's death, his widow and children continued to go to it. But whereas the Lockwoods had a whole pew to themselves in the middle aisle, the Hunters moved to four cheap seats in a short pew at the side. Even in the House of God, the Hunters took a humble place.

They could not see the altar or the pulpit and rarely got a glimpse of the Vicar from the beginning of the service to the end, but they had a full view of the Lockwoods; Mr Lockwood at one end of the pew with Clare beside him; Mrs Lockwood, rustling in summer silk or muffled in winter furs, at the other with the twins between. Clare sometimes turned to smile at her friend Martin, until her father, with one finger, guided her face to the front again. The twins, their profiles uplifted, tried to appear to sing without the help of the printed page, as if they knew everything and had no need to look at the book. But Thea was watching and knew when they went wrong, which was often.

During the sermon, while Clare leaned against her father, comfortable in the curve of his arm, the twins looked about them, tussled silently over the arrangement of the prayer-books on the ledge before them and, when they were older, surreptitiously did their nails. Thea was scandalised by their behaviour; it did not occur to her that her own was little better. She paid no attention to the service; it was familiar, incomprehensible and, in spite of the distraction afforded by the Lockwoods, always seemed very long.

Over a period of years, the Hunter children saw the Lockwoods again every Sunday afternoon. A Miss Somers wishing to instruct in the Scriptures the children of what she called 'nice families', asked Mrs Lockwood to make out a list of those who might be asked to join a class. Mrs Lockwood, relieved to be able to think of three children at once, appended the Hunters. So to Miss Somers's Bible Class, Molly, Martin and Thea had to go.

After the class, Molly went on in front with the older girls. Martin was always behind with Clare. He usually had something to show or give her. They would stand in the street, their heads together, while he carefully lifted the cotton-wool to disclose a bird's egg, pale blue and scattered with freckles as faint and small as those Clare got on her nose in summer-time. Martin and Clare seemed to have been born friends. Going home, they straggled far behind the others, digging moss out of walls with Martin's penknife, puncturing bubbles that rose in the gas-tar in hot weather, doing all sorts of things Clare would never have thought of but for Martin.

Sunday after Sunday, Thea walked home with the twins, their butt and victim. It was her own fault. She could have gone home alone, but for quite a long time, she stuck with them. The discrepancy between what the twins appeared to be and what their mother said they were, puzzled her. She was always hanging about them, gaping, saying nothing, which perhaps excusably, annoyed the twins. They taunted her about one thing or another.

'You've got your sister's hat on!'

'I haven't,' said Thea unconvincingly, because she had.

''Course you've got your sister's hat on!'

The twins intoxicated themselves with their own boasting and taunting. They swaggered along in their best coats, turning their feet out like their father, spluttering with laughter at their own sallies.

'Huh, the High School! We wouldn't be *allowed* to go to the High School. It's common. It doesn't cost half as much as Miss Paton's.'

It was worse when other girls were with them. Led by the twins, they played humiliating tricks on Thea. Going home through the park one winter Sunday, they played hide and seek. But when it was Thea's turn to seek, nobody hid. They all made off for home as swiftly and silently as possible while she counted a hundred with her hands over her eyes. She sought them until the light was almost gone from the sky. She called, but nobody answered. At last, frightened by the solitude and the gathering dark, she went home.

'Where were you?' she asked the following Sunday. 'I couldn't find any of you.'

They only laughed and said they would play again and she could hide this time. She hid in a bush, the sooty leaves against her face. She held her coat round her, making herself small. She smiled with excitement. Nobody came. She grew doubtful. But still she waited to be found. The bare trees drooped above her, the rocks were dark, there was a sound of running water and no other. A sense of desolation came over her. They had left her. She realised that they had left her last Sunday, too. Anger and resentment almost drove out her fear of the deserted park, but not quite. She ran until she was out of it, then, safe among people in the streets, she walked. It was borne in on her that those who wore pale blue coats and hats trimmed with beaver, had important fathers and went to schools like Miss Paton's, would treat badly those who wore their sisters' hats, had no father at all and went to a school you could scoff at. They would treat you badly if you let them.

She realised, too, that there was no one to go to for consolation. It was no use telling her mother. Her mother would only conclude that the Lockwoods, in spite of appearances, hadn't meant it. They couldn't; they were so nice. It was no use telling Molly; she didn't mind about the Lockwoods. No use telling Martin; the twins were Clare's sisters, so there couldn't be much wrong with them. She must keep it to herself.

From this time onwards, she went home alone.

CHAPTER FIVE

I

But the Bible Class came to an end and the twins went away to school in the south with Angela Harvey. When the project was first formed, Mrs Lockwood, calling in Byron Place, wept.

'We didn't want any of the girls to leave home until they all go abroad to finish,' she said. 'Of course we know we shall have to part with them then. They must be fitted for their position in life.'

'Oh, of course,' agreed Mrs Hunter.

'We didn't want to part with them until then. But how can we refuse when Lady Harvey asks us to let them go with Angela?' Mrs Lockwood was torn between gratified snobbery and maternal affection. 'Angela's so difficult, you know, and Lady Harvey thinks she'll settle better if she has the twins with her. I'm afraid we'll have to let them go. It might mean a breach between the families if we didn't, and that would never do.'

The twins went to boarding school the following term, but Clare did not go. Her father wouldn't hear of it. So she stayed at home to be her parents' pet and continued to go to Miss Paton's.

During one Easter holiday, Thea came face to face with Angela Harvey for the first time. She had always known Angela by sight, as everyone in the town knew her. Angela didn't know Thea.

Thea had formed a habit of wandering off alone into the country on Saturdays and holidays. Her friend, Helen Millard, lived out of the town and could not be got at on Saturday. Martin played football or cricket according to the season. Her mother had gradually given up walks, and Molly's idea of spending Saturday afternoon was to cook in the kitchen.

Out of the blue, this passion for cooking had come upon Molly. She didn't shine at school; praise rarely came her way there. But at home now she astonished and delighted her family. To have something really good to eat was something so very new. At weekends now the house was quite a different place to come into. Comfortable smells filled it; smells of soup simmering, cakes baking, sometimes even of toffee. Martin and Thea came bursting in clamouring to know what smelled so good and at table their appetites startled their mother.

'I don't know where you put it all,' she marvelled.

Good cooking is a form of benevolence. Molly gladly sacrificed a fine afternoon to give pleasure by a cake at tea-time. She would lay her afternoon and fresh air on the table with the cake and be rewarded by the glow of pleasure she felt when they enjoyed it. Leggy, pale, freckled, she smiled her sweet, shy smile when they praised her. But she couldn't both cook and walk, so it was no use looking to her for company.

On Saturday mornings, Thea had to do the errands. She had to go up Byron Place, dive through the covered alleyway known locally as the 'back' and come out into Wells Road where a few little shops stood at the corners. She had usually to go to Mr Bowen's, the chemist's, to renew her mother's supply of headache powders, and she always had to go to Miss Riley's for the bread.

Miss Riley was a small, taciturn woman who seemed anxious to keep out of sight. At the ping of the door-bell, her red face popped up between an erection of glass domes on the counter. The domes covered little piles of Eccles cakes, buns, biscuits, Victoria sandwiches. At the sight of Thea, Miss Riley hastily assembled two large loaves in flimsy yellow paper. She then reached for the weekend Victoria sandwich. It was an embarrassing day for Thea when she had to say they didn't want it, because Molly was making a cake at home.

'Huh,' said Miss Riley shortly. 'Funny sort of cake, I'll be bound, girl of that age.'

'Why doesn't she mek bread, too?' she asked sourly, throwing the change down.

'Oh, I don't think she could manage that,' said Thea.

But Miss Riley was not placated by the implied compliment. She skimmed the rejected Victoria back to the pile, clapped the dome on and did her usual, but none the less startling, disappearing trick. She ducked so suddenly that Thea thought she must have a hole under the counter.

The errands done, Thea was free for the country.

One of the advantages of living in Aldworth was the speed with which you could get out of it. You had only to climb to the ridge of the steep hills and drop down the other side to leave the town behind as if it did not exist. Before you lay a great stretch of open country, the plains rising to the fells, the fells to the Pennines, with Helvellyn blue in the distance, sometimes peaked with snow. The fields were criss-crossed with stone walls, the woods were dark. Often you came upon an assemblage, an old house under gaunt trees, the single stone arch of a bridge over a stream, a lonely church, that haunted the imagination as gentler scenes did not.

It was not long after she had turned her back on the town and started downhill that Thea began to skip and sing. She was one of those, born not made, to whom walking in the country is a happiness in itself. She went from one interest to another, poking into streams, looking into banks and hedges for flowers and nests, loitering round farmyards – an odd little figure in bunchy clothes, carrying her hat, since her mother would not let her go without it.

At some point in her wanderings, she turned for home. Up to this point, her interest and energy had never flagged, but all at once, she wanted to go home. It always seemed longer going back than coming out and to enliven the return journey, she often went past Firbank Hall.

Her imagination was lively and often misleading. It worked on Firbank and the Harveys as it worked on Oakfield and the Lockwoods. She had come painfully up against the real Lockwoods, however, and felt resentment now and a wish to avoid them. But the Harveys seemed different because she didn't know them, and Firbank was like a house in a tale.

It stood alone in what she called the real country. When the gates were closed, it meant that no car was expected in or out, and it was safe to go up and look through at the old Tudor house.

Beside the gates to the right was a paved slope leading to the stables, and once she saw Angela and the Lockwoods running down, their hair flying. She drew back so that they shouldn't see her, but she wished she was with them. How wonderful to be inside the gates, to run down to the stables, to go all over the garden. In one place there was a fountain, a single jet of water, not spraying, but rising and falling, rising and falling, in the centre of a small stone basin. How lovely to lean over and let the water fall into your hand! She would have done that every day, she told herself; she would have done it by the hour.

When she had looked enough at the house, she took the path that ran between iron railings through a little wood. A stream ran along with the path, and if Thea saw flowers, she climbed over the railings to pick them.

One spring Saturday, she saw the first bluebells, a blue haze seemingly suspended between the trees and the grass. She scrambled over the railings and knelt on the damp mould, carefully feeling for the base of the stems. She hadn't gathered more than half a dozen when she realised that someone was standing on the grassy mound above her. She looked up and saw Angela Harvey, her dark hair in a bush, her puckish dimples showing high in her cheeks, her hands behind her back.

'You're trespassing,' said Angela blandly. 'This is our wood.'

Thea stared up from below, slowly reddening, the bluebells falling from her hand.

'I didn't know it was your wood.'

Angela was surprised by the way she spoke. Angela was interested in the way people spoke and could hardly ever refrain from immediately imitating them. She was naïvely surprised now that a girl so badly dressed should speak in such cool, clear, even cutting accents. The girl got up from the ground with such a look of anger and humiliation that Angela laughed outright.

'Don't look like that,' she said. 'What do a few bluebells matter? Take them. Take as many as you like. There are plenty more in the other spinney.'

Thea didn't want the bluebells if they were to be given to her. She had thought they were free, anybody's.

'Do take them,' said Angela with a brilliant smile, during which her eyes almost disappeared behind their dark lashes. 'Or I shall feel a pig because I said that about trespassing.'

Thea stopped and lifted the few limp flowers from the earth.

'Thank you,' she said with constraint and, under Angela's eyes climbed the railings and hurried away along the path.

She didn't climb into the wood again. For a long time she didn't even go past the house.

II

Visiting Mr Lockwood on quite another matter, Mrs Hunter was startled to be asked how old her elder daughter was. She was so startled that she couldn't immediately think and turned helplessly to Thea who, as usual, was with her.

'Fifteen,' Thea supplied.

Thea had come straight from school. She had rushed out of the school gates, meaning to get home and snatch something to eat as quickly as possible, but was met by her mother who said they must go to see Mr Lockwood.

So now she sat, her hair in tails under her school hat, her fingers inky under her old brown kid gloves, in Mr Lockwood's private office, and on the other side of the fire, her mother sat, too. It was at the end of the November afternoon, and Mr Lockwood should have been signing his letters.

At the back of the fire a fleece of soot hung trembling violently. If she had been alone, Thea would have enjoyed shearing it off with the poker. But she wasn't alone and she had to keep her attention on Mr Lockwood.

Under the light, the lawyer's hand tapped the desk. He was perpetually amazed by Mrs Hunter's pertinacity. She was, in his opinion, nothing but a rabbit of a woman and he knew he frightened her, but she kept on coming, keeping other clients out, bothering him about one thing after another. And today he wanted to give his full attention to the Searby Development Scheme. It needed it. He could, of course, lay his hands on quite a considerable sum. That mortgage. Cooper's, too, if necessary. But here was this tiresome woman sitting before him, waiting for him to find a way out of her trifling troubles again. She was in money difficulties as usual, and Heaven alone knew what was to be done to cut down her expenses. God, what a nuisance she was! He sighed heavily and put his hands over his face. Let him get the Hunter family into focus, take a look at them since he must, let him settle something, anything, so as to be rid of them. He considered in silence. Thea wondered if he was praying for patience; she didn't feel it could be for them.

'How old is what's-her-name, the elder girl?' he pounced suddenly, dropping his hands.

And the woman didn't even seem to know how old her own daughter was. The child had to answer. What an untidy girl, too! Clare never looked like that.

'How old?' he snapped at Thea.

'Fifteen.'

It did not occur to Thea to look at the situation from Mr Lockwood's point of view. For her, a child, there was only one point of view and that was her own. In her opinion, Mr Lockwood didn't care what happened to her family, but took advantage of his position in regard to them (she wasn't at all clear what this was) to bully them for the sheer love of bullying. Thea regarded Mr Lockwood rather as the mouse must regard the cat, which seems not to take any interest in it, yet deals it the cruellest, most unlooked-for blows. He was, it appeared, about to pounce on Molly now.

'It's time she left school,' said Mr Lockwood. 'You'd better send in her notice at once. It should have been in at the beginning of the term, but I'll get Miss Eardley to accept it.' He made a rapid note on a pad and pushed it from him. 'And now, Mrs Hunter, I must ask you to excuse me.' He rose and made her an ironic bow. 'I have no more time to give you.'

Mrs Hunter rose, too, looking desperate.

'But what work can Molly do at fifteen, Mr Lockwood?'

'You should know, she's your child,' said the lawyer. 'Anyway,

I can't go into it now. Take her away from school, and put her to some kind of work, any kind of work so that one of them will bring some money into the house instead of everlastingly taking it out.'

The youth of the Hunter children seemed interminable. He felt he would never get them off his hands.

'And now good afternoon, Mrs Hunter,' he said.

'I'm so sorry,' said Mrs Hunter, nervously but doggedly, standing her ground, 'but you haven't told me what to do about the money yet.'

'Oh, I'll speak to the bank,' he groaned, giving in for the sake of peace. 'But this sort of thing can't go on. For God's sake – no, for your own sake, Mrs Hunter, use your common sense. The more money you draw out the less you have left. I should have thought even you would see that.'

'I do see it, Mr Lockwood,' said poor Mrs Hunter. 'But what can I do?'

'I've told you what to do for the time being,' said Mr Lockwood, sitting down abruptly and pressing a bell on his desk. 'So allow me to bid you once more – good afternoon.' His voice rose alarmingly and Mrs Hunter and Thea hurried from the room, passing Bromley, the chief clerk, coming in at last with the letters.

Outside in the fog, Thea took her mother's arm.

'I wish we hadn't to go and see Mr Lockwood, Mother,' she said.

'So do I, dear,' sighed Mrs Hunter.

'Why do we go then?'

'We have to, dear.'

'But why?'

'We couldn't manage if we didn't, dear.'

'Couldn't we try?'

'Oh, no, that's impossible,' said Mrs Hunter, drawing in a sharp breath at the very idea.

Baffled and oppressed, Thea waited with her mother for the tram. She was hungry and the fog stung her eyes. The tram clanging its bell could be heard, but not seen. It loomed up at last and the would-be passengers surged towards it, but it clanged past without stopping. 'Full up,' called the conductor and the unlucky travellers fell back to wait for another.

They got home at last. There was a light in the front room where Martin was doing his homework. Molly was getting tea in the kitchen.

She was making toast and as they came in, carried a slice to the table to spread it with butter.

'Do be careful of the butter, dear,' said her mother anxiously.

'Now I know where you've been,' said Molly. 'You've been to see Mr Lockwood. What's he cutting us down on now?'

Neither her mother nor her sister answered, so Molly looked up from the toast.

'Is it anything about me?' she asked intuitively.

'He says it's time you left school, dear,' said Mrs Hunter.

Knife poised, Molly considered this.

'I don't think I mind,' she said.

Thea thought she ought to know the whole of it.

'He says you have to work,' she said.

Molly finished buttering the toast.

'I know I have to work. We shall all have to work for Mother. But I don't know what I can do. I've never been much good at lessons,' she said humbly.

'You can do all sorts of things,' said Thea. 'Look what good cakes you make.'

'That's not work. It's only fun. I suppose I can't go out as a cook, Mother?'

'Of course not,' said Mrs Hunter in a stifled voice.

The girls turned sharply to look at her. She had sunk into the rocking-chair, where she now sat with her hat off and her eyes closed.

'Are you getting a headache, Mother?' Molly darted to the cupboard for the teapot. 'You must have some tea straight away. Tell Martin, Thea, will you?'

'Tea, Martin,' called Thea from the passage, and he appeared, hair on end, hands blue with cold.

'Well, where've you been, you two?' he began cheerfully, but Molly frowned at him.

'Poor Mum, is it a headache?' he murmured, bending to kiss her cheek.

'It's not bad, dear,' she said, opening her eyes to smile at him.

What good children they were, she thought gratefully, watching them from the rocking chair, her head against the woollen antimacassar, once the comfort of cooks in the kitchen at Hill House. Her heart yearned over Molly, no more than a child in a gym tunic. To think she had to go out into the world and earn her living at fifteen!

She sighed and at once three heads turned towards her.

'Are you all right, Mother?' asked Molly.

'Yes. I think my headache is better already,' she said, smiling at them.

Their faces cleared and Martin took another large helping of jam. The second jar this week, thought Mrs Hunter, but hadn't the heart to restrain him. Relaxed in the chair, shelving her problems for the moment, she smiled again at her children.

Thea, biting into toast, smiled back. Such a rush of love for her mother came over her that the mouthful of toast almost choked her. Why were things always so mixed up? Her mother's headache was getting better now, the kitchen was warm and cosy after the fog outside, jam and toast were good, but Mr Lockwood still loomed over everything. He was making Molly go out to work now. Thea knew, although she was careful not to show it, that Molly had had a shock.

When tea was over and the washing-up done, the children brought their homework to the table. Mrs Hunter brought hers, too. She pored over the penny notebook she kept accounts in. The children's sums came out; they ruled lines under them and disposed of them one by one, but their mother's problems were insoluble. If Molly had a new coat, Martin couldn't have shoes. If the coal bill was paid this month, it meant leaving the rates. But if she didn't pay the rates on the right date, she would miss the discount. But if she didn't pay the coal bill, they would be without fire before long, because the man had refused to deliver any more coal until he was paid. Mrs Hunter sat helplessly before the notebook.

Across the table, Molly found it hard to concentrate on her

homework. It seemed no good doing lessons when an abyss yawned two months ahead. There was one question she burned to ask. 'He won't send me away from home, will he?' But she wouldn't ask, because she knew it would upset her mother, even to put such a thought into her head. In other families, parents conspired to keep anxieties from their children; in this one, the children kept them from their mother. Molly knew she must let the question gnaw in secret.

With the years, a curious situation, fostered perhaps unconsciously by Mrs Hunter, had grown up. She didn't want the children ever to blame their father for anything. To a lesser degree she didn't want them to blame her. Mutely, she allowed them to blame Mr Lockwood. From allowing them to blame him, she had almost come to blame him herself. The Hunter family had now almost lost sight of the cause of their own privations, which was, after all, their own poverty. For them, now, it wasn't so much that they hadn't got the money as that Mr Lockwood wouldn't let them have it. Mr Lockwood seemed to be, if not the author of their misfortunes, then the one who imposed them.

III

Preparing for bed, Mr and Mrs Lockwood, according to habit, talked over their day. Mrs Lockwood in a peach velvet wrap, her plump feet in feathered mules, sat at her dressing table arranging her hair for the night. From time to time, tilting backwards, she looked at herself in the glass with approval, first on this side, then on that.

William wandered in and out from his dressing room, in various stages of disrobement, taking money from his pockets, removing cuff links and collar studs.

These two got on very well together. As a boy, William had had no home life. His father, left a widower, married the housekeeper, who didn't like his sons. They didn't like her either and kept out of the house as much as possible. After such an upbringing, William appreciated to the full the home Effie made for him. She surrounded him with comfort and good management and gave him three daughters. Girls were what he wanted; in his own harsh home there had been no girls, and the femininity of his wife and daughters never failed to charm and refresh him. Whatever their faults the Lockwoods were a devoted family.

Surveying the comfortable haze of her day, at the end of it, Mrs Lockwood couldn't quite think of anything in particular that had happened.

'Except that Clare was sick before I took her to the dentist, and when she got there, there was nothing whatever to be done to her teeth, the silly child.'

'She gets it from me,' said her father. 'I'm scared of going to dentists whether they do anything to my teeth or not.'

'And we started airing the twins' beds today for the holidays,' said Effie, putting another curler in.

'Bit soon, isn't it?'

'Well, it seems to bring them nearer,' said Mrs Lockwood, indulgent of her maternal feelings. 'Anything interesting at the office, dear?'

'Well, I've had rather a worrying day, with one thing and

another, and to crown it all, Mrs Hunter arrived at about quarter to five and held up the letters. She always chooses the worst time to come and there's no moving her once she's got in. What a vague creature she is, Effie! She can't collect herself to answer anything I ask her. She didn't even know the age of her own child today.'

'Which one?' Effie covered the curlers by a satin cap, deeply frilled with lace.

'The elder girl.'

'I could have told you myself,' said Mrs Lockwood promptly. 'She's fifteen. But why did you want to know?'

'It's time she left school and started to earn her living.'

'What's she going to do?' Mrs Lockwood manipulated switches, leaving the room pleasantly lit by the bedside lamp and the fire she always indulged in as soon as the cold nights began.

'How do I know what she's going to do?' said William, rather testily, from his dressing room. 'That's what her mother asked me. What do you do with girls? If anyone asked me what to do with ours, I shouldn't know.'

'I don't think the question will arise, dear,' said Mrs Lockwood complacently.

'No, we'll be mobbed by young men wanting to marry them. But it'll have to be a very exceptional young man who'll get Clare away from me,' said William.

'You and your Clare,' said Mrs Lockwood, fondly mocking, getting into bed. 'Well, I wonder what Molly Hunter will do. What can she do?'

'Nothing that I know of. I rang up Miss Eardley before I left the office to ask her to accept the girl's notice. That's the sort of thing I have to keep on doing for your Mrs Hunter,' he said with a slight recrudescence of irritation. 'Miss Eardley says the girl shows no ability for anything in particular. The young one's clever, it seems, but not this one.'

'And the poor girl isn't very attractive either,' said Mrs Lockwood. 'All those freckles, summer and winter alike. It's most unfortunate.'

William now appeared in striped pyjamas, which though silk, made him look like a convict. His jowl was very dark from the day's growth of beard. It was a good thing Mrs Lockwood was used to him; anybody else would have been startled. But Mrs Lockwood welcomed him smilingly into bed, smoothing his pillow for him and he sank into it with a sigh of relief. Good to get into bed after a long day. The firelight was pleasant, everything was very comfortable.

'Ah well!' he sighed aloud, as if life had its compensations.

Effie had been preoccupied since she put out the light.

'William,' she said at length, 'I think I know what you can do with Molly Hunter.'

'Mm?'

'Mrs Watson's desperate for a nursery governess.'

'What – again?'

'Yes, the children are very difficult, you know. She asked me only yesterday if I knew of anybody. She'd be delighted to get Molly Hunter who is, after all, a lady and has good manners and everything. Now isn't that the very thing?'

'It'll do, anyway,' mumbled William from his pillow. 'You'd better arrange it.'

'I will. I'll ring up Mrs Watson in the morning. I'm so glad I thought of it,' said Mrs Lockwood. 'Mrs Watson will be so grateful. Good night, dear,' she said. 'Sleep well.'

'Mm,' murmured William comfortably. 'You, too.'

CHAPTER SIX

After promising Molly to Mrs Watson over the telephone in the morning, Mrs Lockwood went round to Byron Place in the afternoon to make sure of delivery. She had little doubt of bringing it off; but she took an old blouse with her to be on the safe side.

At the scrape of the gate on the path, Thea appeared at the window of the front room and Mrs Lockwood frowned. She had forgotten that this was the High School half-holiday. She had counted on seeing Mrs Hunter alone. Molly didn't matter, but this girl stared so, it made one quite self-conscious. Several times, under Thea's steady stare, Mrs Lockwood had actually found herself thinking what she was saying and of course that ruined conversation. However, the girl was at home and must be put up with.

Mrs Hunter welcomed her with exclamations of welcome and apology. The only fire was in the kitchen. Of course the sitting room fire should be lit at once, but it wouldn't warm the room for quite some time, she feared.

'It certainly would not,' said Mrs Lockwood. 'Let me go into the kitchen. It will be a change for me. I hardly ever see my own, you know.'

She led the way into the kitchen where Molly was just taking a sheet of biscuits from the oven.

'Molly, they smell delicious!' exclaimed Mrs Lockwood, going to lean over them. 'Did you really make them? They look most professional.'

Molly smiled, shyly gratified.

'I'm glad I came,' said Mrs Lockwood, seating herself in the rocking chair and throwing back her sables. 'I hope I shall be offered one with my cup of tea.'

'Of course,' said Mrs Hunter. 'They'll be cool by the time the kettle boils, won't they, Molly?'

Thea had come into the kitchen and was standing by the dresser. She didn't welcome Mrs Lockwood's arrival, but didn't want to miss anything.

'Well, Thea, you're growing,' said that lady, running her eyes over Thea's much too short gym tunic and tangled hair. What a blessing it had been to have had a nanny to train her own three to see to their looks before making any appearance.

Thea smiled, but said nothing, keeping her eyes on Mrs Lockwood.

'You don't often see me in the kitchen, do you?' said Mrs Lockwood, herself conscious of fatuity, but unable to help it. 'Molly, when you make the tea, put plenty in,' she urged with a cosy wriggle. 'I like mine strong.'

'Yes, Mrs Lockwood,' said Molly, who had brought the best teacloth and now told Thea by a look to do something about getting out the best cups.

'By the way, Mrs Hunter, I thought you might like this,' said Mrs Lockwood, unwrapping a tissue paper parcel and holding up a strawberry chiffon blouse with pearl buttons down the back and only a little gone under the arms. 'I've quite done with it,' she continued through Mrs Hunter's exclamations of pleasure. 'I don't know whether it's any use to you, perhaps it *is* a little elaborate? But if you don't want it, I can easily give it to someone else.'

'But I should love to have it,' said Mrs Hunter. 'Thank you very much. What a lovely colour! This will cheer me up, won't it, children?'

She held the pink chiffon under her chin and looked to them to second the vote of thanks.

'It suits you, Mother,' said Molly.

Thea murmured: 'Mmm.' There was something in the situation that made her feel awkward. But her mother was obviously pleased and was still thanking Mrs Lockwood.

'I could never buy anything like this for myself. Look at all the work in these tucks.'

'That's all right,' said Mrs Lockwood, as if she had done them herself. 'I'm glad you like it. It was always a favourite of mine, but it's getting just a little passy for me. I can't wear anything the least bit past its first freshness, you know. I simply haven't the opportunity.'

'No, of course not,' agreed Mrs Hunter.

'Though I suppose I could still have worn it under a coat.' Mrs Lockwood looked for a moment as if she might take the blouse back, but Molly handed her tea and she took that.

'Now for one of those biscuits,' she said.

Molly handed them.

'Mmmm. Mmmm,' mumbled Mrs Lockwood appreciatively, crumbs flying out of her full mouth into her fur. 'I must have the recipe for these. Cook must make some. The children will love them. May I have another?'

'Oh, do,' said Mrs Hunter happily.

The Hunter family, by common consent, always made a batch of biscuits last two days, but now from the way Mrs Lockwood was enjoying them Thea began to have fears for the second day's supply. She thought she had better make sure of her own share while she could. Her hand stretched tentatively towards the plate, she raised her eyebrows enquiringly at her mother. Her mother nodded and Thea took another biscuit. But it soon became preposterous to think of keeping up with Mrs Lockwood. Thea was first alarmed, then indignant. At this rate, there would not only be no biscuits for tomorrow, there wouldn't even be any for Martin when he came in from football today. Thea was so taken up with watching Mrs Lockwood's plump, beringed hand reaching out for biscuits that she did not realise for some time that the atmosphere had changed and that her Mother and Molly were looking intently at the visitor.

'I've got Mrs Watson to take her as a nursery governess,' Mrs Lockwood was saying.

Mrs Watson! Thea at once visualised large overbearing Mrs Watson and her four children with their rough red cheeks and bulging eyes.

'Oh, I couldn't teach,' faltered Molly, who had gone pale under her freckles. 'I don't know anything.'

'You don't need to,' said Mrs Lockwood, taking another biscuit. 'All you need is to be firm.'

'But I'm not firm,' said Molly desperately. 'I don't feel I could ever be firm with the Watsons,' she said.

'Rubbish, child,' said Mrs Lockwood. 'You don't know what you can do till you try.'

'Molly is always nervous with strangers,' put in Mrs Hunter.

'She'll have to get over that,' said Mrs Lockwood, 'if she's going to earn her living.'

The Hunters gazed mutely.

'You see, Molly,' said Mrs Lockwood, in a reasoning way, 'Miss Eardley has told Mr Lockwood that you haven't done well at school. She says you show no ability for anything in particular. So what are we to do for you, dear? I thought it was very nice of Mrs Watson to say she was willing to take you on my recommendation, even though you have no qualifications and no experience and are far younger than she would wish. You see, Molly,' she said, turning stiffly in her direction – there were times when Mrs Lockwood seemed all whalebone – 'I was *almost* going to say: "Beggars can't be choosers," but you know what I mean.'

Thea, staring, wondered why she said she was almost going to say it when she did say it.

'When you have nothing to recommend you but a friend, you almost have to take anything,' said Mrs Lockwood. 'You do understand that, don't you?'

Molly said nothing. She looked miserably at her mother, who murmured sadly that what Mrs Lockwood said was only too true.

'Well,' said Mrs Lockwood, brushing the crumbs of nine biscuits – Thea had counted them – from her furs, 'I went to considerable trouble to get this situation for Molly . . .'

'Oh, it was most kind of you,' said poor Mrs Hunter, thus prompted. 'Very, very kind and I know Molly thanks you as I do. But what makes us hesitate is the fear that she isn't suitable for the post.'

'What post is she suitable for?' asked Mrs Lockwood.

There was no answer.

'My advice to Molly,' said Mrs Lockwood firmly, 'is to take the post and *make* herself suitable.'

After a silence, Mrs Hunter said: 'Perhaps that is the best thing for you to do, Molly. Unless the Watsons will think she is going to them under false pretences,' she added, trying again, to Mrs Lockwood.

'False pretences won't trouble the Watsons,' said Mrs Lockwood bluntly. 'They want somebody.'

She arranged her sables round her neck.

'That's settled then,' she announced. 'She's to start the second of January. I managed to get a week's holiday for her beforehand. The hours are nine till six. You have lunch and tea with the children, of course, Molly. Saturday you leave at four, Sunday at half-past twelve. So it's quite good, isn't it? And you are to have the usual salary, twenty-six pounds a year, even though you are so young and inexperienced.'

While her mother was seeing Mrs Lockwood off at the front door, Molly stole upstairs and shut herself into the bedroom she shared with Thea. When they were hurt, the Hunter children drew themselves in like sea-anemones and shrank into their own particular crevices. By tacit consent, the others forbore to mention the cause of injury until it was broached by the victim in question. Thea, though bursting with sympathy and indignation, was obliged to let Molly leave the kitchen without a word.

'Goodbye, Mrs Lockwood,' Mrs Hunter was saying at the front door. 'And my most grateful thanks for the blouse.'

Thea, standing by the fire, thought her mother was too polite. Far too polite. That was why Mrs Lockwood felt she could be so rude to them all. Thea turned to the door, feeling she must say this to her mother when she came back to the kitchen.

But Mrs Hunter didn't come back. She, in her turn, shut herself into the front room, and sat down abruptly at the table. She felt she had sacrificed Molly to Mrs Lockwood. She felt Molly ought not to be made to go to the Watsons, she oughtn't to try to be a governess at all. How could she, no more than a child herself, manage the unruly Watson children? And Mrs Watson was a most unpleasant woman. She had never been able to keep a governess yet; Mrs Lockwood had said so herself many a time.

Yet what else was there that Molly could do, Mrs Hunter asked? What else? And Mrs Lockwood was always so kind. Look how kind she was when Richard died, Mrs Hunter reminded herself. And Mr Lockwood, too. 'I'm sure they would never, either of them, do anything that wasn't for our good,' thought Mrs Hunter.

Sighing, she got out pencil and paper, without which she could not make any calculation, however small. She worked out how much twenty-six pounds a year meant by the week, and was disturbed again when she found it only came to ten shillings. Ten shillings a week wouldn't cover Molly's clothes and car-fares. The child would be making herself miserable for nothing.

Though, of course, reasoned poor Mrs Hunter, whose life, since Richard's death, had been spent in swaying between the pros and the cons, of course she would get her food, which would make a difference. And perhaps the Watsons wouldn't be so bad after all, perhaps it was just Mrs Watson's manner, and perhaps the children might take to Molly and become quite manageable, perhaps . . .

In the kitchen, Thea, sitting on the fender, talked to herself.

'The Lockwoods shan't make *me* do what they want,' she vowed. 'If ever they want me to do a thing, that'll be enough. I won't do it!'

The fire had formed itself into a hollow cave over which mysterious breaths passed, now glowing, now dark. The kettle on the hob dribbled steam. On the mantelpiece the alarm clock ticked so energetically that it moved itself infinitesimally to the right. By the time Thea went up to bed, it would have reached the tea-caddy. Martin called it the travelling clock.

Thea sat on, revengeful, pugnacious.

'Wait till I'm grown up, I'll fight them,' she vowed.

The front door opened and closed. She heard Martin's football boots clumping down the passage. He appeared, a lanky figure in shorts and sweater, plastered with mud from head to foot, his hair streaked over his forehead.

'Hullo,' he said, coming to the fire and taking off his knobbly boots. 'Where is everybody? Oh, I say, biscuits!' He reached for one. 'Mmmm,' he mumbled appreciatively. 'Who's been?'

'Mrs Lockwood.'

'Mmmm,' said Martin, taking another biscuit.

'It's a wonder there are any left,' said Thea. 'She ate nine.'

'Nine!' ejaculated Martin. 'Cripes!'

'And what's worse she's making Molly go to be the Watsons' governess after Christmas,' said Thea.

Martin burst out laughing. 'Molly a governess! Why she can't spell to save her life!'

'Don't laugh,' frowned Thea. 'Molly minds. She'll be miserable. She's miserable now.'

'Why's she going then?' asked Martin. 'She doesn't need to go if she doesn't want to. They can't make her.'

'They *have* made her. Mother says there's nothing else she can do.'

Martin, steaming before the fire, considered this.

'I don't suppose there is,' he said. 'Poor Moll, she was never much good at lessons.'

They were both silent for a time.

'What're you going to be when you're grown up?' Thea asked.

'Me? A doctor,' he said.

CHAPTER SEVEN

I

But when he left school, Mr Lockwood 'got him into' a bank. 'Anybody want a boy?' Mr Lockwood had thrown out testily at his club.

The Borough Treasurer looked up from his paper and said he might have a vacancy later, but Platt, the manager of one of the town banks, said he could take a boy at once, if he were suitable. So Mr Lockwood sent for Martin to come to his office.

He hadn't seen Martin for some time; in fact, it may be doubted if he had ever really seen him at all. Clare used to talk a good deal about him at one time, but the Bible Classes were over long ago and the New Year parties had fallen into abeyance for the last few years, and Clare had seen no more of Martin than her father had. So when the lawyer looked up from his desk at the end of one afternoon, he was momentarily taken aback at being confronted by a tall, quiet boy instead of the rough-haired child he vaguely remembered seeing on some occasion or other at Oakfield.

Martin stood at the desk, smiling as at someone he was shy of, but trusted. Another man might have been touched by his youth and defencelessness, but not Mr Lockwood. Mr Lockwood hadn't time to bother about anything but the main point at issue. Besides he hardly thought of the Hunters as individuals; to him they were a nuisance to be disposed of as quickly as possible. They were like parcels put before him to tie up for the post; he tied them up without examining the contents. The Hunters were something he had to get off.

He dealt briskly with Martin.

'Well, now, about this career of yours,' he said. 'Have you any suggestion to offer?'

'Yes, sir,' said Martin, encouraged, 'I should like to be a doctor.'

Mr Lockwood gave a short bark of a laugh and Martin flushed. He brushed his hair from his forehead with one hand.

'A doctor, eh?' said Mr Lockwood with amusement. 'And where's the money to come from for another two years at school and university afterwards until you are about twenty-three?'

'I should have to get scholarships, of course, sir. I've looked everything up.' Martin began to draw papers from his frayed pocket.

'Not a bit of use, my boy,' said Mr Lockwood with finality. 'There isn't the money to keep you in food and clothes, let alone pay your fees. You're like these politicians. They promise free places, maintenance grants and goodness knows what, but they conveniently forget that the parents, even though they pay nothing for extended education, are nevertheless losing money because their children aren't earning any. That's your case, my boy. Your mother needs your earnings.'

Martin looked at him, the flush dying in his cheek. His hopes died with it. He stuffed the papers back into his pocket.

'You see that, don't you?' said the lawyer.

'Yes, sir.'

He felt humiliated to have been such a fool. He had never thought about having to be kept, having to eat and be clothed. All his plans, his writing backwards and forwards about prospectuses – what an ass he must look never to have thought of the first essential, the means to live while he was learning.

'No need to be so cut up about it,' said Mr Lockwood. 'There are other jobs, you know. How about going into the bank?'

Mr Lockwood spoke highly of the bank. The hours were short, he said, viewing them from the customer's side of the counter. The prospects were good, he said, as if everybody who went into a bank became a manager. The work wasn't very exacting, he said, knowing nothing about it, but comparing it contemptuously with his own. And on the whole, he concluded, it was a gentlemanly sort of job, which should please his mother. He could, with influence, get Martin in and all that remained then was for Martin to work himself up.

'Take Platt as your example,' advised Mr Lockwood. 'He has a nice job, his salary's about six hundred a year, which is quite fairly adequate for a man in his position. He knows everybody's business, he's respected, mixes with everybody. In fact, he's a friend of mine,' he said, as if to be recognised as a friend of William Lockwood was to have succeeded indeed. And he was right. In Aldworth, it was.

Martin went into the bank. He hurried into it, only too glad to get somewhere, so that it should never appear that he had expected to be kept for eight years. He must show everybody that he meant to keep himself. His salary worked out at precisely eight shillings and fourpence a week.

Mrs Hunter went to the office to thank Mr Lockwood. It was so kind of him to use his influence on Martin's behalf, and it was such a relief to her that he was making such a good start in life. How she wished she could repay Mr Lockwood for all his kindness.

Mr Lockwood implied that all he asked from Mrs Hunter was that she should let him get on with his work, and Mrs Hunter went home to enthuse further about the bank to her children.

She felt it was fitting that an architect's son should spend his working life in such a spacious, impressive building. All that marble and mahogany, she said. It reminded her of a Roman basilica. And the young men in banks always seemed particularly kind and nice . . .

But Thea looked at Martin and saw that he was silent to hide his feelings. She knew he was badly hit by having to go into a bank instead of being a doctor.

There were two of them now, put into work they didn't like by the Lockwoods, Thea reflected. Would Martin go all quiet like Molly? He was quiet enough already; if he got any quieter, he would be hardly speaking to them at all. She looked at her sister and brother with misgiving. They weren't happy.

'And they used to be,' she thought with distress. 'We used to have fun once.'

Molly had stayed with the Watsons for two years. She stayed because she daren't give notice. Every night she tossed about in her bed, rehearsing how she would give notice next day. Every morning she went out pale and determined to give it. Every evening she came home without having given it. She acquired a hunted look. She was always ailing. She had headaches, colds, chilblains, pains of one sort and another. There was always something wrong with Molly in these days.

She might have been at the Watsons' for longer than two years, since the family was continually being added to and they would never have parted with a girl they could so easily put upon. She couldn't release herself, and no one would have released her, but fortunately, though the spirit would have had to go on, the flesh rebelled. She had such a bad breakdown that she had to stay in bed for several weeks, and by the time she was up again, Mrs Watson had replaced her. Molly was profoundly relieved, and Mrs Lockwood found her another place, with the Hallidays.

But the young Hallidays, though mild compared with the Watsons, soon found their new governess had no discipline and proceeded to make her life a misery. Mrs Halliday complained that the children, under Molly, became worse instead of better, and it was not long before Molly went to the Bensons. She was there at present, doing no better than before.

Still, there was always Sunday. Molly was free then of her difficult charges and Martin was free of the bank. The weight of the week's uncongenial work was lifted, and though it would be back the next day, there was this respite. Thea and her mother were relieved for them and with them, and Sunday tea, for which Molly made cakes and biscuits, was the happiest hour of the week for them all. Thea, as she ate, would often worm her hand into her mother's as it lay on the table beside her. That was her way of expressing the deep family contentment that lay over teatime on Sunday.

What the young Hunters chiefly felt during their youth was that there was no security. The only compensation they had, and, as on these Sunday afternoons, they often had it, was that they were all in the same boat together. They were knit closer by the anxieties of their situation. Mrs Hunter wasn't the sort of parent to be able to give security to her children, but they didn't blame her. She was one of them, as defenceless, as uncertain as they were.

II

Christmas, being the season of goodwill, usually reminded Mrs Lockwood to do something about the Hunters. She no longer invited them for the New Year; the twins wouldn't let her. But she usually had Mrs Hunter and the girls up to tea. Sometimes it was just before Christmas and then she showed them the presents she was giving to other people. There was a no-present-giving arrangement between Mrs Hunter and Mrs Lockwood. Mrs Hunter couldn't afford presents and Mrs Lockwood didn't consider it necessary to give to the Hunters at Christmas, since her husband did so much work for them all the year round for nothing.

The presents were laid out in one of the spare rooms at

Oakfield and the Hunters went round admiring them. The handsomest of all were for the Harvey family.

'I have to give them the best,' said Mrs Lockwood. 'Because, you see, they have absolutely everything.'

'"To him that hath shall be given,"' said Thea later. 'I always wondered why. Now I know.'

'Thea,' said her mother reprovingly, 'you shouldn't twist the Bible like that, dear.'

Every summer, while the twins were at home for the holidays, Mrs Lockwood held a Garden Fête in aid of charity and Mrs Hunter took tickets for herself and Thea.

Thea would have preferred not to go. Her policy was to evade Mr Lockwood's notice. She was nearly fifteen. When the others were fifteen, he made them leave school and do work they hated. Although she was determined that he shouldn't make her do work she didn't like, she didn't want to be made to leave school. She liked school. She liked the neck-and-neck race she kept up with Helen Millard for the top place in form, and before she left she wanted to have reached the Sixth and taken Higher Certificate like the others. Every day was a day gained towards this end, every day a day snatched from under the nose of Mr Lockwood.

So when her mother spoke with pleasurable anticipation of the fête this year, Thea was restrained about it. She accompanied her mother as usual but she hoped to be lost in the crowd and escape notice.

Mrs Lockwood had come to look upon it as a special dispensation of Providence that she always had a fine day for her fête. This year it was fine again and she anticipated with satisfaction the congratulations she would receive upon her weather.

In the afternoon, towards three o'clock, ant-like streams of human beings could have been seen converging upon Oakfield. The fête was a social event. It was opened by Lady Harvey and all the notable matrons had stalls. Their daughters presided over Bran Pies, Raffles and whatever the Lockwood girls didn't want to preside over themselves.

Mrs Hunter and Thea proceeded with the others up the hill towards the house. Mrs Hunter had a new rose in last summer's hat and a bow of mauve tulle at her neck, which made her look very distinguished, Thea thought. Thea herself wore a tussore frock, papery from many washings, and a mushroom straw hat. She had a coltish look with her long legs and swinging hair.

'Good afternoon, Mrs Hunter. Good afternoon, Thea,' cried little Mrs Barrett, hurrying by with her friend, tall Miss Wood. Their hats bobbed in animated conversation, though they had been talking all morning, since they always went into town together, stopping everybody they met to pick up the news.

The Vicar of Aldworth went past in his car; he had to be in time to appear on the platform.

The two Arnold girls were with their mother: they had just finished a year in Germany and had acquired an interesting foreign air. So many girls were going abroad these days. It must be marvellous, thought Thea, turning in at the gates with her mother.

The stream of people was borne by the drive almost up to the open door of the house, but was diverted at the last moment by an arrow pointing to the left and lettered firmly: 'This Way'. Passing the house, Thea looked in at the hall, cool and full of flowers.

'I wish we lived there,' she thought.

The stream poured round the drawing-room windows and emptied itself onto the big lawn, where from a small platform, the fête was in the act of being opened.

Too far off to hear, the Hunters watched what was to them a dumb show. The Vicar was evidently paying compliments to both Lady Harvey and Mrs Lockwood because those ladies were smiling, Mrs Lockwood looking up coyly as if to say he really shouldn't. Mrs Lockwood was in deep pink Irish lace with ospreys to match in her toque. Lady Harvey was plain by comparison in dark blue. Smiling now, she rose and clapping rippled round the lawn. She said something, the Hunters didn't know what. Clare, very pretty in a dress that blazed white in the sunshine, appeared to present the usual bouquet. More smiling, more clapping and the opening ceremony was over.

It was always rather awkward going round the stalls. Mrs Hunter felt she had to pay attention to them, she had to admire without buying anything very much. She couldn't afford that. So she went smilingly round with Thea, ready to shy away if pressed. She felt lucky to get off with no more than the purchase of a hand-knitted dish-cloth or a velvet kettle-holder. When these were wrapped up, nobody could tell how little had been spent, and Mrs Hunter had the satisfaction of showing that she had bought something.

Conversation buzzed like bees. Children laughed and ran about and clamoured to dip in the bran pie and ride on the pony. Hot sunshine lay over the scene. There was a smell of trampled grass, raw wood and sweet peas massing the flower stall. From the shrubbery came the strains of 'William Tell' or 'The Gondoliers' played by the Police Band.

As soon as they decently could, Mrs Hunter and Thea made for the side lawn where tea was served. If you didn't grab a table at once, you might stand the whole afternoon, waiting for tea. It was odd, remarked Mrs Hunter, sitting down to one, that people seemed to make for the tables earlier every year.

People smiled from other tables and the Hunters smiled back, but they were, as usual, a little out of it. Mrs Hunter had certainly come to the town as a stranger, but children usually draw their parents into the life of a place. Mrs Hunter had kept hers apart, so that they were strangers, too, or almost.

The Hunters were just finishing tea when Mrs Lockwood appeared to do the honours. As she proceeded from table to table, bending benevolently in the tightly-fitting pink gown with the ospreys waving, Thea thought she looked like a boiled lobster walking on its tail.

The twins joined their mother. Since they had gone away to school, they had become remote and haughty. They were by this time tall, well-developed girls with thick golden hair, thick legs, good complexions, slightly hooked noses and full chins. Roman matrons, thought Thea, watching them. Or those strong females holding up Greek temples. A couple of caryatides, she summed up to her own satisfaction.

Behind their mother, the twins looked over the heads of tea-takers, implying that this going the round was a great bore, but as daughters of the house they supposed it must be done. When their mother moved on, they moved too, coming to a stop with a still higher lift of the eyebrow as if they were almost at the limit of endurance. But Thea knew they were enjoying their own arrogance.

The party reached the Hunters' table. The twins made a faint smile, but Mrs Lockwood bent graciously and laid a hand on Mrs Hunter's shoulder.

'I haven't a moment, really,' she said in a confidential voice. 'But I know you understand. So many people I must speak to. They expect it, you know. You've had tea? That's right. Didn't you think the strawberries were rather wonderful?'

Mrs Hunter murmured that they hadn't had the strawberries.

'Dear, dear,' said Mrs Lockwood, 'that won't do.'

She laid a hand on the arm of a passing waitress and told her to bring strawberries and cream to the table. 'And charge them to me,' she whispered conspiratorially, the ospreys tickling the waitress's cheek.

Mrs Hunter, though protesting, thanked Mrs Lockwood warmly, but Thea blushed. She hated to be given strawberries while the twins stood by and she hated it when they went on, removing their solid persons and leaving the table exposed for all to see that the Hunters had only been able to afford the shilling tea.

The strawberries came.

'Isn't this nice?' said Mrs Hunter. 'Isn't it kind?'

But Thea kept her head down so that the mushroom hat should hide her while she ate them. The afternoon had been shot through with dislike, envy and anger, all the disrupting, damaging emotions that beset her when in proximity to the Lockwoods. 'I ought to keep out of their way,' she said to herself. 'I ought never to come near them.'

The strawberries finished, Thea, still feeling that everybody was looking at them, followed her mother from the table. When they reached the big lawn, Bee Lockwood was making an announcement from the platform. While the band was having tea, announced Bee, Angela Harvey would give some recitations.

Everybody clapped, delighted to have the chance of a prolonged view of the daughter of Aldworth's only title.

'Thea, how interesting!' said Mrs Hunter. 'Mrs Lockwood says the twins say she's wonderful.'

If the twins said she was wonderful, Thea was ready to wager she wasn't. But she was as interested as anyone to observe Angela, who now came to the front of the platform, smiling so that her long eyes almost disappeared behind their dark lashes. She was quite unlike other girls, thought Thea, with her hair in a dark cloud on her shoulders, her face white above her white dress. She was sixteen, but not girlish. There was a cool sparkle about her not usual in girls.

Waiting with self-possession until the applause ceased, she recited something in broken English. Her voice was gay and clear, but it was a silly thing to choose, thought Thea. The twins were wrong as usual; there was nothing wonderful about the recitation.

'Very clever,' said Mrs Hunter admiringly, and from the prolonged applause, everyone else seemed to think so too.

Angela waited again, then came to the very front of the platform and with grave simplicity began:

'Does the road wind uphill all the way?'

Everyone stood still.

'Yes, to the very end.'
'Will the day's journey take the whole long day?'
'From morn till night, my friend.'

Thea, her face upturned, was suddenly rapt. Was it the voice or the words? Both were so apt to each other. Both fell like balm on the spirit that had shrunk small under pinpricks of Lockwood behaviour. Under the spell of the voice and the poem, Thea made one of those exhilarating recoveries in which life abounds, and since it was through Angela that she made it, she smiled at her in warm admiration.

'Shall I meet other wayfarers at night?'
'Those that have gone before.'

'It's too sad,' thought Mrs Hunter, and looked down at her gloves, her lips trembling.
It was over. Angela was bowing, leaving the platform amid applause. To hide her emotion, Mrs Hunter took Thea by the arm.
'Shall we go this way, dear?' she said, drawing her down the little path that led to the conservatory.

Mother and daughter went under the cool canopy of leaves and came out a moment later into the sunlight concentrated on the glittering conservatory. Angela stood basking by the door, gazing before her in a fit of abstraction.

Spurred out of self-consciousness by admiration, Thea darted forward.

'You were wonderful!' she said warmly. 'That last poem . . .' Angela brought her faculties to bear upon the leggy girl, badly dressed but somehow worth looking at.

'Oh, you liked it, did you?' Her eyes did their disappearing trick. 'I said the first to please the people, but the second to please myself.'

'What is it?' asked Thea.

'Christina Rossetti.'

'Oh, is it? Perhaps I've read it then. But I didn't know it was so lovely till you said it.'

'That's a compliment,' said Angela with satisfaction. 'Here . . .' She fished in her sash and brought out a folded paper. 'You can have it. I never forget my lines, but I wrote it out to be safe.'

'Oh, thank you!' Thea blushed with pleasure. 'Thanks awfully.'

Bee came out of the conservatory with treasure-hunt cards in her hands. She looked with haughty astonishment at Thea.

'Hello,' said Thea without warmth.

'Hello.'

Bee put a proprietary arm through Angela's and drew her away.

'Who's that?' asked Angela, not out of hearing.

'Oh, just someone we know,' said Bee dismissingly.

CHAPTER EIGHT

Thea had reached the sixth form and still Mr Lockwood hadn't said anything. She couldn't understand why. He had disposed of Molly and Martin, why didn't he try to dispose of her?

The truth was that Mr Lockwood was not concerning himself with her. He had long ago calculated the expenditure of Mrs Hunter's capital. It was to last a definite time. That time wasn't up yet, the money wasn't done. The youngest Hunter could stay at school for all he cared. Miss Eardley could arrange something for her.

It would have been a great relief to Thea to know this, but she didn't know it. She schemed and worried in secret. She was exultant to have stayed so long at school, but she also felt guilty. She felt she ought not to have stayed on when Molly and Martin had been made to leave. In the house, she waited on them, running up and downstairs for them, fetching and carrying. They thought it was most unselfish in her. They didn't know she was trying to atone to them for staying on at school.

She felt guilty at school as well as at home. When she passed School Certificate with many credits, Miss Eardley congratulated her on shaping so well for her career as a teacher. Thea was startled. This was the first she had heard about being a teacher. Miss Eardley must have settled it with Mr Lockwood, she thought angrily. But she had no intention of being a teacher. Teaching was for her inextricably mixed up with Molly's governessing. She herself could be a qualified teacher, no doubt, and teach in a school, but it would still be teaching.

For five years Molly had afforded an object lesson, an awful warning to her young sister. Under Thea's eyes, Molly had become year by year more spiritless, ailing and defeated. Thea was passionately sorry for her, but she was as passionately determined never to be like that herself. Never a teacher, she determined. Never.

But she didn't say so. She said nothing to her headmistress, merely smiled in a constrained way at the congratulations and went back to the sixth form to another year of school and her preparation for Higher Certificate at the end of it.

No one would have guessed from her pure brow and candid eyes that she felt she was deceiving her own family and the mistress at school. But underneath the regret at the necessity for deception was a firm determination to get what she wanted, which was to stay at school and beat Helen Millard to the end. Helen was going to Girton, but before they parted, Thea would show her who was the cleverer.

This competition with Helen was open and exhilarating. It was fun, sharpened by the necessity of getting the better of Mr Lockwood. Beyond the school year, when she should have taken Higher Certificate, the future was a blank. She had no idea what would happen to her, no idea what she wanted to do. She refused to think of it, because she didn't know what to think of.

Then suddenly one Wednesday afternoon in February, her desires took another leap forward and fastened as tenaciously on the future objective as they were fastened on the present one.

Wednesday was misnamed, for a sixth-former, a half-holiday. The only difference between Wednesday afternoon and any other was that Thea did lessons at home instead of at school.

Thea's scholastic prowess was treated with such respect at home that on Wednesday afternoons in the winter a fire was lit specially in the front room so that she could work alone. As a matter of fact, her mother always crept in to sit in the armchair, laying her fingers to her lips and whispering: 'Don't mind me.' Mrs Hunter was happy on Wednesday afternoons, darning and dozing by the fire, and only occasionally making some remark to which Thea, from long habit, was able to reply without being too much distracted from her work.

On this afternoon, she sat at the ornate table, her books spread over the shabby cloth, translating Cicero into English and putting her translation back into Latin. Mrs Hunter, by the fire, drew her needle in and out of Martin's sock. The blue dusk of the winter afternoon gathered in the street. Footsteps passed occasionally, now and then a gate clanged. There was the muffled rumble of traffic at the end of Byron Place.

'Look at this hole, Thea,' said Mrs Hunter, exhibiting the sock.

Thea glanced and smiled rather absently.

'I shouldn't darn that,' she said. 'It's not worth it.'

'It must be made to do a little longer,' said her mother.

Silence fell again. The flames licked softly at the coal. Mrs Hunter looked at Thea, who, cheek on hand, calmly translated. Thea was changing, thought her mother, she was growing into a very pretty girl. She was more like Richard than any of them. She had his brains, she was critical, impatient, and even, as he was, a little secretive. She didn't tell everything.

In a little while, Thea, glancing up, saw that her mother had fallen asleep. She smiled and got up to retrieve the needle threaded with brown wool that had fallen from her mother's hand. Then, carefully straightening the pleats of her skirt – Thea was at last beginning to mind what she looked like – she sat down and plunged back into Cicero. She was enjoying herself, her brain was working vigorously. Sometimes it was heavy and had to be flogged along; but not this afternoon.

She looked up, her attention caught. Was that a car coming up the street?

'I bet that's Mrs Lockwood,' she said, springing up to look through the curtains.

'Mother,' she cried, 'Mrs Lockwood's here. Oh, bother, I did want to finish before tea.'

'Oh, dear,' fluttered Mrs Hunter, waking. 'My hair's coming down. We've no cake, Thea.'

'She was here on Friday,' said Thea crossly, piling Cicero on Political Economy, throwing in Hamlet and European History.

'Thea dear,' said Mrs Hunter apologetically, putting on the light, 'could you possibly run to Miss Riley's for a sandwich cake?'

'I suppose I'll have to,' said Thea with bad grace.

'All right. Don't worry,' she said, crushing through the door with her books. 'I'll get something. I'll bring tea in.'

She got herself into the kitchen as Mrs Lockwood came into the house. She threw down her books, poked up the fire, put the kettle on and stole out to get her coat from the pegs in the passage. The ladies were already trilling and exclaiming in the front room and Thea smiled to herself: 'Each generation must have its own ways,' she thought. 'Helen and I would never dream of going on like that to each other.' Mrs Lockwood and her mother, although they met so often, kept their distance, across which they addressed each other with formality. 'Funny,' reflected Thea. 'Either we wouldn't keep up all that politesse, or we wouldn't bother to see each other.'

She closed the front door behind her in the quiet dusk. It was cold and slightly foggy. Her collar turned up and her hands in her pockets, she ran up Byron Place, through the back and along Wells Road to Miss Riley's. The shop was melancholy with a glitter of glass domes under a poor light and as Thea entered, Miss Riley's little red face popped up from under the counter.

'May I have a Victoria sandwich, please?'

'Jam or curd?' enquired Miss Riley dispassionately.

'Oh, lemon curd would be nice,' said Thea with enthusiasm, because you couldn't often get it.

Miss Riley removed a sandwich cake from under a dome

and disappeared to fill it. Thea heard her give a long sigh as she scraped the knife against the jar and wondered why.

'One-and-two,' said Miss Riley, appearing.

When she carried tea into the front room, Thea found the ladies with handkerchiefs to their eyes.

'Good afternoon, Thea,' said Mrs Lockwood.

'It's all right, dear,' said Mrs Hunter, explaining the handkerchiefs. 'It's just that Mrs Lockwood is telling me that all her girls, Clare, too, are to go to France in September. It will be very nice for them, but very lonely for their mother.'

'It will,' said Mrs Lockwood, blowing her nose.

France! They were going to France!

France! The word was enough. It stung Thea into sharp longing to go, too. They were going to France. It wasn't fair. It would be wasted on them. They wouldn't appreciate it. To think they should have the glorious chance to see France, to live there and speak French, while she had to stay in Aldworth. She was so taken up by her own thoughts that her mother had to ask twice if she were going to have tea with them.

'No, thank you, Mother, I'd rather get on with my work,' she said, and left them.

But work was out of the question. She stood by the fire saying over and over, 'Oh, if only I could go to France! If only I could!'

That the Lockwoods should be going was altogether too much. They were poaching on her preserves now. The rich, stupid Lockwoods could have the advantages of the rich and stupid – clothes, money, pleasures, all that sort of thing – but that they should *know* anything Thea Hunter couldn't know was too much. She wanted violently to go to France for its own sake, but she also couldn't bear the idea that the Lockwoods should have the immense privilege of going there when she couldn't. Because it would be so wasted on them, she said feverishly to herself.

She reappeared abruptly in the front room.

'Where are they going to in France?' she asked the astonished Mrs Lockwood.

'We don't know yet,' said that lady rather stiffly. She was always rather stiff with Thea. 'We've only just decided it with Sir Robert and Lady Harvey. Mr Lockwood is going to ask Miss Eardley to find a suitable finishing school.'

'How long will they be there?' asked Thea.

'They will stay for twelve months. Until they have acquired the language.'

'Oh,' said Thea, and went back to the kitchen.

At the gate, the fog swirled round the yellow lamps of the car. The chauffeur, humped at the wheel, longed for his tea and wished Mrs Lockwood would put an end to her visit. Thea, restless in the kitchen, possessed by her burning new desire, wished so too.

When Mrs Lockwood at last went, Thea was in the passage to face her mother as she turned from the door.

'Oh, Mother,' she burst out, 'is there any way I could go too? Could I possibly go?'

'Go? Go where?' asked her mystified mother.

'Oh, Mother – to France!'

Mrs Hunter, on her way back to the sitting-room fire, turned in amazement.

'To France, child? How could you possibly . . .?'

'I could teach. I wouldn't mind teaching there, it wouldn't be the same . . .'

'Thea, how could you go? We haven't the money, dear.'

'Oh, Mother,' pleaded Thea, 'would it cost very much – the fare, I mean? If I taught English and they taught me French and boarded me, it wouldn't cost any more than the fare. Oh, Mother, could we manage that?'

Mrs Hunter looked bewildered. It was all so sudden.

'Mother!' urged Thea. 'Say something. Tell me what you think.'

'I don't know what to think, dear,' said Mrs Hunter, who hardly ever did. 'It seems impossible at first sight, but perhaps some way could be found if you want to go so much . . .'

'Want to go!' said Thea vehemently. She clasped both hands on the broken edge of the mantelpiece and pressed her forehead against them. 'If you knew how much I want to go, Mother!'

Mrs Hunter regarded her helplessly. This was how Richard used to want things, and how he used to get them. She had been swirled along in the current of Richard's desires and she felt she was going to be swirled along in Thea's. Though how Thea was ever to get to France, she could not imagine.

CHAPTER NINE

I

'You want me, when I arrange for the Lockwood girls to go to a French pensionnat, to ask the headmistress to take you au pair – is that what you mean?' asked Miss Eardley, looking across her desk at Thea.

Thea swallowed visibly, her already wide eyes widening still further on her headmistress. Miss Eardley, used to the nervousness of the young, gave her time, and Thea struggled with inner confusion.

It wasn't what she had meant at all. What she had meant was, would Miss Eardley find her a place in some French school, any French school. It had not occurred to her to go *with* the Lockwoods. But she was so eager to go, so anxious to make it seem easy that she should – to Miss Eardley, Mr Lockwood, her mother, everybody concerned – that she would agree to anything. The way Miss Eardley put it sounded so easy: that she should be slipped casually in with the Lockwood party. So, youthfully, unnecessarily, she rushed to accept Miss Eardley's idea as if it had been her own.

'Yes,' she said breathlessly. 'Please. If you could possibly. . . if you think . . .'

'Well,' said Miss Eardley, 'I think it's a good idea. You could specialise in French then.'

Thea supposed she meant 'later' or 'afterwards'. But she had no concern with later or afterwards: what she wanted, burningly, was that Miss Eardley should say now, straight off, that she could go to France. If she had to go with the Lockwoods, she would go with the Lockwoods. She would go with anybody, put up with anything, to get there.

'I'll speak to Mr Lockwood,' said Miss Eardley, and Thea's face showed such a radiance of gratitude and happiness that the mistress was quite taken aback.

She had often wondered why she could not get to know this girl. She wondered why Thea avoided her, on the stairs, in the hall; and why, when sent for, she always had a watchful expression. For the first time she seemed to see the real girl at last, all reserve gone. The child glowed with life, and what a pretty creature she was!

'I'll do my best for you,' she said, smiling.

'Oh, thank you, Miss Eardley, thank you so very much,' breathed Thea, and sped away to nurse her hopes ecstatically in secret. France, France, she kept saying to herself.

It happened that Miss Eardley made her proposal about Thea not to Mr but to Mrs Lockwood, and in Lady Harvey's presence, which made it difficult, in fact impossible, for Mrs Lockwood to make any reasonable objection.

Lady Harvey invited Miss Eardley to Firbank so that the mothers could hear what the headmistress had to suggest, and, sitting in the long drawing room, Miss Eardley, almost as soon as the discussion started, said: 'By the way, would you mind if Thea Hunter went to the same school – au pair, of course – if it could be arranged?'

Mrs Lockwood was completely taken aback. She almost gaped.

'Thea Hunter . . .' she said blankly.

'It would be a good thing for her,' said Miss Eardley briskly. 'She's going to be a teacher, but she's too young to go to a training college. She has to put in time, and to spend a year in France would be an excellent way of doing it. I should be very glad if she could be included in your party. She's rather young to go alone – though, of course, you know all about her since she is Mr Lockwood's ward.'

'No, no, she's not his ward,' corrected Mrs Lockwood. 'There's nothing legal about it. He merely does his best for the family out of kindness. We are sorry for them,' explained Mrs Lockwood.

'Well, you will be doing a kindness to Thea by allowing her to go with your girls,' said Miss Eardley, taking the wind out of Mrs Lockwood's sails.

'Yes, of course,' said Lady Harvey, 'there can be no objection at all. Her mother is that sweet, tired-looking woman I see with you sometimes, isn't she, Mrs Lockwood? For my part, I am perfectly willing, Miss Eardley. It will be much better for the girl to go with our party. I shouldn't like my girl to go abroad alone.'

After that, Mrs Lockwood didn't know how to object. But it seemed extraordinary that Thea Hunter could have the same privileges as her girls and without paying for them. She was sure the girls wouldn't want Thea.

'I really don't think her mother can afford to let her go,' she said, trying again.

'It won't cost much,' said Miss Eardley. 'Only her fare and pocket money. She'll teach English, you know. Now what kind of a school do you want?' She led them briskly into discussion.

Miss Eardley took her task seriously. She earnestly considered the girls she was to place. Their education had not been entrusted to her, which was, in her opinion, a pity. The Lockwood twins, from what she had seen of them, thought altogether too much of themselves. The youngest Lockwood girl, though pretty and sweet-natured, lacked, in Miss Eardley's opinion, backbone. The Harvey girl was said to be unmanageable. A Parisian finishing school where they would fritter their time away and learn no more than how to put their hats on was no place for any of them. They would be far better in a good provincial school. Miss Eardley, therefore, proceeded to frighten Lady Harvey and Mrs Lockwood off Paris.

They were easily frightened. France, to Mrs Lockwood and almost equally so to Lady Harvey, was a place where drains were bad, men amorous and the religion Roman Catholic or none at all.

'We must be very, very careful to choose the right sort of school,' said Mrs Lockwood solemnly.

Miss Eardley went away armed with their instructions and began her researches into French provincial schools.

Mrs Lockwood at once went round to Byron Place to express herself as extremely astonished to have had it sprung upon her in Lady Harvey's drawing room that Thea was to be one of the party.

'It would have looked better, Mrs Hunter,' she said with displeasure, 'if I had been approached beforehand.'

'I agree, Mrs Lockwood,' said Mrs Hunter, her lids fluttering nervously. 'But Thea is so impetuous. She got this idea into her head and rushed off to Miss Eardley. I didn't think anything could possibly come of it or I would certainly have spoken to you.'

All the same she was relieved she hadn't had to. It was bad enough this way, but it would have been far worse if she had had to beard Mr Lockwood in his office, or make the proposal herself to Mrs Lockwood. She felt she would never have had the courage to do either.

'I don't think Thea will trouble anyone much, Mrs Lockwood,' she said. 'She won't have much time, will she? If only you will be so kind as to allow her to travel with your party, there and back, I should be most grateful.'

'It's out of my hands,' said Mrs Lockwood coldly. 'It's been decided that she shall go and I suppose she'll go and that's all there is to it. But this was started as an affair purely between the two families, Mrs Hunter, and now not only Thea, but two other girls, called Kenworthy, from Nottingham, have asked to join. They're friends of the Harveys, of course, but it's altogether too bad. My girls might just as well stay at home as take half England with them.'

They drank tea in silence. Mrs Hunter felt dreadfully in the wrong; Thea had really put her in a very awkward position.

Mrs Lockwood always felt resentment that the Hunters should be 'in at' anything, unless she herself invited them. For Thea Hunter to push herself in like this was unheard-of impertinence. The twins were so furious they might have refused to go at all if they hadn't been afraid that the others – Angela, the Kenworthys and Thea – would go without them. Mrs Lockwood was galled by Lady Harvey's easy acceptance of Thea. She said to William that she couldn't understand it at all. But she didn't say anything to Lady Harvey. Somehow one didn't say anything to Lady Harvey. She said plenty, however, to poor Mrs Hunter.

'Mrs Lockwood has been,' said Mrs Hunter unhappily when Thea came in from school.

'Oh – is anything settled yet?' asked Thea eagerly.

'She didn't say. But she's not at all pleased, Thea.'

'Oh, she'll get over it,' said Thea callously. 'What does it matter? When I get there, her precious girls will soon see I don't mean to cling to them any more than they mean to cling to me.'

She stood with her back to the kitchen fire, her eyes bright, careless of Mrs Lockwood's absurd feelings.

After much discussion and enquiry, Miss Eardley's recommendation fell upon the Pensionnat Jeanne d'Arc in the little town of Villeneuve and all was arranged. Between the headmistress of the High School and the Directrice of the Pensionnat Jeanne d'Arc passed letters equally illegible to either. Mademoiselle Duchêne could no more make out Miss Eardley's neat Girton hand than Miss Eardley could make out Mademoiselle Duchêne's calligraphy, tall and jointed like the legs of a cranefly and covering both sides of extremely thin paper. There was, fortunately, a printed prospectus which Miss Eardley was able to pass on to the parents, though she was soon summoned, this time to Oakfield, to explain it.

'It says each girl must take a "couvert", Miss Eardley,' said Mrs Lockwood, sitting plump and bewildered in her drawing-room. 'But how can I possibly get three eiderdowns into the trunks?'

Miss Eardley explained that 'couvert' meant something more portable, merely, in fact, spoons, forks and knives.

'Well, then, "gobelet", Miss Eardley,' continued Mrs Lockwood, again pronouncing the 't'. 'What ever does "gobelet" mean?'

When Miss Eardley explained that the French drank wine from silver or horn beakers, Mrs Lockwood was horrified.

'Wine!' she cried. 'But the girls mustn't drink wine!'

Miss Eardley explained that everyone drank wine in France, but that it was very weak. In the schools, the wine was called 'Abondance', so Mrs Lockwood could gather from that what the wine was like. Mrs Lockwood couldn't and was cast back into her former doubts about France being at all the sort of place for the girls. But Lady Harvey said she was sure the wine was nothing to worry about and that water could always be arranged. In Lady Harvey's experience, everything could always be arranged.

'Have the girls christening mugs?' asked Miss Eardley. 'Because they are the very thing for "gobelets", in fact, they are "gobelets".'

Certainly all the girls had christening mugs, said Mrs

Lockwood and expressed herself heartily glad the mugs were at last going to come in useful for something.

Miss Eardley explained 'gobelet' to Thea, who also had a christening mug, a relic of better days. Her mother hunted it up and gave it, tarnished black as coal, into her excited hands. She cleaned it vigorously every night and was in despair of getting it right in time to take away. It seemed thrilling beyond words that she should be going to drink wine, which she had never tasted, from this hitherto unused silver cup in a country she had not yet seen.

Every detail of the prospectus thrilled her. 'La costume des pensionnaires est uniforme,' she read, and thought how wonderful that they should all have to be dressed in black. She was sure Charlotte and Emily Brontë were dressed in black when they went to the Pensionnat Heger in Brussels.

By Easter all arrangements were concluded; there was nothing to do now but wait, which Thea found hard.

She found it hard to give attention to lessons, but she had to do it. The Higher Certificate examination lay between her and France. It was not so bad at school where everyone else was working, but at home on Wednesday afternoons, her thoughts kept wandering to the prospect of France and it was a temptation to talk of it to her mother. To spur herself on she wrote the word 'France' on a card and propped it up before her. She told herself that she was working to get there. By way of relaxation now and then she allowed herself to loll on the sofa for a few moments or look through the curtains into the street.

One April afternoon all was as usual. There was 'France' on a postcard, her mother in the plush armchair, her books spread out on the table, and by and by Thea came stretching to the window for a break.

'Mother,' she said, 'the new people are moving into the Smiths' house. There's a furniture van at the gate.'

'Really,' said Mrs Hunter, who took no interest in her neighbours. She bowed to them indiscriminately in passing, but hardly knew their names. To the Wests who lived on one side, or the Pentlands who lived on the other, she had hardly spoken two dozen words during all the years she had lived between them. If she took so little interest in the people who lived at numbers nineteen and twenty-three, she took still less in the people moving into number fifteen.

Thea looked idly out. A young man, without coat or waistcoat, displaying a pair of braces, waspishly striped in black and yellow, was directing the carrying-in of a cheap wardrobe, stained oak in front and raw deal behind. Thea took him for the head furniture-remover.

It was a gusty day and the wind took part in the removal, tearing newspaper wrappings and straw from the van and strewing them over the front gardens and the street. Thea frowned. Byron Place was quite ugly enough without litter.

She went back to her work and by and by she finished it. She put her books together with relief and went stretching to the window again. The van was just going away, but the young man in braces remained, watching it go. He was evidently the new tenant, or one of them. Not a desirable neighbour, thought Thea emphatically, since he stood in the street in braces.

The young man stood with his fists on his hips, the wind lashing his dark hair. He turned his head from side to side, surveying Byron Place. As he turned his profile towards Thea she realised that she had seen him before. She was already familiar with this high-bridged nose, short upper lip, rather full lower one, strong teeth and square chin. He looked bossy, cheerful, healthy and when she had last seen him, he had been standing in some other place, just as he was standing now, but with a bowler hat, she was sure, on the back of his head. But where? And how did she know that he could talk a lot and was good-humoured and common, or what she thought of as common?

'Mother,' she said in outraged astonishment, 'do you know that the people moving into the Smiths' house had a stall on the Pot Fair? At least, the man had.'

'I can well believe it,' said Mrs Hunter with resignation. 'This neighbourhood just goes from bad to worse.'

Yes, Thea remembered, pressing her face to the window to look at him, this young man had been selling and shouting at the Pot Fair, when she went with her mother to match up the willow pattern service. While her mother was rummaging for saucers, Thea had watched the young man. She hadn't been able to miss him, he made such a noise. And here he was, actually making himself into a neighbour.

'He's standing in the street in his braces,' said Thea in disgust. 'And the street's all straw and paper as if he'd brought the Pot Fair with him. He looks as if he might start shouting and selling at any minute. Do look, Mother.'

Mrs Hunter came to the window, and as they looked, an old woman came out of the house, a little old woman with white hair and a black shawl folded tidily over her shoulders. She laid her hands round the iron spikes of the gate and stood there, looking through. A girl, with the same cheerful, healthy aspect as the young man, came out, wiping her hands on an apron, to join the others at the gate. There they stood, surveying Byron Place as if it were the Promised Land and the young man the Joshua who had brought them to it. After surveying the Place, they turned to survey their house, and Thea saw that the woman looked happy and the young man proud and gratified.

'Imagine being pleased to come to this place,' said Thea in amazement.

'It all depends what one has been used to, you know,' said Mrs Hunter, turning from the window.

II

Two days later, the young man, whose name was Oliver Reade, came face to face with Thea in Byron Place. She was going back to school towards quarter to two as he was coming home. As he approached, he ran his eye over her with male interest. He began to whistle silently, raising his eyebrows. His smiling gaze ran over her with obvious approval, but when she came up with him and he met her eyes, his own fell. Abashed, he raised his bowler hat and hurried into his own gate. But before he reached his front door, he had recovered and halted to look after her.

'By gum, Edie,' he said to his sister, who now came out of the house on her way back to the afternoon session at the cash-desk of Pond's the drapers, 'you should have seen that girl.

She's a winner. I was going to give her the glad eye, but, when she got up to me, I daren't.'

'Serves you right,' said Edie good-humouredly. 'You're too fond of giving the glad eye. D'you mean that girl going down? She lives three doors higher up. Their name's Hunter,' said Edie who, with feminine perspicacity, already knew all about the neighbourhood. 'They think a lot of themselves and don't mix with anybody. There's another girl about my age. She mightn't be so bad, though she doesn't look as if she's got much life in her. I don't like the look of the young one much.'

'By gum but I do,' said her brother.

'She looks stuck up to me,' said Edie. 'But do go in, Noll. Mother's done nothing but try to keep your dinner hot for the last hour.'

'Aye, I'm late,' admitted Oliver. 'But it was worth it. I've got a grand lot of shirts out of that burnt warehouse. Scarcely any damage to speak of in what I've got. Send them to the laundry and they'll look fine. They'll sell like hot cakes on Saturday night.'

'Good lad,' said Edie. 'But bye-bye.'

'Ta-ta,' said Oliver with a last look down the street at Thea.

CHAPTER TEN

I

It dawned gradually upon Thea that she was always coming across the young man from number fifteen. If she went down Byron Place, he was coming up. If she got on the tram, he was on it, too. When, reaching her favourite place on the outside platform of the upper deck, she found him there before her, she took to travelling inside. It was not until he also took to travelling inside, staring fixedly at her, that she realised he must be following her about on purpose. He was trying to get to know her. She was amazed and incredulous. Why should he want to know her? She had no wish at all to know him. She looked at him with deepening suspicion. Was he trying to flirt with her or something?

There were girls at school who wrote notes to boys, met them in secret, giggled about them, but Thea was not among them. Unawakened, uninterested, she stalked past boys. She now stalked past Oliver Reade, though in her view he was not a boy, but a man. He must be more than twenty, she thought. As if she would look at him, or any other man or boy! Romance for her lay not in man or boy, but in going to France in September. She ceased to look at Oliver Reade with scorn; she didn't look at him at all.

Oliver Reade changed his tactics. He began to cultivate her brother. Martin was courteous in all his dealings; he had never been known to snub anybody. So when Oliver Reade nodded to him, he nodded back. When Oliver spoke, Martin answered, and before long they were walking up or down Byron Place together. When Martin appeared in the small front garden after supper, as he often did on these early summer evenings, Oliver walked up from number fifteen to lean over the railings and talk, in the hope of being asked in. But it did not occur to Martin to ask him in and he continued to talk from the garden.

On these evenings the sash windows of the front room were thrown up as far as they would go and Thea, doing lessons at the table, could hear, though she had no wish to, what they were saying. One evening she heard them talking about her.

'Your young sister's very pretty, isn't she?' said Oliver.

In the room behind him, Thea stretched up to look into the Empire glass over the fireplace. Am I? she asked herself, blushing with gratification.

'Thea?' Martin said with brotherly indifference. 'Do you think so?'

'I should think she's a proud sort of girl, though,' said Oliver.

'Pooh,' thought Thea indignantly. 'Just because I won't know him.'

'I don't know what she or any of us has to be proud about,' said Martin gloomily.

'What's wrong? Feeling down?' enquired Oliver.

'Oh, I don't know,' said Martin. 'No more than usual.'

'Chronic, eh?' said the other cheerfully. 'Don't you like your job? You're in a bank, aren't you?'

'Yes,' said Martin, disinclined to talk further about himself, which did not deter Oliver, who was not at all disinclined to talk about himself, especially as he had now glimpsed Thea through the curtains.

'I don't believe in working for other people,' he said, raising his voice. 'I believe in working for myself. You should be on your own, like me.'

'How can I?' said Martin. 'I haven't a penny.'

'Had I?' asked Oliver.

'I don't know. Hadn't you?'

Oliver Reade gave a snort. Thea saw his bold profile turned on Martin.

'My dad walked out one Saturday night fourteen years ago and we've never seen him since. He left Mother and Edie and me stone cold. Mother had thirty bob in the world. I was eleven, Edie was eight. Not much help to Mother, eh? But she managed. She managed,' he said, his voice dropping from its confident, self-congratulatory note. 'But it made an old woman of her. She's old before her time. I bet she's no older than your mother, but look at the difference.'

'My mother's had a lot of trouble,' said Martin.

Thea lifted her head. She hoped Martin wasn't going to copy the Reade man and pour out his family history over the railings. But he wasn't. He said no more.

'Your mother's not had to work like mine,' said Oliver. 'You had money.'

Martin laughed.

'Yes, what you'd call no money at all,' said Oliver, 'would seem riches to people like us. We'd nothing. People like you can't understand what nothing means. So it's really not much good talking. But we were brought up in Gas Street. Ever seen Gas Street? No? Well, if you had, you'd see the difference between what we came from and where we are now.' He glanced about the Place with satisfaction. 'And who's done it?' he asked. 'Me,' he answered himself triumphantly.

He actually looks on Byron Place as an achievement, thought Thea.

'I went half-time to the mill like everybody else, but I hated it. I mortally hated the mill,' he said vibrantly. 'So I left. I pushed a cart for a man on the market. I cleared up for him on market nights. I began to help him to sell. I began to help him to buy. Now he's selling for me. Not buying. No, thanks. I buy for myself. I bought a warehouse for myself two days ago,' he said with assumed nonchalance.

'Good,' said Martin kindly.

'What I'm telling you this for,' said Oliver, with a glance at the window – it had suddenly struck him that she might think he was boasting and she wasn't a girl to like boasting, 'what I'm telling you for is to show that you don't need to stick to any job you don't like. Give it up and get out after another. Move about and don't be so bl – don't be so frightened,' he amended.

'Look at me,' he began again. 'I started from nothing, much lower down than you, and I haven't done so bad, have I!' he pleaded.

Thea heard him with astonishment. He thought himself a success because he had a stall on the market where he sold damaged goods, things that couldn't be sold anywhere else? And he was holding himself up as an example to Martin? As if Martin wanted to be anything like him, she thought with scorn.

She went to the window and whisked the curtains apart with both hands.

'I'm sorry to have to shut the window,' she said, 'but I can't do my homework while I can hear you talking.'

The window was closed, the curtains swung back into place. Oliver Reade remained at the railings a little longer, then he went slowly away. It didn't seem worthwhile to go on talking if she wasn't listening.

II

It was August before he got himself asked into the Hunters' house. One evening, by dint of keeping Martin at the gate in the rain, he achieved it.

'You'd better come in,' said Martin at last, fearing for his unprotected Bank suit.

'Thanks,' said Oliver, and followed him to the door with alacrity. He swished the rain from his bowler hat, scooped his hair back with one hand and stepped into the front room like a policeman about to serve a warrant and nervous of his reception.

'Mother,' said Martin, 'here's a neighbour of ours, Mr Reade. D'you know my mother and sister, Reade?'

'Well, I've seen them about' – Oliver proffered a hand to Mrs Hunter – 'but I doubt whether they've seen me,' he said significantly, going over to proffer the hand to Thea where she sat on the sofa. 'Pleased to meet you at last, Miss Hunter.'

Thea disengaged her hand from her sewing and laid it unwillingly in his. So he was forcing her to know him, was he?

'I'll go and change, I'm rather wet,' said Martin. 'I'll be down in a moment, Reade.'

'Sit down, Mr Reade,' said Mrs Hunter in a formal voice. Who was this young man? This was the first time anyone from Byron Place had come into the house. She didn't want to encourage it. 'Will you lift the material from that chair? I don't want to take my hand from these tucks for a moment. I've just got them fixed.'

'Thanks,' said Oliver, lifting the black stuff and letting it flow through his fingers in a knowledgeable way. 'Why, I had a lot of this very stuff myself last week. Sold it at one-and-eleven a yard. I bet you paid more than that?'

It was Thea he challenged, but she sewed on, making no response. She was indignant that he had pursued her into the house.

Oliver Reade turned to Mrs Hunter.

'I bet you paid more than that,' he repeated.

Mrs Hunter's eyelids fluttered. The young man shocked her. In the polite world, one did not behave like this. But Mrs Hunter, boldly tackled, could not keep up an attitude of her own. If the neighbours had made a determined attempt to be friendly, she would probably have succumbed to them long ago and been happier in consequence.

'Well... er...' she said. 'As a matter of fact, we paid three-and-eleven a yard.'

'So you see, you've been done,' said Oliver, sitting down. He sniffed cheerfully. 'You'd have done better to get it off the market.'

Thea looked up.

'All stuff sold in the market has flaws in it, hasn't it?' she said. 'Yours had flaws in it, I suppose?'

'Well, what can you expect?' asked Oliver. 'It had – a few.'

'I shouldn't have had it then,' said Thea, resuming her sewing.

'They were absolutely unnoticeable,' urged Oliver.

'It makes no difference,' said Thea. 'I should have known they were there.'

He looked deeply at her.

'You're very particular,' he said.

'I am,' said Thea.

He continued to look at her. There was something different about her. She didn't look like a schoolgirl any longer. He couldn't immediately make out what had changed her overnight. Then he realised that her hair no longer touched her shoulders. She had curled it up or something, and now, with her little neck revealed, she looked more like a young queen than ever.

He hadn't known a girl like this one before. He was used to response in girls. Those he knew liked a bit of horse-play, but the idea of attempting horse-play with this one made him shudder. In her company, his self-confidence fell away, which was something new to him. He didn't know how to behave, he felt at a loss. The bold tactics he employed for his onslaught on life in general were no use here. He would have to manœuvre cautiously for a look or a word and then, as likely as not, the word would cut him and the look pierce him through and through.

But it would be worth it, he decided. And at any rate, he had made a start. He'd got into the house and that made it easier to get in again. He was actually sitting in the same room with her – some good-class stuff in this room; bit out of date, but must have cost a lot in its time. It had taken him nearly six months to get into this room. But she hadn't got up and walked out, as he'd half-expected her to do.

Like a dog settling down into his place on the rug, after some doubt as to whether he would be allowed there, Oliver drew a long breath and sank lower in his chair. He relaxed. The longer Martin stayed away the better. It gave him more chance to talk to Thea. He must make the most of it, improve their acquaintance. He wondered what she would like him to talk about. A look of masculine indulgence came into his face. His rather heavy eyelids drooped at her.

'You're busy,' he said. 'Doing a bit of dressmaking?'

It was Mrs Hunter who replied.

'We're getting Thea's things ready for France. She goes in September, you know.'

He turned an astonished face. France? He wouldn't have thought they could afford continental trips. But perhaps those grand friends of theirs, the ones who called in a car, were taking her.

'France?' he said. 'A holiday, eh?'

'Dear me, no,' said Mrs Hunter. 'To a school. For a year.'

'A year?' he repeated. He couldn't believe his ears. He turned on Thea. 'You're not going away for a year?' he demanded.

'Yes,' said Thea. 'Yes, I am.'

She smiled. She wasn't smiling at him, she was smiling at the prospect of going away for a year. He stared at her. She was going away. Just when he'd got into the house. Having carefully prepared the way, there was now nothing to proceed to. Where he had expected a beginning, there was a blank.

A year. She would have put a greater distance than ever between them by that time. Seeing things, travelling, he thought, as silent, subdued, he spun his bowler hat between his hands.

'Thea is going with our friends the Lockwoods; the three girls, you know, and Sir Robert Harvey's daughter,' explained Mrs Hunter, in a formal but kindly way. 'They are going to a pensionnat at Villeneuve, about sixty miles from Paris.'

'Oh, yes,' said Oliver in a flat voice.

Mixing with people like that, he thought. Where would he come in?

Something in his face and voice touched Mrs Hunter without her knowing why. She discarded formality.

'The Lockwoods and the others are going to finish,' she said. 'But of course we can't afford that for Thea. She is going au pair.'

Oliver lifted his head. 'What's au pair?'

He suddenly didn't care how little he knew or how he exposed his ignorance.

'She'll give English lessons in return for French lessons and her board. She won't pay anything and they won't pay her anything.'

'I see.' He looked at the carpet for a moment.

'Well, I think I'll be going,' he said, getting up.

They looked at him in astonishment.

'I'm sure Martin will be down in a moment, Mr Reade,' said Mrs Hunter. 'Do sit down again.'

'No, I'll be going,' said Oliver, looking down at the doorhandle he was now holding. He looked heavy, crushed. 'I can see him another time. So I'll say good evening,' he said, nodding first towards Mrs Hunter and then towards Thea. 'Good evening.'

'But wait at least until we can let you out,' said Mrs Hunter, beginning to lay aside her sewing. 'Thea!'

'Nay, I can let myself out,' said Oliver. 'There's nothing in that. Don't you move. Good night.'

In two strides he was down the passage and out of the door.

'What a strange young man!' said Mrs Hunter, taking up her tucks. 'What possessed him to rush away like that?'

'Oh, he has no manners,' said Thea dismissingly, although she knew why he had rushed off. He was disappointed that she was going away for a year. As if she would have had anything to do with him if she had stayed at home!

CHAPTER ELEVEN

■·■

I

Oliver Reade meant to give up. No use starting something you couldn't go on with. That wasn't his way. He liked to get on with things. Nothing he hated like kicking his heels, waiting about in uncertainty. Besides, he could see she didn't want to have anything to do with him, and it wasn't as if he enjoyed being snubbed and looked down on. And he'd been keen on girls before and it had worn off. He reflected on all this, putting his infatuation in the worst possible light to himself.

But it was no good. For a few days, when he met her on the way to or from Miss Riley's, he himself going on the same bread-errand, he raised his hat as if she were a middle-aged woman in whom he took no interest. But before long he was back again, contriving ways and means of seeing her.

Now that she had left school she no longer went up and down Byron Place twice a day. To see her at all, he was obliged to walk past her house, walk up Byron Place as if he were going somewhere, though there was nowhere to go, since it was a blind alley. When he had walked to the top, he turned and walked back again, looking sideways at the windows of number twenty-one. It was all very obvious, but Thea, sitting on the sofa with her sewing, gave him no help. She let him embarrass and exert himself as he chose.

There she sat, her head bowed over her sewing, cool, unattainable. She was absorbed into a life of her own, into which he could not break. It gave him a feeling of frustration and obstinacy, it bewildered him. Why wouldn't she speak? Why wouldn't she lift her head and look at him?

In the end, he would come to a stop at the railings and say good evening.

'Bother,' muttered Thea to herself before raising her head. 'Good evening,' she said with reserve.

Then he would say the day had been hot or something else she already knew. Gradually he would settle down, with one elbow on the bar between the spikes of the railings.

He was anxious to be of service to her.

'If you want anything cheap, you know,' he said, 'I can get it for you. I can get practically anything.'

'Thank you,' said Thea. 'I have all I want.'

'Mackintosh or anything like that,' he suggested. 'Cost price, of course,' he added hastily, blushing in case she should think he wanted to make a profit out of her.

'I have a mackintosh,' said Thea.

'Oh, well, if there is anything, you've only to let me know,' he said.

He told her about his mother and sister. He explained himself, hoping she would tell him about herself in return. But she didn't. The more he talked the less she said. She was a close one, he thought, but admiringly. He admired her power of keeping silence, but she made him feel he said too much. Sometimes, when he felt he was making a fool of himself, he tore himself from the railings even before he was dismissed, as he usually was, by her getting up from the sofa and saying she must go.

Time was getting short. If only he could get her out of that room, off that sofa, make her listen, make her really look at him as if she saw him.

'I suppose you wouldn't like to come for a stroll?' he said desperately.

Thea raised her head in amazement.

'A stroll?' she said.

Her inflection cut him.

'Well, a walk then or whatever you want to call it,' he said roughly. He thought he'd put it wrong, or something. She was so particular, perhaps she didn't call walks strolls, but if she only knew what it had cost him to get the invitation out at all, she would overlook the wording of it. Or would she? He rather thought she wouldn't. He took off his bowler hat and mopped round the leather band that had rimmed his forehead with red.

'You won't come, then?' he said, putting the hat back.

'No, thank you,' said Thea.

'Right,' he said. 'Well' – with resolution, removing his elbow from the railings – 'I'll go for one myself.'

He walked off, but Thea only thought thank goodness, and went on with what she was doing.

II

September was drawing near. In her driving urge to go to France, Thea had not reckoned on the parting. Sometimes at table, when she looked at her mother and Molly and Martin, she could hardly swallow.

They were so good to her. They were so good to let her go at all. And they kept bringing the most touching things to go into the trunk. Molly's gloves were darned at the tip of every finger, but she gave Thea a pair of warmly-lined ones for the French winter. Martin had only one good tie, but he bought her a scarf. For weeks they had been contributing such things as one handkerchief at a time, a few yards of ribbon or lace. The trunk was slowly filling with the deprivations of her family, and though Thea was delighted with her things – she had never had such a stock in her life – she felt guilty, too. The more she had, the less there was for them.

'But I'll make it up to them,' she promised herself. 'When I begin to earn money I'll repay them over and over again.'

She said to herself that she was taking from them now in order to give back more later. She was the one, she felt secretly. She felt special, different. It was she who would retrieve the family fortunes. She said nothing about this, but she often gazed dumbly at them, hoping they realised that their sacrifices were so much bread cast upon the waters.

The trunk was filled at last, everything was ready. The family resources had been strained to the utmost, but there was nothing else to be bought now, they felt with relief.

Then they realised that Thea must have something to hold

the things she would need for the journey. A night was to be spent in London. Sir Robert Harvey and his friend, Mr Kenworthy from Nottingham, were taking the girls to Paris, where they would be met by the Directrice. Since a night had to be spent somewhere, the mothers decided that their girls would be better in London.

'I shall take a parcel,' said Thea with outward firmness and inward misgiving. She could imagine how the Lockwoods would eye a parcel. Now that the day of departure was almost upon her, she was beginning to be nervous of going with the Lockwoods. She wished she had tried to go to another place in France by herself. But it was done. She must put up with being the poor one of the party and carry her night things in a brown-paper parcel. She would not allow anyone to buy her a case. 'Not another thing,' she said firmly.

'Thea,' said her mother suddenly one afternoon, 'd'you know – I do believe that little bag is still in the loft.'

'What little bag?'

'The little bag your father kept his receipts and bills and things in. When we removed, the men stored several old things away for me up there and I do believe that bag is among them.'

Martin was the only one who had ever been into the loft, a place between the landing and the roof very awkward to come at. You had to stand on the tallest pair of steps, push open the trapdoor, leap at the ceiling and haul yourself through. It was the sort of thing only a young man could enjoy.

'I'll go up now,' said Thea.

'I don't think you can manage, dear. I think you'd better wait until Martin comes home.'

But a few moments later she was watching Thea's legs disappearing through the trapdoor.

Thea lit her candle. It was strange in the loft among the ribs of the roof, and close after the hot day. Things that had not been touched for fifteen years lay dimly about. A dressmaker's dummy loomed up, startling her, an old screen, a packing-case. Thea felt oppressed, as if the unhappiness her mother felt that removal day had been stored up there with the things. She peered down the trapdoor to look at her mother again.

'Are you all right, Mother?' she asked unaccountably.

'Yes, dear,' smiled her mother, surprised. 'It's you. Are you all right? Don't come through the ceiling, will you? Have you found the bag?'

'Wait a minute,' Thea replied hollowly from the roof.

'There's only this,' she said, dangling through the ceiling a stiff little bag of unfashionable shape, so long and narrow that it was almost like a roly-poly with a handle.

'That's it.' Mrs Hunter welcomed it eagerly. 'Now didn't I tell you? Could anything be better?'

Thea thought with dismay that nothing could be worse. She felt she could never be seen with it but she didn't know how she was going to say so. Carrying the bag downstairs, Mrs Hunter purred like a cat over a newly-rescued kitten. Coming behind with the steps, Thea felt that every moment of her mother's pleasure in the bag was making it more difficult to say she would rather take a parcel.

'The lining's torn at the bottom,' said Mrs Hunter, peering into the bag's interior. 'But I'll just stick the edges down with a little glue and you'll never notice it.'

'I am glad I remembered this,' she said happily, removing the dust of fifteen years in the kitchen.

She became aware of Thea's lack of response.

'You do like it, don't you, dear?' she asked. 'You think it will do, don't you?'

'Oh, yes, I'm sure it will, Mother,' said Thea hastily, smitten by the anxiety in her mother's face. 'It will hold everything nicely, I'm sure.'

So she was committed to the bag. Committed but not reconciled. Alone in the bedroom, she paraded with it before the glass and groaned. It was like a little empty pig, she thought, beating its stiff sides with the flat of her hand. And rubbed into bright orange at the corners, too. To think she had to step out into the world for the first time with a bag like this. She naïvely imagined she would be much more conspicuous in places like London and Paris than in her native town. She felt everybody would be looking at her and the bag. It humiliated her, and no one would know she was carrying it out of love for her family, because, if she didn't, her mother would be hurt and the others spend money they couldn't afford on another.

It came to the last evening at home. They were being so sweet to her she could hardly bear it. There were all the things she liked best for supper, sausage and bread sauce, apples in red jelly with whipped cream on top, and she couldn't enjoy them. They stuck in her throat. She kept looking at her mother, at Molly, and Martin, who kept making jokes. A year was a long time. Anything might happen to them in a year. She felt it was only by being with them that she could keep them safe. When

Molly went out and came in again to lay on the table a splendid cake covered in pink icing with 'Goodbye' on it in silver balls, Thea smiled fixedly at it for a moment, then got up and rushed into the front room. Molly rushed after her. 'It's my fault. I shouldn't have put "Goodbye" on it,' she wept. 'I thought after I'd got it on, I shouldn't have done it, it looked so awful. But I couldn't get it off again without ruining the cake. Don't let's cry, darling, we'll only upset Mother. I'll make you a grand cake when you come back and it'll have "Welcome Home" on it then.' They pressed their tears back, composed their faces and went back to table.

Time dragged. There was nothing left to do. The trunk stood strapped and ready in the front room, waiting for the out-porter to fetch it away first thing in the morning. Since no one thought it fitting to do anything unconnected with Thea, no one did anything at all. Mrs Hunter swayed gently in the rocking-chair, Molly stood about, Martin paced the kitchen rattling the stem of his pipe over his front teeth. He had lately taken to a pipe and it now occupied his hands so much that his family wondered what he had done till he got it. He continually screwed and unscrewed it, blew down it, knocked it out, pointed to things with its stem, used it to reinforce argument, contemplated it, clenched his teeth on it, but rarely did anything so simple with it as to smoke it.

'You should have gone to tennis, Martin,' said Thea. 'You shouldn't have stayed at home for me.'

'Oh, that's all right,' said Martin. 'When you come home, I'll make you a member of the club, shall I? Then we'll go together.'

'Oh, Martin,' glowed Thea, who loved to play tennis. She flew to kiss him and he smiled at her affectionately.

They were too good, too nice, they made her ache. She took refuge in the front room again.

But the sight of the trunk sent a stab of excitement through her. All the evening her emotions had been so variable they made her feel slightly sick, like going up and down perpetually in a lift. One moment they swooped up into excitement, the next dropped plumb into grief and apprehension. At the sight of the trunk they swooped upwards again and at that moment she saw Oliver Reade at the railings. She sprang to the window and leaning out, bestowed on him a smile of pure delight.

'I'm going tomorrow,' she said.

He laughed shortly. It was the first time she had spoken to him of her own accord and it was to tell him she was going tomorrow!

'I know that,' he said.

She looked kindly upon him. Even he, with the glow of parting over him, seemed not so bad.

'Goodbye,' she said, and letting the curtains fall, she turned from the window.

CHAPTER TWELVE

Over the pit of the town, the haze of the September morning was thickened by the admixture of smoke and soot into fog, in which the hidden mills clacked and pounded. But the hills surrounding Aldworth rose bland and tawny into clear day and, round Firbank Hall, the sun was plucking away the last fine shawls of mist, leaving in the hedges and bushes the perfect circular webs of the garden-spider, every thread diamonded with dew.

Sir Robert Harvey had gone to the library with the intention of communicating with his four mills by telephone. Before leaving home for any length of time he had always done that. But this morning he put the receiver back. There was really no point in struggling further with the cotton problem. He would leave it to the men who meant to stay in cotton no matter what happened to it. For his part, he meant to get out.

The pity was he hadn't sold the mills during the boom. He would lose a great deal of money by selling now, but not so much, he calculated, as by keeping them. And there was no point in keeping them in the hope of better times, since Anthony didn't want them. Once Sir Robert had been hurt and angry that his only son refused to follow the Harvey tradition of land- and mill-owning, but now he was resigned. Let Anthony stay on at Oxford as don or fellow of his college if he wished; there was nothing in cotton for him.

Ah, children, reflected Sir Robert. Of course one had to have them, everyone pitied you if you didn't, but secretly he often felt that, as blessings, they were over-rated. Here was Anthony going his own way and Angela with some mad idea of going on the stage. But that he would never tolerate. A Harvey on the stage! It was unthinkable. Good thing she was being packed off to the French provinces. It was a relief to get someone to take her off their hands for twelve months.

Once the mills were sold there would be no point in keeping the house. It looked as if the children would never be in it much again, and it was a great expense to keep up. Let it go, thought Sir Robert, who was in the mood to give up. An era had come to an end. He and Sybil would go and live in a smallish way at Tunbridge Wells or somewhere. And probably be a damned sight more comfortable, he said to himself. In the meantime he could shelve his troubles for a few days at any rate. He was off to Paris within the hour. The thought of his few days in Paris with Kenworthy when they had disposed of the girls cheered him and he strode with vigour towards the dining room and breakfast.

His wife was still in her room. At the sight of her daughter on the terrace below, she paused at her window. Although only Angela's back was visible as she stood at the stone balustrade, all the sorrow of farewell was in the droop of the young figure.

'I didn't realise,' thought Lady Harvey self-reproachfully,

'that she minds leaving us so much. I must hurry down to her. Her last few hours . . .'

But at that moment, Angela swung round and, with a completely clear face, threw up her arms and went skipping across the terrace to the house.

Her mother frowned. A trick again. This everlasting play-acting. It was so peculiar, unladylike and persistent. It was so insincere, thought Lady Harvey.

Once when she saw Angela, at seven or eight years of age, watching herself in the glass as she played at being a queen, her mother said reprovingly: 'You're rather a vain little girl, aren't you?'

Angela turned.

'I'm seeing if I'm right, Mother,' she said gravely, and her mother was silenced by the authenticity of the reply. The child was certainly in earnest about something, but whatever it was, her mother didn't like it.

Perhaps she would lose her foolish notions in France. Lady Harvey had her misgivings about the Pensionnat Jeanne d'Arc. The fees were not high enough for her to feel that it was quite the place for a daughter of the Harveys. But the deciding factor had been that the Lockwood girls were going there. Angela was used to the Lockwood girls. She had been to boarding-school with them, and had remained. In sending Angela to Villeneuve with the Lockwoods, the Harveys were working on the same principle as the farmer who keeps a donkey in the field with the horse. So long as the donkey is there, the horse stays. But if the donkey is removed, the horse breaks out and goes somewhere else.

Her maid now brought her outdoor things and confronting her own haggard beauty in the glass, Lady Harvey finished dressing to accompany her husband and daughter to the station.

At Oakfield, no one had eaten any breakfast, though all tried to disguise the fact. Mrs Lockwood, the twins and the maids kept up an incessant bustle, but Mr Lockwood stood at the library window, his back turned, and Clare stayed in her room. Boz, her dog, who knew she was going away without him, nevertheless sat beside her dressing-table in mute appeal. Every time she passed him, he butted her legs gently with his nose to remind her of himself. It was almost too much for Clare.

The twins had been away before. Clare had never left home, never, except for holidays at the sea when they were all together still, slept anywhere but in her own bedroom. She loved home. She had been trained to love home. 'A real home girl,' her mother always said fondly, and now she had to leave it. She was determined not to cry. If she began, everybody else would cry, too. But she had to stay alone in her room to keep to her resolve.

In Byron Place, the out-porter had been for the trunk. Molly and Martin had said goodbye and left the house at the usual time. When they were gone, Thea rushed upstairs. To keep back the tears, to be doing something, she put on her outdoor things, the black coat over the black dress with the round white collar, the black felt hat turned up all the way round which gave her a child-like air. Picking up the bag, she tried to see herself with other people's eyes. What did she look like to the outside world? She decided that, because of the bag, she looked as if she were 'travelling in something'. Something long and rolled up, probably stays. She felt all the misery of the self-conscious young.

'Thea,' called her mother in a gentle voice – it sounded as if she had been standing at the foot of the stairs, plucking up courage to say it. 'I think we ought to be going.'

The closing of the front door had a final sound, and it was strange to walk down Byron Place, knowing you would not walk up again until a year had gone.

They boarded a tramcar and sat just inside, Thea with her arm closely through her mother's. Withdrawing from all she knew, she was very alert, noticing everything for the last time.

The car entered the wide square before the station and stopped. Getting out Thea looked back in farewell at the statue of Queen Victoria, whose soot-streaked face had struck awe into her heart as a child. The soot, gathered thickly in all the lines and pouches faithfully reproduced by the sculptor, gave the venerable queen a terrible and haggard aspect. Pigeon-droppings encrusted her robes and regalia. What with the soot and the pigeons, almost the worst thing you could do for anybody was to raise a statue to them in Aldworth.

Thea looked at the station clock and wished she could skip the next half-hour. She looked at her mother and saw that though she smiled, her lips trembled. It was too much, thought Thea. Prolonged goodbyes were too painful. You should just wave a hand and go.

The Hunters were the first of their party to arrive. They

were much too soon. The fog had cleared and strong sunlight struck horizontally in from each end of the covered platform. In the revealing light, Mrs Hunter, looking at Thea, thought with a pang how young she was. And Thea, looking at her mother, thought, 'Why, Mother's *old*.' The look of age in the beloved face made her feel weak, lost. She took her mother's arm again and pressed against her.

The platform was filling up. Important-looking men and well-dressed women were assembling. Only those with urgent business or plenty of time and money went to London. London was five hours away, and when you went, you had to stay at least one night, preferably several. The ordinary townspeople of Aldworth did not lightly incur the expense of such a journey. So that it was the leisurely and the important who paced the platform now, glancing without interest, if at all, at the mother and daughter.

Then, rising from the subway, came the Harveys and the Lockwoods and a tide of animation ran over the platform. People turned eagerly towards them. Hats were raised, heads bowed, smiles and greetings exchanged.

Thea, however, experienced her first shock. From this time forward she was to have many moments of discomfiture, but this was the first. The girls were not in uniform. It had never occurred to her that they would be in anything else. But Angela Harvey was in grey, carrying a fur coat, the three Lockwoods were in dark green suits and top coats. They all looked very fashionable. Thea would have shrunk back out of sight, but the party came on towards her, making royal progress down the platform.

As they approached, Mrs Lockwood said in a low voice to Lady Harvey: 'This is Mrs Hunter and her daughter.'

Lady Harvey said, equally low, to her husband: 'Now, dear, this is the girl you are to take with you. And her mother. Hunter is the name, you remember.'

Lady Harvey always prompted Sir Robert, who needed it. She was fully alive to the responsibilities of their position. The Harveys were the royalty of Aldworth. When the King visited the town once, someone remarked admiringly that Sir Robert was very nice with him. But Lady Harvey always had to prompt him and he owed much of his popularity to her. He himself had a bad memory for names and faces, but at balls, garden-parties, gatherings of all sorts, she was beside him to remind him whom to speak to.

'The Sandersons, dear,' she would say.

'The Waterhouses, Robert.'

'Ah, yes. Where?' Sir Robert would exclaim, peering through his eyeglass, and having focused on them, would greet with geniality the waiting Waterhouses, the Sandersons and anyone else his wife indicated. On being confronted with them, he always managed, with great tact, to disguise the fact that he hadn't the least idea who they were.

Now, steered towards Mrs Hunter, he affably shook hands.

'Another of my charges, eh?' he said, taking Thea's hand. 'I hope I get 'em all there, Mrs Hunter. I shall have to check up on 'em occasionally, eh?'

Mrs Hunter blushed faintly. It was a long time since she had been spoken to in this hearty, masculine way.

'You have a charming daughter,' said Lady Harvey, looking at Thea, who was speaking to the Lockwoods and Angela. 'Only the young should wear black, I think.'

Mrs Hunter smiled. How kind they were.

People came up to say goodbye to the girls, and Mrs Hunter and Thea fell back. They stood apart, looking away. Nobody comes to say goodbye to me, thought Thea. How strange that we don't know anybody.

Then, looking down the platform, she saw that someone was in fact coming to say goodbye to her, the very last person she wished for. His bowler hat on the back of his head, a large unwrapped box of chocolates, destined, she was sure, for her, under his arm, Oliver Reade was advancing.

She looked wildly round for a way of escape. But she was hemmed in by the fashionable friends of the Harveys and the Lockwoods, now cleft apart by the oncoming Oliver. There she had to stand, awaiting him.

''Morning,' said Oliver, raising the bowler.

Under the eyes of the others, he brought the chocolate box from under his arm and held it out with assumed nonchalance to Thea. He himself was impressed by the size of the box and hoped she was.

'Thought you might like a few chocolates to eat on the way,' he said.

Thea, looking down at the box, flushed crimson. Not only did he thrust himself in where he wasn't wanted, but he offered her a vulgar thing like this. The box was much too big and the postcard beauty on the lid showed far too much bosom. He had no taste and no sense. It was just like him to choose such a box, she thought. In this, she was unjust. He had simply said to the girl in the shop: 'Give me the biggest box you've got,' and this was it.

He stared in acute anxiety at Thea. What was the matter? Wasn't she going to take it?

At that moment, the train came round the bend, mercifully distracting the attention of the others. Thea almost snatched the box from Oliver's hand. 'Thank you,' she said, 'but you shouldn't have troubled. Mother, the train . . .'

'Don't wait,' she said, flashing dismissal at him.

'Goodbye, then,' he said, raising his hat.

But she had already turned to the train. There was nothing left for him to do but go. He walked down the platform into the subway. She'd fairly snubbed him, he thought burningly.

Thea thrust the offending box into her mother's hands.

'You take it, Mother. I can't travel with a thing like that. Keep the picture out of sight. Turn it to you.'

'But, Thea, it was for you.'

'I don't want it. Goodbye, Mother. Goodbye, darling.'

'Goodbye, child. Goodbye, Thea dear. Take care of yourself. We mustn't cry before all these people. Don't get your feet wet. Put your warmer vests on in good time . . . when the weather begins to get cold . . .'

Blinded by tears, Thea climbed into the carriage.

Angela Harvey waved kindly to her mother and said a few words about nothing in particular. Her mother smiled back.

But the Lockwoods' hearts were wrung. The girls stood at the window, smiling determinedly, but with swimming eyes. Mrs Lockwood's chin quivered in a way that fascinated Angela

Harvey, who withdrew to the back of the compartment to see if she could make hers do the same. Mr Lockwood's bloodshot eyes were suffused with tears. Since he was a man, he could not openly wipe them away and was in consequence acutely occupied with the problem of getting rid of them. He kept his eyes on the stretch because to blink, he knew, would be fatal. But a year! Twelve months before he saw them again! What would the house be without them? Bee and Muriel were such a lively pair and Clare had the sweetest face and the sweetest nature in the world. He daren't look at her, she looked so wan. 'Why must I go?' she had asked him, and he had explained that to make oneself fit for the world one had to go out in it. But why should she go when she wanted to stay, and he so wanted her to stay?

The guard blew his whistle. The train began to move.

'Goodbye. . . goodbye . . .' their almost despairing young voices called out to the last. Thea crushed her face under their elbows and took a last look at her mother, standing apart with her handkerchief to her lips.

Mr Lockwood plunged away. He hurried into the obscurity of the subway and buried his face in a large handkerchief. He sobbed once, and then, hearing footsteps, wiped his eyes in feverish haste and put the handkerchief away. He straightened his shoulders and emerged into the daylight. Passing through the barrier, he tendered his platform-ticket to the right, while seeming to take a deep interest in the poster to the left. He even smiled at it, but the collector was not deceived. The chap had been crying and he thought none the worse of him for it. In fact, he was glad to see that Lockwood could cry. According to some, he was a hard, sharp customer, but he couldn't be so bad, reasoned the collector, if he blubbered a bit when his daughters went away.

Above, the three mothers waved the train out of sight. When there was nothing more to be seen but the empty rails glittering in the sun, Mrs Hunter turned one way with her handkerchief, Mrs Lockwood another. Lady Harvey walked slowly down the platform leaving them to recover.

Mrs Lockwood approached Mrs Hunter and said quiveringly that she was going to Firbank Hall for the day. 'Just to make the break,' she said, and Mrs Hunter nodded.

'But I'm sure Lady Harvey will give you a lift home in the car,' quavered Mrs Lockwood.

Mrs Hunter shook her head.

'I'd rather be alone, if you don't mind,' she said.

'I understand,' said Mrs Lockwood, and unable to say more went after Lady Harvey.

In a few moments, Mrs Hunter in her turn left the station. And Oliver Reade, who had been hanging about with some idea of supporting the bereaved mother, saw her going across the square with his chocolate-box under her arm.

'So that's where it's got to,' he thought grimly, and changed his mind about offering support.

He breasted the stream of people approaching the station. He swaggered, his hat at its usual angle, but he was sore. Sore and self-conscious. He glanced sideways at the people as they passed to see if they noticed that the mother had got the box of chocolates he had offered to the girl.

'I'll be damned,' he said, 'if I ever give her anything again.'

'She was ashamed of me,' he thought, walking down Station Street between the blackened buildings.

He laughed shortly. 'As if I shan't knock spots off any of those people she was with before I've finished.'

But would he?

He came to a halt before a tripe-shop wedged incongruously between an insurance office and a travel bureau. He stared unseeingly at the chilly merchandise laid out on a marble slab. He knew he'd make money all right, but wouldn't these people always be able to come it over him because of his lack of education? They would.

'But why should she be the only one who can finish herself?' he thought pugnaciously.

'Trouble with me is I've not even begun,' he thought, noting mechanically that there was what his mother would call a 'nice bit of seam' in the window.

'I don't relish the idea of making a fool of myself at nightschool,' he argued. Awful to have to put his pride in his business achievements in his pocket and eat humble pie at a desk in the Technical School. And what should he set about learning? How should he begin?

He walked on. The place to find out about education was the Education Office, he supposed. In Town Hall Street. Better take the plunge straight off. It was like a cold bath. Better get in.

He walked slowly to Town Hall Street, and slowly up the steps of the Education Office. A window to the right said 'Enquiries,' and pushing his hat back, he tapped.

'This is the daftest errand ever I was on,' he said to himself, feeling his ears redden.

The window opened and an office boy's head appeared low down in the aperture.

'I want to see the chap in charge of this place,' said Oliver sternly.

'D'you mean the Director of Education, sir?' piped the boy.

Mollified by the form of address, Oliver said he supposed so.

'What name, sir?'

'Reade.'

'One minute, please, sir.'

Oliver looked uncertainly at the door he had just come through. He felt like bolting, but the sudden remembrance of the look Thea had flashed at him kept him where he was.

'Mr Vulliamy will see you, sir.'

'What's his name?' said Oliver, following.

'Vulliamy, sir.'

'Funny name,' said Oliver surlily, as if the boy could help it.

'Good morning,' said a long, lean man, rising from his desk. 'You want to see me?'

With deliberation Oliver watched the boy go out of the room. He wasn't going to talk about being educated in front of this kid.

'Sit down,' said Mr Vulliamy, drawing out a chair. He had thought the man had come to make a complaint, he looked like it as he came in. But he was too young for a parent with a child of school-age. Also a parent coming to make a complaint usually didn't wait until the door closed.

'What can I do for you?' he said.

Oliver drew a long breath and fixed his very blue eyes on the Director of Education.

'Well,' he said, 'it's like this. I want to get myself more educated.'

'You do?'

'Yes,' said Oliver, and gave a short laugh. 'I don't suppose you've ever heard of a chap my age wanting to go back to school, have you?'

'Many a time,' said Mr Vulliamy calmly.

'Oh,' said Oliver.

'One of our best students at the Technical School is a weaver who's learning Chinese.'

'Oh,' said Oliver, feeling easier. 'Well, I don't want to learn Chinese myself, but I want to get some education.'

'What d'you mean by education? D'you mean education for a job?'

'Oh, no, thank you,' repudiated Oliver. 'Nobody could teach me anything about my job.'

'What is your job?'

'Well, it's hard to put a name to it,' said Oliver. 'It's buying and selling. But in quite a big way,' he said anxiously. 'I mean, I made well over a thousand pounds last year.'

'Good,' said Mr Vulliamy again calmly. 'Well, if you don't want to be educated for a job, you want to be educated for – shall we say social life?'

Oliver blushed.

'That's about it,' he said.

'I see,' said Mr Vulliamy.

'I suppose you think that's daft,' said Oliver.

'Not at all. I think it's very sensible.'

Oliver relaxed and drew another long breath.

'How long will it take for me to get educated?' he asked.

'All your life.'

Oliver frowned.

'But I've only got a year. I want to do it in a year.'

'All your life,' repeated Vulliamy firmly. 'And then you'll die knowing nothing.'

'What's the good of beginning then?' said Oliver.

'You've got to begin, to know that you know nothing.'

'But why begin at all?'

'Because it makes life immensely interesting to know that there is so much to know that you can know nothing.'

Mr Vulliamy smiled. A gleam of such enthusiasm flashed behind his spectacles that Oliver was kindled.

'Right you are,' he said. 'I'll begin.'

'Well, there it all is,' said Mr Vulliamy with a wave of the hand. 'A bottomless well of beauty and wisdom for anybody to dip into. What d'you want to begin with?'

'French,' said Oliver.

'French?' Mr Vulliamy considered this.

'I should leave that till later,' he said. 'What about your own language – the richest in literature in the world? There's a good course at the Technical School. And what about History?'

'Yes, I wouldn't mind knowing a bit about History,' conceded Oliver, drawing up his chair.

CHAPTER THIRTEEN

I

The Lockwoods and Thea, sitting in silence, their faces averted, had the carriage to themselves. Angela, untroubled by home-sickness, roamed the corridors, looking with interest at other travellers, going from time to time to sit with her father in his first-class apartment. Thea supposed the girls were travelling third because of her, but they needn't have bothered, she thought ungratefully, she would rather have been alone.

All the same, hearing Bee and Muriel blow their noses now and again, she was more favourably disposed towards them than ever before in her life. They were her companions in misery and she was sorry for them.

She, who had never been farther than Manchester before and had looked forward with excitement to this journey down the length of England, now that she was making it, saw nothing. Blinking her tears back, or removing them surreptitiously with the tip of a gloved finger, she thought only of home. She didn't know it, but the black from her gloves had dyed her wet cheek.

A bell rang somewhere down the train and Angela reappeared.

'Come, eat, my weeping willows,' she said, swinging through the door at them. 'What's happened to your face?' she said to Thea. 'You're like a wet sweep.'

Thea jumped up to look in the glass. Blushing, humiliated, she murmured she must go and wash.

When she came back, the carriage was empty. They hadn't waited for her. They had left all their things, even their coats. Must she do the same? To be like them, must she display a nonchalance she didn't feel? She decided she couldn't; her things were too hardly come by. Besides, the prospect of finding herself without nightgown and toothbrush appalled her. She compromised by taking the bag with her and leaving her umbrella in the rack.

She swayed down the length of the train in apprehensive search of the dining-car. She had never been in one before. At home, she bore herself with youthful dignity, keeping Oliver Reade in his place, thinking, poor thing, he doesn't know any better. But out in the world now she knew she was inexperienced, uncertain, provincial.

She came into the dining-car and found the others sitting at a table for four. She blushed to find there was no room for her and stood at a loss beside them. She saw the twins glance at her bag and then at each other, suppressing, too late, a smile. The smile was like the flick of a whip to Thea. It steadied her. She held her head higher, the blush ebbed.

'Where are you going to sit?' asked Angela cheerfully.

'I shall find a place,' said Thea, moving on.

'May I sit here?' she said nervously to a waiter, pausing at an empty table for two.

'Certainly, miss,' said the waiter over his shoulder as he rushed past. In a moment he came back to ask if she would take soup.

'Yes, please,' said Thea. Her eyes, wide with anxiety, were on a level with his as he bent over her, and his were reassuring, kind. 'I'll look after you,' said the waiter's eyes.

Thea sank back with relief.

Down the car, Bee Lockwood put her large fair face round the partition to see where Thea had got to, but not from solicitude. Thea saw from her hostile look that it was going to be as it had always been. She wasn't going to be able to get on with the twins.

Bee and Muriel Lockwood resented Thea's inclusion in the party. They didn't want her and they meant her to know it. They didn't want her to have access to their friend Angela, a girl everyone in Aldworth would have liked to know. They didn't want Thea to be doing the things they were doing. They never had liked her and they never would, they said to each other. They didn't like the cool way she returned their stares. She needed keeping down, keeping at a distance. Their behaviour was childishly malicious and an adult would have laughed at it. But Thea was little more than a child herself. She took it all in dead earnest, blowing hot with vengeance one moment and cold with scorn the next. The twins could not have found a better target; every dart went home.

The solitary lunch was a respite, but Thea was thrown into an agony of indecision again when it was over. Other people were tipping the waiter, but he had been kind to her, like a friend, and could you tip a friend? She fingered her money in miserable hesitation, then laid a shilling down and plunged away before he came to take it up. She would have liked to say goodbye, but with the shilling lying there she couldn't.

Over and over again throughout the journey, she didn't know what to do. She would sooner have died than ask the others; they weren't kind enough. Clare, the only one who might have helped, was too homesick to notice anything. Pale, her lips set, Clare followed the others in dumb misery.

The discreet splendour of the London hotel was so awesome that Thea almost tiptoed up the marble steps. The entrance hall seemed to be full of attendants in green uniform. One took her bag from her and though she felt acute anxiety, she daren't resist him. The curl of his fingers as he dangled it implied that he was used to very different luggage.

She followed the others to the reception desk. They were given their numbers and keys. They were all together on the first floor; she was alone on the fourth. Mrs Lockwood had stipulated for a cheap room for her. She followed the others to the lift, but could not help saying to Clare as they came behind: 'What about my bag?'

'Your bag?' said Clare, bringing her attention to bear with difficulty on Thea. 'Oh – they'll take it to your room.'

Thea, unused to such super-organisation, could not believe it, but when she reached her room, the bag was already there, lonely on the stand. She greeted it with relief. She no longer despised it, she had an affinity with it. Like the bag, she was too poor for her company.

Dinner, said a notice, was from seven-thirty until nine o'clock. She decided to go down at twenty-five past seven to see what the others intended to do.

In the meantime, this room was her refuge and she was alone. She went about switching on lights, opening cupboards and drawers, feeling the thick towels and fine sheets with childish pleasure. It was all very sumptuous. She turned on the taps. This was a beautiful basin, she said to herself, not like the one at home. She bathed her eyes, which felt strained from looking at so much that was new. She unpacked her things for the night and thrills of excitement rose again like bubbles in a well. 'I'm on my way,' she thought, recovering from the buffetings of the journey.

She turned off the lights and went to lean out of the window over London. She clasped the wooden window frame and felt a secret steady throb. It was like holding an electric battery, she was galvanised by the strong life of London. She felt it running through her.

She leaned out, her hair blowing. The subdued roar of London went on, but the square below was quiet, wide, noble, with cars silently gliding over a surface that shone like a lake, reflecting the lighted lamps.

As the sky gradually ceased to shed light down on London, London began to shed light up into the sky. The glow of London brightened in the dark.

At last, she drew her head in and found her hands dirty and her hair wild. She had to wash and do her hair again in a hurry, because it was time to go down.

Leaning out over London had invigorated her. She had

taken breaths of the big world. She felt different, stronger – but unfortunately, the reinforcement lasted no farther than three flights of stairs.

Unused to giving trouble, Thea thought it was too much to bring up the lift for her alone. She ran down the stairs. But for the descent into the great hall, the staircase divided into two curving marble flights, and at the foot of the one upon which Thea had started, the Lockwoods and Angela stood with two other girls, presumably the Kenworthys from Nottingham. And, noted Thea, shrinking back, they were all in silk or chiffon dresses with satin slippers. They were in evening dress, everyone in the hall was in evening dress and she was still in the black uniform. She had never thought . . . No one had told her . . .

She stood, her hand on the bland marble, looking down on the groups of beautiful women and handsome men in dress clothes, the lordly attendants, the lights. An orchestra was playing, there were flowers everywhere. She wished she was at home. 'Why did I ever try to come out?' she said to herself.

The girls looked up from below. They saw her and she had to go on. To have everyone looking at her because she wasn't properly dressed was like the nightmare where you found yourself in the street with nothing on but your vest.

'You'd better come and be introduced to the Kenworthys,' said Bee, coming to the foot of the stairs. She looked coldly at Thea. Not dressed for dinner. Didn't she know anything? She disgraces us, she thought.

The young act, speak, think mostly in groups. Uncertain themselves, they follow the least uncertain among them. The

Kenworthys from Nottingham, Anne and Nora, ordinarily two pleasant enough girls, at once took their cue from the Lockwoods. The girl in uniform was evidently of no importance. She was going to teach. She wouldn't be with them. They needn't know her, at least not properly. So they smiled indifferently, said how d'you do, and went on chattering excitedly to the Lockwoods.

Thea moved apart; she pretended to be interested in what was going on around her, but her heart burned. Angela Harvey stood apart, too, but she had no need to pretend to be interested; she was. Her hands behind her, her dimples showing, the scene might have been spread for her amusement. In the colourful, varied assembly, Angela expanded; Thea contracted.

'Come along,' said Bee coldly over her shoulder to Thea. Then seeing that Angela did not stir, she went to take her possessively by the arm.

Moving into the dining room, so immense that the innumerable tables were merely incidental, Thea saw, going in before them, Sir Robert with someone who was presumably Mr Kenworthy. She noted with surprise that Sir Robert, who looked so important in Aldworth, looked quite ordinary here. She was taken up by this metamorphosis until, at the three tables indicated by a waiter, she realised that a struggle was going on as to who should not sit with her.

'I'll be here with Clare and Thea,' said Angela, sitting down.

Bee Lockwood was annoyed. She wanted to be with Angela, but Angela had pointed Thea and Clare to their chairs.

'I look like the lady's maid allowed to dine with them for tonight,' thought Thea, sitting up very straight.

'You look very haughty,' said Angela.

Thea blushed and let her back go. She smiled for the first time that day.

'I don't feel haughty,' she said.

'Perhaps you were trying to make yourself feel it then,' said Angela.

'Yes – yes, I was,' Thea admitted. Her heart warmed at what she took for kind understanding, but Angela did not proceed with it.

'I wish they'd hurry up with this dinner,' she said, drumming with the long fingers of both hands on the polished damask. 'I'm going out.'

'You're going out?' said Thea in amazement. Even Clare was roused and looked at Angela with reddened eyes.

'Yes,' said Angela calmly. 'But don't say anything, Clare,' she warned.

'What's this, Angela?' said Bee, leaning from the other table to put a hand on the back of Angela's chair.

'Nothing,' said Angela shortly. 'Hurray – here's the soup.'

At table with Angela, Thea forgot her discomfort.

'Have you been reciting anything lately?' she asked, as having finished the soup, Angela ate with rapidity roll after roll of bread.

Angela turned from her interested observation of other diners.

'I'm always reciting, as you call it. But how did you know I recited?'

Thea was astonished. 'Why – I spoke to you at the Garden Fête two years ago. When you did "Does The Road Wind

Uphill All The Way?". You gave it to me, on a paper you had in your sash. Don't you remember?' she asked in amazement.

'Oh, was it you?' said Angela pleasantly. 'Yes, I remember now that someone did like "Does The Road Wind". Hurray – sole! Waiter, I'm hungry. I hope you've brought me a lot.'

'You can always have more, miss,' said the waiter devotedly.

'I probably shall,' said Angela.

Thea, thinking how delicious sole was, puzzled about Angela. You'd think that one who could say 'Does The Road Wind Uphill' so movingly, must herself feel deeply. But when Angela was not acting, was just herself, there seemed to be a kind of clear impermeability about her. She certainly kept other people off. Thea looked long and searchingly at Angela, which was possible because Angela was looking long and searchingly at other people. It wasn't a pretty face, Thea decided, but it was the sort of face you wanted to look at all the time.

Being served roast chicken, Thea thought suddenly of her mother and Molly and Martin having boiled eggs at home. Perhaps they would even be economising on eggs tonight; not having them so that she could eat chicken in this magnificent hotel. At the thought of them, a wave of homesickness engulfed her and she looked steadily aside for a moment to keep the tears out of her eyes.

She recovered and turned back to the table. Across it, Clare had already given up trying to eat. Thea leaned forward.

'D'you like your room?' she said, for the sake of saying something to distract Clare's thoughts from home.

But Clare was stiff with misery.

'My room?' she frowned. 'Oh – I suppose it's all right.' She turned away with sick irritation and Thea, rebuffed, gave up.

As they trooped out after dinner, Sir Robert fell back to say good night to Angela and tell her to go to bed early. Mr Kenworthy said the same to his girls. They then made their way to some other part of the hotel.

'Bridge or drinks, probably both,' said Angela. 'We shan't see them till morning, and that's just what I wanted. Now, girls, I'm off myself. So good night, too.'

'Angela,' cried Bee in alarm, rushing after her. 'Where are you going?'

'Out,' said Angela.

Bee, several stairs below, caught at her dress. 'Angela – you can't. In London at this time of night! Angela, your mother told me. . . I shall have to tell your father,' she finished.

'Don't you dare!' Angela suddenly blazed with anger. 'It's nothing to do with you what I do. You're not responsible for *me*. How could you be?' she said with scorn. 'Don't be so fussy. You're like an old hen. And don't make me late.'

She tore her flimsy flounces from Bee's hand and sped on up the stairs.

Bee turned and came down, her blush of humiliation succeeded by an expression of worthy anxiety.

'It places me in such an awkward position,' she said to the others, and Thea's lip curled. This was pure Lockwood. 'Whatever Angela says, I am responsible. Lady Harvey asked us to look after her, didn't she, Mew-mew?'

'Yes, she did,' said Muriel, wrinkling her brow to match her twin's. 'What on earth can she be going out for? We must just stand here until she comes down, Bee, and try to stop her again.'

'Yes, that's what we'll have to do, Mew-mew,' said Bee.

They posted themselves at the foot of the stairs, waiting for Angela to come down.

But Angela didn't; at least not that way.

II

At breakfast, which they ate with their hats on, gloves and bags on their knees, at eight o'clock next morning, Angela airily disclosed that she had been to the theatre.

'The theatre!' gasped the others.

'Then I might have waited at the bottom of the stairs till midnight,' said Bee, aggrieved.

'What good did you think waiting would do?' asked Angela.

Thea looked at her in amazed admiration. While she herself had tossed in the strange bed, worn out with the emotions of the day yet unable to sleep, quivering with impressions and apprehensions, feeling that she was far from home and would be farther still tomorrow, turning on the light to look round the unfamiliar room, listening to the pad of footsteps on the thickly carpeted corridor outside her door – while she was shrinking from experience, Angela had gone boldly out in search of it.

'How did you get there, Angela? What did you go to see?' the others craned from their tables towards her, while the unsuspecting Sir Robert read *The Times* half a dozen yards away.

'In a taxi. I saw Anna Moore in *Hedda Gabler*. I had it all fixed. I wasn't going to miss a chance like that.'

'Was she good?'

'Superb.'

'What was the play about?'

'Well,' said Angela, eating bacon and eggs with appetite, 'it wasn't what I expected. I expected magnificent drama because she looks as if she should play magnificent drama, doesn't she? Well, it was a funny little dowdy setting for a big play. It was something big crushed into something little. I can't explain. But she was so bored.'

'Bored?' said Thea. How funny for a play to be about being bored.

'Bored. Bored with her husband, he was so good, bored with her life, with the place, a provincial town like ours, but much worse. She was bored with herself, she was so bored she ruined everybody's life around her and then she shot herself. Waiter, I'd like sausage now. I'm going to France in a minute and this is the last decent breakfast I shall eat until next August.'

'Oh, it isn't, is it?' cried the girls in alarm.

'It is. Mother says you only get chocolate and bread, or coffee and bread – dry, too – in France.'

'It can't be true,' said Bee, who knew it was no good keeping up her aggrieved attitude with her idol for long, because the idol wouldn't notice. 'I couldn't bear that.'

'You'll have to,' said Angela. 'So fill up now, everybody.'

They did, until the moment came when Sir Robert and Mr Kenworthy folded their papers and gave the signal for departure.

Sir Robert and his friend, Mr Kenworthy, who had been as prosperous in lace as Sir Robert in cotton, resumed their places at the head of the party, the sort of head that does not look round to see what the body is doing, but expects to be followed as a matter of course. Unlike mothers, Sir Robert and Mr Kenworthy did not cling, expect to be clung to, or fuss. They sat comfortably masculine with cigars and talk in their first-class compartment a few doors from the girls in their second. They walked down platforms with papers under their arms and sensibly left the luggage to porters.

Sir Robert and Mr Kenworthy conducted their charges through what remained of England, across the Channel, from the French port to Paris, by the simple expedient of leading the way, and they fetched them up towards five o'clock in the afternoon in the hall of the hotel near the Gare de Lyon where they were to be handed over to the Directrice of the Pensionnat Jeanne d'Arc.

The two men had not concerned themselves much about the business of 'taking the girls to school'. If the girls had been bound for a dull place it is doubtful whether Sir Robert and Mr Kenworthy would have offered to conduct them, but a visit to Paris never comes amiss and after disposing of the girls the two men would stay at the Crillon for a few days by way of a change from Aldworth and Nottingham.

They had not concerned themselves much with their charges; girls lived in a world they knew nothing of and never tried to enter, but in the hall of the hotel, awaiting the arrival of the headmistress, the men were ill at ease. Seven girls and all so different when you came to look at them. And another female due to arrive at any moment, the sort of person they left to their wives, but must now deal with themselves. Sir Robert and Mr Kenworthy had come to inspect the schoolmistress but now felt as if they had come to be inspected by her. They supposed, too, that they would have to speak French to her and they didn't feel they had any. Altogether an uncomfortable half-hour was before them and they strained beyond it to the thought of the Crillon and liberty.

Mr Kenworthy had a last conversation with his girls, saying the same things over and over again as if he were on a station waiting for the train to go out. Sir Robert, too, would have spent the last moments with his daughter if she had let him, but she was prowling round some screens behind which a wedding-party was in progress. Sir Robert looked at her with disapproval. No well-bred girl, in his opinion, would go peering about like that.

The Lockwood twins were occupied with Clare who, now that the last moorings in the shape of Sir Robert and Mr Kenworthy, were about to be cast off, was overwhelmed with misery. Bee pushed and pulled at her hat, scolding her, while Muriel held her hand and sympathised.

Thea sat apart, forlorn and full of dread. She was tired. She felt dirty. The grit of the French train was in her eyes. She sagged on the chair, one leg wrapped round the other, the bag on her knee.

Suddenly she sat up, the colour rushing into her cheeks. A tall woman was coming through the hotel doors. She advanced, gaunt in black clothes. She had a long face and showed long yellow teeth in a fixed smile. Angela Harvey, turning from the screens, thought: 'Enter a funeral horse.'

Mademoiselle advanced unerringly on Sir Robert, who rose with bolting eyes.

'Sirrarvy?' she said, extending a cotton-gloved hand.

Sir Robert bowed. Presenting her card, Mademoiselle Duchêne disclosed a greater length of tooth. She turned, looking for the girls who, as if fascinated, slowly rose and gathered round. Her eyes did not smile, but remained dead. The whites showed under the iris, Angela noticed, like the eyes of a mastiff. Yes, she was more like a mastiff than a horse, Angela decided, being presented by her father. Mr Kenworthy introduced his daughters. Sir Robert brought up the Lockwoods and beckoned to Thea.

'Ah, c'est Miss,' said the Directrice.

Nine pairs of eyes stared uncomprehendingly. Thea stared as blankly as anybody.

'C'est Miss, n'est-ce pas?' repeated Mademoiselle Duchêne, raspingly. 'It is you who come to teach English?' she said.

'Oh,' said Thea. 'Yes.'

'Eh, bien,' said Mademoiselle Duchêne, with a dismissing shrug, 'you are Miss.'

Thea blushed. She had not thought of being labelled. The others looked at her as if she had suddenly become something different. She felt different, too.

Mademoiselle Duchêne, in imperfect English, explained that she must now take her pupils to the train. There was no need for the gentlemen to come with them, unless they wished. It was better not, she thought. They thought so too. Angela kissed her father, the Kenworthys kissed theirs, the others shook hands, said thank you and goodbye.

The two men conducted the party to the doors and watched them cross the square to the station, the Directrice a grim figure in their midst.

'Poor kids,' said Mr Kenworthy.

'We had to go through it in our time,' said Sir Robert. 'They'll be all right. Now let's get across to the Crillon. We'll have to hurry if we're to get seats for the opera tonight.'

CHAPTER FOURTEEN

It was dark when the station omnibus put down its passengers at the Pensionnat Jeanne d'Arc. Tired and subdued, the girls followed the Directrice to a great door set in a façade of shuttered windows. She jerked at an iron ring and a bell jangled somewhere in the interior. Except for the rattle of the trunks being got down from the bus, it was quiet, the air was fresh; it felt like a country town. The cobbled street was narrow and the houses high. Thea had the feeling that they had stepped not only into a foreign place, but backwards fifty years in time.

A small door cut in the big one opened, seemingly of its own accord. A woman in a black apron came forward saying something which was, to them, unintelligible.

'Entrez, mes enfants,' said the Directrice. She was on her own ground now and no longer a figure of fun as she had been, at least in Angela's eyes. 'Leave your affairs here. The pensionnaires are at dinner. This way.'

Even Angela was taken aback to be plunged so suddenly into the seething life of the pensionnat. The Directrice led them straight into the refectory, where the roar of voices fell at once to silence, followed by the scrape of benches as the school rose.

'Sit down,' said the Directrice shortly. 'Sit here,' she said to the girls, indicating an empty table. 'Miss also for this evening.' She went immediately from the room by another door.

The girls stood stock-still at the table. Then concerned, by common consent, to hide their shocked surprise at the absence of tablecloth – the table was covered by brown oilcloth nailed into place – at the black-handled knives, two-pronged forks, hunks of dark bread, they stepped over the benches and sat down. Thea's eyes met Angela's across the table and Angela's nostrils quivered with suppressed amusement, though how she could be amused, Thea couldn't imagine.

'There must be some mistake,' said Bee Lockwood haughtily.

The babble of voices, which had been rising steadily since the exit of the Directrice, was now deafening. The pensionnaires commented with interest on the newcomers.

The English girls had no idea what was being said about them. To them, the pensionnaires looked wild and rough, tearing bread to pieces, drinking wine, eating with amazing gusto. They had dark hair, dark eyes, flashing teeth and a restless animation and vigour the English, pale and restrained, were not prepared for.

Two small, thickset serving maids, padding about in felt boots, set plates of soup before the girls. Clare turned her head in sick aversion.

'Clare, you must eat,' said Muriel. 'She's not eaten a thing since she left home,' she told the others.

Bee looked haughtily about. This was the wrong type of school. Miss Eardley had made a hideous blunder. Someone ought to have come to inspect the place before they were committed to it.

The Directrice reappeared and the school scrambled to its feet. Taking her place at her own small table at the head of the room, she flapped a hand at them and they sat down again.

The Directrice looked even grimmer without a hat. Her black hair streaked with iron grey, was parted in the middle and arranged in a small plaited mat on the crown of her head. Her long face was preternaturally stern. She wore a high-necked black satin blouse and a long grey cloth skirt.

'Funny,' remarked Angela, forking up slithering macaroni. 'In an English schoolmistress, it would be the other way round. A grey blouse with a black skirt. If it had to be. Though I think only pew-openers wear that combination now.'

She was deeply interested in the Directrice. 'A stock figure,' she said. 'When I take a part like that I shall know how to do it now.'

But Thea looked at the Directrice with misgiving. She had to work under her. 'I don't like her,' she thought, watching the Directrice being served with special dishes.

'Do eat some macaroni, Clare,' urged Muriel. 'She'll be ill if she doesn't eat,' she warned the others.

Clare tried. But she raised her eyes and looked round with fear and repulsion and put down her fork again.

'Is there no meat?' asked a Kenworthy in surprise as a plate of Marie biscuits, arranged in pairs, was put on the table with a small dish of jam.

'How can we spread jam without knives?'

'Let's see what the French do,' said Angela. She took a smiling look at the next table and was met with smiles in return.

'You eat jam with a teaspoon,' she announced. 'And these girls aren't at all bad.'

Thea looked at the girls, too; but she couldn't smile.

After the biscuits, the English were astonished to see a large tin dish of hot water set upon the table.

'Now what?' Muriel challenged Angela. 'Do we drink it?' Explain that, her tone implied.

Angela mutely consulted the next table.

'We wash up in it,' she said. 'We dip knives and forks in and dry them on this cloth.'

'Of course I shan't stay,' said Bee, dipping cutlery with hauteur. 'What sort of a place is this where we have to do the washing-up?'

'Oh, Bee,' said Clare, colour and life rushing into her pale face. 'D'you mean we shall go home?'

'I can't decide anything yet,' said Bee in an elderly way. 'But I don't see how we can possibly stay here.'

'Oh, if we could only go home,' said Clare, her eyes brimming over so that large, bright tears splashed to the brown oilcloth.

'Clare,' warned Angela, 'don't let us down here.'

'No,' quavered Clare, smiling in a watery way. 'But if we could only go home . . .'

'See,' said Angela cheerfully, polishing spoon and fork, 'they're putting their own things into linen cases and handing them up to be put away in the drawer at the top of the table.'

'We have a drawer,' said Anne Kenworthy, trying it, 'but no cases.'

The woman who had met them in the hall now appeared and motioned to them to leave the cutlery on the table.

'Suivez-moi,' she said.

They gaped. They had all been learning French for a dozen years or so, but none of them could understand even so little when spoken by a native.

The housekeeper beckoned; they got up from the benches and followed her from the room amid the interested silence of the French.

The housekeeper led the way up the stairs, stone and railed with iron. The sad light of an occasional and inadequate electric bulb showed plastered walls. 'This might be an orphanage,' said Bee.

'Or a prison,' said Angela.

But the dormitory, containing six beds, into which the housekeeper led them, was better than the staircase promised. The beds, with square white pillows and plump eiderdowns, looked inviting and the parquet shone.

'Voilà,' said the housekeeper, who knew it was no good saying more. 'Et vous, Miss,' she said to Thea. 'Suivez-moi.'

As at the hotel, Thea was to go up higher. She followed the housekeeper to the fourth floor. Here the infrequent light showed a labyrinth of whitewashed low-ceilinged passages, the floor dipped and rose, the doors were rickety. These were the attics of an old, old house.

The housekeeper forced open a door, wadded with a burst sausage of canvas and horsehair against draught, turned on a light and revealed a room with, Thea saw with a shock, two beds. It had not occurred to her that she would have to 'sleep with anybody' as she put it to herself. To have to sleep in the company of a stranger, breathe, wash, weep, think, with a stranger there! 'I wish I'd never come,' she thought, as she had thought many times since she left home.

The housekeeper crossed the room and opened another door to show a cupboard-like room within. 'Cabinet de toilette,' said the housekeeper, speaking very distinctly. On two wooden stands were minute jugs and basins more suitable to the tea than the toilet table. Thea's trunk and the bag were already there.

The housekeeper, re-crossing the attic, indicated the bed opposite the window. 'À vous,' she said, and pointing to the other: 'À Jeanne Audet.'

'Bonsoir,' she said.

'Good night,' said Thea shyly. 'And thank you.'

The housekeeper shrugged her shoulders to imply that English was beyond her and went.

Thea looked at the room. The ceiling was fairly high over her bed but sloped low on each side of the dormer window. The wallpaper was a cracked and faded pink, the floor was of highly-polished red tiles. There was a strip of carpet beside each bed, there were two chairs, two small tables, one piled with books, the other presumably for herself.

She tiptoed, though there was no one there, to the cabinet de toilette. It struck her that if she hurried into bed, she could pretend to be asleep when the strange girl came in. She swiftly unpacked a towel and dressing-gown and went in search of a bathroom. In vain. She couldn't find one. She knocked on her compatriots' door.

'There's no bathroom,' said Angela, putting her head out. 'No. No bathroom.'

'No bathroom?' echoed Thea, aghast.

'There's a wash-room, but no hot water,' said Angela.

'No hot water?' echoed Thea again. 'But what do we do?'

'Wash in cold.'

'Close the door, Angela,' said Bee from within. 'Everybody can see us.'

'There's no one here but Thea,' said Angela. 'But I'm frightfully sleepy, so good night.'

She smiled and shut the door. Thea stood outside, looking at it. There was a buzz of voices as a door opened briefly below; someone struck up tinnily on a piano. She went back to the attic, undressed quickly, washed in the absurd basin, put out the light and went stealthily to the window. Fumbling with the fastenings, she put back the shutters and leaned out into the night. Over dark irregular roofs the sky was pricked with stars. There was a fir tree so close at hand she could hear it creak as its branches stirred. A clock struck nearby with a deep note, and another, light, quick, silvery from farther off. When the clocks had struck, silence, fresh and pure like water, flowed in again.

'I'm in France,' she thought.

The bed was surprisingly comfortable, much more comfortable than her own at home. She was grateful for the bed. And the pillow was smooth and soothing. It was square with a little round sausage of a bolster underneath. She lay in the dark with a vivid procession of the day's events streaming through her head. But by and by, the inward cinematograph-show dazzled less; it blurred gently away. She relaxed, her head settled into the pillow. She slept.

Later, she opened her eyes and lay looking at the wall without moving. There was someone in the room. The strange girl must have come in. The light wasn't the same. Cautiously she turned her head.

A girl with dark hair was studying by candlelight at her table. Her face was hidden by her hand, but when she dropped the hand to turn a page, Thea saw that she was pale and had fine dark brows and dark lashes. Her face was still and grave, and Thea, who had herself pored over books for hours, knew that she was tired.

In spite of the interest she felt in the girl whose room she shared, Thea's lids drooped and she slept again.

Later, she woke with a start. The girl was just getting up from the table, candle in hand. She saw that she had disturbed Thea, who lay now with wide-open eyes, looking at her.

The girl raised a hand as if to hush a child.

'Sleep,' she said quietly in English.

Thea smiled drowsily and closed her eyes. She dimly felt she had found somebody kind.

CHAPTER FIFTEEN

I

If the Pensionnat Jeanne d'Arc was not in the least what the English girls expected, it was hardly the fault of the pensionnat, which was merely the ordinary provincial day and boarding school and had not pretended to be anything else. The fault, if any, lay with Miss Eardley, who either had not known provincial France as well as she imagined, or had considered it would do the girls no harm to live in France as the French live.

The three Lockwoods and the two Kenworthys wanted to go home at once, if only for reasons of plumbing. No bathroom! No hot water, except what you took up in a jug from the kitchen two or three nights a week! Sanitation primitive beyond belief! No means of washing one's hair! And, they added in horror, no tablecloths! 'We owe it to our parents to go home,' said Bee, and the others agreed.

Except Angela. 'Here I am and here I stay,' she said. 'We can go to the établissement des bains in the town and what do I care about tablecloths?'

Her one disappointment was the discovery that she couldn't go to the theatre. In France, it appeared, no young girl ever went to the theatre. 'What it is to be a young girl,' said Angela. 'It's bad enough in England, but seems fifty times worse in France.'

'Angela,' said Bee. 'It's five to one against staying here. I think you ought to consider us.'

'Have I asked you to stay?' said Angela. 'You must do as you please. All I say is that *I* am staying.'

So of course they stayed.

'I shouldn't be doing my duty,' said Bee loftily, 'if I left her. Lady Harvey trusts me to look after her. We shall just have to put up with the place. Abroad evidently isn't like England. We can't expect it. They're backward. But I'll speak to the Directrice and make better arrangements for us if I can. Oh, Clare, don't cry, please. As if I haven't enough to put up with in Angela.' Bee passed her hand across her brow like a much-harassed housewife, which was what she subconsciously liked to imagine she was.

She spoke to the Directrice. Her first complaint was about the classrooms, which were, she pointed out, too cold, too unpleasant, and not what they were used to. 'Very well,' said the Directrice, showing her teeth in an accommodating smile, the English need not go into them. The English were paying far more than other pupils and she did not mean to lose them. They had come to learn French, she supposed, but if they did not want to, that was their affair. It was her affair, however, to keep them at the school, so she gave them all they asked. They were treated with tolerance and indifference. It was taken for granted that they didn't want to learn anything. It was arranged that they should have their few lessons in the Grande Salle and that Mademoiselle Françoise, who was not much use anywhere else, should teach them. No one minded if they were late for their lessons, or did not turn up at all. They took baths in the town, went to the hairdresser, always accompanied, practised the piano and generally did as they liked. They sat together at table, they slept together in a dormitory. They were in the school, but in no way of it.

Bee was very satisfied with the Grande Salle, the pensionnat's showpiece, a great room with a shining parquet, filet net at the six long windows, and handsome Empire furniture. Bee looked upon the Grande Salle as peculiarly her own and took charge of it. Between lessons she opened the windows, like a mother airing the nursery while the children were out. She straightened the chairs, kept a duster in a drawer to give things a rub over, even bought flowers for the long table when she went into the town to the hairdresser's or the baths.

And no sooner had she made all these satisfactory and creditable arrangements and got things into what she called working order, than Angela deserted. The Grande Salle bored her, so she went into class with the French. She got her place moved at meals and no longer sat with her compatriots, but with the French. She no longer walked round and round the courtyard with the others at recreation, but instructed the French in a wild kind of golf played with croquet mallets.

'When I'm in France, I'll do as the French do,' she said.

She was determined to speak French because, she said, she adored the sound of it.

'So please don't hang round me,' she said to the outraged Bee. 'I can't learn French if you are always speaking English to me and wanting me to speak it to you. French is going to be useful to me, so please don't get in the way. You've got your sisters and the Kenworthys. You must make them do.'

Bee's possessive soul was deeply wounded. She was also permanently aggrieved. This was what came, she said to the others, of doing your best for somebody. This is how she repays me, she pointed out. If it hadn't been for Angela, she reminded them, we should all have gone home at once.

Bee had lost not only her friend Angela, but her enemy Thea. Both had put themselves out of her reach.

There had never been any question of going home for Thea. It had cost too much to get here. Thea knew, from the beginning, that she must put up with everything, and everything proved to be a good deal. More, at times, than she felt she could bear.

She was at once faced with the ordeal of controlling classes of girls who were only too glad to take advantage of a foreigner and have fun in reaction to the stern discipline of their other teachers. At her first class, she stood at the rostrum as if she were facing a pack of wolves. Unable to speak a word of French except that which sent them into fits of laughter, she had to control them somehow. She did it from sheer desperation. She did it because she had to. She simply stood there waiting for the din to die down, and by some miracle she never understood, it died. Without a word spoken she compelled the class to be quiet. White in the face, her eyes dark with nervous distension of the pupils, her hands clasped behind her back so that no one should see they trembled, she compelled them.

After the first time, she did not utter a word they could laugh at. She spoke cool, clear English and left it to them to puzzle and be stupid. After three or four classes, some of the girls began to admire her and these admirers helped her to control the class, rounding on anyone who ventured to annoy her. Gradually she relaxed. She began to translate into her faltering French when it was impossible to make them understand otherwise and this baby talk endeared her still further to those who liked her already. Gradually she got her classes under way, but it had been a stiff ordeal and she emerged from it tougher and a little grim.

She soon found that the more she proved herself capable of doing, the more she was given to do. The Directrice piled classes and supervision upon her. Even out of class she wasn't free. At meals she sat with the 'little ones'. She served and kept an eye on fourteen small girls. At first it was torment. She couldn't understand what they said. They were quarrelsome, they spilled things – salt, soup, water – embarrassing her dreadfully because she didn't know how to call the maids to get the spillings wiped up, making the boarders, including the Lockwoods, giggle. And the children were always vociferously wanting more bread. 'Du pain, Miss. Du pain,' they cried incessantly. They were like ravenous young sparrows. But she got used to them. She came to like them. She found peace and relaxation in their prattle, and she was touched when they ran to her in the courtyard with their troubles and joys.

She knew the Directrice meant to get as much out of her as she could. She wasn't singled out in this, because the Directrice got as much as she could out of everybody. Pupils and teachers slaved at the Pensionnat Jeanne d'Arc and Thea had to slave with them.

The French lessons she had expected did not materialise. The weeks went on and no lessons were mentioned. Wondering how she dared to, Thea nevertheless approached the Directrice.

The Directrice smiled one of her glassy smiles. 'But your lessons are all around you,' she said. 'You hear French all the time. It is your fault if you do not learn. Also you are professeur. It is not suitable that you should sit in the classroom with your pupils.'

Thea withdrew defeated, but she returned to protest that her letters were read before they were given to her. The Directrice said coldly that all pupils' letters were read.

'But you said I wasn't a pupil, Mademoiselle,' said Thea.

The adversaries measured each other. The eyes of the woman looked into the eyes of the young girl. Thea felt a shiver of apprehension, but her eyes did not flinch. After this, her letters were unopened.

She wrung another privilege from the Directrice. She asked to be allowed to go into town unaccompanied and without seeking permission.

'The pupils are not allowed to go out alone,' said the Directice.

'But I am not a pupil,' said Thea.

Triumphant, she sped up the four flights of stairs to tell Jeanne she had defeated the Directrice again.

Jeanne looked grave. 'Méfiez-vous de Mademoiselle Duchêne,' was all she would say.

'Pooh,' said Thea. 'What can she do? I'm not afraid of her.'

'Beware of her,' said Jeanne again.

Thea laughed. She felt she knew her way about now. She could manage, she said to herself.

One thing at least this coming to France had done for her, she sometimes said to herself: it had freed her from the Lockwoods. During those first miserable weeks at the pensionnat, the pinprick tactics of Bee and Muriel Lockwood had lost their power to hurt her. Thea, struggling against so many other difficulties, had barely noticed the Lockwoods. She forgot the hateful journey she had made in their company, she forgot the humiliations she had suffered at their hands. They might be at Timbuctoo now for all she cared or felt about them. She congratulated herself that what she had been through had given her a better sense of proportion; she was at least able not to mind any more about the Lockwoods.

Bee knew and resented her loss of power. She had always been able to flick Thea on the raw and move her to envy and dissatisfaction; and now she couldn't. Bee was her father's daughter, she liked power. But her sojourn in France was depriving her of it. She had lost Angela to the French and could no longer hurt Thea. Also, in this place, she herself was without importance. No one here knew what a big house they lived in or how many servants they kept. No one knew how well she spoke in her own tongue, or what she was in her own country. She objected to making a fool of herself, so she wouldn't speak French if she could help it. To stammer and stumble in French did not suit her haughty bearing. Still, she ruled in the Grande Salle and getting Clare through the hard winter exercised almost to the full her faculty for fussing.

It had been very cold. The French took to felt boots, mittens, shawls, old fur tippets, in which they sat in classrooms where all the windows were closed and the air was moted thick with chalk from the blackboards. The English had no such protective coverings, nor, they declared, would they have worn them if they had.

'I thought the French were supposed to be smart,' said a Kenworthy.

'Another illusion,' said Bee.

The English persisted in wearing their fine stockings and thin slippers and in consequence suffered from chilblains. Clare wept over hers and fretted for home.

Thin, shrinking, her hair out of curl, her eyes too big, Clare was a ghost of her former self. She was simply getting through the days, marking them off on her calendar as they crept past. She couldn't get used to France, she couldn't settle, she didn't like any of it. Not any of it, she wept to herself. She couldn't get used to eating with so many noisy people, to being always surrounded by them, to hearing the incessant tinkle of so many pianos, to going to bed in a dormitory, weeping herself to sleep and waking in a fright at the dark bulk of the huge puffed eiderdown looming over the edge of the blankets.

She longed for her fire-lit room at home, with all her treasures round her – all those darling little china animals on the mantelpiece, Boz, her dog, at the foot of her bed and her parents sleeping across the landing. Not only was she homesick here, but she was so bored, she told herself. She couldn't understand what they were saying and didn't want to. There was nothing to do. Every day was the same. There were so many things to do at home. She went out in the car, paid visits with her mother, played tennis, walked with her father, and everybody smiled at her. Here nobody smiled at her. They were always in a hurry here, pushing her out of the way as they rushed from place to place, always violently engaged on something she didn't know anything about.

Why had she to suffer like this? What was the use of it? She didn't want to speak French. What use would French be at home? Because she would never leave home again. Never, she vowed. Dear Oakfield, darling Daddy, I'll never leave you again, she wept. Her letters, always blistered with tears, brought tears to her father's eyes as he read them. 'It was a mistake,' he said over and over again. 'It was a mistake to send that child away from home.'

When Thea came across Clare with her wan, listless looks, she hardened her heart. Clare was a Lockwood, everything was made easy for her. She could do as she liked; she was always with her sisters, the Grande Salle was heated, she never suffered from hard work, cold, and the inability to buy the cakes displayed in the pâtisseries, so tempting to a hungry girl who got nothing to eat but a hunk of dry bread between twelve o'clock lunch and seven o'clock dinner. The others had tea which they bought and made themselves, and if they didn't get out into the town to buy cakes themselves, they prevailed upon others, sometimes Thea herself, to bring cakes in boxes for them.

'Clare hasn't had anything like I have had to put up with,' said Thea to herself. 'What would she have done if she'd been me?'

II

Winter in the attic had been rigorous indeed. The steam heating did not go up so high and the water was often frozen in the absurd little jugs.

On winter nights, when their duties were over downstairs, Jeanne and Thea put their candles together on Jeanne's table. The single electric light was so bad they bought candles out of their own pockets to supplement it and two candles on one table gave more light than one candle on each. They put on coats and mufflers and wrapping their eiderdowns like mermaids' tails about them, they settled down to work; Jeanne to prepare lessons – she was a pupil-teacher and was also working for her Brevet Supérieur – Thea to prepare lessons, too, and to teach herself French.

Sometimes the wind tore at the shutters and the fir tree in the courtyard groaned as if it would break at any minute, sometimes there was an absolute silence and Thea, taking a last look out, would find the roofs deep in snow. The dark and the cold and the storms without made the attic more of a refuge than ever. Weather might be bad outside and things often disagreeable downstairs, but up here, with Jeanne, there was peace and companionship and a sense of what Thea thought of as 'being in the same boat'. Looking round the attic, which had horrified her at first sight, Thea realised that she was happy to be in it.

The girls worked, but often broke off to talk. They leaned across the table, looking into each other's eyes, clear in the candle-light. Each burned to find out what the other thought about things. They spoke a mixture of French and English that served them very well.

Sometimes, as they talked, the door was flung open and the Directrice loomed above the candles.

'Why are you talking? You are here to work. And I heard you speaking French. You must speak English, Miss. Jeanne must speak English to pass her examination and prepare herself to take your place when you are no longer here. Jeanne, you share this room with Miss to profit from her English, not to waste your time in chatter.'

'Oui, Mademoiselle,' said Jeanne, dropping her eyes.

She always spoke calmly and, judging from the words only, with a humility that seemed almost servile. But there was an undertone of the mockery which Thea thought must be peculiar to the French. Jeanne fell in with the Directrice's orders, she did as she was told and the quiet mockery that no one could put a finger on seemed to make up to her for having to do it.

Jeanne was an orphan, brought up by a grandmother who had died when she was fourteen. The priest of the parish arranged with the Directrice that she should be taken into the pensionnat on condition that she became a teacher there in due course. She was without money, relations or friends. She had to resign herself to spending the rest of her life at the Jeanne d'Arc or some similar institution, because she must live in. She could not be allowed to go into a shop or into any business where she would live out, because at her age she would be constantly open to the temptation, the outstanding temptation in France, it appeared, of becoming somebody's mistress. Thea, fresh from Aldworth High School and little Byron Place, was aghast. There was no hope of marriage for a girl without a dowry, Jeanne explained.

'It can't be true,' said Thea.

'It is,' said Jeanne. 'No dot, no marriage. Even the poorest working man demands something.'

'No love unless you bring money in your hand?' said Thea, unable to believe it.

'Ah, love – yes,' said the realist Jeanne. 'Love, that's another thing. I could become someone's mistress, but the prospect does not attract me. One passes from one man to another until one becomes old and dies in poverty. I shouldn't like that,' said eighteen-year-old Jeanne. 'Besides, I think I am serious by nature, though I didn't wish to be serious all the time. However, I shall have to be. But it's sad not to be able to look forward to your life.'

'Sad!' cried Thea. 'It's terrible!'

She burned with indignation. Thea had never really had a friend before. She had never plunged into another mind as she plunged into Jeanne's and a mind so like her own, though more cynical, more mocking and at the same time more accepting of life as it is, without fighting or hoping for anything better. Thea had more of the malady of the ideal in her composition than Jeanne, who no longer considered the ideal at all. And that of itself made Thea burn with fiercer indignation. That was what the pensionnat had done to her friend. Jeanne must get out, she insisted. They must find a way. She put wild plans of rescue before Jeanne, who shrugged them away as absurd.

'I shall never get out. But don't concern yourself.'

'But you are nothing but a prisoner here,' cried Thea. 'You're a prisoner!'

'Yes, I am a prisoner,' said Jeanne. 'But few women are free, you know. Or men either, for that matter. But look at the time. We must work.'

Thea, baffled by this defeatist attitude, had to return to her books.

She wrote home that, thanks to Jeanne, she was quite settled at the pensionnat. She had to work hard, the Directrice was a stern taskmistress, but she didn't wish to be anywhere else, even if better, she wrote, because of Jeanne.

Her mother, Molly and Martin wrote every week, mostly to say they really had no news. Their letters seemed to be both wistful and flat. Now that she was at a distance from her family, with only their letters to represent them, she noticed a factor common to all three: a lack of interest in what they were doing, in the way they had to spend their lives. Her mother wasn't interested in housework, Molly wasn't interested in governessing, Martin wasn't interested in the bank. Thea was shocked to make this discovery. Not only was it a waste of life, but she wondered, too, if it was a fault inherent in the family. With anxiety, she examined herself to see if it was in her as well. But though she had to admit to frequent dissatisfaction, resentment, indignation, she didn't think she could be accused of lack of interest.

Strange that the letters she didn't want and was annoyed to get should breathe such strong and individual interest in life that the writer seemed to stand before her in the flesh as she read them. Oliver Reade had begun by sending a few picture postcards, which she ignored. But at Christmas he had sent a copy of *Villette*, and she had to thank him for it. She had written home to ask for the book, but it was he who sent it. She was annoyed that they should have let him. They must allow him to read her letters, she thought indignantly. If so, he was on far too intimate terms with her family. 'Why do they encourage him?' she thought angrily.

Since Christmas he had written several times, but she hadn't answered. She didn't want to enter into a correspondence with him and had no money for unnecessary stamps.

III

The winter was over. One morning there was balm in the air; spring had noticeably arrived. The buds on the pollarded fig trees in the courtyard seemed suddenly very much bigger and the fir tree was newly tipped with bright green. A sunny silence brooded over the long grey façade of the pensionnat.

The cathedral clock began to strike eleven, the town clocks hurried to join in and the air was full of bells. Mademoiselle Françoise, clutching in spite of the sun a little black shawl at her neck, crossed the court and pulled at a bellrope. At the resultant clangour, all the doors on the school side seemed to burst open simultaneously and girls poured out into the courtyard, a dark, dishevelled crowd in black sateen overalls.

From the french windows of the Grande Salle, the Lockwoods and the Kenworthys stepped out, neat in white collars, their fair hair shining in the sun. They began to walk round and round, arm in arm, with Clare tagging along at the end of the row, taking no interest. She was like a child out with its elders, accompanied, but not companioned.

From the school side, Thea came out with an armful of books.

'Gare à vous,' shouted Angela and Thea dodged, just in time, a great wooden ball. Without noticing the Lockwoods, Thea hurried across the court and rushed upstairs to Jeanne, whom she had seen at the open window.

'Here you are,' said Jeanne, turning with a smile. She blinked in the strong sunlight.

'Here I am,' said Thea, throwing her books on the bed and going over to the window. She was about to lean companionably on Jeanne's shoulder to look down into the court, but Jeanne drew back.

'Mademoiselle Petit is looking at us,' she warned.

Close friendships were discouraged at the pensionnat; they were, in fact, viewed with suspicion, though Thea could not understand why.

'It's a lovely day,' said Thea, keeping well away from Jeanne as she leaned out of the window. 'I hope I'll be able to rush out for quarter of an hour at four o'clock. I wish you could come, too.'

Jeanne shrugged her shoulders. She didn't even consider the wish since it was hopeless.

Exercising her privilege to the full, Thea went out almost

every day, even if only for quarter of an hour. When she went down the Grande Rue, heads were turned and people came to shop doors to look at the spectacle of a young girl, attractive and not of the working class, walking alone. Thea had not been wrong in her first impression that in coming to Villeneuve she stepped back fifty years in time. Young girls in Villeneuve did not walk about the town, or anywhere else for that matter, unaccompanied and for no apparent reason. People did not know what to make of the Miss at the pensionnat. Was she respectable? They supposed she must be, since she was there. Of course, the English were singular and one understood that young girls in her country had more liberty than in France. But they were surprised, all the same, that the Directrice should allow the Miss to promenade in this way, alone.

'Yes, I shall try to get quarter of an hour's walk on the boulevard this afternoon,' said Thea cheerfully, leaning farther out of the window to get the full warmth of the sun.

There was a knock at the door. Mademoiselle Petit put her sallow face into the room, glancing round it instead of looking at the occupants.

'Miss,' she said, 'la Directrice vous demande en bas.'

'Oh, dear,' said Thea.

With a look of apprehensive enquiry at Jeanne and another into the pocked glass on the wall to see if her hair was all right, she hurried from the attic.

CHAPTER SIXTEEN

I

The Directrice's room opened off the Grande Salle and might once have been a powder-closet. It was so small it was almost entirely filled by the Directrice's large, littered desk and the Directrice herself. Half the terror of an interview with the Directrice came from being at such close quarters with her. It was like being in the cage with a tiger.

When Thea, having knocked, was bidden to enter, she did so with difficulty because there was already a second person with the Directrice. Squeezing in, Thea found this to be a middle-aged woman in deep mourning, than which, in France, there is nothing deeper.

'Madame, this is Miss,' announced the Directrice. 'Miss, Madame Farnet, the mother of Simone, you understand. Sit down.'

Thea sat, finding herself almost knee to knee with both the Directrice and the stranger. From the grouping it looked as if the three of them had come together for a cosy chat, though Thea knew it could be nothing of the kind.

Simone Farnet was in the cours supérieur, a prim girl with a narrow face, and here under the widow's coif, was the face repeated, but older, shrewder, even narrower. Madame Farnet kept her face still, but her eyes were active. She kept her lips pressed together and when she had something under consideration, she tightened them still more, so that white lines rayed out from them, giving her a look of age and extreme severity. The lines were marked now as she considered Thea.

'She is young,' she said suddenly in a harsh voice, as if Thea's youth were an affront she had not expected.

'Oh, Madame,' cried the Directrice, throwing a hand into the air, 'that is precisely what I said when I first saw her. These English look like that. But Miss is eighteen and she has sense. Oh, yes, believe me,' said the Directrice with a sudden hard note in her voice, 'she knows how to look after herself. But she teaches English well. Better than anyone we have ever had.'

Thea looked at the Directrice in surprise. Was this genuine praise, or was she trying to sell something?

'Have no fear, Madame. Miss is exactly your affair. Since Simone must improve her English for her examination, and Monsieur Jacques for his business, you cannot do better than employ Miss to take English with them twice a week. If you wish – and for Simone at least there is no time to lose – Miss can give the first lesson at your house this afternoon at four-thirty,' said the Directrice, consulting a timetable on her desk. 'Miss, you can go to your class now. The bell has rung. I will let you know what Madame Farnet decides.'

Thea left the room and recrossed the Salle. She was both indignant with the Directrice and angry with herself for not having refused then and there to be sent to teach in the town. The Directrice had no right to do it. The arrangement was that she should teach in the school for board and French lessons. She hadn't got the lessons and now she was to be sent out to teach. The Directrice was going to make money out of her and not one penny, she knew, would come her way.

She stood before the door in the Salle without opening it. She wished she had the courage to go back and refuse to teach the Farnet man or boy, whichever he was. She might have done it, if the door had not at that moment opened to admit the Lockwoods and the Kenworthys coming back to lessons.

'Oh, Thea, you're the very person we wanted to see!' said Muriel. 'Are you going out this afternoon? If you are, will you bring us some cakes in? We're simply starving.'

'Starving,' chorused the others.

'Bring me two rhum babas, will you, and an éclair.'

'I want one of those things with a kind of custard in the middle and two madeleines. . . .'

'We'll give you the money after lunch,' said Bee, proceeding to the table.

'I may not go,' said Thea. 'Let me pass, please,' she said, thrusting through the others.

'But if you do . . .' they besought her.

'Make out a list then,' said Thea shortly. 'Though I may not go . . .' she called back at them.

But when she had discussed it with Jeanne, she decided to go.

'The old camel shouldn't send you out, perhaps, but go,' counselled Jeanne. 'At least it gets you out of this box for a while. I only wish I could go. But they wouldn't let me come into contact with a young man. No fear. They wouldn't risk it. The English are said to be different. Colder.'

'But is he grown up?' asked Thea apprehensively.

Jeanne couldn't say. Thea decided that she would go for this once to the house in the Rue Victor Hugo, and if she didn't like it, she would refuse to go again.

She collected money and cake-list from her compatriots after lunch, but rather ungraciously. They were always stuffing themselves, she thought testily. It was a mild form of torture to buy cakes for other people when you couldn't afford any yourself.

II

On the spring afternoon, Villeneuve was like a pastel drawing, with all its colours soft and chalky: the houses pale grey and white, the cobbles of the streets the varying greys of a pigeon's breast, the old cathedral a weathered buff, the river pale cloudy green, with the sanded boulevard alongside stumped with trees newly burst into leaf.

But Thea paid no attention to the placid scene as she hurried through it on her way to the Rue Victor Hugo. She was nervous. She hadn't liked the look of Madame Farnet. She was grim. Judging from the Directrice, Madame Farnet, the women at the cash desks in the shops, there were a good many grim Frenchwomen. They were so terribly single-minded, thought Thea. They had no sidelines, no softnesses, no leisure. Whereas their counterparts in England, the middle-aged women whose work, after bringing up their families, seemed to be over, were often so vague and at a loose end. Funny, the difference, thought Thea, and gave up comparisons. She had arrived at the Rue Victor Hugo.

It was a street of high walls and great closed doors. For their domestic life, the French shut themselves away, and Thea, remembering the little houses in Byron Place into whose front rooms anyone could look, thought it very sensible of them. She walked down the middle of the paved street looking for number twenty-four and found it carved in curly figures on a stone medallion over an enormous wooden door.

The Farnets, Jeanne had told her, were wholesale grocers on a large scale. The warehouse was behind the private house and the business was conducted, since her husband's death, under the close supervision of Madame Farnet herself.

Thea rang the bell and when the small door (cut, as usual, in the big one) opened she stepped through. Across the small court which, with the house within it, was like an eighteenth-century illustration to Voltaire, a woman in an apron waited. She admitted Thea to the house, ushered her through a door to the right and withdrew.

Thea found herself in an astonishing place. In the middle of a large, otherwise bare room was a tubular enclosure of glass, within which, protected from draughts like a plant by a cloche, was Madame Farnet at a desk. She took no notice of Thea, but continued to stoop over a ledger. She had a hot-water bottle at her feet and a black shawl round her shoulders. Though it was spring in the world, in Madame Farnet's veins it was winter. She had a bad circulation, not surprising since she rarely moved out of the tube, and she suffered from indigestion, for which she continually sipped tisanes of peppermint and camomile.

Thea stood unregarded, until Madame Farnet laid down her pen, clutched with one bony hand the shawl more closely about her, emerged from the tube and said unsmilingly: 'This way.'

Crossing the hall, she pulled at a bell which clanged somewhere outside, then led the way into a dining room, which was dim and warm, with a stove, a dark parquet, a long table set with chairs and a window shrouded in filet through which Thea could see the bulky shapes of lorries and covered wagons in the back court.

Simone Farnet was waiting. Her hair screwed back, her dress thriftily covered by a black sateen overall, she was prim, dutiful and full of self-importance at having English lessons at home.

'Good afternoon, Miss,' she said.

'Good afternoon,' said Thea nervously.

The door opened and a young man came in.

'Good day, Mademoiselle,' he said, bowing.

Thea bowed in return. She had a confused impression of vigour, good looks, good humour. And he was quite grown up.

Madame Farnet pulled out a chair at the table.

'Sit here, my son,' she said.

Speaking to him, her voice changed. It was like warm oil, thick with maternal passion and possessiveness. It surprised Thea, and she was surprised again by the submission of the son's voice when he said: 'Merci, Maman,' and went to stand behind the chair.

In her surprise she looked at him, and at that moment he shot a glance at her. It was no more than a glance, but its amused irony made hay of his filial attitude. A typical French glance. Thea had seen it many a time. 'Moquer,' she thought. But the glance was gone in a flash and his eyes were lowered to the table.

'Simone, sit here,' indicated Madame Farnet. 'And, Miss, put yourself at the head of the table.'

Thea sat down.

'You can begin,' said Madame Farnet.

Thea was taken aback. She had hoped Madame Farnet would go away before she had to begin. But there was no help for it. She had to start.

She turned to Jacques Farnet, who sat on her left, his back to the window.

'I don't know how much English you have done, Monsieur,' she said.

He raised his eyes. They were fine dark eyes. His hair was crisp and dark. He corrugated his forehead; he had a slightly squared tip to his nose and two deep, short lines, two nicks, on each side of his well-shaped mouth. His expression at the moment was of such extreme solemnity as to be absurd. His mother stood by, waiting.

'I have passed my Baccalauréat, Mademoiselle,' he said. 'And English was one of my subjects.'

He pinched in his lips and gazed at her. Thea was seized with a crazy desire to laugh. But under the watchful eyes of the mother and sister, she controlled it.

'Then you are even more advanced than your sister?'

'I hope so,' said the young man.

'Let us begin with grammar then,' said Thea.

Madame Farnet, after standing for a moment longer, went out of the room.

When she came back, Thea was showing Jacques Farnet how to pronounce the English 'th,' because, though he had passed his Baccalauréat, his accent was bad.

'Say "the,"' she said. 'Like this.'

She tilted her chin. He gazed obediently at the charming foreshortened view of her face thus presented.

Madame Farnet made Thea jump by coming up behind and pressing two bony fingers into her collarbone.

'Tenez, Miss,' she said harshly, 'it is not necessary for my son to *speak* English. It is necessary for him to write it and understand letters we receive from England. For my daughter, it is necessary that she has a good accent for her examination. Occupy yourself as you like with her accent, but for my son, take a dictation. You understand?'

Thea blushed violently. To be prodded and spoken to in such a way humiliated and startled her.

'Very well, Madame,' she said, reaching swiftly for her dictation book.

She opened it at random. She could hardly see. The violence of the blush had brought tears to her eyes. She began to dictate too soon, before her pupils could get their exercise books and pencils ready. She felt she was cutting a poor figure as a teacher.

'"Having regained my room,"' read Thea.

Madame Farnet hovered watchfully; and again withdrew.

'If she keeps coming in like this,' thought Thea, 'I shall never get on with the lesson.'

'"I set myself to turn over in my mind,"' she read.

The blush was subsiding, but her lashes felt damp and she surreptitiously put up a finger to one eye, and in a moment to the other.

'"The incident of the evening,"' she read, carefully spacing out the words.

She looked up. The young man looked up, too, and their eyes met. His were grave. They mutely begged her pardon for his mother's behaviour. They told her not to mind.

It was a moment of contact so unexpected that she paused in the dictation. But before Simone could look up, she recovered. She bent over the book, but she was happier. She went on with the lesson with confidence, almost with gaiety.

Simone Farnet looked up enquiringly once or twice. Miss was showing a side of herself she had not seen before. Some of the girls at school were crazy about her, but Miss did not encourage them; she had always been very discreet. When Simone had suggested that she might have special tuition for her examination, her thrifty mother consented on condition that the utmost should be got out of the lessons. One lesson must be made to do for two people. Jacques, and incidentally the business, must profit at the same time. But Madame Farnet had enquired very searchingly if this Miss was entirely serious and convenable, and Simone had replied without hesitation that she was. Simone therefore felt responsible for Miss's behaviour.

Madame Farnet came in to put an end to the lesson.

'Jacques, go and check the consignment that has just come in. Simone, replace me at the bureau. I have indigestion and I am going to take a little of something.'

'I am sorry you are suffering, Maman,' said Simone.

It gave her satisfaction, Thea thought, to pinch in her lips and say the dutiful thing.

'It is nothing,' said Madame Farnet, implying that in the stern interests of business such a thing as bodily discomfort must be ignored. 'Miss, good afternoon. The servant is waiting to conduct you to the door.'

Out in the street, Thea still hurried, impelled by Madame Farnet's urgent wish to be rid of her and get on with the business. Hurrying over the cobbles, passing under the giant shadow of the cathedral, she went back over the moment when the young man raised his eyes and looked with sympathy into hers.

She was so preoccupied that she almost forgot the cakes for the girls and had to go back down the Grande Rue to the shop.

Madame Blanchot, the pâtissier's wife, was behind the counter and was as inquisitive, Thea found, as ever. She always tried to draw Thea and Thea always tried to resist being drawn.

'So you went to the Farnet house today?' lisped Madame Blanchot, slowly assembling the cakes on a wire tray.

'Yes,' Thea was forced to admit. How did she find out? she wondered. What a place! It was worse than Aldworth. It was a whispering gallery.

'You give English lessons to Jacques Farnet as well as to Simone, perhaps?' said Madame Blanchot, putting the cakes into cardboard boxes.

'Yes,' said Thea.

'Ah, I thought it must be like that,' cried Madame Blanchot with satisfaction. 'Otherwise you would have given lessons to Simone at the pensionnat, wouldn't you?'

'I suppose so,' said Thea, fidgeting on the tessellated floor.

'He is nice, Jacques Farnet, isn't he?' trilled Madame Blanchot. She spoke in an infantile, guileless way.

'Yes.'

'I don't know why, but he isn't at all like his mother or his sister,' prattled Madame Blanchot. 'He is like his father, that young man.'

'Ah?' said Thea. 'How much do I owe you, please?'

'That makes two francs the babas, that makes five francs, that makes twelve francs fifty in all, Mademoiselle. And thank you. It is lucky for us that you like cakes so much, Mademoiselle,' she simpered.

Thea held up the boxes tied together by blue cord.

'You thought these cakes were for me?' she asked in astonishment.

'They aren't for you, then?' asked Madame Blanchot innocently. She knew they were not, but she wanted to know whom they were for.

Thea laughed. 'They are for the English pupils at the pensionnat,' she said.

'Ah, the young English girls. Very rich probably. All the English are rich, aren't they?'

What a silly woman, thought Thea.

'Good evening, Madame,' she said.

'Good evening, Mademoiselle, and thank you again. Thank you,' fluted Madame Blanchot.

'I don't like that young girl,' she called inwards to her husband when the door closed on Thea. 'She doesn't tell you anything.'

CHAPTER SEVENTEEN

At noon the refectory was warm, noisy and full of the savoury smell of haricot beans. At Thea's table there were not enough to go round. She tried to give Anne-Marie less so that Francine, whose eyes were round and anxious on the dish, should not be the only child left unserved. But it was no good. There were not enough to divide.

'Oh, Miss!' wailed Francine.

'Yes, it's a pity,' sympathised Thea. 'But I'll hold the dish high and Marie will soon bring some more.'

In a moment the felt-booted maid came to take the dish to the kitchen.

'Oh, Miss, I'm so hungry,' said Francine, pressing against the table and looking piteously at Thea.

'So am I,' said Thea. 'But they'll be here in a minute.'

Everybody else was eating. At the English table they had finished their beans. They were always served first. Everybody looked at the English table to see what there was going to be.

'Voilà,' said Marie, planting a smoking dish before her.

'Oh, good!' said Thea, spooning beans at a great rate on to Francine's plate and at last serving herself.

But no sooner had she begun to eat than the Directrice came in with the letters. Silence fell and the girls rose irregularly, standing as best they could between the tables and the benches.

'Sit down,' said the Directrice. She always seemed to be irritated to have to tell them to sit. She travelled about the refectory so smoothly she might have had wheels under her skirts.

Thea did not expect letters; she had heard from home the day before. But suddenly a picture postcard appeared face upwards beside her plate with a long, discoloured fingernail laid upon it.

'I paid twenty-five centimes for you on that card,' said the Directrice coldly.

Thea rose hastily. 'I'll get the money, Mademoiselle,' she said.

The Directrice waved her back to her place.

'Remain with the children. You may repay me later. But in France, Miss,' she said, again laying on the card her fingernail, shaped, ridged like, and something of the colour of, a matured acorn, 'we do not consider such things in good taste. That is a strange affair to come through the post to an establishment for the education of young girls. You should tell your friends.'

Thea blushed hotly. Everybody was looking at her. She hid the card, the back view of a fat woman with views of Blackpool folded up into her skirts, and hastened to serve the children, who were now proffering their plates like prayers for a second helping.

'Oliver Reade,' she thought furiously, spooning out the beans. Humiliating her at this distance. Not that in England one would have thought anything of such a card, but in France it was full of hidden meanings. 'I'll write to Martin,' she said to herself. 'The moment lunch is over, I'll write and make him stop that man sending things to me.'

The children ate, their eyes, over their spoons, on Miss who had been reproved by the Directrice. Poor Miss, their eyes said.

The Directrice left the refectory and talk burst out again. Under cover of the noise, Thea glanced frowningly to see what was written on the card. What could Oliver Reade possibly say that was worth twenty-five centimes? She could have bought a piece of soap for that.

In Oliver Reade's well-formed hand – his handwriting always surprised her – was written:

Spending Easter here. Bit of an improvement on the Pot-Fair, isn't it? Sea grand. Hope you are all right.

O Reade.

'As if I want to know how he spends Easter,' fumed Thea. 'And why does he mention the Pot-Fair? You'd think he'd like to forget he was ever on it.'

Beans were eaten. Prunes followed. Lunch was soon over. Too soon. Thea was still hungry. Benches scraped the floor, girls poured out of the refectory into the courtyard. Thea, having put the linen cases into the drawer at the top of the table, went up to the attic.

'Well?' asked Jeanne, from her place at the window. 'What was the trouble?'

'This,' said Thea, showing the card.

'Perhaps a little robust,' commented Jeanne, 'but nothing to make a scene about. It was simply an excuse to humiliate you.'

'I wish he'd stop sending cards. I don't want anything to do with this person,' she said vehemently. 'But he lives practically next door.'

'You are lucky to have any sort of a young man to send you postcards, even vulgar,' said Jeanne. 'If a young man sent me cards the Directrice could say what she liked. I'd send cards back with enthusiasm.'

'You wouldn't,' said Thea.

'Wouldn't I? Let me get the chance,' said Jeanne. 'But I am due below, so au revoir.'

Thea sat down and seized her pen. She was in such a hurry to dispose of Oliver Reade that she spluttered ink over the paper. She drew a ring round the blot, wrote 'sorry' beside it, and continued rapidly:

Please stop that Reade man from sending postcards. I have just got into a row about the last affair from Blackpool. The Directrice spoke to me about it before the whole school. Why should I be disgraced by a person I hardly know? The way he bothers me amounts to persecution. Please stop him. And I had to *pay* to receive the card. Twenty-five centimes. That's adding injury to insult. He shouldn't have written any more than his name on a card like that. Tell him not to send any more cards. Tell him as soon as you get this letter.

She thrust the sheet into an envelope, licked it up, clapped on a stamp and threw on her hat and coat. She would go out and post it at once, she would put it on its way. She wished she could have wired, she was so indignant.

In the vestibule she met the Directrice.

'Where are you going at this hour, Miss?' demanded Mademoiselle Duchêne.

'To the post, Mademoiselle.'

'Why do you not put your letter with the others? Is there some secret about it?'

'No, it is to my brother,' said Thea, showing it.

'You have a class at half-past one,' said the Directrice.

'I shall be back,' said Thea. She opened her purse. 'May I give you the twenty-five centimes, Mademoiselle? This letter,' she said awkwardly, showing it again, 'is to say I don't want any more cards like that.'

'So much the better,' said the Directrice coldly.

She went away and Thea slipped through the door. There was no one about. The sky was blue above the roofs. She almost skipped to be out. To escape from restraint, even for a few moments, filled her with exhilaration.

The cathedral stood in splendour at the end of the street. Beside her as she walked along, water flowed through little stone ducts in the gutters, washing away wisps of straw, matches, scraps of paper, swirling them out of sight. A nice way to clean a town, she thought, leaping over the water.

She turned into the Grande Rue. It was empty, too. At this hour, probably, all were making their digestion. Digestion was a serious matter in France; it was respected.

She passed the Pâtisserie Blanchot and it was empty, too. Empty, even, of Madame Blanchot, which was a relief. Thea took a good look in, unimpeded. The interior was cool and elegant in pale grey with a tall mirror let into the panelling. There was one round table with a marble top and a chair beside it, mutely inviting to a cup of chocolate or an ice. All sorts of nice things you could have, thought Thea, if you had the money.

She went on down the street. Far behind her there was the sound of an approaching bicycle bell. In France, bicycle bells rang all the time, not just when necessary. A bicycle in France was belled like a cow. Horses were belled, too, not once but a dozen times over. There seemed to be no national objection to noise. Thea walked on, lost in vague pleasant dreaming, taking no notice of the bicycle bell, now coming nearer and nearer.

Suddenly the cyclist, passing immediately in front of her, came to rest at the kerb, one foot lowered to the pavement.

'Bonjour, Mademoiselle,' said Jacques Farnet.

Thea's eyes flew wide, her mouth rounded to an 'oh' of astonished pleasure. Both showed a naïve delight at meeting like this in the empty street.

'Did I startle you?' he asked.

'No, but it was a surprise.'

He smiled warmly at her. No mother, no sister to watch now. No need to be guarded. They looked openly at each other for the first time, each exploring the face of the other with eagerness, as if to confirm what had been merely glanced at before.

Easy, entirely himself, Jacques stood with one leg over the saddle of his bicycle.

'How is it that you are out at this time?' he asked.

'I am going to the post.'

'Do you come out when you like?'

'I can come out when I have time.'

'Really?' He turned this over in his mind.

'Do you ever walk by the river?' he asked. 'We have a little property there, hardly more than a kilometre out of the town. It is a little wood. Very pretty. You could go there if you liked. You could take a book and spend the afternoon there.'

Thea blushed at the offer.

'I should like to, thank you, but I don't see how I can. Madame Farnet . . .'

'My mother never goes there,' he said quickly. 'My father loved the place, but since his death nobody goes. There never seems to be time.'

He frowned.

'But you can easily find it,' he urged. 'There is a notice: "Private Property", and in the corner of the board, which is painted blue, there is the name "Farnet". Please go, if it would amuse you. The wood gives pleasure to no one at present, alas!'

'Thank you very much,' said Thea. She didn't think she could possibly go, but didn't like to say so. 'I don't often get time enough to go so far. Except sometimes on Saturday or Sunday perhaps.'

'Saturday would be a good day,' said Jacques. 'There are so many people about on Sunday. But nobody would be out that way on a Saturday. There are wild lilies of the valley in the wood,' he said. 'They should be out now.'

'How lovely! I've never seen lilies of the valley growing wild.' It seemed suddenly possible to go now – to see the lilies of the valley.

'Well, there they will be, in the grass,' said Jacques, smiling at her. 'I've been to see a client in a village out that way this morning. I'm late. Maman will not be pleased,' he said unperturbed, making no move to go.

'So you walk alone,' he went on. 'In France young girls don't do that much.'

'It's different in England,' said Thea.

'Yes, I've heard it's different in England. So much the better for England. This place is all eyes and ears. Probably someone is watching us now.'

'Oh, surely not. Why should they?' said Thea, laughing.

But they both turned and there at the door of the pâtisserie was Madame Blanchot. When she saw they had seen her, she drew back out of sight, as she fancied. But the tips of her shoes and the curve of her ample stomach were still visible in the doorway.

Thea laughed. She thought it was funny. But Jacques Farnet looked annoyed.

'That woman gets her sugar and chocolate and stuff from us. I know her. She has her nose into everything.'

The cathedral clock struck three times, shaking out its notes over the empty street.

'Quarter-past one,' cried Thea. 'I must go. I shan't be able to go to the post after all.'

'If you will give me the letter, I'll post it for you.'

She put it into his hand. 'It's to my brother,' she felt called upon to explain.

'Well,' he said, smiling and touching his beret, 'till half-past four.'

'Half-past four,' she repeated happily. 'Au revoir, Monsieur,' she finished correctly.

'Au revoir, Mademoiselle.'

They drew apart, he jangling down the street on his bicycle, she retracing her steps past the pâtisserie, which now seemed empty again.

Madame Blanchot hurried into the back premises.

'Would you believe me?' she said, narrowing her eyes at her husband, who was picking his teeth over *Le Journal*. 'She was meeting young Farnet by arrangement! Because she transferred a letter into his hand. Ah, there will be something there before long,' she prophesied. 'I can see it at this distance.'

Monsier Blanchot received this with indifference. His wife was always bringing tales in and half of them had no foundation in fact.

'The éclairs are ready,' he said. 'You can put them in the window.'

CHAPTER EIGHTEEN

I

Oliver Reade was a bluebottle you couldn't get rid of. You flapped him away, there was peace for a time; then he began again. Here he was coming back with a letter.

Sorry you had to pay on the card. Enclosed, please find, money-order value one shilling. You can refund yourself and spend the rest on letters to me. What a hope! How are you getting on? You will be home in about five months now, and then things will begin to look up in Byron Place.

We all go on much as usual here, except that I have been doing rather well one way and another. Mostly with things with flaws in them, but most of us have to be content with things with flaws in them. Anyway, by dealing with things with flaws in them, I shall come in time to deal in things without flaws, and then perhaps you'll think better of me!

Your family seems all right. Bit depressed perhaps. I went in to supper last night and Molly had made a first-class pie. I asked her why she didn't go in for cooking or start a pie-shop, instead of trying to teach kids and being miserable. I told her to think it over. I shall think it over myself, and when I think a thing over, I generally do something about it.

I thought of taking a trip to Paris, but have given up the idea because I am putting all the money I can get back into my business at present. Still, the day will come. That's what I say to myself about a lot of things. Should have liked to have seen you, though. It seems a long time. Hoping to hear from you,

O Reade.

PS Have you read *Antony and Cleopatra?*

Thea almost laughed with helpless irritation. What a man! What a nuisance! And passing his opinion on her family! 'Bit depressed', indeed! Unfortunately it was true. But nothing to do with him. Why did they have him to supper? He had got into the house, and when she went home she would have the greatest difficulty in getting him out again.

She tore the letter up. She would ignore it. It was a mistake not to ignore the card. Why had he reminded her that in five months she must go home? She didn't want to think of it. She didn't want to look backwards or forwards, she wanted to live in the present; and the present consisted solely of Tuesdays and Fridays, the days she went to the house in the Rue Victor Hugo.

Today it was Tuesday and so fine and warm that, leaning out of the window at recreation, she decided suddenly that it was time to bring out her thin dress, the one for summer. She ran to the cabinet de toilette to take it from its wrapper. She held it up, admiring it. She held it against her and looked into the glass. It's nice, she thought rapturously.

The sunlight poured in through the bull's-eye window behind her, illuminating the whitewashed walls, striking spears of light from the water in the jugs. The voices of the girls rose from the courtyard below, where Jeanne was taking recreation. Thea stood, her dress clasped under her chin, conscious of light and warmth and happiness. She wanted it to go on. She wanted it to be always like this.

'I hope I can come back next year,' she said fervently.

The bell clanged. Recreation was over. Thea went down and found the Lockwoods and the Kenworthys waiting in the passage. She knew why. They only waited when they wanted cakes.

'I'm not going to Blanchot's any more,' she said.

Their faces registered consternation. Weren't they going to get their cakes?

'Oh, why?' they asked in alarm.

'I don't like the woman there,' said Thea. 'I shall have to go to Moret's in the Avenue de la Gare, I suppose,' she said crossly.

'Moret's will do just as well,' they assured her.

'All right,' said Thea, taking the money and the list. What they ate, these people, she thought, glancing at it.

The afternoon was marked off by the strokes of the cathedral clock. The windows of the classroom were wide open to the warm air. The cours supérieur went out, the cours moyen came in, the cours élémentaire came last. Four o'clock. The bell clanged and the girls rushed out to rifle the bread-baskets.

Taking two hunks of bread as she passed, Thea flew up to the attic, tearing at the bread as vigorously as any French girl. She hadn't time to eat more than one piece, so she put the other into a drawer for later. Then she shut herself into the cabinet de toilette to put on her new dress. She heard Jeanne come into the other room as she changed.

'Ah,' said Jeanne when she emerged. 'You have been making yourself beautiful.'

'Do you like it?' asked Thea diffidently.

'You look very pretty,' said Jeanne, smoothing Thea's white collar with long, sallow fingers. 'Va, ma fille,' she said, like an old priest dismissing a child with a benediction.

II

At the house in the Rue Victor Hugo, the procedure was usually the same. The middle-aged servant, as unsmiling as her mistress, ushered Thea into the bureau where she stood, awaiting Madame Farnet's pleasure. Once, while Madame Farnet was engaged, Thea was left in the hall and stood there alone, feeling what a grim house it was, and how little given over to happiness or leisure. It was a strange place for Jacques Farnet, so full of life and vigour, to have grown up in. Through a half-open door she saw the formal salon with stiff, tasteless furniture on which were arranged cushions no bigger than handkerchief sachets. In the whole house there seemed to be nowhere to sit down and read a book in comfort.

Madame Farnet emerged in due time from the glass tube and conducted Thea to the dining room, ringing the bell for her son on the way. Simone was always there already, and Jacques appeared with suspicious alacrity. He always greeted Thea very correctly. The atmosphere was at once electric for these two, but mother and sister were insulated. They were for ever on the watch, but they were insulated.

Today, somewhere in the back premises, they were roasting coffee and the air was pungent with the smell of it. As soon as Madame Farnet had made her first exit, Jacques leaned towards Thea.

'The coffee smells very strong,' he said anxiously. 'Does it annoy you?'

'Not at all,' said Thea, raising her eyes.

Simone looked in cold astonishment at her brother. What did it matter if the smell of coffee annoyed Miss? It was not as if she were a visitor.

'We will take translation first,' said Thea.

Jacques began. When he stumbled among the English words, Thea felt a mixture of amusement and tenderness she was careful to hide. The next moment she was full of admiration for his vivid use of his own language. It was the same for him. English, when she spoke it, sounded like the tongues of angels. When she helped him with the French, she sounded like a little girl.

When the translation passed to Simone, it was their chance to look at each other. Thea resisted as long as she could. She kept her eyes lowered. As a teacher she could not lend herself to these games with a pupil, her face said. But she had to give way in the end. She looked up and he was always waiting. Their eyes rested gravely on each other, or they smiled with sudden mischief, which was dangerous because they had to compose their faces quickly before Simone looked up or Madame Farnet came in. The situation was shocking, Thea told herself. Shocking, dangerous and exciting, and with every lesson it became more of all three.

'Now we'll have dictation,' said Thea.

Madame Farnet came noiselessly into the room in her felt slippers, eyed them for a moment and went out again.

'"The day of departure came,"' read Thea.

His head was bent over his exercise book. His hair was so crisp and dark, she had an almost irresistible desire to touch it . . .

'"Throwing the household into commotion,"' she read.

The pencil leapt from Jacques's hand, described a remarkable parabola and fell to the floor.

'Ah, my pencil,' he said, diving under the table.

'It's not under the table, it's there,' said Thea, pointing.

She was startled to feel a small object laid on her knee. In a flash, Jacques had emerged, pencil in hand, and was in his place again. Thea retained enough presence of mind to grasp the object. Her fingers explored it. It was something rocky, wrapped in silver paper. It must be a bouchée pralinée. She almost laughed aloud. She leaned forward against the table and continued in a gay voice:

'"After dinner, Maggie was the recipient of three amazing muslin aprons."'

He looked up smiling and she smiled into his eyes. They were like two children at this moment, happy, friendly. Simone looked up and this time they were startled. They had forgotten her. In her confusion, Thea lost her place in the dictation.

Madame Farnet came in to put an end to the lesson, and as usual they were all dispersed in different directions.

Out in the street, Thea took the bouchée from her handkerchief.

'I shan't eat it,' she thought. 'I'll keep it as long as possible.'

She noticed then that the silver foil had been undone and a minute piece of white paper inserted. She unfolded it. On it was written very small: 'Have you been to the wood yet?'

Hastily she hid the message in her glove, put the bouchée in her bag and went down the street with a fast-beating heart.

Did he mean to go to the wood, too? Did he mean to meet her there?

'I daren't go,' she thought. To be alone with him in the wood, it would be too much, too exciting. At the mere thought of it, she was breathless. No, she could never go.

She halted. She had wandered into the wrong street without looking where she was going. There was something she had to do. She stood still, her lips parted, her breath coming fast as if she had been running, trying to think what she had to do. The little piece of paper pricked the palm of her hand under her glove. Ah – it was the cakes for the girls. She must go to the Avenue de la Gare.

When she came back up the Grande Rue, she was carrying the pink cardboard boxes tied with yellow cord, the Moret trademark. Madame Blanchot, looking out for her, ready to serve her with the usual large purchase of cakes and avid to find out more of the affair with young Farnet, saw her pass by.

'Mon Dieu!' she called out to her husband. 'Miss has been to Moret. She daren't come here any more. She saw that I had observed her with young Farnet, so she dare not confront me. Perhaps you will believe me now, eh?'

'Indeed?' said Blanchot, appearing, floured, from the back premises. 'That is too much. There must be something in it after all.'

That two young people should meet in the street was a matter of indifference to him, but when custom was taken elsewhere, that came home to a man.

'I told you there was something wrong, didn't I?' said Madame Blanchot, flashing her black eyes in triumph. She was highly gratified to have piqued her husband at last. It didn't often happen. 'I told you, didn't I?' she repeated.

'You did, and for once you seem to be right,' admitted Blanchot, going back to his oven.

III

Thea, hurrying up to the attic, hoped for the first time that Jeanne would not be there. Until now, she had always looked forward to getting back to Jeanne, but now she wanted to be alone, to pore over the scrap of paper that burned the palm of her hand. She opened the attic door with anxiety. The room was empty.

She shut the door behind her, threw hat, gloves and books on the bed and took deeper refuge in the cabinet de toilette. She locked the door and with trembling fingers, unfolded the small creased piece of paper.

'Have you been to the wood yet?'

It was the most thrilling question she had ever been asked.

'But I daren't go, I daren't go,' she whispered.

She looked and looked at it without its growing any more familiar or less thrilling. Every time she said it over, it seemed more wonderful. That he should have written to her, that he should have found a way to give it to her. . . that he should want to see her alone in the wood. . . 'But I daren't, I daren't . . .' she whispered.

The cathedral clock struck. In a few moments, she must go down and take supervision. She was always being hurried on, there was no time to stand, to dwell on happiness. She must hide away her treasure and come back to it later. But where could she hide it? It must be somewhere very secret and safe.

Her eyes fell on the little travelling bag, thrust, since her arrival, beneath the shelf she kept her shoes on. She stooped, pulled it out and emptied it of a few oddments. The lining her mother had glued down was loose again, her hurried fingers caught and tore it further. When she attempted to put the lining back again, she saw that a piece of paper had worked itself quite a long way underneath. She poked it out. What was it? It was worn in the fold and discoloured on the back, but quite clean inside. She read it:

Received from Richard Hunter the sum of Three Hundred Pounds (£300) in repayment of loan to him secured by promissory note.

Wm. Lockwood.

Puzzled, Thea pored over it. What did it mean? 'Received from Richard Hunter . . .' she read. 'Repayment of loan . . .'

It meant, she told herself, crouching on the floor, her back against the wall, that her father had once borrowed three hundred pounds from Mr Lockwood. True, he had repaid it, but he had borrowed it, and Thea was deeply humiliated. The one thing with which she had bolstered up her pride when it smarted under the patronage of the Lockwoods was that when her father was alive, they hadn't needed help from anybody, that they had been a self-contained, self-supporting family like any other, and that it was only because her father had died that they were laid open to the grudged help and petty slights of the Lockwoods. But this little paper was a complete refutation of that notion. Her father himself had borrowed money from Mr Lockwood. The obligations of the Hunters to the Lockwoods had run like twitch through their family life from the beginning.

She screwed up the evidence of this fact and threw it into the waste-paper basket. She remained where she was, crouched against the wall. Then she reached over and picked the paper from the basket. She would take it home and ask her mother about it some time. She smoothed it out, refolded it and put it into the ticket-holder provided by Thos. Cook, which she had kept, though empty. She snapped the elastic band round it and put it into the pocket of the bag.

Then she remembered Jacques's note and looked about for it in alarm. It had drifted, no more than a shaving of paper, under her washstand. With a shocked murmur, as if she had subjected it to very unworthy treatment, she retrieved it. But the finding of one note had tempered her excitement in the other. At this distance of time, the fact that her father had borrowed money from Mr Lockwood had the power to depress her spirits. She read Jacques's note again and thought: 'I shan't go!'

She folded it and thrust it under the lining where the receipt had been. If the receipt could lie undiscovered for more than sixteen years, the note should be safe for an hour to two.

She got up from the floor. Chilled, checked, she went downstairs. As she was beginning on the last flight, she saw the Lockwoods going along the passage below, and drew back until they had gone. The Lockwoods. There was no getting away from them. She supposed the twins knew about the borrowed money. They'd probably told everybody, too.

It wasn't until the middle of the night that excitement came back. The moon waked her. It had moved round until it shone full upon her bed. She sat up. Across the room, in the shadow, Jeanne was asleep. The cathedral clock struck the quarter after some night hour. The moonlight was wonderful, she was bathed in moonlight.

'Have you been to the wood?' he asked her.

'I shall go,' she determined suddenly, and lay down again, her face turned to the moon, smiling.

CHAPTER NINETEEN

▄▀▄

The boarders were getting ready for the walk. Every Saturday afternoon, if fine, the boarders passed, a giant black caterpillar rippling from head to tail, along the Route Vernet. At the white post on the side of the road, motion was reversed and the caterpillar rippled back the way it had come. The walk was the most monotonous that could have been chosen and it was chosen for that very reason. No encounter dangerous or exciting to young girls could possibly be made on the Route Vernet, because there would be no encounter of any kind at all.

The boarders, including the English girls, hated this weekly sortie, and protest, though useless, was finding expression now in the thudding of shoes to the floor and the banging of drawers and cupboards.

Thea, in the attic, waited for them to go. She sat at the table, pretending to read, but she had a strange bright look and every time Jeanne spoke, she started. She laughed unnecessarily and in the wrong places. It was one of Jeanne's duties to accompany the girls on the weekly walk, and Thea waited for her, too, to go.

Jeanne moved about, getting ready. Putting on her old black hat before the glass she said: 'I am condemned to walk along the Route Vernet every Saturday for the rest of my life, or at least until I am too old to walk any more.'

'Poor Jeanne,' said Thea, but almost mechanically.

'I feel worse about things since you came,' said Jeanne.

'Do you?' said Thea. 'Why?'

'Well, you go after what you want, you know, and it makes me think I might do the same. But I must go down,' she said. 'Au revoir.'

At the door, she paused.

'What's the matter?' she asked.

Thea almost gulped. 'Nothing,' she said.

Jeanne gave her an amused, ironic glance and disappeared.

After a moment, Thea tiptoed to the door to listen. The thudding below was diminishing. Girls clattered down the stone stairs, at first in a torrent then at longer intervals. When none had clattered for some time, Thea stole to the top of the stairs and looked over. She saw the last boarder emerge from the dormitory, muttering to herself. All the ennui of Saturday afternoon at school was in her face. She clattered down the stairs in her turn and a door banged behind her.

Thea flew soundlessly to her window to watch them off the premises. Below, like sheep through a gap, they were pressing through the door into the street. Thea fancied herself hidden, but Jeanne seemed to know she was there for, without looking round, she lifted an arm in resigned farewell before stepping through after the others and closing the door behind her.

Silence fell. The way was clear. Now she must either go or not go. To go was almost unbearably exciting, nerve-racking; but not to go was unthinkable.

She put her hat on before the pocked glass. No wonder Jeanne had asked her what was the matter. She looked too alive, somehow. She pressed her hands over her face to banish that too vivid look. To get out, how you had to listen, wait, watch! Her pride revolted against these precautions. She would have liked to go boldly, flaunting the consequences, but she daren't. Her courage didn't match her pride.

She stood in the doorway. The whitewashed passages were full of light from the dormer windows. Mademoiselle Petit was coughing in her room. That was all. The great house seemed otherwise empty.

But as she began to go down the staircase, the sound of a piano rose from below and she drew back with an exclamation of annoyance. It was unmistakably one of the Lockwoods playing 'Rustle of Spring'. All the Lockwoods were learning 'Rustle of Spring'. Poised, Thea listened. The piano, she could tell, was the one in the couloir. She must pass the player on the way out.

'Well, it can't be helped,' she thought with exasperation. A Lockwood in the way again. Always a Lockwood.

As she entered the couloir, Clare Lockwood's hands fell listlessly from the keys.

'Hello, Thea,' she said.

'Hello,' murmured Thea, passing swiftly.

'I made an excuse not to go for the walk,' said Clare. 'But now I wish I'd gone. Saturday afternoons were so nice at

Oakfield, Thea. Daddy was at home then and we used to take Boz for that walk behind Firbank – you know . . .'

'Sorry,' said Thea, opening the far door, 'I can't wait.'

Clare's face, which had brightened as she spoke of home, fell again.

'Sorry,' she murmured in her turn.

Thea stepped through the door. At the end of the street the cathedral hung like a backcloth. For centuries, little figures had hurried to and fro before it. Now Thea Hunter was hurrying across it in her turn, engaged on her small rôle.

She turned into the Grand Rue. In the pâtisserie, Madame Blanchot looked aside from a customer. Thea bowed. In France you must always bow; not to bow amounts to insult. Thea disliked bowing to people she didn't like, but bowed, though stiffly. Madame Blanchot inclined her head in response, but with reserve.

'She's annoyed because I don't go there any more,' thought Thea.

But Madame Blanchot was too inquisitive. It was too much if every time you went in for cakes you had to submit to a battery of questions. Besides, Jacques didn't like her. Besides again, she shouldn't have been looking out at them the day they met in the Grande Rue. Or rather, since she was looking out, she shouldn't have drawn back. It was the drawing back that condemned Madame Blanchot.

Thea turned into the sanded boulevard by the river and walked under the trees, now thickening into shade. On the one hand were houses beyond the trees; on the other, without parapet, ran the river, opaque, green, swift and silent.

The town curved away inside its trees and Thea struck out across the open country, still following the river. There was a bare exposed piece to cross before the woods began, but there were only a few men working on a lock. No one else on the road along which Thea hurried.

The men raised their heads to stare at the unusual sight of a young girl walking alone in this deserted place. They began to make ribald remarks. But when she reached them, they were abashed in spite of themselves. She was English and used to looking men in the eye. She looked at them and passed on, and they made more ribald remarks.

'She must be the English girl,' said one youth. 'My Aunt Blanchot speaks of one in the town.'

'Pity for her to be alone,' said another. 'Shall I propose myself?'

But Thea was out of sight round the bend of the road. Woods now lay on either hand and she looked about for the notice board Jacques had spoken of. She wanted to find it quickly. She wanted to be hidden. She saw a board leaning crookedly out of the wood. There was his name in the corner: 'Farnet'. Her heart gave a leap. With a swift look about her, she ducked under the wire fence and ran in under the trees.

But inside the wood, her apprehension did not lessen. Where was she to find him? He hadn't said. Where were they to meet? She stood still, trying to breathe more steadily. At any moment now, he might appear. She must be ready. She took off her hat. The birds sang, the trees held their leaves quite still. But where was he? They might be all afternoon in this wood and never meet.

She advanced timidly from tree to tree, hat in hand. One path seemed more marked than others; she followed it and suddenly, at the end of the silent ride, she came upon a wooden hut, the kind the French call a chalet, raised on a platform. Startled, she drew back quickly behind a tree.

Its boards blackened and shrunken from exposure, it looked sinister. The door and window frames had once been painted light blue, but the paint was bleached and livid now. The windows were covered with filet curtains. Curtains in the middle of a wood, she thought. That was Madame Farnet's touch. The curtained windows gave the hut a secretive, furtive air.

From behind the tree, she watched to see if the curtains moved, if the livid door would open. But nothing stirred, and by and by she crept up to the hut. She went up the three steps and put her face to a window. Dimly she could see an old divan covered with a dark rug, a round table lurching sideways, two chairs, a fishing-rod in one corner, some paper-backed books swollen to twice their size with damp.

'I don't like it,' she said to herself.

A low whistle startled her. She turned and saw Jacques Farnet bumping down the ride on his bicycle, from which he had removed the betraying bell. Bent low over his handlebars, he smiled at her as he came, his teeth white in his brown face.

She went down the three steps towards him. Her emotions this afternoon were bewildering, they changed so quickly. Her face changed with them, light and shade ran over her face, her colour came and went. She had been nervous getting out of the pensionnat, startled by the chalet, startled again by his whistle and was now shy. Shyness in the young may be charming to look at but is painful to the one who suffers it. She turned her hat in her hand and looked away from him. How stupid to have come, she thought, to have got here in spite of everything and then to have nothing to say.

'I hope you haven't been here long,' he said, getting off his bicycle. 'I couldn't escape.'

'No, not long,' murmured Thea.

He propped his bicycle against a tree. She stood where she was, foot-fast, tongue-tied, the sun striking light from her hair. He came back to her.

'You are so nice to come,' he said, taking her hand.

Thea smiled, but in a moment took her hand away. She pretended she needed it to put her hair back.

'Let's open the chalet,' he said. 'See, the key's here.'

He reached under the wooden platform and brought out a rusty key. 'It's always there,' he said.

He went up the steps and put the key in the lock. It was hard to turn. The swollen door resisted, but he pushed it open.

'No one has been here for so long,' he said, standing aside for Thea to go in.

But she didn't. She stood on the threshold, looking in with mistrust.

There was a mute invitation offered by Jacques as he stood aside for her to enter – an invitation that Thea didn't even know of. Innocent, ignorant, young, she merely said: 'I don't like it,' and didn't go in.

Jacques was neither innocent nor ignorant. He was as experienced as any young Frenchman of his age. But he was deeply in love with Thea and love made him diffident, unconfident. When she shook her head at the intimate, if mouldering, interior of the chalet, he handed over the reins to her. She should drive and he would go her way, and as slowly or as fast as she wished.

'Let's sit on the steps in the sun,' said Thea.

They sat down, their feet on the steps, their knees almost under their chins, their sleeves touching.

To the left, through the trees, the river slid, full and silent. Even looking straight ahead at the sunlit wood, you could see the river running furiously beyond the trees, Thea noticed. There were strange elements in this place and meeting; the chalet sinister behind, the swift swollen river, and underlying their pleasure in each other, an almost unbearable tension. And fear lurked behind them, fear of discovery, fear of other people, the old, the people with the power.

'Oh,' cried Thea suddenly, glad to remember something so uncomplicated. 'Where are the lilies of the valley?'

'Ah, yes,' he said. 'They grow over there.'

'Let's go and find them,' said Thea.

They walked under the trees together. Here the wood was wholly candid. The trees were young, their leaves delicate and pale green, the grass was lush, every blade broad, even sharp like a sword. The place seemed illuminated, not only from above, but from below; light dappled everything.

'This is a lovely wood,' said Thea.

'My father was very fond of it. Every Sunday we used to have picnics here. We don't see much of it now. My mother talks of selling it. We were gayer when my father was alive, you know. I'm afraid you find ours a gloomy house to come to.'

'Oh, no,' said Thea. 'You're there.'

He smiled, touched by the simplicity of her statement. Her lack of coquetry enchanted him.

'Oh, the lilies,' she said, dropping to her knees in the grass.

He knelt beside her.

'Don't let's pick them. They're so lovely growing,' she said.

'You must have one little bouquet,' he said, beginning to gather them.

'Only a few then,' said Thea, picking carefully. She held up one flower with its minute rounded bells. 'And smell,' she said, holding it out.

He smelled obediently.

'When you speak French,' he said, sitting back on his heels, 'you have the most adorable accent.'

'Oh,' said Thea, with a rueful face, 'have I an accent? I don't want an accent. I must get rid of it.'

He laughed. 'No, don't lose your pretty accent.'

'Yes, I must,' she insisted. 'I must speak French with perfection.'

'Perfection is so dull,' he said. 'Classic, cold. Imperfection is much more lovable.'

He put the lilies he had gathered into her hand, his brown fingers closing over her doubled fist. They knelt in the grass.

'Your eyes are perfect, anyway,' he said in a low voice.

'No,' disclaimed Thea, her head bent.

'They are,' he said. 'The eyes of young girls are so often empty. But yours . . .'

She daren't lift the eyes he praised. He took her other hand from the grass and pressed his lips against it. Still holding it, he said anxiously: 'I don't annoy you?'

He was afraid of going too far, of overstepping the mark, the mark he didn't know about, the mark drawn by an English girl. So he asked if he annoyed her by kissing her hand, and Thea, smiling, shook her head, but withdrew the hand and got up from the grass.

They went slowly back under the trees and came to a halt before the chalet. Jacques looked at the watch on his wrist.

'Do you know, it is time for me to go?' he said gloomily. 'We work on Saturday afternoons since my father died and I must get back before my mother misses me. You don't think I have brought you too far for so short a time, do you?' he asked, anxious again. 'I wanted so much to see you alone. I wish I could stay. But I am afraid of involving you. My mother is very severe. I fear her severity, not for myself, but for you. So to avoid suspicion I ought to go back.'

'But I must go, too,' said Thea, thinking that the boarders must have turned at the white post and be now on their homeward way.

'Will you come again?' asked Jacques. 'Dare you? I know it's a great risk for you. I know I ought not to ask you to come.'

'I'll come,' she said.

'Next week?'

She nodded.

'Oh, you make me so happy,' he said. 'All I ask is to be with you, even for so short a time. But perhaps we shall have longer next week. I may be able to get away earlier or stay later. I'll lock the chalet now; then I'll come with you to the edge of the wood. You'll go first, won't you? I don't want to leave you in the wood alone. When I'm on my way and you know I'll soon be here, it's not so bad to be alone. But I wouldn't like to leave you behind. So you'll go first, won't you?'

He sprang up the steps to lock the door and leaped down again. At the prospect of another meeting, he was gay.

'You'll remember where the key is,' he said, putting it back under the platform.

Together, he pushing his bicycle, they went up the grassy ride, under the delicate, light-pierced canopy of leaves. Now and again a bird, chirping sharply, fled at their approach.

'There's the road,' said Thea, halting. 'I'll go quickly. Give me fifteen minutes and I'll have disappeared.'

She gave him her hand and he kissed it again. He stood for a moment, looking down at her hand in his, then let it go.

'Goodbye,' he said. 'Since it must be.'

Thea started down the path, but before she disappeared from sight, she turned. Standing with his bicycle under the trees, he threw out a hand as if to beg her to come back. But Thea, though she stretched out her own hand towards him, turned and ran on.

The men working on the lock watched her come with interest. Had not young Farnet from the Épicerie en Gros gone that way too? Was it a rendez-vous?

Thea passed them. She reached the boulevard and turned into the Grande Rue. Madame Blanchot noticed the lilies of the valley in her hand.

The boarders had not yet returned. Clare was looking listlessly out of the window in the couloir. Thea hurried in as she had hurried out and Clare this time made no attempt to detain her.

CHAPTER TWENTY

I

When letters came from home these days, Thea found it an effort to bring her attention to bear upon them. To read them and take them in was like having to come a long way through a house to answer a ring at the bell. She took three letters from the Directrice's hand and noted that one was from her mother, one from Molly and the third from Oliver Reade. Even that last fact she registered without annoyance, merely with an absence of any feeling whatever.

Climbing the stairs, she opened Molly's letter first and went to the window to read it. As her eyes ran over it, she was wishing she could go to the wood on this lovely afternoon and find Jacques under the trees. Last Saturday had been much better. They had been completely happy last Saturday...

She was giving only divided attention to the letter. She thought that was why it seemed so muddled. But clearing her brain and beginning again, she found that it was muddled in reality. Molly had been too excited to be coherent.

Oliver Reade, wrote Molly, was setting her up in Miss Riley's shop.

Miss Riley's shop? Thea looked down into the courtyard where the girls seethed like bees. Reluctantly, her memory pierced together a picture of Wells Road with its brick houses, little front gardens and corner shops. It conjured up Miss Riley's red face popping out between the glass domes. Having placed Miss Riley, she returned to the letter.

During the winter, on Oliver Read's advice, Molly wrote, she had taken a confectionery course at the Technical School. 'I didn't want to tell you what I was doing, in case I didn't pass,' she wrote. 'But now I've got a Diploma. It's framed and hangs in the shop. And outside there's a swinging sign with "The Bun Shop" painted on it. Oh, think of me in a shop!' scribbled Molly. 'Can you believe it? Oh, the relief of not having to deal with children any more. I would so much rather deal with buns. With me, buns always turn out all right, children never!'

What can all this be about, thought Thea, opening her mother's letter. But it was hardly any more explicit.

Mrs Hunter wrote that she didn't know what Thea would think of Molly being in a shop. She hardly knew herself. But Mrs Lockwood had been quite nice about it. She said since it was obvious that Molly would never make a governess she might as well be in a shop. She also very kindly said she would probably give Molly an order now and again.

Thea opened Oliver's letter and at last had a clear account of what had happened.

Perhaps you'd like to hear about this confectionery business from the inside. It came into my hands in a funny sort of way. I've been dabbling in the patent-medicine line lately – the public will always buy medicine, you know – and it caused me to spend a lot of time in the dispensary of a chemist pal of mine. Daw his name is. When I was in the other night after shop hours, who should come in but Miss Riley! Daw went out to attend to her. She couldn't see me, you know, but I could hear everything, and I found out that she came in every night to get him to bandage her hands up till morning. She's got baker's eczema. Nice thing, isn't it? Baking people's bread and cakes with eczema? Not that it isn't often done, but when it's your bread and you know about it, it makes you feel a bit squeamish, doesn't it? Well, I daren't let on I'd got to know, through being behind the shop, since it might have cost Daw a customer, so I went round next day on the pretext of calling for our bread. And when she was wrapping it up, I leaned through all those glass domes and said: 'What's up with your hands, Miss Riley? Looks very like eczema to me.' The poor woman burst out crying and we had to go into the kitchen behind until she could get over it and 'explain' as she put it. She'd been worried to death in case anybody should find out. She was hanging on to the business until she'd put by enough to retire on. Well, to make a long story short, I told her I'd try to find a way out. And, by Jove, the idea came to me that I'd put Molly into the shop and pay Miss Riley something on account, with a percentage on the profits until we could buy her out altogether. And it all came off. Miss Riley's out and Molly's in. And Edie's going to help her until she gets married to Joe, which will be before long. I'm pleased about this deal because (*a*) I've fixed your sister up, (*b*) saved Miss R. a lot of worry and (*c*) done the public a good turn.

This man is unique, thought Thea, sitting on the window-sill. He came crashing into her dreaming thoughts of Jacques with talk of Miss Riley's eczema. Who else would do such things? Who else would dump such an unsavoury subject before someone he apparently wanted to attract.?

And to think of Molly in a shop! Oliver Reade must have faith in her capacity to manage. Thea herself was doubtful. Molly could certainly cook, but she was always being ill, always having colds and headaches. How could she run a shop? There was the sister, of course, but imagine letting herself in for being all day and every day with Oliver Reade's sister! 'Well, it's Molly's concern, not mine,' she thought, and was shocked by her own detachment.

She was ashamed of her own variability; she who, six months ago had been so sick for home she could neither eat nor sleep, could hardly think about it at all now. She could think only of Jacques and herself. She looked upon everything else as an interruption of the dreaming happiness that possessed her, or would have possessed her, if only people would leave her alone. Her consuming desire all day was to be alone. She was ashamed of herself, but she was secretly glad when Jeanne had to take music lessons for Mademoiselle Drouet or supervision for Mademoiselle Petit, or do one or another of the tasks heaped upon her by the Directrice.

Jeanne, with tacit acknowledgment of the fact that Thea no longer wanted to talk, withdrew into herself. She asked for no explanation, she did not twit or tease, but she guessed. She really knew. Jeanne delicately, cynically, withdrew, and kept the surface of things as smooth, shallow and ordinary as possible.

Love is not only blind about the beloved; it is blind about other people, too. Thea went dreamily on with no idea that she was startling the Lockwoods and many of the boarders by her looks alone. In the pensionnat, many girls were putting on the bloom of young womanhood, but Thea outshone them. Her hair glowed and curled with vitality, her eyes were full of light. The French began to use her for comparison. 'Almost as pretty as Miss,' they would say of someone. Or, 'She wasn't as pretty as Miss, of course.' The eyes of the Lockwoods followed her uneasily. It looked as if their snubbing days were entirely over; you couldn't snub a girl who was turning into a beauty under your eyes.

Thea was indifferent to the Lockwoods, as she was to the Directrice and had no idea that her present attitude annoyed that lady even more than her former independence and hostility.

During the day, Thea had to make an effort to do her work, but the nights were all hers. In her bed facing the open window, she lay looking into the soft blank of the night. Sometimes the sky was pierced by stars, sometimes lit by the moon which travelled slowly round until it shone full upon her. In the silence the town clocks struck the hours away, the old fir tree creaked. Jeanne stirred and sighed in her sleep. Thea lay, reluctant to sleep. Sleep seemed too much waste of happiness.

What the end of this love was to be, or even how it was to continue, she did not know or conjecture. It was enough in itself.

During lessons at the house in the Rue Victor Hugo, Thea and Jacques remembered to be on their guard only at times. Thea was always on her guard when Madame Farnet was there; she was much too conscious of that grim presence to be otherwise. But she often forgot Simone, and it was a mistake to forget Simone.

In the Farnet family, Simone might have been entirely thrust aside by her mother's twin ruling passions – Jacques and the business – if she had not kept in with, and made herself important to her mother by sharing both. Almost the only way Simone could make sure of getting notice for herself from her mother was to report on Jacques and she lost no opportunity of doing it.

Jacques was far from discreet in his behaviour. Sometimes when his mother came to lean her hard fist on the table and watch beside him, he indulged in almost farcical acting. It wasn't done so much to deceive his mother as to amuse Thea, to remind her that they shared a secret in spite of those watching eyes. Thea wished this kind of thing could be avoided, but Jacques enjoyed it. A situation in which he could indulge his wit and mockery, even though his mother was the dupe, amused him. He admired and respected his mother, but he thought it permissible to deceive her in the matter of a love-affair. She would not have let him have any love-affairs if she could help it, and that was, of course, ludicrous. So he played, and when his mother had gone out of the room, he gave Thea a smiling glance from his dark eyes.

When he was at these games, Thea felt all the nervous apprehension of a mother whose child might at any moment go too far. Jacques was showing off, she knew, but since she was charmed by whatever he did, she was helpless. Sometimes she longed to laugh with him, laugh at solemn Madame Farnet and prim Simone, laugh because they took things with such deadly seriousness and life was really so wonderful, if they only knew it.

Love has a dangerous way of simplifying, for the lovers, things that cannot be simplified. Lovers can rarely see why they cannot be allowed to love, to be together. Why not, they naïvely wonder, since nothing else matters?

CHAPTER TWENTY-ONE

Saturday afternoon, and fine again. Five fine Saturdays in succession. Five walks for the boarders, poor things, thought Thea, without much compunction, because if they hadn't gone, she wouldn't have been able to go either. She stood now, waiting to go, listening, as usual, before flying down the stairs. Mademoiselle Petit was coughing as usual in her room, but, there was no sound this time of 'Rustle of Spring' on the couloir piano. Clare Lockwood had gone for the walk, finding it even more boring to remain behind.

Noiselessly, Thea ran down the stairs. Once she paused thinking she heard a door close somewhere. But there was no further sound and she ran on. Everything was easy this afternoon, she thought, escaping into the warm air of the street.

She hurried past the cathedral and turned into the Grande Rue, preoccupied, happy, pressing forward.

'She has passed,' said Madame Blanchot, and thin-lipped, went to the telephone.

Thea went on, the shop windows reflecting her in her thin dress with the white collar and her new wide-brimmed straw hat. She owed this hat to Molly. Molly had sent some of the first money she had made in her shop to Thea. Thus, cakes sold in Aldworth materialised into a straw hat from the Nouvelles Galeries to charm Jacques Farnet in Villeneuve.

Thea passed down the cool canyon of the street, under the green shade of the trees by the river, out into the sunlight of the exposed ground beyond the town. Were the men still working on the lock? As she was about to turn the bend in the road, she remembered that she hadn't noticed and looked round to see. They were there, and as she turned, they whistled after her.

She sped up the road between the trees and looking swiftly around as usual, plunged into the wood.

When she came into sight of the chalet, she stopped dead. Her heart seemed to stop, too. The door was open. But as she stood, rooted, Jacques himself came out and, seeing her, sprang over the rail to meet her. He took both her hands.

'Oh,' she breathed. 'You gave me a fright.'

'I'm always giving you frights. If I'm not here, I give you a fright. If I am here, I give you a fright. What shall we do about it?'

They laughed, walking towards the hut, their fingers locked.

'Did you get away all right?' he asked.

'Yes, I don't think anyone saw me leave.'

'I got away well, too,' he said. 'Maman was nowhere about, so I slipped out early. We're going to have a real picnic today. I've brought a bottle of muscatel and some madeleines.'

Thea laughed at the French idea of a picnic. In Aldworth it would have been tea and jam sandwiches; in Villeneuve it was wine and sponge cakes.

They went up the steps of the chalet. The bottle of wine stood on the table with two glasses and the madeleines.

'Not from Madame Blanchot, the old camel,' said Jacques, proffering them. 'You must have a glass of wine,' he said.

'Not yet,' protested Thea.

But he poured it out.

They sat side by side on the sagging divan and drank to each other. The wine was thick and sweet, and over the rim of her glass as she took small sips, Thea eyed the interior of the chalet with distaste. Everything since the time of the late Monsieur Farnet had been silently mouldering away. It smelled as if the river had been in, it smelled of minnows. Under her fingers, the cover of the divan was hairy and harsh with dust and age.

'You don't like wine, do you?' said Jacques.

'Not much,' she admitted, smiling.

'Give it here,' he said with mock resignation. He took the glass from her and put it with his own empty one on the table. 'What's the good of providing material entertainment for a nymph of light and air?' he said, coming to throw himself full length on the divan beside her. She sat above him, turning towards him, her hands in her lap.

'How beautiful you are,' he said.

She shook her head. When he said she was beautiful, it didn't make her feel beautiful. On the contrary, it made her feel plain, not half beautiful enough for him. But she was glad, all the same, that he thought she was beautiful.

'Isn't it strange that you should come from so far away to be here with me in this wood?' he said.

Her gaze was lost, smiling into his.

'This wood where I came so often when I was a child on Sundays. I wore a sailor suit and a sailor hat with a red pom-pom. What would you be wearing then?'

'Probably a brown velveteen frock,' said Thea, returning in a flash to the party at the Lockwoods, the time the twins gave their concert on New Year's Eve.

'And now we are here together,' he said, taking her hand.

Smiling, she said nothing.

'You'll come back to the pensionnat next year, won't you? You must, because of your accent.'

They laughed, leaning closer. It was warm, sunny, drowsy in the wood. They rested together, her hand in his. Thea's heart filled with happiness.

'Your hair is so lovely,' he said, leaning back to look at it. 'I dream sometimes that I see you with your hair loose. I long to touch your hair, you know.'

'Then touch it,' said Thea, bending her head to him.

He put up his hand to smooth it.

'Let your hair down,' he said. 'Like Mélisande.'

'No, I can't,' said Thea, startled.

'Yes, you can. Take these pins out. Like this. See, they're out. Now shake your head.'

She shook her head and her hair flowed down on either side of her face in two shining waves. Smiling, shy, she leaned above him.

'That's how I dreamed of you,' he said.

They looked deeply at each other.

'I love you,' he said.

Reaching up, he put back her hair with both hands and held it close against her head. They kissed, and having kissed at last, they kissed again and again.

At last he fell back and drew her down by her hair. She could breathe more evenly now and smile. They sighed with happiness and relief and kissed again. They murmured words of love without coherence.

'What adorable little ears,' he said, taking the lobe of one between finger and thumb.

Time was nothing. They lost all count of it.

'Kiss me again,' he said.

She leaned to kiss him and when she had kissed him, he still held her by the hair, keeping her face within reach of his lips. Held down, protesting, smiling, she suddenly raised her eyes.

Her smile froze, every vestige of colour drained from her face, leaving it ashen. Through the open door, at the foot of the wooden steps, were two shapes, dark against the blinding light of the sun. Two figures in black.

'What is it?' asked Jacques, putting aside her hair that had fallen over his eyes. 'What's the matter? Good God, what is it?' he cried, seeing her face.

He rolled outwards on the divan and saw the figures at the steps.

'Good God!' he exclaimed again, getting to his feet to stare at them.

There was silence. Thea remained, her fists deep in the divan, her face white between the folds of her hair.

'You were right, Madame,' said the Directrice, breaking the spell with her harsh voice. 'She is here.'

Grim, angular, the two middle-aged women stared in at the lovers.

'Jacques,' said Madame Farnet, climbing the steps. 'Go home. At once. Home.' She ordered him home like a dog that has got loose.

Thea, recovering sufficiently to move, bundled up her hair with trembling hands. She couldn't find the pins he had taken out. They were scattered over the divan and she couldn't see. Her heart seemed to be beating in her eyes. She felt over the surface of the divan with frantic hands. She must get her hair up. To be caught by these women with her hair down filled her with shame out of all proportion. She might have been caught naked she was so ashamed. Her breath came fast and loud as if she were going to cry.

The Directrice and Madame Farnet were in the room now, looming in it. They pointed at the bottle of wine, the glasses, the crumbs on the table. They turned and pointed at Thea, at the crushed divan. She couldn't make out what they were saying. She couldn't hear; her heart drummed in her ears.

But she heard Jacques.

'Mademoiselle Thea came here at my invitation,' he was saying. 'There has been nothing wrong. No wrong must be attributed to her. . . .'

'Hold your tongue!' said his mother.

'Maman, I insist!'

'Am I blind?' said his mother, a dark flush on her cheek bones. 'Go home. I will speak to you at home.'

'I shall leave when Mademoiselle Thea leaves and not before,' he said. 'It is my fault she is here. I asked her to come.

She had no wrong thought in coming. In England young men and girls mix freely . . .'

'And the young girls let down their hair and go into the woods to drink wine and lie on beds with young men, I suppose? If that is the sort they are, let them stay in England and not come to France, corrupting our own young girls. Eh, Mademoiselle Duchêne? You no doubt agree?'

But the Directrice was darting instructions to Thea.

'Finish with your hair, if you please. Get your hat on. Put your gloves on and shake out your dress. At least look convenable, even if you are not. And now have the goodness to precede me down the steps.' She waved Thea out of the hut. 'I will keep my eye on you in future, Mademoiselle,' said the Directrice, stalking after her. 'I will keep my eye on you until you have left this town, as you will now assuredly do. Go on. March!'

The brutality of her tone brought a flush to Jacques's face. 'Quel type,' he muttered furiously, getting his bicycle.

'Jacques,' said his mother, 'go home. I have told you. Go home!'

He took no notice, but wheeled his bicycle behind Thea and the Directrice. Madame Farnet locked the door of the chalet and put the key in her pocket.

'This is the end of the place,' she said, hurrying after him. 'I shall sell it. I will leave you no more place for a rendez-vous.'

'My dear Maman,' he said, with the first open scorn he had ever shown her, 'you may be sure that if I want a rendez-vous I shall always find one.'

'Silence,' said his mother. 'Monsieur l'abbé shall speak to you.'

He laughed.

The grotesque procession passed up the ride, grotesque because Thea was taking a form of revenge she was unconscious of. They made her go first alone, but she walked so fast that the two elderly women had difficulty in keeping up with her. Unused to walking over rough grass, or indeed to walking at all, they hurried, tripping over their long skirts, stumbling over the bumps and hollows, their faces red, their black hats awry. But though breathless, they were still voluble.

'Ah, Madame, I promise you she shall pay for this.'

'The prayers, Mademoiselle, the prayers I have said for my son. But I shall hand him over to Monsieur l'abbé . . .'

'All the time going out, escaping down the stairs and out of the door. I might have known . . .'

'Simone told me, she warned me. . . then Madame Blanchot . . .'

Thea did not hear them. She walked swiftly on. Her thoughts were incoherent from shock. She was burningly ashamed, burningly angry. 'They were watching. They saw . . .' she kept saying, passing her tongue over her dry lips, clenching her fingers into the palms of her hands. 'They were watching . . .'

Love should never be watched. Under other people's eyes, it changes, it becomes something else . . .

'And my hair down,' thought Thea. She hated that. She hated the whole situation. She couldn't bear it, she told herself, hearing the breathless, voluble women stumbling behind her and the bump of Jacques's bicycle.

She knew what they had come to discover and she burned with anger. But she was as ashamed as if she were guilty of it.

'This way,' called out the Directrice and, turning, Thea saw her pointing imperiously to a gate at the side of the wood.

She went towards it, but faltered at the sight of an open carriage standing in the road, an old-fashioned hired landau, lined with linen for the summer, with a corpulent, extremely interested coachman on the box and a tired horse dozing between the shafts.

'Am I to ride in that? With them?' thought Thea, halting. 'Through the town?'

'Get in,' said the Directrice.

Thea got in and sat with her back to the horse.

'Tiens,' said the fat coachman, craning down at her over his tight collar. All this fuss, this palaver and out of the wood had come no more than this little young girl.

'Jacques,' said his mother, 'I command you to go home.'

Jacques ignored her. He waited with his bicycle for the landau to start.

'Jacques, I beseech you,' said his mother. 'What is the good of advertising this affair by remaining?'

'It is you who are advertising it,' he said coldly.

'Allez,' said the Directrice harshly. 'Drive on, coachman, and have the goodness to mind your own business.'

'Very good, Mademoiselle,' wheezed the coachman, and with another look at Thea, roused the horse.

The landau moved off. Side by side, the two women, black, angular, swayed rigidly with the movement of the carriage. They were still voluble. Now that they stumbled no longer over the painful ground, now that they had put their hats straight and the breeze cooled their hot faces, they could remember the French code of manners. They became apologetic to each other.

'I cannot forgive myself,' said the Directrice, with a passionate shrug of the shoulders. 'Ever to have allowed this girl to go out alone.'

'I am profoundly ashamed of my son, Mademoiselle. If Madame Blanchot had not told me what was going on, I should never have believed it of him. Never. He has been a good son, pious and obedient till now. She has corrupted him.'

'Ah, she is depraved, depraved,' said the Directrice with another shrug, equally passionate.

The coachman kept his ear cocked.

Thea kept her face turned away, away from the two women and from Jacques riding silently, slowly, beside the carriage. She would not look at him; she couldn't.

The men on the lock had watched the landau go and now they watched it return. Thea travelled backwards into their view. They waved to her, shouting: 'Courage. Du courage. T'a pas eu de chance, va!'

Thea blushed violently and turned her head still farther away over her shoulder.

'Ach,' cried the Directrice, outraged. 'See – everybody knows. It is shameful.'

Her hand twitched on her knee, the acorn-thumbnail working over her clenched fingers.

The landau bowled under the trees of the boulevard and entered the Grande Rue.

'At the corner,' announced Madame Farnet, gripping her meagre breast, 'I must go home. I have palpitation of the heart.'

'Ah, Madame, you have my sympathy,' said the Directrice with false gush. 'Let the carriage take you to your door.'

'Thank you, no,' said Madame Farnet firmly. 'I prefer to enter unnoticed. The scandal will be bad enough later. It will be all round the town by the end of the afternoon.'

'And my poor school, eh?' demanded the Directrice.

'Mademoiselle, you have my sympathy,' said Madame Farnet in her turn. 'Jacques, I need your arm,' she said, descending from the carriage. 'You must take me home. I am not well.'

He stood, dumbly stubborn, his eyes on Thea. She turned her head and met his eyes at last.

'Go,' she said. 'You can't help me.'

'I am so sorry,' he said humbly, coming to the side of the landau. 'Forgive me.'

She smiled faintly and murmured goodbye. It was all over.

'Allez,' said the Directrice, sharp as a goad to the coachman. 'Drive straight to the pensionnat. I have had enough.'

With a jerk the carriage was off again, dragging Thea backwards. The Grande Rue was crowded with Saturday afternoon shoppers and she was raised above them, like a penitent in a shift. She didn't know where to look to avoid meeting the staring eyes. Her chin up, she kept her own eyes at a level beyond the Directrice, who displayed her anger as if she were taking part in a show, shrugging and muttering without pause.

Madame Blanchot was standing at her door to see them pass. She nodded her head in self-congratulation. Her husband's high white cap showed behind her and some customers, about to enter, stood on the pavement and were told the tale.

The carriage turned at the cathedral and as ill luck would have it, the boarders were just returning from their walk. Clustering at the entrance of the pensionnat, they gaped, open-mouthed. What was Miss doing in a carriage with the Directrice? Where was she being brought back from? Why was she in disgrace? What was it? The Lockwoods and Angela Harvey worked their way through the others. What had Thea done? One of their number had disgraced herself and, through herself, them. They were English in a foreign country and now one of them had done something the French could taunt them with.

The Directrice alighted: 'Out of my way,' she said, sweeping the girls aside. At the moment she would willingly have exterminated them all.

'Follow me,' she threw back at Thea.

'Pay the carriage,' she said to the housekeeper in the hall.

She threw open the door of the Grande Salle and a little maid who was polishing the parquet looked up in alarm.

'Out,' said the Directrice, and the little maid scuttled, closing the door behind her.

The Directrice did not go further. She stood inside the door, drawing off her gloves.

'Well, Miss,' she said, with an ugly smile, 'it is pretty what you have done, eh?'

Thea was white, her eyes dark. She felt fear, shame, anger. She also felt sick.

'You have disgraced this school,' said the Directrice. She could not control the saliva that flowed too freely between her yellow teeth. She literally spat out her words. 'You have done more harm to this school in one afternoon than has ever been done to it in its whole previous existence. You, a stranger, a person we do not care anything for, you come here and disgrace us. From the beginning you have been a nuisance – independent, proud, and now it turns out that you are also sly and depraved. Stealing out from this place of innocent young girls to meet your lover and coming back to it after your amorous meetings. In this place consecrated to the education of young girls by women who have taken vows of chastity, you have been amongst us, unchaste, deceitful. You have betrayed the trust of everyone who has had anything to do with you. The trust of Mademoiselle Eardley who sent you here, the trust I placed in you, the trust of that good Madame Farnet, that excellent mother . . .'

'Wait!' Thea struggled to speak. 'What is it you suppose I have done?'

'I do not suppose,' said the Directrice with a sneer, 'I know.'

'I've done nothing wrong,' said Thea. 'Nothing.'

'Tell that fairy tale to someone else. Tell it at home. Tell it to Mademoiselle Eardley. No one will believe you.'

'I've done nothing wrong,' said Thea. To have to say it at all galled her beyond bearing.

The Directrice laughed.

'You don't believe me?' asked Thea.

The Directrice laughed again, a mirthless sound.

'I do not,' she said.

'Then I shall leave. I shall go home,' said Thea.

'You will certainly go home. But don't imagine you are choosing in this matter. I am dismissing you. You will oblige me by leaving this house as soon as possible. I have no further responsibility for you. There is no reason why you should not return home alone, since there is no object in protecting you further, Miss Hunter,' said the Directrice with insult. 'You can therefore find your own way to your home, whatever it is. I should have taken more pains to find someone who came from a respectable family. I have no more to say. You will have no further contact with the girls. You will take your meals after the others have finished, when the refectory is empty. Jeanne Audet will take over your classes. I shall give you instructions about your train from Villeneuve. On Tuesday morning, you go. If you have not the money for your fare, I shall provide it and reclaim it from Mademoiselle Eardley.'

'I don't need to borrow from you,' said Thea.

Rolling her gloves into a ball, the Directrice proceeded to her room.

Thea, her lips white, went out of the Salle. Beyond, in the passage, were the Lockwoods, the Kenworthys and Angela Harvey. Beyond them, through the open door of the couloir, were more girls. In the refectory, more again. All silent, all staring. The news had got round. Miss had been caught in the woods with a man; some said it was young Farnet, some said it was the baker, Monsieur Blanchot. The girls stared avidly, some sniggered, some compressed their lips in disapproval. All believed the worst.

Thea walked through the silence to the stairs. Then she turned and went back to her compatriots. The Lockwoods and the Kenworthys recoiled, as if they didn't want to have anything to do with her.

'Can you lend me five pounds?' said Thea, looking at no one in particular. 'I'll send it back as soon as I get home.'

'Home!' cried Clare. 'Thea, are you going home?'

'Can you lend me five pounds – between you?' asked Thea desperately.

'No,' said Bee Lockwood. 'We wouldn't if we could. How do we know where you'd go with it. I won't take the responsibility of lending you money. You'll find it hard enough to explain to Father as it is, without involving us in it.'

'I shall explain nothing to your father,' said Thea. 'There's nothing to explain.'

'I'll lend you the money,' said Angela. 'Come to the dormitory and I'll give it to you now.'

They turned away together and went upstairs.

'What's all the fuss about?' asked Angela in a conversational way. 'They say you were in the woods with a man and the old dragon caught you. What a situation!'

'I mean for a play,' she added. 'Are you going home alone?'

'Yes,' said Thea.

'Then you'll be able to look round Paris,' said Angela.

Thea laughed shortly.

'Why do you take things so hard?' asked Angela, as they reached the dormitory. 'This affair isn't so desperate as all that, surely? Nothing but a flutter in the dovecot. Do cheer up. Will five be enough? I can spare another pound.'

'I have some of my own,' said Thea, receiving French and English notes into her hand from Angela's. 'I'll send this back as soon as I get home. And thank you. Thank you very much.'

'Ce n'est rien,' said Angela, with an essentially French gesture, slightly turning out her hand and dismissing the obligation with grace.

Like a scale in contrary motion, one girl went down the stairs, the other up.

CHAPTER TWENTY-TWO

I

'The Directrice insists that this door,' said Mademoiselle Petit, flinging it back and startling Thea and Jeanne, 'shall remain open. Jeanne, it is forbidden to speak to Miss, and you ought to be downstairs at this time. Go at once, please.'

She waited until Jeanne passed her and then, leaving the door open, went away herself.

But Mademoiselle Petit had to go to bed some time, and in the night, when everything was quiet, Jeanne and Thea talked in whispers.

'Was it love?' asked Jeanne from her bed in the dark corner. 'Or was it just an affair?'

'No, it wasn't an affair,' said Thea, staring wanly at the moon.

'Don't pity yourself then.'

'But it's over. I shall never see him again.' A tear ran from the corner of Thea's eye to the pillow, but she dashed it away. She was determined not to cry, not to have red eyes the next day. The Directrice might think she was sorry, or guilty, or wanting to stay. No tears, she told herself.

'The great love stories of the world,' said Jeanne, 'are great because they had to end at their height. Death or separation ended them all.'

'Not much consolation to the lovers,' said Thea grimly.

'No, mais c'est beau quand même,' said Jeanne.

Thea preferred happiness.

There was silence. The cold radiance of the moon increased.

'Why did she drag me through the town in that carriage? Why did she make a show of me?' asked Thea, sitting up suddenly in bed. 'You'd think it would be against her own interests to let anyone know.'

'Not at all,' said Jeanne. 'She knew that people knew. How could they miss knowing in a place like this? In a provincial town these affairs have an importance out of all proportion. In Paris, who would have known or cared about this? But here, once the Directrice knew that people knew, she had to show she was dealing severely with you. For the sake of the school, she has to punish you openly. All the same, I hate her.'

Thea flung herself back on her pillows.

'Go to sleep, Jeanne,' she said wearily. 'You'll be tired in the morning.'

Jeanne protested. She went on whispering, listening, consoling. She meant to stay awake to comfort her friend, but in spite of herself she went to sleep.

Thea lay plucking at the crack in the ancient brittle wallpaper beside her bed. Her thoughts whirred distractedly like a clock with the spring broken. What was I doing when they were looking at us in the wood? My hair was down. I hadn't got my hair up properly under my hat and I had to ride through the town. I must have looked tumbled... as if... as if... I shall never see Jacques again. Those old women... I shall have to write home tomorrow, and what shall I say? They'll never understand. They'll be kind, but they'll never understand. The Lockwoods – to have given the Lockwoods something they can use against me for the rest of my life, and they will. They'll come home and tell everybody – and I haven't done anything wrong, but to keep *saying* I haven't is too much. I can't bear it. I loathe the Directrice. I'll come back some day and make her eat her words. I'll come back. I wish I hadn't to go home. I wish there was somewhere else I could go. I don't want to face them at home.

Her thoughts jostled unceasingly on. She groaned to get away from them. She groaned for sleep, but it wouldn't come. The house sank deeper into the night. There were faint sounds, of girls stirring in their beds, of Mademoiselle Petit's intermittent cough, of an occasional drip from the tap on the stairs. Across these small interior sounds the striking of the church clocks cut the night into quarters. She had loved these striking clocks, they had always reminded her that she was actually in France where she had longed to be. But now they were indifferent and relentless, striking her out of the town.

'To have to go home like this . . .' she said again, plucking at the wallpaper.

In the street outside, Jacques Farnet was padding up and down, his eyes ranging every inch of the façade of the pensionnat, looking for some sign that she was there. But, every shutter closed, it was blind, deaf, dumb, in the moonlight.

Earlier in the evening, he had been to the pensionnat and asked to see the Directrice, but was turned away. He had handed in a letter, but it was returned to his mother. He had tried to bribe, to cajole his sister into taking a message to Thea, but, thin-lipped, she refused.

He ranged up and down, up and down. But he had to give up in the end. His collar turned up, his hands in his pockets, tears of desperation in his eyes, he had to go home in the end.

II

Sunday, and the great bell of the cathedral shaking the air. Below in the courtyard the girls were pressing through the door on their way to mass. Thea, stretching up from the floor where she knelt beside her trunk, saw their faces turned up to her window, as if it were the condemned cell and they hoped for sight of the prisoner.

She put more books into the trunks. She got up from the floor and took more things from the cupboard. To remove all traces of herself from the room she had loved because it had given her refuge and a friend was like pulling up her own roots. In this room, though she had often been unhappy, angry, homesick, she had, all the same and all the time, been immensely interested, and now she had to leave it.

On her table lay a paper with the times of her trains, tabulated by Mademoiselle Petit, who had been sent to the station the night before by the Directrice. Two days from now she would be home. There would be hundreds of miles, there would be the sea, between Jacques and her.

She sat down at the table and drew a sheet of writing-paper from her drawer. She didn't know what to say to her mother, An immense reluctance to write anything at all weighed upon her; a reluctance to explain, excuse, tell anything to anybody.

'I am coming home [she wrote]. I shall be home some time on Wednesday evening, but don't meet me. I am afraid you will have a shock to get this letter, if you haven't had one from the Directrice already. But if Mrs Lockwood comes round with any tale, don't believe it. Wait until you hear the truth from me. I haven't done anything, whatever they say.'

What she couldn't bear was to keep on repeating that she 'hadn't done anything'. It was the horrid ambiguity of the phrase that she hated, but she couldn't find another, she daren't say anything else. What did they call it – what they thought? She didn't know.

She'd thought she had a rose in her hand, but when other people looked at it, it changed into a nameless stinking mess that she couldn't get rid of. She saw in their eyes that she couldn't get rid of it. It was their idea of it that had worked this hideous transformation. What people can do, what power they have!

'I haven't done anything.' She had to keep saying it. She had said it that morning, when after the others had left the refectory, she went down and Marie, the little maid, brought her a bowl of cocoa, her eyes round and scared above it.

'Don't look like that,' Thea was goaded into saying. 'As if I'd done something awful. I haven't done anything, I tell you. Nothing!'

But Marie scurried off in her felt boots. She wasn't going

to put herself in the wrong by talking with Miss, who must have done something, or why should she be sent away? Thea, drinking cold cocoa, saw her with the other maid, having another look through the crack of the door. There were eyes everywhere, all looking at her. She hated everybody in the place; except Jeanne.

Or so she thought until, coming out of the refectory, she met the little ones being led down the passage by Mademoiselle Petit. The children broke their ranks at the sight of Thea and crowded round clamouring to know why she hadn't been at breakfast. 'Have you a headache, Miss?' 'Are you ill?' 'They say you won't be at our table any more, but it isn't true, is it, Miss?' 'See, Miss, I've cut my finger. I've got a bandage on it.' 'Miss, Hélène pushed me at table and made me spill my chocolate. She wouldn't have done it if you'd been there, would she, Miss?'

The partings of their hair, their little plaits, the backs of their necks, their round pure cheeks and chins were intolerably endearing. The children had wound themselves round her heart and now she had to leave them; and probably someone would tell them some shameful story about her.

Mademoiselle Petit, who had gone on, expecting to be followed, now came back like a fury, and pushing one here, pulling another there, but without a glance at Thea, hustled the children out of sight.

Thea, her eyes pricking with tears, went back upstairs. The trunk filled slowly up, the day went slowly by.

'Why didn't she let me go at once?' she managed to say to Jeanne, in spite of Mademoiselle Petit in the passage. 'Why does she keep me here?'

'To get her tale in first,' said Jeanne. 'She'll have written at once to your home, your guardian, your headmistress. She's warned them of your coming. Now your journey is their responsibility. She's washed her hands of you, but it has taken a day or two.'

'No talking,' said Mademoiselle Petit, appearing.

On Monday, Clare Lockwood managed to reach the open door.

'Thea,' she whispered, 'are you really going home?'

'Yes.'

'When?'

'Tomorrow.'

'Oh, Thea, could I come with you? Could I run away and come with you?'

'No, of course you can't.'

'Oh, Thea, I'd so gladly risk it, if you'd let me.'

'Well, I won't, so don't be stupid.'

Clare's blue eyes filled with tears, her lips trembled.

'Now go away,' said Thea, speaking from the depths of her own misery to one whose misery was so much less – couldn't be anything, she told herself. Lockwood misery couldn't be the same as anyone else's, there was no *reason* for it. 'You've only got another two months,' she said roughly, but moved in spite of herself by Clare's face. 'You must stick it out.'

Clare was silent, then she tried again.

'Well, will you ask Daddy to come for us in June instead of July? One more month won't make any difference to our French. None of us knows any and we never will. Beg him to come for us in June, Thea.'

'Can you see me begging your father for anything?' said Thea grimly. 'I don't intend even to see him.'

'Oh, Thea . . .'

'Mademoiselle Clare, what are you doing here? You must go down,' said Mademoiselle Petit, reappearing. She spoke with the simulated severity due to a rich, spoilt pupil who would never be punished. Clare needn't have taken any notice of a voice like that, thought Thea, but she did, and Thea despised her as she allowed herself to be sent away down the stairs. 'If I'd been a Lockwood they'd never have dared to treat me like this. They'd never have sent Angela Harvey home like this . . .'

Bringing out the little bag to pack it for the journey, she pictured to herself the possibility of coming back some day, rich and powerful, to get her own back on the Directrice somehow, and Madame Farnet too. And to compensate herself for being humiliated by Mr and Mrs Lockwood at home, she told herself that one day she would get the better of all these people. 'I'll show them,' she said to herself.

But she picked up the Thos. Cook's folder and saw the receipted note for the money her father had borrowed from Mr Lockwood, and was brought down again. There never had been a time, evidently, when the Hunters stood on their own feet without help from the Lockwoods. Perhaps, after all, the Lockwoods were justified in their insufferable patronising of the Hunters, perhaps the Hunters had asked for it.

She swung ceaselessly from one point of view to another. One minute she was sorry and ashamed, the next she was proud and defiant. One moment she longed to get away from the pensionnat, the next she wept to be leaving it. One minute she was swept away on a tide of anger and resentment, only to be swirled back into an eddy of self-reproach and anxiety. She was too young to cope with the situation. She had no armour.

But the last night, she thought only of Jacques. She was leaving him, she was really going.

When she was sure that Jeanne was asleep, she got out of bed and went to the open window. She stood there, the warm breath of the night stirring her hair. She couldn't believe he wouldn't come, that somehow he wouldn't get to her. She leaned out and looked down into the silent court. It was barricaded round by school buildings, it was a prison yard, he couldn't get in there. She went to her open door and looked out into the dark passages. There was not a sound. She stole to the only window that looked out on to the street. It was high and small and she had to pull herself up by her hands and hang there, her chin just reaching to the ledge. But she couldn't hang there long enough to see the street, her hands weren't strong enough. She went back to bed and lay down in hopelessness, but by and by she went to the window again. She knew he couldn't reach her, but she couldn't believe that he wouldn't. She knew he was thinking of her. She felt the strong pull of his thought. It kept her at the window until the sky was flushed with dawn.

Exhausted, she fell asleep then only to be awakened at once, it seemed, by Marie, who brought her chocolate and shook her shoulder.

Thea opened her heavy eyes.

'All right,' she said, and Marie, after lingering with interest, went away.

It was like the morning of the execution. Time was up. People kept arriving to tell her so. Her trunk was strapped, the bag filled, her hat and coat were on. She said goodbye to Jeanne in spite of Mademoiselle Petit, who stood by.

'I hate to leave you,' said Thea. 'Some day I shall try to come back and get you out of here.'

'You won't be able to do that,' said Jeanne, smiling. 'But never mind. You will soon forget this. Remember, though you feel it bad to go, it's much worse to have to stay. Make a good life for yourself. I shall not find anyone like you again in this box. It was nice, you and I with our books on those winter nights, eh?'

Thea's eyes filled with tears.

'Don't cry. Don't let them see they can make you cry . . . they would like that,' said Jeanne, squeezing Thea's hands hard.

They kissed each other in spite of Mademoiselle Petit's protest.

Heavy boots were heard on the stairs. The omnibus driver, the one who had brought the trunk up, now came to carry it down. Groaning, he hoisted it to his back, Thea took up the little bag and smiling again at Jeanne went down the stairs.

Heads were poked out of the dormitory doors to watch her go.

'Cheer up,' cried Angela Harvey, appearing in her petticoat. 'Good lord, no one can eat you!'

'Oh, Thea,' cried Clare distressfully, 'will you be all right going home alone? Will you be safe?'

She was plucked out of sight, presumably by her sisters, but reappeared to call out: 'Try to get Daddy to come for me . . . try, Thea!'

'Adieu, Miss,' murmured one girl, weeping, and others said 'Adieu, bon voyage.' The rest stared with their girls' eyes, awed, relishing to the full the drama of this exit.

The maids were looking through the refectory door, their eyes round, their hands rolled in their aprons, thinking that this was what happened if you did anything wrong. It taught you to be careful, to see someone sent away like this.

Thea went through the couloir and out into the street. Stepping into the omnibus, she recoiled. The Directrice sat within.

'I should prefer to go alone, Mademoiselle,' Thea said.

'It is a matter of indifference to me what you prefer,' said the Directrice, leaning forward to shut the door of the omnibus. 'I shall give myself the satisfaction of seeing you leave the town. You may have an assignation with young Farnet for all I know. You may have it in your mind to set up an establishment with him and create more scandal. But at least you shall not do it from this house. It is not my affair what happens to you afterwards.'

She did not speak again.

The omnibus rattled through the cobbled street past the cathedral. (It had been commissioned specially for this journey; no one else got in.) It passed the pâtisserie where Madame Blanchot was setting out the dishes for the cakes. It passed the corner of the Rue Victor Hugo. It crossed the bridge over the river and drew up before the station.

Thea got out. The Directrice walked onto the platform. Thea took her ticket, registered her luggage and went onto the platform herself. The train came in, Thea climbed into an empty carriage marked 'Dames Seules'. The Directrice stood afar off, long, black, like a maypole in mourning.

Thea, her heart beating heavily, stood at the carriage window looking past the station buildings to the square before the Hôtel de la Gare. Anyone coming to the station must cross that square. Would he come? Would he hear at the last minute that she was going this morning and come? Would she see him again – if only to say goodbye? But the square remained empty, the mattresses lolling through the hotel windows in the sun.

The guard blew his toy trumpet, the train began to move. The Directrice walked out of the station. The train gathered speed. The town passed before Thea, strung out by streets and squares, embosomed in trees, pierced by spires, spanned by bridges, dominated by the cathedral towers. Then receding, the town drew together, closer, tighter, until it grew so small she could see it no longer.

CHAPTER TWENTY-THREE

As the train drew in to Aldworth station, Thea saw her mother and Martin among the people on the platform. Even passing at considerable speed she saw that their faces were anxious, not eager. They looked as if they had come to meet someone in disgrace.

The train carried her far down the platform. Creased, begrimed from the long overnight journey, she got out. They hadn't seen her. She asked a porter to get her trunk from the luggage van and looked again towards them. They still hadn't seen her. She walked reluctantly towards them. She had no impulse to fling herself into her mother's arms. She had withdrawn too far into herself these last days to be able to come freely out now. And their faces had given them away, she told herself.

She came up behind them and said in a flat voice: 'Here I am, Mother.'

Mrs Hunter turned swiftly.

'Oh, Thea,' she said tremulously, and clasped her daughter in her arms.

Her embrace said: 'Whatever you've done, you're my dear child.'

But even this loving acceptance seemed out of key to Thea, who would rather it had been taken as a matter of course that she hadn't done anything. Like an adult receiving the demonstrations of a child, she submitted to her mother's embrace, then turned to get the next welcome over.

Gravely, hat in hand, Martin bent to kiss her cheek. She knew at once that he was embarrassed.

'I'll get your trunk and meet you at the front of the station,' he said, and she knew he was glad to get away.

During the last few days, many blows had been dealt to Thea's pride, but after every blow it stiffened and waxed stronger. It stiffened now. 'Mrs Lockwood's been round,' she thought at once. 'And they've believed her. But if they think I am going to begin explaining and excusing myself, they're very mistaken.'

'What a fuss,' she thought wearily. 'About nothing.'

Her head up, she stalked through the subway, her mother hurrying alongside, her eyes full of the questions she would not ask.

'You must be very tired, dear,' ventured Mrs Hunter.

'Yes, I am,' said Thea.

They came out at the front of the station. Thea saw Queen Victoria again, and the few trees round the sooty church. She felt she was seeing them altogether too soon. Time hadn't lapped her gently, expectedly, to their feet, but flung her abruptly up.

Martin came back with a taxi. Thea got in and resisted a powerful urge to close her eyes. The taxi moved off. More movement. Things had been swimming past her for days.

Martin sat with his back to the driver, carefully keeping his knees out of her way.

'How's Molly?' said Thea, for something to say.

'Very well indeed,' said her mother brightly, glad to be able to be bright about something. 'It's wonderful what a difference the shop has made to her. You'll be surprised.'

'Mmm?' said Thea, making a smile with her dry lips. 'I'm glad.'

'She was so sorry she couldn't come and meet you. But Wednesday is a busy day for her. She won't be home until about eight tonight.'

'Won't she?' said Thea.

She looked steadily out of the window. Everything seemed unutterably drab. The summer sky that had been so clear over the country was smudged with smoke. The people in the streets looked plain and shapeless in their dark clothes. There was a dreadful sameness about the rows of houses. They passed the High School. She supposed she would be expected to explain to Miss Eardley. But she wouldn't. No explanations, she said stubbornly to herself.

Mrs Hunter looked out of the window, too, making remarks from time to time.

'Don't you think the park beds are pretty this year, dear? Darwin tulips.'

'You see they've taken down the hoardings here. Such an improvement, isn't it?'

But Mrs Hunter was even more perturbed than before. To find Thea pale, silent, obviously having done something she didn't want to talk about, removed Mrs Hunter's last hope that there might be nothing in the dreadful affair after all. Since yesterday morning when Mrs Lockwood read Bee's letter to her in the front room, the only hope Mrs Hunter had to cling to was that Thea, when she arrived, would be able to refute everything.

If Thea had come home cheerful and indifferent to other people's opinion, her mother might have been able to be the same. She had counted on Thea, but unfortunately Thea had counted on her mother. At least, if Thea did not, from experience, expect too much, she needed warm indignation on somebody's part and she wasn't getting it. Each failed the other and withdrew into unshared distress. Mrs Hunter made an effort. She tried to sound as if nothing very much had happened, she drew Thea's limp hand through her arm and held it there as they sat side by side. But her expression was piteous in the extreme.

Since the previous morning, Mrs Hunter had been in a sad state. Molly and Martin were on the point of leaving the house when the post brought Thea's letter. In spite of the resulting confusion, in spite of the necessity there was of calming their mother, they had to go. Customers wait for no man and customers would present themselves at the counter of the bank and the shop no matter what Thea had done. They hurried out, and on the way down Byron Place Martin told Oliver Reade that Thea was coming home unexpectedly, and at the shop Molly told his sister.

Left with the letter, Mrs Hunter went in a dazed way from one household task to another without getting any done. No sooner had she started one than she had to come back to the letter to see if she could possibly find out anything from it. Baffled, she put it down again and started something else. Only to come, in a moment, to the letter again. The beds were unmade, the breakfast table was still uncleared, she had got no further in her preparations for lunch than the laying of the stewing beef on the board for cutting up, when she was summoned from her first shock to receive a second and much worse one. Mrs Lockwood arrived in a state of outrage with a letter from Bee and, the stew abandoned, Mrs Hunter had to accompany Mrs Lockwood into the front room to have the letter read to her.

Sitting on the sofa, Mrs Hunter fixed her eyes in horrified incredulity on Mrs Lockwood's lips from which the dreadful words fell. Mrs Lockwood didn't spare Mrs Hunter; she didn't sympathise, because, as she stopped reading to say, she had always held that Thea should never have gone.

'I was very much against it,' said Mrs Lockwood. 'I felt it at the time. I didn't quite know why, but this was it, you see. I was right,' she said triumphantly, and continued to read.

The Directrice, wrote Bee, had asked her to put the facts before her parents so that they should realise that there was every justification for sending Thea home. The Directrice had been informed that Thea was meeting a young man in the woods and had gone there with the young man's mother and found them together.

'"Lying on a bed in a hut,"' wrote Bee. '"They had been drinking wine together."'

'Oh, stop! Please!' implored Mrs Hunter. 'I can't believe it. She was never like that. She has never shown the slightest interest in men. You saw for yourself, Mrs Lockwood, that when our neighbour, Mr Reade, brought a box of chocolates to the station, and such a big one, too, she wouldn't have it. She made me take it. She wouldn't have anything to do with him.'

'That doesn't follow,' said Mrs Lockwood dismissingly, and read on.

'"Thea borrowed five pounds from Angela,"' wrote Bee. '"You will see she gets it back, won't you, Mother. It places us in such an awkward position, doesn't it, since it was through us that Angela ever met Thea."'

'Oh, dear!' said Mrs Hunter piteously.

'I must say,' said Mrs Lockwood, finishing the letter and putting it into her bag, 'that I am grieved and distressed beyond words.'

She spoke as if she, and not the culprit's mother, were the prime sufferer in the affair. She was outraged that Mrs Hunter, instead of apologising to her, should occupy herself with her own distress. In fact, she wouldn't have it. She spent the rest of the morning in trying to bring Mrs Hunter round to a proper attitude.

She was still there, still sitting in the front room, when Mrs Hunter saw, with great increase of agitation, that Molly and Martin were both arriving at the gate for lunch. She was in a panic lest they should come into the front room and have Bee's letter read to them by Mrs Lockwood. That part about lying on a bed with a young man in a hut must never fall upon their ears, especially if she had to be with them when it fell. No, shuddered Mrs Hunter, they mustn't hear it put like that.

She got Mrs Lockwood out of the house without knowing how she did it and hurried into the kitchen. But her children could not make out whether she was wringing her hands because she had forgotten to cook anything for them or because of bad news from Mrs Lockwood. And they couldn't find out. She was so vague and guarded in answer to their questions, yet so distressed, that they could hardly do otherwise than conclude that Thea had disgraced herself and them.

So as they rode home Martin in his turn looked out of the windows. Thea, watching him with a cynical eye, noticed that not once since they got into the cab had he looked directly at her.

'How's the bank, Martin?' she had asked.

'Oh, just as usual,' he said, craning forward to look at the Baptist Chapel he passed every day of his life.

'So that's how he's going to take it,' thought Thea. Her heart burned. Kind, quiet Martin to be so unjust.

She looked at him with the cold considering eye of the injured. He was completely spoiling the shape of his mouth by holding his upper lip so tightly down on his lower one. It was a habit that had grown on him with the years, but now it was very marked. It didn't, Thea admitted though angry with him, give his face a mean or censorious expression. But it made him look as if he kept a tight rein on himself, which probably made him expect that she should do the same.

Martin was not, if she had known it, judging his sister harshly. He was embarrassed and estranged. He felt that Thea had become someone he didn't know. He had never thought of her as anything but his sister, cool and young. He had taken a vicarious pride in her achievements at school and had been glad that she had been able to do what he hadn't. But now that she had grown up and grown away so far as to get herself mixed up in some unsavoury love-affair, he couldn't understand her at all. It was the sort of thing no brother could bear to think or have said of his sister.

The whole thing was distasteful to him. If she had come home weeping and appealing to their protection and affection, his heart would have melted, but she hadn't. She sat there looking as if the fault was theirs, not hers. His hands in his trouser pockets, his profile turned steadily to Thea, Martin looked out of the window.

The taxi turned into Byron Place. It looked just the same. Nothing worse could be said for it. A feeling of revulsion shook Thea.

'Now, dear,' said Mrs Hunter. 'Here we are at home.'

Thea got out and waited for her mother to open the door with her key. As she went in, the suddenness of the stairs struck her as never before. They seemed to be pouring in a cataract out of the front door, and the passage seemed so narrow it didn't look possible to push past the hall table to get in to the front room. Had it really always been like this, thought Thea, distracted for a moment from her own misery. She went into the front room and stood there while Martin and the driver carried her trunk upstairs. This small shabby place cluttered with large unsuitable furniture – was this the room she had thought of with such nostalgia those first weeks in France? And described subsequently, she feared, to Jeanne, as if it were an elegant drawing room. Mrs Hunter had hurried through to put the kettle on and now came back, rolling up her gloves.

'I'm sure you want something to eat, dear,' she said.

'I'd much rather go to bed, Mother, if you don't mind,' said Thea. 'I've been travelling for two days and a night, you know. I wish I could have a bath.'

'Well, I don't know if the water is hot enough. I've been out, you see. But wait a moment.' She hurried upstairs to lay her hand to the cistern in the bathroom cupboard and called out with relief: 'Yes, it's nice and hot, dear. So come along.' Far better for her to go to bed, she thought, it will all be easier tomorrow. She turned on the taps and the house was filled with the cheerful sound of running water.

Thea climbed the stairs, bringing her white face slowly to her mother's level.

'We've given you the little room over the door, dear,' said Mrs Hunter. 'We were going to have it done up for you. Martin and Molly were going to paint and paper it. But – well – coming suddenly – but later they'll do it, I know.'

Thea felt a pang to think she had spoilt her homecoming for them as well as for herself. The little room had a pallid air, with its white bed-cover, pale blue wallpaper and a pink rug faded to silver on the floor. Thea had always wanted this room for her own, but now it was no more than a place to sleep in.

Her bath was ready. She took off the clothes she had put on in the cabinet de toilette thirty-six hours before. How strange it was to be carried so far away in so short a time, she thought wearily, getting into the bath. But oh, warm water, how lovely, how kind! She smiled, stretching to full length. For the first time for five days and nights, she felt pleasure. The body knows its own consolations even when the mind has none. The hot bath at the end of the long journey made up, temporarily, for the lack of understanding in her family. She was conscious only of the lovely laving of her tired body by the water. She was soothed and comforted. But only temporarily.

Soon she sat up, her face on her wet knees, her arms along her legs, her hands along her feet. They ought to have rushed to welcome her, they ought to have been angry for her, they ought to have believed in her. People hardly ever do as you hope they will, she thought. Except Jacques. Jacques was always what she hoped; he was more. She would always remember him as he rode beside the carriage, holding on to it, being with her. Slow tears rolled down her face into the bathwater.

'I'm bringing you some hot milk in a moment, dear,' said her mother's voice at the door.

Thea got out of the bath.

When she was in bed, which felt thin and unwelcoming after her plump French bed, her mother came up with a tray.

Something in the way she carried it, loving, anxious, careful, smote Thea. She felt the self-reproach of one who is not so glad to see a beloved face as one ought to be or would once have been. The change is in me, she thought, blaming herself.

Receiving the tray on her knees, she said: 'So Mrs Lockwood has been round, Mother?'

Mrs Hunter looked cornered.

'Well, she came yesterday, dear,' she admitted. 'She brought a letter from Bee.'

'And what did Bee say?'

Mrs Hunter looked distressfully at her daughter.

'Mother, tell me.'

'Well, she said the Directrice found you in a hut with a young man and you were lying on a bed . . .'

'It's true, Mother, but it wasn't like that at all.'

'Oh, Thea, dear, it sounds so dreadful. . . .'

'I know, but it wasn't. I gave him English lessons, you know, with his sister. He was a young man like Martin, or the Cunningham boys. Like anybody else, only nicer.' She looked anxiously to see if she had been able to replace the sensual villain of her mother's imagination by the idea of Jacques as he was. But her mother still looked doubtful. 'I. . . we . . . fell in love, we couldn't help it,' said Thea. 'We could never speak to each other alone anywhere. So on Saturday afternoons we went to the wood his family owned. There was a hut with an old divan in it. We'd never even kissed each other before, but we did then and they sneaked up and watched us. It's all so ugly, Mother, smeared over. And it was nothing. I did nothing wrong.'

'If you didn't, Thea, and if you say you didn't, I'm sure you didn't, how dare that woman, the Directrice, send you home?'

'I suppose, from her point of view, she was justified,' said Thea wearily. 'There are no half-shades in the French provinces. Either you stick to the conventions and are respectable and respected, or you don't and you aren't. I knew, really,' she said bitterly, 'but I risked it.'

'I'm glad you've told me, Thea,' said her mother. 'I'm sure we shall be able to explain everything satisfactorily to Mrs Lockwood.'

'We shan't,' said Thea, drinking the milk. 'She *wants* to think I've done something disgraceful. She'd feel cheated if she had to be convinced I hadn't. But go down and have supper, darling. We'll talk tomorrow. You go. Martin will be waiting for you. I'll see Molly in the morning, shall I? I'm so tired I'm afraid I shan't be able to keep awake until she comes home.'

'She'll understand. No one shall disturb you. Good night, dear. I'm so glad you're safely home. I'm so glad you've explained everything to me, dear.' Mother and daughter kissed each other warmly and, wiping her eyes, Mrs Hunter went away, closing the door quietly as if Thea were already asleep.

Thea, eating sandwiches – queer bread, she thought – felt like an adult who has settled a child. Herself she had not settled. The strangeness of this rôle made her feel lonely. It is by these painful stages that one grows up.

She got out of bed, drew down the blind, and got into bed again. Lying there, her eyes wandered over the dimmed room. There was nothing in it to annoy, nothing to please; it was merely insipid. Beside the chest of drawers, the little bag had collapsed after its travels. It was unlikely it would ever go on any more. It still held, under the lining, the note from Jacques – strange how all the thrilling excitement had gone out of it since Saturday – and in the otherwise empty Cook's folder, the receipt for the money her father had borrowed from Mr Lockwood. Let them stay there, Thea thought.

Her lids drooped. Sleeping, her mind was a confusion of images; the harsh figure of the Directrice, the river flowing swift and silent through the wood, Jacques riding beside the carriage, Jeanne's smile when she said goodbye. In spirit, she was still in France.

Outside in Byron Place, Oliver Reade, without hat, came out of the gate of number fifteen and walked swiftly up the road. He had had his hair cut by a good barber. Instead of having the clippers on it all round the back and the sides, he'd had it done all over with comb and scissors by the best Manchester barber and, by gum, it had made a difference, he thought with satisfaction, looking at it through Edie's handglass.

It was this haircut, the day Thea was coming home, that had given him away to Edie and moved her to tell him that Thea had been sent home because of a man. Molly wouldn't say much, Edie said, which showed that there was something to be hushed up. Oliver saw again Edie's side-glance as she said it. But if she wanted to put him off this girl, she was mistaken in thinking she could do it by hinting at another man. Since Edie had mentioned the man at tea-time, he hadn't known what to do with himself, he couldn't settle anywhere. He was possessed with a fury of wanting to know what had happened. But now when he reached the gate he was checked by the drawn blind. She must have gone to bed. There was no chance of seeing her tonight, of finding out about the other man.

He stood with his hands round the spikes of the gate, looking up at the blind, struggling against an impulse to go in and find out from Martin or her mother. But if he so much as opened the gate, it would scrape and squeak as it always did, and wake her. She must be tired. He stood there. His imagination could always supply him with vivid pictures of her and now he saw her lying asleep, tired out.

His hands fell from the gate and he turned away.

CHAPTER TWENTY-FOUR

I

Thea opened her eyes and lay without stirring. The day was bright round the edges of the blind. The wallpaper within a few inches of her face was not the French cracked pink, but the English white and pale blue. Time, damp and the lime in the walls had been at work making faint rings, blotches, infinitesimal growths. Mysterious things were going on even in wallpaper. For a moment, Thea lived in a strange world, then, painfully, her mind came back to herself.

Someone was moving on the landing. It must be Molly, she thought, but did not call out. She felt a recoil from, instead of a movement towards, the members of her family. She hoped Molly wouldn't come in, but the door was cautiously opened and Molly's nice freckled face appeared round it.

'Oh, you're awake!' She made a rush to the bed and the sisters kissed each other.

Thea's thought was that Molly was fatter, that she looked different, altogether happy and sure of herself. Molly's was that Thea was prettier – more than pretty, lovely even. Yes, she looked like a girl men would fall in love with. Molly had no pang to stifle at that. No envy. The shop was enough for her. She didn't want any unsatisfactory love-affairs, or even any love-affairs at all. She was rather scared of being told about any, too.

'I looked in last night, but you were asleep. How are you this morning, love?' Molly remained bending over the recumbent Thea, who looked up into her sister's eyes.

A spell binds human beings. A wrapping keeps them from one another. Thea couldn't burst out about what had happened to Molly, though one would think that to a sister it would be easy. But she couldn't.

'You look very well, Molly,' was what she said, smiling palely.

'I am,' said Molly emphatically. 'I never have a headache these days. Now I'm just going to bring up your breakfast, before I go.'

'Oh, no,' protested Thea, throwing back the blankets.

'Yes,' said Molly, covering her up again. 'Just for this morning. It's all ready. You're going to have sausage made at the shop,' she beamed. Far easier to keep to sausage and that sort of thing, she thought.

'Do you make sausage?' said Thea, opening her eyes wide.

'Well, Edie makes the sausage and the toffee. She's rather heavy-handed for pastry and cakes.'

'To think of you with a shop! D'you really like it?' asked Thea, wondering how anybody could.

Molly, leaning her fists in Thea's eiderdown, said seriously: 'I enjoy every minute of every day.'

'D'you really?' said Thea wonderingly.

'And I owe it all to Oliver Reade. What a man, Thea! The things he does and the way he gets them done! Everything seems so easy, so sort of *possible* when he's about.'

Thea wondered what women almost always wonder if another woman speaks warmly of a man. Was Molly in love with him? But Molly's eyes were tranquil and unabashed and Thea felt sure she was in love with nothing but the shop.

'How d'you get on with his sister?' she asked.

'Very well. She's good-natured and she works hard. She does the books. She's got a young man in Manchester, though, and they're going to be married soon.'

'D'you have to call her Edie?' asked Thea.

'Oh, yes,' said Molly. They sent one of their old smiling glances at each other. Thea knew that Molly must have jibbed at saying 'Edie' because she would have jibbed at it herself. 'Edith' could be managed without difficulty; but 'Edie' – no!

'The money I bring home,' said Molly in an awed voice. 'You'd scarcely believe it. D'you know that twice I've brought home five pounds in one week?'

'Five pounds in a week!' echoed Thea.

Her face changed and she grasped her sister's arm.

'Molly, five pounds reminds me. I borrowed five pounds from Angela Harvey to come home with. I've two pounds left. Could you possibly lend me three? I want to send it at once. I hate to ask you. I won't be able to repay you until I get some sort of a job.'

'Of course. I'll give it you,' said Molly.

'No, I'll pay it back.'

'I'll give it to you,' said Molly firmly. 'It's something new for me to have anything to give, isn't it? But it's not only the money the shop brings in, Thea,' she said. 'It's making things and making them good. I made apricot tarts yesterday. You know, glazed with strawberry jam and piped with cream. And no sooner had I put them in the window than it got round and people came flocking to the shop. And when I was handing them out over the counter, I thought: "Yes, you'll enjoy those. They're good."'

Thea laughed. It was so typical of Molly.

'We don't bake bread, we couldn't possibly – Oh, your sausage – they must be done!' cried Molly, dashing from the room and down the stairs.

Thea sat up, waiting for her to come back. She wished she could be satisfied with a shop. It must be fun; like a little girl's dream come true. But it wouldn't do for her. She had wanted something marvellous. . . . She didn't know what it had been, but it was there no longer. There didn't seem to be anything to want now. If anybody had asked her what she wanted, she couldn't have thought of a thing.

'Here I am,' said Molly, throwing open the door.

Thea straightened her knees to receive the tray and sniffed up the appetising smell of grilled sausage and tomato, coffee and toast.

'Oh, Molly, there's a lot to be said for the English breakfast. Now I see this, I know I'm hungry. I can't remember if I ate anything yesterday or not.'

'Eat it all up then.' Molly tucked Thea's dressing-gown round her shoulders. She scooped up Thea's curls and pinned them in a childish knot on the top of her head. You could do this sort of thing much more easily than talk about love-affairs. 'There you are! I've taken Mother's tray and Martin is having breakfast. It's early-closing today, so will you come round and see the shop while Mother's resting after lunch? I'm dying to show you everything. And here's the money.' She took it from her apron pocket and put it on the tray. 'Now I must fly.' She stooped and kissed her sister's cheek and escaping from thanks, ran down the stairs.

II

From childhood, Thea had been used to helping to make beds, clear tables, dust and sweep, but though she had not enjoyed it, never until this first morning of her return had she actually suffered in doing it. She suffered now, standing at one side of a bed waiting for her mother to find her corner of the sheet, or tuck in one blanket before bringing up another, standing with a tea-towel in her hand waiting for her mother to bring a cup or plate out of the water. Such an accumulation of desperate irritation seethed within her that she put up a mute petition: 'Please God, at any rate help me not to upset Mother.'

She had felt, vaguely, that being discovered in the wood with Jacques was not a thing to appeal for help about. Besides, it was done, it was too late for help. But surely to ask to be helped not to wound your mother by cutting remarks that threatened to burst out of you at any minute was the sort of thing God might be expected to listen to? It was His province surely?

Perhaps the prayer was answered, because by and by Mrs Hunter mildly suggested that, while she did the vegetables, Thea should go upstairs and unpack her trunk.

'Then Martin can put it back in the loft and it will be out of the way.'

'Must the little bag go up, too, or may I keep it?' asked Thea.

'Keep it by all means, dear. No one else wants it.'

Thea paused by the door wondering whether to mention the receipt she had found in the lining. 'No, I can't be bothered,' she decided, crushed with the new inertia that had come upon her. She escaped upstairs to the comparative relief of being alone.

Slowly she unpacked the trunk, taking out the things she had put in such a long time ago; or so it seemed. Was it really only Sunday then? Today must be Thursday. Only four days since she left Jacques. What would it be like to have to spend not four days, but four weeks without seeing him, a year, years, her whole life? She would never see him again. She would never have the money to go back. Besides, what would be the good if she went? You couldn't marry without the consent of parents in France. And perhaps he wouldn't even want to, since she had no 'dot'. Love had no chance against these filial and financial considerations.

She sorted out her things. She hung up her dresses, hid the little bag in the corner of the wardrobe and went down with her arms full of books.

'I'll put these back on the shelves in the front room, shall I, Mother?' she asked, going into the kitchen where her mother was still very carefully shredding French beans.

'Yes, dear,' said Mrs Hunter.

So Thea was kneeling at the shelves when the front door opened and a voice said: 'Mrs Hunter?'

Thea got swiftly to her feet. It was Mrs Lockwood. Now it would be all gone through again. She was never allowed to settle. She had to keep beginning again with somebody different, explaining, excusing, going through it all again. She stood, gone pale, her eyes on the door through which Mrs Lockwood now appeared, followed by Mrs Hunter, so agitated that her fingers wouldn't undo her apron at the back.

The protagonists observed each other. It struck Mrs Lockwood unpleasantly that the girl had increased in beauty; unpleasantly, because she felt obscurely that what Thea had must be subtracted from her daughters. As if Thea's being more beautiful made them less so. It struck Thea that Mrs Lockwood was older, heavier and if possible more self-satisfied than before.

'Well, Thea?' said Mrs Lockwood.

There was nothing Thea could return to this except 'Well, Mrs Lockwood?' and she dismissed that as too rude. She said nothing.

'Do sit down, Mrs Lockwood,' urged Mrs Hunter anxiously.

'Just here then,' conceded Mrs Lockwood, indicating with dignity a chair at the table, and when Mrs Hunter had drawn it out, taking it.

'Well, Thea?' she said again.

Thea still said nothing and her mother looked at her imploringly.

Mrs Lockwood had to try another opening.

'I'm very sorry to find you home before your time and for such a reason.'

Still nothing from Thea. Mrs Lockwood turned to talk at her through her mother.

'The whole thing has been most unfortunate from our point of view,' she said. 'We sent the girls away in a party so that they could keep to themselves without getting mixed up with undesirable girls and hearing things we didn't want them to hear. Then one of their number behaves so disgracefully that she has to be expelled, Mrs Hunter.'

Anger was coming to Thea's rescue. Invigorating trickles were creeping through her veins, brightening her eyes, stiffening her spine.

'It was a favour to allow Thea to go with the girls and their friends. I should have thought she would realise that. It wasn't as though she was one of them,' said Mrs Lockwood. 'And then she, the one who was allowed in, the one who shouldn't have been there, disgraces them all. Bee says they feel it dreadfully. And we have to apologise to the Harveys and the Kenworthys now, because it was through us that Thea came into contact with their girls. I'm sure they'll wonder why we aren't more careful about the people our own girls associate with. If the girls can be said to associate with Thea. Though I must say they have never done it willingly, but only for old times' sake, as I shall explain . . .'

'Mrs Lockwood,' Thea broke in, 'Bee wrote to you what the Directrice told her to write. But whatever she has said, I did nothing wrong. In England no one would have thought anything of it. In France it seemed like something it wasn't.

You don't understand the French provinces. How can you, since you have never been there?'

'Is she throwing it in my face that I have never travelled, Mrs Hunter?' asked Mrs Lockwood with hauteur.

'Oh, I don't think so for a moment,' said Mrs Hunter hurriedly. 'You aren't, are you, Thea?'

'I'm trying to put the situation plainly,' said Thea.

'The Directrice has already put it plainly,' said Mrs Lockwood. 'And a responsible woman like that wouldn't have told Bee such things if they weren't true. I prefer to believe the Directrice,' announced Mrs Lockwood.

'Then it's no good saying any more,' said Thea. 'Except this. I've done nothing wrong and I'm not answerable to anyone, certainly not to you, Mrs Lockwood. If one of your girls had been sent home, would my mother have walked into your house – without ringing, too – and asked Bee or Muriel or Clare to give an account of herself?'

Mrs Lockwood's mouth fell open.

'What right have you to ask me anything, or to badger Mother the way you do? Why should you come here and say: "Well, Thea?" to me?'

Mrs Lockwood turned in outraged astonishment to Mrs Hunter.

'Because we're poor and you're rich,' said Thea, bright with anger. 'You treat us without courtesy. You treat us as you'd never dream of treating your rich friends.'

'Thea!' cried her horrified mother.

'After all I've done, after all Mr Lockwood's done . . .' cried Mrs Lockwood.

'What have you done? I can't think of one good, kind thing you've ever done,' pursued the ruthless girl. 'Was it kind to hand Molly over to the Watsons and make her into a governess to oblige your friends when it made her ill and wretched for years? Was it kind to put Martin into a bank that he hates because Mr Lockwood couldn't be bothered to do anything else for him?'

'Thea!' Mrs Hunter rushed at her daughter, but Thea put her aside and spoke round her.

'You've done nothing but patronise us and humiliate us. You used to have us up to the house to show us the grand presents you were giving to other people and then give Mother some messy blouse you'd finished with . . .'

'*Thea!*' Mrs Hunter's voice rose to a despairing shriek. This was terrible. 'Mrs Lockwood,' she implored, clasping her hands, 'how can I sufficiently apologise?'

'You can't,' said Mrs Lockwood, rising from her chair. 'I'm leaving your house, Mrs Hunter, and I shall never come into it again. I have never been so insulted in my life. The outrageous girl to speak to me like this! To *me*, Mrs Hunter,' said Mrs Lockwood, laying a tightly gloved hand upon an innocent bosom. 'Our long friendship is at an end. Your daughter has finished it.' She made uncertainly for the door. Her legs were trembling. 'You understand that my husband will sever his connection, too,' she said, turning. 'You won't expect him to do anything more for you, of course. We have finished, Mrs Hunter. Good morning.'

'Mrs Lockwood, Mrs Lockwood – please . . .' cried Mrs Hunter, darting after her in tears.

But the front door closed.

'Mrs Lockwood . . .' called Mrs Hunter despairingly.

'Let her go, Mother,' said Thea, who was nevertheless considerably shaken.

While Mrs Hunter wept and Thea tried to soothe, Mrs Lockwood hurried, not down Byron Place as she had intended, but into the back alley, which was the only place she knew of to hide in. In this place of closed doors and high brick walls she stood, struggling with unusual emotions, dabbing her eyes with her handkerchief, talking to herself, telling herself how awful it was that that girl should say such things to her. 'Why, everybody likes me,' said Mrs Lockwood to herself, 'I know they do. The tradespeople – everybody. Everybody says there's no one like me. The girl at the glove counter in Spray's – she'd do anything for me. Anything. And Johnson's – look how they rush to serve me there. I'm always so nice with everybody. It's not fair. That awful girl. No wonder she was sent home. Messy blouses. That's what I can't forgive. Mrs Hunter always thanked me, she was always so grateful. She *encouraged* me to give her them. That girl said I'd never done anything kind. Why, there's nobody kinder than I am. I'm always being kind in one way or another.'

'I never heard how my girls were,' said Mrs Lockwood, breaking into fresh tears. 'I never heard how my girls were and that's what I went for. I really only went to hear how the girls were.'

Deeply outraged and hurt she wanted somebody to tell it all to, but who was there? She would tell William later, but it was another woman she needed. Lady Harvey wouldn't do. She couldn't tell Lady Harvey about the messy blouses. Strange, but the only person she wanted to tell, the only one who would really have felt for her, was Mrs Hunter. And that was all over now.

'I can't go into town looking like this,' thought Mrs Lockwood, peering at her red eyes in her little glass. 'I shall have to go home, that's all!'

CHAPTER TWENTY-FIVE

I

Thea and Martin were alone at lunch. They sat down to cold meat and boiled cabbage in a state of acute embarrassment. Molly didn't come home on early-closing day and Mrs Hunter, shattered by the events of the morning, was lying down with a headache. When Thea told Martin their mother would not be down, his upper lip tightened.

'Upsetting Mother like this,' said his expression.

It was extraordinary that a brother could become a stranger, and a hostile stranger, too, but that was what he was, thought Thea. And why? 'Why think the worst of me?' she thought in weary resentment.

Briefly, she entertained the idea of telling him that he was being idiotic, unjust, unkind. But she gave it up. She had had too many scenes lately. She hadn't the courage or the energy to begin another. She let the silence go on. But when she brought the rice pudding in, she murmured she had something to see to and left him. It was with relief that she heard him leave the house.

Clearing the table, she stood with the plates, looking out at the yard. The ash sapling by the dustbin was taller than when she had seen it last. 'Poor thing, having to grow there,' she thought. 'It's as bad for it here as it is for me – for all of us,' she amended, and went to wash up in the kitchen.

And now she must go to see Molly's shop, she said to herself, though she could feel no interest in it. She felt no interest in the shop, in the house, and worse still, none in anyone or anything in this place. She was a limb cut off from the family tree. No family sap reached her; she wasn't nourished from it. She felt she had already withered.

She stole upstairs so as not to disturb her mother, she put on her thin black dress and the wide-brimmed hat she had bought at the Nouvelles Galeries; not from coquetry but because it was a hot day and those were the coolest things she had. She went quietly from the house and turned up Byron Place.

It was, even in manufacturing Aldworth, a lovely day. Sunlight lay over streets and houses, the sky was softly blue above the slate roofs. Sparrows chirped and scrimmaged in the privet hedges, the front gardens were very neat. The scraps of lawn had little flower beds in fancy shapes, as if they had been cut out with a pastry cutter, in diamonds, rounds, triangles, trefoils. There was no end to the fanciness, the effort to make a difference in the shape of flower beds, but there was no profusion of flowers, the smoke would not allow it. Anyone from the country would have pitied the gardens, but their owners found pride and solace in them, greeting the seasons with three or four snowdrops under the sooty laurels, with the secret march of lilies of the valley among the privet sticks, and now, as Thea saw when she turned into the Wells Road, with laburnum flinging its golden light from almost every garden.

But it stirred no pleasure in Thea. She was occupied with the banality of it all, with the stone, brick and asphalt, the hard sunlight and sharp shadow. Her feelings matched the scene; they were set and stony too.

She passed Mr Small's, the dentist, to whom Mrs Hunter went when she had to go anywhere. Her children had long ago protested that Mr Small wasn't qualified. 'Well, dear, he's an American dentist,' said Mrs Hunter mildly, as if American dentists had no need of qualification. The fact, if Mrs Hunter would have admitted it, was that Mr Small was cheap, close at hand and didn't hurt.

At each corner, where tributary streets debouched into the larger Wells Road, a shop was set: Bowen's, the chemist; farther along another chemist, Daw's, where Oliver Reade had made his discovery about poor Miss Riley; a haberdashery, a grocer's, and now a shop newly painted bright blue with a swinging sign proclaiming it 'The Bun Shop'.

Thea examined it from across the road and smiled in spite of herself to think that it was actually Molly's.

At his desk in the room over the shop which he used as an office, Oliver Reade looked up and saw her. His heart gave a great leap. He was startled to find that the sight of her affected him with the old violence. What was there about her that enslaved him? He stared fixedly at her, trying to make out what it was. When she had gone away, snubbing him, he had tried, nay more – he had succeeded in having what he thought of as a bit of fun with Doris Barnes. But it was no more than a bit of fun, a pastime. It was negligible beside the misery and splendour of his feeling for Thea. And here she was, mixed up with some Frenchman, torturing him in a new way.

She didn't want him, she'd chosen another man, and she'd spoilt all other women for him. He used to like women, he said to himself, and now she'd taken all his pleasure out of them. He saw himself lonely, lost, forever without women because of Thea.

She crossed the road, her thin dress flowing over her long limbs, the wide brim of her hat dipping and waving round her head. She looked as if she were moving on the wind, though there wasn't a breath in Wells Road. She disappeared under his window and in a moment he heard her being greeted by Molly.

He went to look cautiously over the banisters. He saw her being conducted about by Molly, followed at a distance by Edie, who, her arms folded, leaned against the door, watching Thea. Oliver knew Edie. He knew what the expression on her healthy face meant. 'I'm as good as you are,' Edie was implying. 'You don't need to put on airs with me.' But Thea had no thought of putting on airs. She and Molly were going about naturally, one showing, the other admiring. Edie had no need to look like that about them, thought Oliver. But he understood.

'We may have guts,' he thought. 'But they've got grace. It's the same with Martin and me. He makes me look a rough chap, and by gum, I *am* a rough chap. She'll never look at me as I am. I've got to do something about myself.'

Thea, who did not know he had an office upstairs or could be watching her, went about admiring everything. There was a comfortable smell of toffee and tea-cakes. It was all very English, all very unlike the cool vanilla airs of the Pâtisserie Blanchot.

At that reminder, her temporary respite was at an end. Misery flooded over her again. She must get away, she must be by herself.

'I'll go now,' she said to Molly.

'Oh, wait for me. I won't be long. Mrs Haines is just going to make tea.'

'No, I think I'll go now,' said Thea, determined to escape. She smiled at the unsmiling Edie and went out of the door.

She went back along the Wells Road. She supposed she would go home, and when she got there, she would have to leave the house again. One of the worst things about this affair was the restlessness it induced in her. She couldn't settle anywhere, she couldn't find any peace.

She heard someone coming rapidly along the road behind her and turned her head. It was Oliver Reade. She turned abruptly to the front again. He was the very last person she could bear to see. She quickened her steps, feeling persecuted, hunted. But there was no escape. His long stride soon brought him up with her.

'Good afternoon,' he said, his eyes intent upon her face.

'Good afternoon,' said Thea, turning her head away. She drew in a long breath and let it out again, like a child in distress.

He heard it and was disturbed. He didn't know what to say. They walked in silence.

Then he said hoarsely: 'You came home very suddenly, didn't you?'

A tide of red rushed over Thea's pale cheek. Every time this subject was broached, she blushed. She was silent for what seemed to him such a long time that he thought she wasn't going to answer. He looked anxiously at the curve of her cheek, which was all he could see under the wide brim of her hat. Then she turned on him in such a blaze of anger that he recoiled.

'It's no concern of yours why I came home,' she said. 'But I'll tell you and then perhaps you'll leave me alone. I knew a man in France. I taught him English. I used to meet him on Saturday afternoons in a wood and last Saturday the Directrice of the pensionnat and his mother followed us, and I was sent home.'

He flinched as if she had struck him in the face. He had expected something like this, but when she said it, he couldn't bear to hear it. His face pale, he stared at her.

'So now you know,' said Thea tersely.

They walked on, their faces rigidly averted.

He stepped off the pavement to avoid the lamp-posts and stepped on again, stumbling once, going on beside her.

'Did he – were you in love with him?' he asked with difficulty.

'Yes, I was,' said Thea.

'I am,' she amended.

They walked on.

She said she loved him. He knew, without knowing how, that he had no cause for mere physical jealousy. But he felt no relief. She said she loved the French fellow. What was he like? Nothing like me, he thought, since she doesn't like me.

The afternoon felt very hot, his bowler hat bound his brow, his collar was too tight. He walked in physical and mental discomfort.

But Thea felt a sort of ease. As if she had passed some of her pain to him, as if, by sharing it, he made it less. She realised that he, of all people, cared more vitally than anyone else what happened to her. He was, in fact, the only one who realised what she felt.

They emerged from the back alley into Byron Place. Thea, keeping her head steadily turned from him, looked into a garden as she passed and saw late lilies of the valley growing under the hedge. She remembered the last time she had seen lilies. In the wood. She remembered the dappled light and felt Jacques's fingers on hers. Tears stung her eyes and became acute embarrassment. Her gate was near now. She would have to turn as she went in and he would see them. She tried to blink them back, but it was no good. She was at the gate, she had to turn and let him see her face. Humbled by her own tears, she raised her eyes and smiled with shame to be caught crying.

A pang pierced him. His face changed. Unable to believe she was letting him take part in what she felt, that she would admit him, he smiled back. Not the smile of man to woman, but of one fellow creature to another. Then she turned away, and he closed the gate and went down to his own house.

II

No sooner had Thea cleared one hurdle, bruising herself in the process, than another was put up before her. The next morning there was a terse request from Miss Eardley that she should present herself at the High School at three o'clock that afternoon.

All morning Thea told herself that she wouldn't go. But habit was strong and at three o'clock she was obediently going in at the school gates, going through the cloakroom which, from the ranks of dark pendent coats and hats, looked like a place of mass suicide. She climbed the stairs. The pupils were collected into classrooms, the core of the school was hollow and empty. She came into the great hall, with its shining parquet and imposing organ behind the rostrum where prayers were read every morning. How different from the Pensionnat Jeanne d'Arc, how much cleaner, more orderly, correct and in consequence less picturesque.

'I won't disparage it,' she said to herself. 'It's a good school. But I've finished with it.'

She knocked on the familiar door. Miss Eardley's voice bade her enter, which, with fast-beating heart, she did.

'Ah, good afternoon. Sit down,' said Miss Eardley coldly.

Miss Eardley looked upon the affair at Villeneuve as vulgar in itself and as a grave defection on the part of an intelligent girl from whom she had, as she put it, expected great things.

'Well, Thea?' she said.

Here it was again. The middle-aged seemed to specialise in this opening, thought Thea. And it was clever of them, because there was no counter-move.

'I have a letter here from Mademoiselle Duchêne,' said Miss Eardley, touching some sheets of mauve paper covered in the

Directrice's spidery hand. 'But I am willing to hear your side of the story.'

She sat back, pressed the tips of her fingers judicially together and prepared to listen. She wished to be strictly fair. The girl must be heard.

'Tell me your version of the affair,' she said.

A vast reluctance overcame Thea.

'I don't want to,' she said.

Miss Eardley was startled. No one ever spoke to her like this.

'You don't want to?' she repeated.

Thea shook her head.

'I've nothing to say. I didn't do anything.' Here it was again.

'But surely you want to defend yourself against these most unpleasant charges?'

Thea shook her head again.

'But you must!' cried Miss Eardley.

'It's too late,' said Thea. 'I've been expelled. I've come home. I can't go back.'

'But you must explain to *me*,' said Miss Eardley. 'I must hear your side of the affair before I can decide whether or not you are a fit and proper person to be allowed to become a teacher.'

'But I'm not going to teach,' said Thea.

'You're not going to teach?' Miss Eardley was surprised again into echo. 'What about your degree?'

Thea shook her head. The long-cherished hope of a degree was certainly hard to relinquish.

'What is the reason for this incredible decision?' asked the headmistress.

Thea looked away.

'I've had enough of schools,' she said. 'I couldn't bear to put myself inside one again.'

'Because one schoolmistress may have shown herself harsh – I don't say she actually has – but suppose it, for the moment, are you, on her account, going to sacrifice a very promising career?'

'I'm not going to teach,' said Thea.

'Thea, listen to me,' said Miss Eardley with much earnestness.

The tables were turned indeed. Miss Eardley had begun by implying that Thea might not be allowed to become a teacher; she ended by pleading with her to become one.

But it was no use. Thea could not be moved. She kept to her stubborn determination to finish with all that had gone before.

'But no one will remember this against you. You're only a child, after all. You're attaching too much importance to the affair altogether.'

Thea shook her head.

'And don't you think it's time you thought of your mother?' said Miss Eardley sternly, veering to another point. 'How are you going to earn your living?'

Thea didn't know.

'Thea, I beg you . . .'

But it was no use. Thea sat pale, mute, mulishly determined.

'I am bitterly disappointed in you,' said Miss Eardley.

Thea got herself out at last. She backed out, rather like a cat evading detaining hands, and, Miss Eardley's reproaches in her ears, left the school.

She walked home up the long main road. The sun shone; it did not warm her spirit. Passing the houses, she was oppressed by the melancholy of glimpsed interiors; bottles of sauce standing on tables where they left the cloth on from one meal to the next: an old woman asleep with her mouth open; dressing-tables standing in upper windows looped with dirty curtains.

It doesn't matter so much what the eye falls on if the imagination and the heart supply their own images and affections, but Thea was at one of those dread stages in life when the secret spring that sustains the human spirit goes quite dry.

She reached home and found her mother in tears, fingering rolls of paper tied with pink tape, flat packets, curled bills and receipts.

'What are they?' asked Thea heavily.

'They're your father's papers,' said her mother. 'Mr Lockwood has sent them back. I'm to manage for myself in future.'

'Is there much to manage now?' asked Thea. 'And what there is, surely Martin can do it.'

'It's not that,' said Mrs Hunter, wiping her eyes. 'It's just that it's such a break after all these years.'

'Oh, Mother,' said Thea with compunction. 'If I'd thought what I was doing, I'd have tried not to do it. But I couldn't stand having all those things said to me without lashing out at her.'

'No, no, dear,' said Mrs Hunter, 'you couldn't. I quite understand. Don't think about it any more. Perhaps it will all come right some day. I'm just sorting these papers out. I don't think Martin will want to look at them yet and there's no need to. I'm afraid Martin is like me. He doesn't like papers.'

'These are what the French call "paperasses", and no wonder,' said Thea. 'Where are you going to put them?'

'Well, we used to keep them in that little bag you've got, but I daresay there's an empty hat box somewhere,' said Mrs Hunter. 'What did Miss Eardley say, dear?'

Thea was slightly startled. She had again an immense reluctance to discuss anything with anybody. But she struggled against it.

'It was more what I said, I'm afraid. I told her I wasn't going to teach.'

'You're not going to teach?' exclaimed her mother, her hands dropping to the table.

Thea shook her head.

'But, Thea, what are you going to do?' asked Mrs Hunter in alarm.

'I'll find some way of earning my living, Mother. Don't worry. You won't have to keep me long, I promise.'

'It's not a question of keeping you, dear. I wish you wouldn't put it like that,' said Mrs Hunter distressfully.

'Don't worry, Mother. Perhaps, as you say, it will all come right in the end. I'll go and make tea. You know tea always cheers you up.'

Mrs Hunter went on sorting the papers. Picking up and putting down the receipted promissory note Mr Lockwood had surrendered when he took over the paddock, Mrs Hunter reflected that in two days Thea had removed two props of the household: Mr Lockwood and Miss Eardley. The child seemed bent on ruining all her chances, and she had had so many more than the other two.

Of course, Mrs Hunter reflected, trying to count her blessings, it was providential that just as her annuity was coming to an end, Molly should be bringing such substantial sums of money into the house. But what, Mrs Hunter asked herself in the strictest secrecy, could be expected *socially* from a shop? No, it wasn't to Molly that her mother had looked to make the comeback of the Hunter family. Nor to Martin, whose progress at the bank was so slow as to be almost imperceptible. It was to Thea that Mrs Hunter had pinned her hopes. Thea had gone to France with the Lockwoods and Angela Harvey. She had had the chance to form a friendship with the very people who could do most for her.

During the lonely hours she spent in the house, Mrs Hunter had often cheered herself by thinking how nice it would be for Thea to be invited to luncheon and dinner at Firbank Hall and Oakfield, to be asked to tennis and taken to the dances. The Lockwoods and the Harveys would, her mother hoped, give Thea an entry to the world she had been born into, but kept out of since her father's death.

And Mrs Hunter had cherished the hope that the ultimate outcome of these dinners and dances would be that Thea would not, like poor Molly, have to work for her living, but would 'meet somebody'. . . .

But now all chance of that was ruined. Thea would never be invited to Oakfield again. She must work now, and yet, this afternoon, she had rejected the quite respectable, the often even highly-looked-up-to profession of schoolmistress. What could there be half so good for her now?

Wiping her eyes, Mrs Hunter went upstairs to look for a hat box to hold the unwelcome papers.

CHAPTER TWENTY-SIX

The Hunters had always maintained that they didn't know anybody, but it seemed to Thea now that they knew far too many people. Whenever she went out, alone or with her mother, there was always someone to stop her and exclaim: 'Have you come home?'

It was quite natural. People knew she had gone to France with the Lockwoods. The Lockwoods weren't due until the end of July; people wanted to know why Thea should be home in May. It was natural, but it filled Thea with irritation and disgust.

'Don't tell them anything, Mother,' she murmured as little Mrs Barrett and tall Miss Wood came towards them like a giraffe out with a small kangaroo.

Mrs Hunter swallowed nervously and looked as if she mightn't be able to help it.

'Oh, you're home, Thea,' exclaimed the friends. 'We *heard* you'd come home. Did you come home before the others then?'

When Thea admitted that she did, they still stood, expecting to be told why. Miss Wood peering down, Mrs Barrett looking up, they waited.

'Didn't it agree with you?' asked Mrs Barrett.

'Yes, thank you, it agreed with me,' said Thea.

They waited. Mrs Hunter couldn't stand the pause.

'Thea had a difference with the headmistress,' she said hurriedly. 'They haven't quite the same ideas in France as we have, you know.'

Mrs Barrett and Miss Wood longed to ask what sort of ideas Mrs Hunter referred to. They were dying to know. Their questions were forming on their eager lips when, coming to Thea's temporary rescue, the tram appeared round the corner of the Town Hall.

'The tram, Mother,' she said, drawing her mother away.

'Oh, yes, dear,' said Mrs Hunter with relief. 'Good morning.'

'Something fishy there,' said Mrs Barrett, sending a sharp glance up to Miss Wood.

'Decidedly,' said Miss Wood with satisfaction. 'What on earth can it be?'

By the time they met Thea and her mother again, they knew. They had heard the whole tale from Mrs Lockwood. They didn't stop the Hunters this time. They bowed and crossed the road. They knew all they wanted to know, and to talk to the Hunters would have been, they felt, a disloyalty to Mrs Lockwood. Besides, the girl had behaved in such a reprehensible fashion. Going into woods with a Frenchman! Those foreigners were so immoral, said Miss Wood and Mrs Barrett, never having met a foreigner in their lives. What young girls were coming to in these days, they simply didn't know, they said, enjoying dark conjectures with mid-morning coffee.

'Who are these people that I should mind what they think

or how they behave?' Thea asked herself haughtily. But the fact remained that she minded. She seethed with resentment and a consciousness of being treated with rank injustice. But she was helpless. She couldn't go about buttonholing every inhabitant of Aldworth to tell them that she hadn't 'done anything'. She couldn't put a notice in the paper. She had to put up with the cold-shouldering, but she was embittered.

She resented it not only for herself but for her mother. Though she did not realise it, her mother made her feel worse. It would have been easier if Mrs Hunter had been the sort of adult who could say: 'Never mind. They'll soon find something else to talk about.' But she wasn't. She was wounded and harassed. She shrank from unpleasantness, and since she couldn't go out without meeting curious stares, she tried to avoid going out at all.

Thea burned to get away from all these frets, to *do something*, as she said fiercely to herself in the little room over the front door where she spent her hours of unease. She had to find a job, but she was severely handicapped. She wasn't trained for a good one and wouldn't take a bad. She began to be alarmed by her inability to fit into the social scheme.

Once she had been full of large vague ideas about earning a living, but when she really came to consider the advertisement columns in the daily papers, these ideas dissolved like the insubstantial things they were. 'Visiting Corsetière', 'Bright young girl wanted for office', 'Companion for Elderly Lady', 'Nanny required, Baby in August', she read in despair.

She went to the Labour Exchange. When she went through the door labelled 'Women', she felt she lost her identity. She became one of a number of other females. 'Am I like these? Am I the same?' she wondered.

But a powerful woman, somehow reminiscent of a hippopotamus in a very large size of white silk blouse, the cuffs protected by enormous funnels of black patent-leather, evidently thought not. She singled Thea out and took her into a room apart where she strongly advised – everything about her was strong – the teaching of the mentally defective.

'Splendid openings there,' she said. 'In fact, here's the very job for you. Birmingham. Start on Monday.'

Her thick fingers negotiating a thin sheet of typescript, she read out details of board, lodging, laundry.

Thea thought of the poor distracted women from the Aldworth asylum being led out for a walk by a stout nurse in a blue cloak lined with red. She was full of pity for the women, but she couldn't take the nurse's place. She couldn't, she protested mutely.

'It's a very good job. I'm telling you and I know,' said the Labour Exchange official. 'The pay's much higher than the pay for ordinary teaching. We can settle it now. You'll take it?'

Thea rose and, making for the door, murmured something about having to think it over.

'Wait a minute,' called the woman. 'I can offer you an alternative.'

But Thea was gone. She hurried home with a hunted look. But though the woman sent literature relating to the teaching of the mentally defective after her, she did not arrive in Byron Place as Thea feared she would.

'Is there anything I could do at the shop?' she asked Molly

in desperation, and at once wished she hadn't. For a second Molly had hesitated. The shop was small; there was hardly room as it was for herself, Edie and the woman who did the washing up. She didn't know how Thea could be fitted in. But Thea immediately concluded that Molly didn't want her and hastily withdrew.

'No, I don't really want to go to the shop,' she said. 'If you don't mind keeping me a little longer, something is sure to turn up.'

Feeling far less Micawberish than she sounded, she went out of the room. She took her hat and went out into the street, laughing shakily. Something in her stood off and was amused by her own discomfiture. It seemed ironically funny that such things should be happening to her.

She went down the street, and when she was half-way down she saw Oliver Reade coming up. She wanted to turn back to avoid him, but she couldn't without being rude, and she no longer wished to be rude to him.

'Hello,' he said. 'Where are you going?' Then he thought he ought not to have asked; she might resent it.

'Nowhere,' she said. 'I'm just walking about.'

She sounded quiet, and she looked at him with the new look, consideringly. There was no doubt that the affair in France had hit her pretty hard; the proud girl was changed.

'Will you walk back with me then?' he asked hopefully, and she turned. 'There's something I've been wanting to ask you,' he began.

She turned swiftly towards him. Not about France, flashed her startled eyes.

'It's only,' he stammered, 'that I wondered if you'd come and have a look at my warehouse some time.'

Her face changed and she laughed. He didn't know why.

'All right,' she said. 'When?'

'Well, any time,' he said, unable to believe his luck. 'Now, if you like.'

'All right.'

She didn't in the least want to go to his warehouse, but she would go as she would have gone with a child who wanted to show her his toy. In her own heaviness, the thought of giving pleasure to somebody, anybody, was a relief. Let somebody be happy at any rate, she thought.

As they walked through the hot streets, she wished they had waited until it was cooler. It was far too hot to come into this part of the town. Dust lay inert in swathes on the pavements, men lounged unbuttoned in the doorways, women clattered about in clogs doing their housework after the day in the mill. Overhead the summer sky blazed and Thea, looking up between the houses, remembered the round burnt-umber tower of the cathedral soaring into the sky over Villeneuve. On many such an evening as this – the heat came sooner there – she had stood at the attic window looking over the old roofs and thinking of Jacques. His face sprang, vigorous, handsome, into her mind.

She looked at the man beside her. His face half-turned away, he smiled down indulgently on the children playing some hopping game over squares on the pavement.

'I used to play that when I was a kid,' he said. 'And not far from here, too. Gas Street is quite near here.'

'Gas Street,' she said. 'What an awful name!'

'It's an awful street,' he said. 'Here's my warehouse.' He unlocked a door and they stepped through into a barn-like place lit by skylights through which the sun had poured all day drawing out the smell of harsh new carpets, sticky new linoleum, new varnish, new cotton goods. Thea advanced into the heat and the smell, looking about at the merchandise gathered into heaps and rolls, stored into shelves, set out on trestle tables covered with protective sheets.

Oliver, starting on his collection of carpets, turned back one after another from the pile on the floor.

'Not bad, that,' he said, displaying an ochre rug.

'This is rather nice, isn't it?' he said, turning up a brown and blue Brussels carpet.

'And here you see,' he said, moving briskly to the shelves, 'I've got a consignment of children's sandshoes. Holidays coming, you know. Bathing suits here. Boys' drawers,' he said, picking out bundles and putting them back again. 'China over there. Job lots, but they go.'

He went to a trestle table and ran nimbly back with the dustsheet, revealing such a collection of rubbish that Thea marvelled he should think it worth covering up. She stood looking down at it. Among the Kewpie dolls with prominent stomachs, the bathing belles, the pot dogs, cats, birds, horses, the money boxes, biscuit boxes, celluloid flowers, there was a card of crucifixes, the figure of Christ blurred, mass-produced. She picked the card up and all the crucifixes swung.

'Yes, those'll sell,' said Oliver. 'They're a novelty. They're luminous. They shine in the dark.'

'Don't you like them?' he asked anxiously as she laid the card down. 'What's wrong?' he asked.

She moved off round the table. She burned with a sudden anger.

'Did Jesus die so that people could tack Him on their bedroom walls, so that when they waked in the night they could see Him hanging there and think: "That's neat. That's a novelty"?'

He stared at her in silence.

'I didn't think of it like that,' he said, and was silent again.

'But I don't see that I have to think of it like that,' he said, rallying. 'These things are made in hundreds. I didn't make them. People buy them. If they don't buy them from me, they'll buy them from somebody else. I don't have to think why they buy. I only have to think what they buy. As a matter of fact,' he charged her, 'you don't like any of the stuff, do you?'

She shook her head.

He stood looking round at the goods he had so busily and cannily accumulated. He stood with one fist on the table, the other doubled on his hip.

'Nay, come,' he said. 'It's not as bad as all that.'

But she would not soften towards it, and her attitude mattered to him. Part of her fascination was that she was different from him. She saw things from a different angle and the angle fascinated him as well as she herself. Her point of view often galled him, but it stimulated him too.

'They'll all sell,' he said.

'More's the pity,' said Thea, but smiling in mitigation.

'Don't say that. I've got my living to make. I give the public what it wants. You can't blame me.'

'Can't you try to make it want something better by choosing better things to put before it?' asked Thea, who had never considered buying and selling before and had to formulate views she didn't know she had.

'Nay, I'm not out to educate people. I haven't time. I'm out to sell this stuff and get a lot more and sell that. Besides, if you'll allow me to say so, I know better than you what these people want. Because I'm one of them. My taste, looked down on by you, is no better than theirs. It *is* theirs – and that's my advantage.'

He looked at her challengingly.

'You don't mean to say you think that's a good colour or a good design,' said Thea, roused, pointing to the topmost rug whereon pinwheels and snakes were imposed in violent green and magenta on an ochre ground.

'It's clean and it's new,' said Oliver Reade firmly. 'When you've lived with everything old and shabby about you, the first thing you ask is that what you are buying shall be clean and new.'

'But if it had been a plain colour, with a border, it would still have been clean and new, wouldn't it?'

'Ah – but it would have been dear. You can't get good colours in cheap things.'

'Why? That's what seems so awful. Why?' She sighed and went on round the table. 'It's sad that you, with all your energy, should be spending it in buying up and distributing things like this. It's sad so many of us have to get our livings in ways that aren't half good enough.'

'It's enough for me at the moment that I *am* getting my

living,' he said. 'And it's a better living every day. I don't much mind how I get it so long as I get it.'

'Oh, you do,' she protested.

'Not I. I don't,' he said pugnaciously.

'Well, I do,' she said. 'I can't bring myself to do anything I don't like.'

'By gum, if you were a man you couldn't be so squeamish,' he said. 'Life's a scramble. It's mostly a question of getting in before the other chap, or doing the other chap down before he can do you.'

'It's all so ugly,' she said.

'Well, speaking for myself,' he said, drawing the cover over the collection on the table, 'I quite enjoy it.'

She burst out laughing.

'I do,' he insisted, laughing himself.

She walked to the door and he followed her, carefully locking up the place she despised.

On the way home, she found herself telling him how hard it was to find a job. It was much easier to talk to him than to her family.

'Can't you give French lessons for a start?' he asked.

'I suppose I could.'

'It must be nice to speak French,' he said wistfully.

'I'll teach you French if you like,' she offered. 'For nothing, of course,' she added hurriedly. 'You've been so good to Molly.'

'I can't speak my own language yet,' he said, saying nothing about the classes at the Technical School. 'You'd better teach me English first.'

'I don't think I dare teach English.'

'That's funny,' said Oliver, his heavy-lidded eyes sliding sideways in amusement. 'You go to France for a few months and feel prepared to teach French, but you daren't teach the language you've been speaking all your life.'

She laughed. She had laughed oftener in the last hour than in all the time since she came home; but she didn't know it.

'Are you coming in?' she said when she reached her gate.

He caught his breath at the invitation.

'Well, just for a minute perhaps,' he said.

They went into the front room where Mrs Hunter was resting on the sofa by the open window.

'How is your head now, Mother?' asked Thea, who felt she was the cause of all her mother's headaches, these days.

'Better, dear, thank you,' said Mrs Hunter, greeting Oliver Reade.

'Funny, but I've got a headache, too,' he said. 'A thing I can't remember when I had last.'

Mrs Hunter was all concern. Headaches were her special province.

'You must have one of my powders,' she said, rising from the sofa. 'I'll get one for you and Thea will make some tea. The kettle's on, Thea; it should be boiling. Your headache will be gone in a few moments, Mr Reade.'

'Nay,' protested Oliver. 'I sell patent medicines, I admit, but I don't reckon to take them.'

'This isn't a patent medicine,' said Mrs Hunter with mild indignation. 'It's a powder made up from my father's prescription. I've taken these powders for years. They're wonderful. You'll take one to please me, won't you?'

'Well, I don't suppose it'll kill me,' he said indulgently.

'It will cure you,' said Mrs Hunter, going upstairs.

Thea came in with the teatray, Mrs Hunter came down with the powder. He sat, with simplicity, being waited on. Mrs Hunter folded the little paper crossways and handed it to him. Thea handed his tea. He tipped the powder down his throat and swallowed some tea.

'Now your headache will disappear as if by magic,' prophesied Mrs Hunter, returning to the sofa.

He sat facing her and the light, and she thought what a healthy fellow he looked and how blue his eyes were.

After the hot streets it was cool in the room. The tea was refreshing. He had a sense of peace sitting with Thea and her mother. He felt carefully about in his mind for topics of conversation. He didn't want to break upon the atmosphere with anything harsh. In fact, he would have liked best to sit and say nothing, but feared it would not be the thing. So he searched for topics. But they were difficult. There were so many he dare not touch upon. France, for instance. The year she had been away yawned like an abyss; he must keep away from the edge.

Since there were no topics at hand, he went after them. After two cups of tea, he got up and moved about the room. He looked at the framed sketches, done in white chalk on rough blue paper. They were of such ruined ruins that he didn't know what they were. Broken pillars and such.

'My husband did those in Greece,' said Mrs Hunter.

'He could draw, couldn't he?' said Oliver admiringly, wondering nevertheless why he hadn't drawn something whole.

He examined the books on the shelves and picked out at random one small battered volume. He looked into it. The illustrations surprised him. Hastily he put the book back. *Sentimental Journey* it was called, but it looked more bawdy than sentimental to him.

This wandering in search of topics seemed full of pitfalls, so he sat down again.

'I don't know what to put it down to,' he said, 'but my headache's gone.'

'There!' exclaimed Mrs Hunter triumphantly. 'What did I tell you?'

'Mmm,' he said. 'Must be good stuff. It certainly does the trick.'

He sat at the table, looking out of the window. His headache had gone, the depression he had felt because she didn't like his warehouse or his goods had gone with it. There were other ways of making money. Many other ways.

Like a fisherman on a placid evening, he cast about pleasurably and lazily in his mind as over a well-stocked lake. He was sure of bringing up an idea sooner or later.

CHAPTER TWENTY-SEVEN

Next morning it was raining. Molly and Martin left the house. Thea took up her mother's tray and came to the table to have her own breakfast, which she took French fashion, a bowl of coffee and a piece of bread. Neither tasted as it had done in Villeneuve; she couldn't think why.

In the dark little dining room, the window was open. After the heat of the previous day, the rain was delicious, even in Aldworth, even in the back yard. Thea, looking down the 'Situations Vacant' column, lifted her head to listen to the patter of the rain on the leaves of the little ash tree.

'O doux chant de la pluie, par terre et sur les toits.' Jeanne and she had liked that.

The front door bell rang shrilly. Every time the bell rang, it set her heart in a commotion. Although she knew he hadn't her address and couldn't get it, she could not cure herself of expecting a letter from Jacques. Worse, she couldn't cure herself of expecting him in person. She kept thinking that surely one day, when she opened the door, he would be there. She sprang up now, ran into the passage and threw open the door.

On the step stood Oliver Reade, his damp dark hair on end. He had shaved, he had taken the cold bath he had trained himself to since he came to the house in Byron Place and had a bathroom, but in his haste he had forgotten his hair.

'I say,' he burst out, 'I know I'm early, but can I come in?'

Rapidly readjusting herself to the sight of one man when she had hoped for another, Thea led the way into the front room, regretting her hot coffee.

'I've got a scheme,' he said, and bringing her attention fully to bear upon him, she saw that he was in a state of excitement, his eyes were wide and alert, he jingled money furiously in both trouser pockets.

'Can you spare time to hear about it? I hope so because it concerns you as well as me, and your mother, too. Is she about?'

'Not yet,' said Thea in mystification. 'Is it urgent? Shall I tell her?'

'Not yet,' he said. 'Let her be for a bit. Till I've told you. You sit down. It'll take time.'

'Won't you sit down, too?' said Thea, taking a chair beside the table. Evidently her coffee must go cold.

'No, I'd rather walk about,' he said.

'But there's no room.'

'I'll make room.' He thrust the furniture aside and began to pace between sofa and door. 'That headache powder,' he said, mystifying Thea still further. 'It worked wonders on me. I was free from pain in a few minutes. We must time it. In the night it suddenly flashed across me that I'd put it on the market.'

Thea stared incredulously.

'But can you?'

'Of course I can. Anyone can put anything on the market. Any dam' thing. Nothing to stop you or me or anybody else making up any old thing, so long as it's not harmful, in any old back parlour and selling it without restrictions.'

Thea, her eyes upon him, took this in.

'But it oughtn't to be allowed,' she said.

'Well, it is, and don't let's bother about that,' said Oliver Reade, pacing. 'Besides there's nothing to bother about in this case. The powder's a good honest painkiller. And I want you to help me sell it.'

Thea's eyes flew wide.

'Me?'

'You. I'm going to use those rooms over the shop for it, and I want you, if you'll agree, to be there to answer the telephone, write the letters, write the adverts – because you'll know what to say and I shan't. Least, I shall know what to say, but not how to say it. I want you even, till we get on our feet, to weigh out the powders, which I shall get made up in bulk by my pal, Daw, the chemist, and fold 'em into the little papers. Pack 'em, in short. Salary to be two pounds a week until we can afford more, and your mother, seeing the prescription's hers, to have a small percentage of sales, say two-and-a-half per cent for ever.'

If he had been a conjurer presenting himself in the front room in the morning to produce rabbits out of a hat, Thea could not have been more astonished.

She gazed at him, her eyes following him backwards and forwards, backwards and forwards.

'Noll's got one of his ideas,' Edie was saying to Molly at the shop. 'There'll be no holding him till he's made something of it.'

'If it's as good as this one . . .' said Molly, taking tarts from the oven.

'It'll probably be better,' said Edie confidently. 'He generally goes one better every time.'

At half-past ten, Oliver Reade was still pacing the front room. The breakfast table was still uncleared, the beds were unmade, no sweeping, dusting, cooking done. Mrs Hunter, after sitting in gentle incomprehension for some time, withdrew to 'see to one or two things'.

It was certainly very kind of Mr Reade to say she must have two-and-a-half per cent, though why such an odd figure, why a half, Mrs Hunter couldn't think. There was no reason why he should pay her anything. He was very welcome to the prescription if it was of any use to him, and it was nice to think she wouldn't have to pay for her headache powders any more. The provision of personal powders was what Mr Reade called one of her 'perks', whatever those might be.

The best feature of the scheme was the fact that it provided work and a salary for Thea. The child would be so much better for having something to do, though it was work no one would have chosen for her before the unfortunate affair at Villeneuve. Mrs Hunter wasn't sure that it was quite the thing for Thea to be shut up in an office with a young man all day. But her sister was below, reflected Mrs Hunter, her mind furnishing her with mild pros only to furnish her with equally mild cons, as she pursued a vague search for a pudding through several cookery books.

In the front room, Thea was still sitting at the table, her chin on her hand, her eyes on Oliver Reade. She was filling the feminine rôle of listening, and the equally feminine rôle of secretly wondering at him and summing him up. That all this energy and ingenuity should be brought to bear on a headache powder! If only it had been something really worthwhile. . .

'Advertise, advertise, advertise,' he was saying, walking up and down. 'I've got so little capital. Though I know where I can get some money. I'll have to make up for lack of capital by personal drive. I'll have to force it on the chemists. If only Woolworths would take it, I'd be made. And Boots. Think of that. Never mind,' he said more to himself than her, 'I'll get it on this town and then on the county and then on the country. You'll see.'

He laughed with pleasure at the fight before him. Then sobering suddenly, he came to lean over the table. His face was directly above hers.

'Don't touch me,' her eyes warned.

'The name, Thea. The name is vitally important.'

'Yes,' she said. 'Yes, it is.'

'Thea, will you let me call the powder by your name? It's a lovely name. It suits you,' he said, looking down into her eyes.

'But it doesn't suit headache powders,' said Thea hurriedly. 'And what's to stop you putting stomach powders on the market next, as an extension? I'm flattered, but let's think of something else.'

'I think "Thea Headache Powders" sounds first-rate,' he urged. 'I'd like to blaze your name all over the world.'

'I'd rather you didn't,' said Thea. 'Not like that. I'm certain we'll be able to think of a good name. Give me till tonight. I'll think all day and you think, too, and come back and we'll pool our ideas.'

He went at last. Making her bed belatedly, Thea reflected that she was now committed to packing powders and writing advertisements in the room over the shop. It was a great relief to be about to keep herself instead of being kept by her family. She was grateful to Oliver Reade, and if she felt that the furthering of the sales of headache powders had little to do with the purpose of her life, and if all that was going on around her and within her at present seemed a bad dream, a dream where you thought you were crying all the time, nothing of that should appear. She would do her best. She would earn the money he would pay her. And to begin with she must find a name.

Finishing her bed, covering it with the faded counterpane, folding the flaccid eiderdown, which lost a little more colour and substance with each successive year, she hunted for a pencil and paper and stood at the chest of drawers, waiting for a name to suggest itself.

Only the most absurd did. Turning her notice for the first time upon them, a flock of silly names trooped out like lunatics she had unsuspectingly harboured for some time. 'Koodoo.' 'Wagman.' 'Poritanian.'

To escape from them she went downstairs.

'Mother, can *you* think of a name for the powders?'

'Well, dear, there used to be some called "Daisy",' said Mrs Hunter, not very helpfully, and could make no further suggestion.

Mrs Hunter told Martin about Oliver Reade's scheme while Thea was bringing in lunch, and Thea looked anxiously towards him for his comment.

It seemed as if Martin was coming round a little. Not much, but a little. And although she still thought he was unjust and unkind, she couldn't help trying to bring him round altogether. She wanted him to be as he was before she went to France. She couldn't bear these strained relations between them.

'I don't suppose anything will come of it,' he said, slicing the ham Molly had cooked for them at the shop. 'Reade's full of madcap ideas.'

'Can you think of a name for the powders, Martin?' asked Thea.

'No, I can't,' he said and didn't try.

Oliver Reade arrived after lunch and went into the front room.

'Well?' they asked simultaneously.

'I haven't got anything possible yet,' said Thea. 'What have you got?'

'Only one or two, but I don't know what you'll think of them,' he said, glancing at a scrap of paper in the palm of his hand. He could hardly be persuaded to disclose it, and when he did, blushed at the back of his neck.

'Cureyew. Instanter. Presto. Surething,' she read and laughed up into his face.

'You're nearly as bad as I am. Not quite, but near enough to comfort me. I daren't show mine.'

'Nay, come on. Fair do's. Let's see 'em.'

'No, no. I'll try again . . .'

But he snatched, and as the crazy list met his eye, he roared with laughter. Mrs Hunter came to see what the matter was and getting no coherent reply to her mild queries, went away again.

Martin, leaving the house, thought: 'Is she at the same game again?'

Still laughing, Thea conducted Oliver to the door, promising to sober up and produce something better by suppertime.

'I think I've got something,' she said, going to meet him as he came through the gate that evening. 'I got on to French words, and suddenly I hit on "Guerison", which means cure, but it's an English word, too, isn't it? How d'you like the sound of "Guerison",' she asked, showing a slip of paper whereon she had printed the word as neatly as possible.

'"Guerison. . . Guerison"'. He tasted the word, rolled it over, looking out of the window, trying it again. '"Guerison". By gum, I believe you've got it. I think I like it. It's got style. And it'll do for any powders at all, not only headache. Thea, you've done a good day's work for me today. It's a name I could never have got for myself. You see how education comes in? I'll sleep on "Guerison", but I bet it sounds as good tomorrow. Now can you start work in the morning? We ought to get that room ship-shape as soon as possible. I've been with Daw all afternoon.'

CHAPTER TWENTY-EIGHT

I

So 'Guerison' made its appearance. Through the summer days, Oliver Reade and his assistants peddled powders from chemist to chemist, from street to street, village to village, town to town, and Thea worked in the room over the shop.

This proved, unexpectedly, to be a haven to which she daily escaped with relief. The room smelled, from the new filing cabinets, of dried beans left too long to soak; it smelled too of toffee and gingerbread. Its two sash windows overlooked the rigid, unlovely set-out of Wells Road. But it was a refuge and Thea had it mostly to herself. She was having a respite, though it could only be brief since, at the end of July, the Lockwoods would come home and stir everything up again.

But for hours together she forgot the Lockwoods as she pored over one of her father's books, choosing the lettering for display cards and boxes, teaching herself to type on a second-hand machine, writing letters, advertisements, pamphlets to submit to Oliver Reade when he came in at the end of the day.

Oliver Reade was fully aware of the piquancy of the situation. That she who had looked down upon him, snubbed him, kept him at a distance should now be at his beck and call, should ask what he wanted her to do, try to please and help him, was a bewildering turn of events. It might be pleasant – it was – but it felt all wrong. He couldn't get used to it.

Outside – with chemists, grocers, haberdashers – he persuaded the most unlikely people that they ought to have Guerison powders on the counters – he knew what he was doing, he was on his own ground. But returning to the office at the end of the day, he wondered extremely to find himself dictating letters, looking at her dark head bowed over the notebook, her pencil putting down his words. Thea sometimes looked up to find him with an expression of blank incredulity on his face.

They were both naïvely new to their rôles. When he gave her her first wages, she blushed with pleasure. But after a few moments, she came to his elbow as he stood at the high desk and said diffidently:

'Are you sure you can spare it?'

His heart filled with tenderness. He smiled and told her she was worth every penny.

'You're too good for this job,' he told her.

'So are you,' she said.

'I'm the rough stuff,' he said. 'You're the style. I couldn't write letters like that, or put out showcards like that. You've got such good taste.'

'You do all the hard work.'

'Who'd have thought you and I would come to form a mutual admiration society?' he teased.

She no longer disliked him, he knew, but she was no nearer being in love with him. He often looked at her from under his hand, wondering if she was beginning to forget the French fellow yet, or if she ever would. When the desire to find out became too pressing, he went out to do some more tramping about. To Thea, he seemed indefatigable. No matter how tired or despondent he was at the end of the day, by the beginning of the next he had renewed himself and set out again, fresh and hopeful.

Thea's wages gave her great satisfaction. She gave up one pound as her contribution to the household and insisted on refunding ten shillings a week to Molly for her loan. There was only ten shillings left for herself, but this remnant seemed exciting and quite unlike any other ten shillings. She said something of the sort to Martin in one of her attempts to regain their old footing.

But Martin, tightening his upper lip, remarked that if she had had the sense to take her degree, she would one day have been in receipt of much more than two pounds a week. Then he went out. It seemed to cost him a good deal to say these things. He didn't seem to like saying them; but he went on making himself do it.

He was evasive, elusive and always going out, getting away. On these summer evenings he went to tennis. In the house they slaved for him as women will for the sole male. They saw to it that his tennis things were always ready, his socks, shirts, sweaters washed and ironed; and his white flannels sent to the laundry week by week, though none of their things went.

Martin played tennis well; so did Thea. He had said that when she came home from France he would make her a member of his club and they would play in tournaments together. But nothing had come of this.

Sometimes, after being cooped up all day in the room over the shop, Thea longed for activity of some kind. She wanted to do as other girls did; play tennis, dance, go out in a car or swim. But evening after evening was the same. She left the shop and walked home. She had supper, washed up, and walked as far as the park. She came back to sit on the sofa to read, or more often to stare out of the window into the darkening street. The melancholy of empty summer evenings ached within her.

One evening, she could bear it no longer. She was sitting on the sofa when Martin came into the room in search of his pipe. She looked at him, immaculate in white, his racquet under his arm, his thumb pressing tobacco into the bowl of the pipe.

'I thought you said you'd take me to tennis when I came home from France,' she said with a quaver in her voice.

He turned and looked at her in genuine surprise.

'Good lord, I didn't think you'd want to come *now*,' he said
'What d'you mean "now"?'

'Well – surely you'd rather the talk died down before you appear at a place like the club?'

'As if I've done anything,' she said, biting her lip, which trembled. 'It's all so unfair. I haven't done anything.'

'It doesn't much matter whether you've done anything or not,' he said. 'If people think you have, they'll talk.'

There was silence in the room for a moment. Thea's heart swelled so that she couldn't speak.

'I didn't ask you to come because it didn't occur to me that you would want to. But you can come now, this minute, if you like,' he said.

Thea shook her head.

'No thanks, I don't want to go really,' she said. 'You needn't have been afraid to ask me,' she added. 'I wouldn't have gone.'

'Come on,' he said, almost like his old self.

She shook her head.

'All right,' he said, with his eyebrows up. 'Please yourself.'

He went out. She heard the soft padding of his rubber shoes dying away down the street. Tears welled into her eyes. She rushed upstairs to the room over the front door, and for the first time since she had come home, she wept. Face downwards on the bed, she sobbed into her eiderdown, making a dark stain of tears.

When she had cried herself out, dusk had thickened in the street, in the house. She stole to the bathroom to bathe her eyes.

'There's no one,' she said to herself; 'no one to understand here.'

Standing at the basin, she pressed the cold sponge to her burning eyelids.

'Except Oliver Reade,' she said. She had to be reasonable. She wouldn't make it worse than it was.

'He's kind,' she admitted.

II

Thea knew that the end of the summer term at Villeneuve must be approaching and with it the end of her respite. The Lockwoods should be home any time now. She looked out for them, her eyes and ears alert for a sight or a rumour of them. But the days went on and they seemed not to have come.

Then suddenly in church on Sunday morning, as she got up from hiding her face briefly in her gloves on entering, she saw them filing into their pew. She turned sharply away and pretended to busy herself with the prayer books Martin was handing to her.

Her heart thumped. They had come, her enemies were on her track again. When the congregation stood for the entrance of the choir and clergy, she looked again.

Her face lit at once with scornful amusement. The twins looked ridiculous. They looked quite as absurd as even she could wish. They must have rigged themselves up in Paris, and at the wrong places. They looked quite thirty from the way their hair was scraped up and from the flowered toques posed on top. Their coats and skirts were matronly in the extreme. Their faces were made up with heavy sophistication, with eye-shadow like the French models in the old fashion plates. Playing at it again, thought Thea scornfully.

Clare had not suffered such treatment at the hands of the French shops. Although her pink organdie was more suited to a garden party than a church service, she looked charming. Clare always looked pretty when she was happy and she was obviously happy now, standing beside her father. To come home had been enough for her to recover her looks.

Across the aisle, Thea saw Angela Harvey with her parents. She was quite unfurbished in a grey coat and skirt and was looking round the church with interest, her prayer book drooping in her hand. Looking at her, Thea felt a pang. She had once hoped to be Angela's friend, but Angela didn't need a friend; she didn't really need anybody.

These people had just left Villeneuve. They had been where Jacques was; they might even be able to tell her something about him if she could have asked. They could give her news of Jeanne and the little ones. But of course she could never ask.

She lost her place in the service and found herself standing when everyone else knelt. Hastily she reached for her hassock and buried her face in her hands, but not to pray. Her thoughts were on the Lockwoods. She took herself to task about them.

'Why should I mind about them? They're so *ordinary*. If they were really enviable, if they were beautiful, or charming, or talented, if I wanted to be like them, there would be some excuse for me. But they're completely ordinary and I don't want to be like them or be in their place at all.'

'It's probably because Mother tried to impress upon us when we were little that they were important and mattered enormously, and I suppose I've been shocked to be finding out ever since that they aren't important at all, or shouldn't be.'

She looked sideways at the probable author of the trouble beside her. Mrs Hunter's face rested on her clasped hands, her eyelids fluttered in an effort to keep them closed, her lips moved with the Vicar's. Her face was defenceless and touching, and Thea was filled with compunction.

When she stood up and looked towards the Lockwoods again, Clare was smiling up at her father and he was smiling down at her. Thea was unwilling to witness this interchange of affection. She didn't want any evidence that the Lockwoods were human. She turned her head and found Martin looking intently at Clare. She was startled by the change in his face; he looked all at once as if he had come to life. His face was tender, half-smiling. With a pang she remembered how fond he and Clare had been of each other in childhood. It would be too much if anything like that were to start again, she thought. Nothing could come of it for Martin.

'Oh, I do hope they won't fall in love,' she thought with apprehension.

In a moment she was acutely engaged with the problem of getting out of church without meeting the Lockwoods. If she had dared, she would have gone out during the last hymn, but convention kept her where she was. The blessing pronounced by the invisible Vicar, the congregation rose raggedly from its knees. Thea, seizing her gloves, waited in agitation for her mother to precede her from the pew. Mrs Hunter was a long time about it and when Thea at last plunged into the aisle it was thronged. When she saw she couldn't hurry, she tried to hang back, but that was equally impossible. She was borne along at a fixed snail-pace and an inexorable fate carried the Hunters into the porch at exactly the same moment as the Lockwoods. Thea was thrust, in spite of herself, into the very bosom of the twins. They closed their eyes at her and turned their toques away and everybody saw. Mrs Lockwood bowed with elaborate coldness to Mrs Hunter. Mr Lockwood took no notice of anyone. The throng pushed them all on and ejected them down the steps, where, no longer jammed together, they could at last detach themselves.

But behind in the porch, Clare's pink hat brushed Martin's shoulder. She turned her radiant face up to his.

'Glad to be home?' he whispered.

'Oh, I am,' she said. 'Nothing will ever induce me to go away again.'

'Good,' he said.

They smiled at each other. Then they in their turn were out in the air and parted.

Thea burned. She hated the Lockwoods. She hated it that her mother should look so crushed by Mrs Lockwood's cool bow. She hated it that her brother should respond to Clare's smiles. She wanted to rush home fast, without speaking to anyone. But she had to subdue herself to walking gently with her mother up the long road home. Martin had seen a man he knew and gone off with him.

Mrs Hunter made a few safe remarks, and Thea disciplined herself to reply with patience. They didn't mention the Lockwoods. Mrs Hunter grieved silently. She would so have liked to tell Mrs Lockwood how glad she was she had her daughters at home again. These harshnesses between old friends were sad and unnecessary, she felt. She also felt they were uncivilised and unlike the old days in Guildford. She couldn't remember that they had ever, in those days, had what she thought of as a wrong word with anybody.

CHAPTER TWENTY-NINE

I

And now, a swan with cygnets, Mrs Lockwood breasted the full tide of prosperity and contentment. Her brood restored, she was to be seen in the street, in the shops, at the theatre, the concerts and in church. Wherever there was anything going on, public or private, the Lockwoods were sure to be.

Their pride of place could only have been disputed by the Harveys, and the Harveys were not often at Firbank in these days. The time had come for Lady Harvey to launch her difficult daughter upon the world and there was a shortage of suitable young men in Aldworth.

With every year, the number of eligible young men decreased. Sons showed a growing disinclination to go into their fathers' mills. After public school and university, many were never seen in their native town again; they entered the services and professions and were dispersed over the face of Britain and the world. To take Angela about in Aldworth would be, to Lady Harvey, like giving a performance to empty stalls.

Pit and gallery might be packed and appreciative, but it was the stalls that mattered to Lady Harvey.

Not so much to the Lockwoods. Mr and Mrs Lockwood took it for granted that their daughters would marry some day but the longer that day was in coming the happier the fond parents would be. In the meantime, they would all make the most of their time together. William and Effie determined, in their bedroom talks, to give their girls the best of everything while they had them.

'Because we perhaps shan't have them long,' said Effie.

'Don't talk like that,' said William sharply.

The more the Lockwoods were in evidence, the less were the Hunters. It was enough for the Lockwoods to be in a street or a shop for the Hunters to be out of it. The Lockwoods swam about, leaving an unpleasant backwash for the Hunters to negotiate. Thea felt the recrudescence of curiosity and everybody, she thought, must have heard the Lockwood version of the affair at Villeneuve by this time. She knew she was pointed out wherever she went. She almost felt the nudge in her own ribs when one said to another, 'That's the girl. . . .'

People stared at her. Some with admiration; some thought she was very pretty, some said she didn't look that sort of girl at all. But Thea didn't discriminate between the kinds of stare. All stares were unwelcome and bitterly resented by her.

Mrs Lockwood had postponed the annual Garden Fête until her daughters should be home, but now it was announced, and Mrs Hunter shed tears in secret to think that, for the first time since its inauguration fifteen years before, she would not be able to go.

But one member of the Hunter family was there. He himself said nothing about it, but the next morning Thea, in the room over the shop, opening the local paper, found, among the photographs of the Fête, one of Clare with Martin behind her.

Abruptly, Thea got up from the desk and took the paper down to Molly who had her hands in the pastry and could only lean sideways to see what was pointed out to her with indignation so acute that it was silent.

'Oh,' said Molly. 'So Martin was there, was he? Isn't it a good photograph?'

Thea looked at her with amazement. Didn't she see the disloyalty, the betrayal? The Lockwoods were cutting his sister, and practically cutting his mother, and yet he would go to their house?

'Surely you don't think he should have gone?'

Molly looked up in surprise. Thea hadn't brought down the paper just as a matter of interest then? No, she hadn't. Molly saw now that she was upset.

'I shouldn't bother about it, love,' she said soothingly.

That was always Molly's advice nowadays. Because it didn't matter to Molly, Molly thought it couldn't matter to Thea. Molly didn't care about the Lockwoods any more. 'Don't bother about them,' she said. It was good advice, but Thea couldn't take it.

She took the paper upstairs and brooded over the picture of Martin and Clare. Were the Lockwoods going to add another crime to their list and take her brother from her?

It soon became obvious that they were. The Lockwoods

were short of young men for their tennis parties and Martin played well. Thea was dumbfounded to see the Lockwoods annex Martin as calmly as if he were entirely unrelated to his mother and sister. How Martin explained the situation to himself, she could not imagine. He made no attempt to explain it to anyone else.

II

So it was Martin, not Thea, who entered the fashionable world and became persona grata at Oakfield. He was fully conscious of the humiliation it entailed, but he would put up with anything, everything, he determined, to be near Clare.

Mrs Lockwood herself encouraged him to come to Oakfield. The girls had to have a young man from somewhere. Popular though they were, and she had no doubt about that – it was nevertheless true that three of them were apt to overbalance any party. When they could take a young man with them, it was very different, she told William. Martin made a useful and personable escort and they must just ignore the fact that his sister had disgraced herself and been intolerably rude into the bargain. The poor boy couldn't help what his sister had done, said Mrs Lockwood, and they ought not, because of her, to deprive him of all the pleasure he could have at Oakfield.

William was at first very doubtful of the advisability of letting such a penniless young man come to the house.

'Effie,' he warned, 'we can't have this boy falling in love with any of our girls. There mustn't be anything of that kind, you know.'

'Of course not,' said Effie reassuringly. 'There won't be.'

'But Clare's enough to turn any man's head,' said William. 'And this boy won't do, you know. He hasn't a cent and never will have. Clare could marry an earl. Not that we want her to, but she certainly can't marry a bank clerk. You'd better speak to her and make it clear from the start what terms that boy comes on, if he's to come at all.'

'That would be most unwise,' said Effie. 'It would just put the idea into her head. Girls are so romantic. If you tell them they can't have a particular young man, that's the one they're certain to want. Leave them alone. I'll keep an eye on them. Clare and he are too used to each other to fall in love. Besides, he'd never presume. On three pounds a week? Of course he wouldn't.'

Mrs Lockwood flattered herself that she fully understood the feelings of a young man who found himself among people with much more money than he had. *She* knew Martin's difficulties, she said to herself, and took him into the drawing room one evening after tennis.

He was suddenly apprehensive. He thought she must have noticed something.

'Now, Martin,' she said, settling herself in a plump armchair, 'there's something you and I must settle.'

A pulse beat noticeably in his temple, but he looked steadily at her. His hair was rough from the game, his shirt open at the neck and she was glad now of the Hunter distinction because it made it nice for the girls to have this personable, and harmless, young man as an escort. Her heart quite warmed towards him.

'Martin,' she said, 'it costs quite a lot of money to take three girls about. Far more than a young man like you can afford. We are very glad for you to go with the girls, but we don't want you to be out of pocket by it, so we propose to pay for you just as if you were the girls' brother.'

Martin reddened. He was embarrassed. But she was right. He couldn't afford to take three girls out; on his salary, he couldn't even afford to take Clare out, except perhaps once or twice a week to the cinema, if she would go.

'I certainly have very little money,' he said grimly.

'I know, my dear boy,' said Mrs Lockwood reasonably. 'I know. And we must be sensible about it. So whenever there is any plan afoot for the girls to go anywhere, you come to me. I'll pay. I'll give you the money beforehand and then there'll be no need for any embarrassment.'

'Thank you,' murmured Martin, deeply embarrassed already.

'Not at all, dear boy. Now go and get the girls in for supper. You'll stay, of course.'

In the shrubbery after supper Clare asked what her mother had said to him in the drawing room and he told her.

'It's very kind of her,' he said. 'But I don't see how I can possibly let her pay for me. I hate the idea.'

'Oh, Martin,' begged Clare, her face lovely in the moonlight. 'Don't stop coming with us because of that. We're having such a marvellous time. Don't spoil it. What does it matter who pays? Please don't mind about such a silly thing, Martin.'

He gave in. If it had to be not fire and water but mud that he had to go through to be with her, he would none the less go through it.

So the next time a party of young people arranged to go in cars to a hotel on the coast for dinner and a dance, Martin took the money from Mrs Lockwood. The first time he hated taking it; it spoiled his evening. The second time, he minded less; and before long he hardly minded at all.

The twins enjoyed rushing up to Martin when they were out and saying: 'Oh, Martin, give me some money, please. I haven't a cent. Martin's our banker, you know,' they said to the other girls, holding out a palm for him to pay something into it.

'The poor chap's paid to take them out,' said one young man to another.

'They'd have to pay somebody,' said the other. 'Nobody'd do it for nothing. Clare's a darling, but those twins terrify me. I loathe dancing with 'em. I feel a perfect fool being run about the floor as if I'd no will of my own.'

'Still, they give good parties,' said the other.

'Oh, agreed. Always first-class grub at Oakfield. I'll put up with a lot for first-class grub,' said the cheerful hedonist.

The fact that he was paid to take the Lockwoods about divided Martin from the other men of the party. He knew it, but he didn't care. He was possessed of a single idea and that was to be with Clare and to know that no other man was with her.

But autumn was approaching. The winter festivities would soon begin in earnest. The twins were making plans, counting up the dances they would go to. They took it for granted that Martin would go with them and Martin had no dress-clothes. He couldn't possibly afford dress-clothes. He had now three pounds a week, out of which he gave his mother thirty shillings. He had never been able to save anything out of his salary and less than ever could he save now that he was going about with the Lockwoods. Mrs Lockwood provided the money for the excursions and so on, but his own expenses had increased enormously. He didn't drink because he couldn't afford to. He only smoked in public now. But he was continually having to buy shirts, socks, ties, shoes. Shamefacedly he asked his mother if she could possibly manage on less money from him now that Molly and Thea were both contributing to the household. Mrs Hunter hurriedly said yes. She would have said yes whether she could manage or not. So he gave her a pound every week instead of thirty shillings; but it didn't make any difference to his situation.

The day came, as he knew it would, when Bee told him her father had bought tickets for the first dance of the season, the Hospital Ball. He paled. He managed to get Clare to the shrubbery and there he stammered wretchedly that he couldn't go, that she must tell them. He had no dress-clothes, he said, and no money to buy them with. They stood in the damp, dark shrubbery together, both crushed by this disclosure.

Martin said despairingly that he couldn't go on. They were too rich, he said, and he was too poor and never so far as he could see would be anything else. It made a gulf that couldn't be bridged. He had thought it could, or at least he had deliberately blinded himself to it, but it was no good. He must stop now, he said, before things got any worse.

Clare stood before him, as pale as he was.

'Oh, Martin, don't talk like this. I can't bear it,' she said. 'Martin, don't leave me. I know it's dreadful for you. Don't think I don't see it all. I do, I do. But don't stop coming, Martin. I couldn't bear it.'

His head low, he pressed moss into the gravel with the toe of his shoe, carefully trimming it round, in silence.

'Martin.'

She put her hands on his shoulders and he trembled. He had never kissed her, so she kissed him. With a groan for the hopelessness of his love and the hopelessness of making resolutions against it, he closed his arms about her.

'What were you and Martin doing all that time in the shrubbery?' asked Bee suspiciously later.

Clare's eyelids fluttered slightly.

'We were – we were talking about going to the dances. Bee, Martin says he has no dress-clothes. He says he can't go.'

'No dress-clothes!' exclaimed Bee aghast, as if she had never heard of a man without dress-clothes. 'Good heavens, how awful! But he must go. He'll have to get them.'

'How can he, Bee? He hasn't the money. They cost an awful lot.'

'I should have thought he'd have enough money to buy dress-clothes,' said Bee, as if she couldn't get over it.

'Well, he hasn't,' said Clare with exasperation. The strain of sharing Martin with her sisters, of pretending he was no more to her than he was to them was sometimes too much for her. But it must be done. They would only tell and ruin everything if they knew.

'We must do something about it,' said Muriel. 'We can't possibly do without Martin at the dances. Let's tell Mother. She'll know what to do.'

They told their mother; their mother told their father and the upshot of it was that Mr Lockwood summoned Martin to the library one evening.

'My boy,' he said genially, 'I hear you are in a fix for dress-clothes. You haven't them, I hear. Well, there's nothing unusual in that. I don't think I had at your age. They cost a lot of money, naturally you can't afford them. But my girls say they can't and won't go to the dances without you. So I think you'll have to let their father pay for the dress-clothes. You go to my tailor and order dinner-jacket and tails. I'll give them a ring to-morrow and tell them you're coming.'

'Oh, sir . . .' stammered Martin. 'It's awfully kind of you, but I can't possibly accept such a thing . . .'

'Now, none of that,' said Mr Lockwood with a wave of the hand. 'It's all part of my girls' fun. I'm very fond of my girls, Martin, and I want to give them whatever they want, within reason. They happen to want you to take them about, and I'm glad to have such a reliable fellow for them to be with. Now I have some work to do. You go back to the girls and set your mind at rest about the dress-clothes. Everything all right at the bank? I suppose you don't know anything about the Moreton deal?' said Mr Lockwood, suddenly narrowing his eyes.

'The what, sir?'

'The Moreton deal.'

'I haven't heard of it,' said Martin, looking blank.

'That's all right. Now be off, there's a good lad. I'm going to be busy tonight.'

Clare was in the hall.

'Martin, Daddy's going to make you a present of the dress-clothes, isn't he? Isn't it lovely?'

Then she looked anxiously into his face.

'It's all right, isn't it, Martin? You're going to let him, aren't you?'

'Oh, yes,' said Martin in a queer tone. 'I'm going to let him all right.'

'Oh, Martin,' she pleaded. 'Don't spoil things. Do let's be happy. It will be such fun. We'll have such a lovely time.'

He cleared his face and smiled down at her. 'All right,' he said. 'We will.'

Clare smiled radiantly up at him. Then, hearing Bee's voice round the corner, she ran forward with a slightly exaggerated guilelessness.

'Daddy's solved the problem, Bee. He's making Martin a present of the dress-clothes.'

'Oh, I know,' said Bee grandly. 'I knew what he was going to do. Hurray, Martin! Let's turn the rugs back and you show me that new step. I thought I'd got it, but I haven't.'

Martin found it difficult to go to the tailor the next day. He walked round the block of shops twice, trying to reason himself out of humiliation and self-disgust. Then, as he came back into the main street, the Lockwood car passed him, carrying Clare and her father home. Clare turned to smile at him and his resistance collapsed. He hurried into Dennisons' where the tailor received him as if the provision of dress-clothes for impoverished young men by his rich patrons was an everyday occurrence.

'You'll do us credit, sir,' he said, busy with his tape, and Martin went away feeling better.

When, one morning, the tailor's boxes were delivered in Byron Place, Mrs Hunter took them in with a sigh. Nothing marked the growing secretiveness of her son like this purchase of what she supposed must be a new suit. Once, the ordering of a suit, a rare event, was the occasion of long discussion by the whole family. Patterns were laid on the table at every meal, so that everyone, while eating, could consider them. Martin fingered patterns for hours. He doubled them on his lapel, observing the effect in the glass. 'Mother, how's that?' 'Molly, what do *you* think?' 'But this is very nice too . . .' he used to say.

But this time he had evidently got a new suit without saying a word about it, Mrs Hunter thought sadly. Still, she supposed he would like her to take it out of the box and hang it up as soon as possible.

She undid the string. He had gone to an expensive tailor this time, she reflected. She took off the lid, removed the tissue paper and her eyes and fingers fell with consternation on the satin lining, the smooth face-cloth and silk lapels of the dress-clothes.

She sat down beside them and stared at them in horror. Martin couldn't possibly afford clothes like this. How was he to pay for them? Where did he propose to get the money from? Dreadful answers flew unbidden into Mrs Hunter's mind. She thought of all the money Martin handled during the day, she saw gold and notes passing through his fingers. She got up and re-packed the dress-clothes into the boxes. She tied them up with the string and carried them up to Martin's bedroom. She must pretend not to know what was in the boxes. Perhaps he would explain them at lunchtime.

But at lunchtime, Martin was a long time upstairs and when he came down he said nothing about the dress-clothes. Thea noticed her mother's nervous anxiety and wondered what had happened. When Martin had left the house, Mrs Hunter hurried up to his room. Perhaps the clothes were a mistake. Perhaps they had been delivered to the wrong house. But they hung in all their richness in the wardrobe and Mrs Hunter, unable to keep it to herself any longer, called to Thea.

'Oh, Thea,' she said, standing with the wardrobe door in her hand, her anxious face turned to her daughter, 'such expensive dress-clothes have come for Martin this morning and I'm so worried about how he's going to pay for them.'

Mystified, Thea came to look into the wardrobe.

'Oh, dear,' she said with concern, 'this is what comes of trying to keep up with the Lockwoods.'

'But how can he possibly pay for them? I'm so worried. You don't think . . .? There's so much money about at the bank, Thea.'

'Mother!' Thea was horrified. 'As if Martin would ever touch the bank money!'

'Don't you think he would? The temptation must be very great.'

'Of course he wouldn't,' said Thea indignantly. 'I don't suppose there's any temptation at all for him. I don't suppose he ever thinks of it. Really, Mother, do put such ideas out of your head.'

Thea's vigorous indignation cleared the idea for an hour or two, but it crept back and after supper her mother brought it out again.

Thea went up to Martin in his room.

'Martin,' she said in the cold voice they used for each other nowadays, 'Mother's worrying about how you're to pay for those dress-clothes. She's afraid you've been borrowing from the bank. You'd better set her mind at rest, or she won't sleep tonight.'

He turned from an open drawer.

'Borrowing from the bank?' he said in mystification. 'The bank wouldn't lend to me. What does she mean?'

'Taking from the bank then,' said Thea bluntly.

He turned back to the drawer in disgust.

'Good heavens,' he said.

'Well, you'd better tell her about the dress-clothes,' persisted Thea. 'Or she'll worry all night.'

'You can tell her they're a present,' he said.

'A present?'

'A present from Mr Lockwood.'

There was silence at the door.

'So they've hired you?' said Thea cuttingly in a moment. 'Are you going to wait at table, too?'

He turned on her.

'You shut up,' he said savagely. 'Shut up, d'you hear? And get out of my room. There's no privacy in this house.'

He darted swiftly to slam and lock the door and Thea went downstairs. She trembled. She hated quarrelling with Martin, but they were always quarrelling these days. What were the Lockwoods doing to him? As if they hadn't done enough to her without starting on Martin. She went slowly to her mother in the front room.

Mrs Hunter was waiting with anxious eyes.

'The dress-clothes are a present from Mr Lockwood,' said Thea.

'From Mr Lockwood!' Mrs Hunter looked incredulous; then her face broadened with relief. 'Oh, how kind!' she breathed.

'Kind, Mother? Surely you're not *glad* Mr Lockwood has given Martin dress-clothes?'

'Well, it's much better than taking money from the bank, dear.'

'Oh, Mother.' In spite of herself, Thea laughed ruefully. It struck her that she never had known and never would know how her mother would react to anything. 'There was never any possibility of Martin's taking money from the bank, darling.'

'No,' said Mrs Hunter with docility, 'I don't suppose there was.'

Once the worry was over, she was quite ready to dismiss it as foolish.

'But I don't see why you should be so cross about Mr Lockwood's giving the dress-clothes to Martin, Thea,' she said. 'It's a magnificent present.'

'It's far too magnificent. Martin shouldn't take it. They're just using him to take the girls about and they'll dress him up so that he can do it. They'll detach him from his family for that, and he lets them.'

'Thea, you're too hard on the Lockwoods,' protested Mrs Hunter. 'This is a very kind action on Mr Lockwood's part. It shows they still have a kindly feeling towards us. In fact, I think if I were to write a little note now, it would just heal the breach.'

'Oh, Mother, don't,' begged Thea in alarm. 'Please don't. They don't understand that kind of thing.'

Mrs Hunter sighed. She sometimes wished she could do as she liked.

'I hate quarrels,' she said in a troubled way.

'I know you do, Mother,' said Thea. 'You're the sort of person no one should ever quarrel with. Perhaps there'll be a better chance – I mean a decenter one – of making it up with Mrs Lockwood later. Not for me,' she said hastily. 'I don't want to make it up with her. But for you.'

Mrs Hunter's face cleared a little. That Thea should allow her to entertain any prospect of making it up with Mrs Lockwood was more than she had expected.

CHAPTER THIRTY

I

When, for a party at Oakfield, Martin put on the dress-clothes for the first time, he came down in his overcoat and went straight out of the house. He didn't mean his family to see his magnificence. But when, the first to arrive by request, he walked into the drawing room at Oakfield, he made all the effect he had missed at home.

At the sight of him, the girls broke away from their parents by the fire and came running over the shining floor with cries of admiration.

'Martin! How grand you are! You look marvellous, Martin!'

Smiling, he let them take him to their parents to be looked at. He stammered thanks to Mr Lockwood, who waved his cigar in genial dismissal.

'Martin, let's try that new step once more,' cried Muriel, sliding over the floor to put on the gramophone.

Seizing him rather forcibly, she propelled him before her to the middle of the room. But Martin didn't mind.

Tonight he was a little intoxicated by his own appearance.

Watching himself, from the tail of his eye, recur in a glass, he marvelled at the difference clothes could make. He was as enraptured with his dress-suit as any girl with her first ball-dress. And the clothes had not only worked wonders on his appearance, but on his spirits. They made him what he rarely was: they made him optimistic. He felt tonight that he could surmount all the barriers between himself and Clare. In fact, looking at the Lockwoods so happy in one another and so welcoming to him, he wasn't even sure there were any barriers. They were so kind, they seemed to like him, they adored Clare – surely they wanted her to be happy? And if she could be happy only with him, why, what then? There seemed to be but one answer, and Martin's spirits soared.

'Left foot, behind, Muriel. Left foot.'

Muriel always had difficulty in distinguishing between left and right.

'It's my turn now,' clamoured Bee. 'Muriel, you've had ages and the others will be here in a minute.'

She took Martin, and Muriel ran into the hall to see if anyone was coming.

Clare, in a mist of rose-coloured tulle, stood with her father by the fire.

'I suppose you don't need lessons, pet,' he said, looking fondly down at her.

She shook her head, smiling. Even if she had needed them, she wouldn't clamour for Martin in public. She always let the twins have him. It was safer.

By twos and threes, the guests began to arrive. Soon the room was full of them, young, lively and too much for Mr

Lockwood, who withdrew to the library. Mrs Lockwood went to the dining room where one of her famous buffet-suppers was set out. Followed by the maids, she ran her expert eye over the silver and glass, the flowers and linen, the creams, the wines, the patties, the cakes. She congratulated the maids and rustled away again. Life was very pleasant. She was very contented.

In the drawing room, Angela Harvey had come late. She waved to Bee not to bother about her and went to stand by the fire. She wore a finely-pleated dress of white chiffon, and with one arm raised to the marble shelf overhead, she leaned into the fire in a lovely pose. As they revolved the dancers turned their heads to keep her in view.

Bee brought Martin up. As the best dancer in the room she offered him to Angela, whose presence was flattering, since she refused to go to other parties.

Martin danced away with her, as light as a lily in his arms.

'Is your sister here?' she asked.

Martin was embarrassed. 'Er – no,' he said.

'Isn't she invited to the house?'

'No.'

'Because of that affair at Villeneuve?'

'I suppose so,' said Martin uncomfortably.

'Good Lord, it was nothing,' she said. 'Nothing that anyone over here would have thought anything of. Give her my love, will you?'

Martin bowed. But he knew he wouldn't. He wouldn't mention this party, or any other at home.

'Are you going to the dances this winter?' he asked, to change the subject.

'No fear!' She showed her puckish dimples. She looked as if she had something secret in prospect, something not connected with dances or girls' sports at all.

What a queer girl, he thought. She didn't listen eagerly like the others, she hardly listened at all. Other girls hung on the young men's words, anxious to laugh in the right place, to show themselves ready to appreciate, be sympathetic. This one didn't put herself out in the least. Other girls fiddled with their hair, their pearls, their dresses. This one made no single unnecessary movement. All the same, other girls were more comfortable to be with and when the dance ended, he returned her to the fire and escaped to Clare with alacrity.

Exhilaration leaped in him as he whirled her over the floor. He could have laughed aloud he was so happy.

'I'm glad you're not a white taper in a Grecian dress,' he whispered into her curls.

'Oh, Angela's most unusual, Martin,' Clare protested. 'And I'm not at all.'

'Aren't you? I've never seen anyone half so lovely and I never shall.'

'Martin, you're so absurd. What are we dancing?'

'Something that has never been danced before. I don't know what it is either, but isn't it marvellous?'

She laughed. His arm was strong to hold her. They were wildly happy. It was something so new in their love that Martin should be gay and confident. So often he was heavy-hearted, almost tragic, about it. But tonight a new thrilling element had come into it.

Martin had more dances with Clare than he had ever dared to have before; and they kept creeping away to the back-stairs, though not for long, in case they should be missed.

The winter festivities came thick and fast now. Thea often went, feeling furtive, into Martin's room to look at the invitation cards and dance programmes strewing his dressing-table. On the dance programmes, there were many 'Bee's and 'Muriel's and comparatively few 'C's. The poor boy seemed to spend most of his time partnering the twins, which was a heavy price to pay, Thea considered, for a few dances with Clare.

Mr and Mrs Lockwood had intended to accompany their girls to all the dances, but there were too many of them. Getting into bed in the small hours for the third time in the week, William remarked that he thought he was getting rather old for much of this sort of thing.

'That's just what I was thinking myself,' said Effie, 'but there's really no need to go to everything. If we take the girls to the important functions, the Mayor's and the Territorial and perhaps the Cripples, Martin can squire them to the rest. You and I will stay at home and be Darby and Joan for a change.'

So instead of picking up Martin at the end of Byron Place as they did when their parents went too, the girls called for him. The bell was not rung. Mysteriously, he was always ready to leave the house as the car glided through the winter dark to the gate. Sometimes the light was on inside the car and Thea, looking round the blind of her darkened room, saw the Lockwoods in white fur wraps, their fair hair shining. The twins were in the best seats; Martin joined Clare on the little collapsible ones with their backs to the driver. The light was put out, the car glided away. The scene – Byron Place on a cold, foggy night – was empty again.

II

Martin didn't speak of the world he now frequented and his family did not ask about it. Thea wouldn't, Molly wasn't interested and Mrs Hunter always avoided awkward subjects. So that, although Martin had heard it discussed for weeks past at Oakfield, the news about the Harveys came like a clap of thunder to Thea's ears.

'Oh, by the way,' said Oliver Reade one morning at the office, 'the Harveys are going.'

Thea looked at him in amazement.

'Going?'

'As a matter of fact they've already gone, I think,' he said, enjoying the effect of his announcement. He liked to bring interest to her face; she looked too quiet, too withdrawn in these days. 'They've gone to live in the south. Funny how people make their money here and when they've made it, they leave the town and go to live somewhere else. Still, we didn't expect it of the Harveys, did we? I suppose they got out quietly to avoid fuss and farewells and all that, and people coming to look at the house while they were still in it. The mills are sold and Firbank is up for sale, you know.'

'Goodness!' murmured Thea.

'Your friend Angela,' he went on, 'ran away weeks ago, it appears.'

'Angela? Ran away?'

'To join a Repertory Company, they say.'

Thea stared at him, taking this in; and he took advantage of her preoccupation to let his eyes dwell unhindered on her face. Her eyes were wide open to his gaze and he lost himself in looking into them. The mystery of eyes, he thought.

Thea was entirely taken up with the Harveys. To think they had gone! And that no one would see them again in the town – not see Sir Robert's eyeglass, or Lady Harvey's elegance; and Angela. Thea said to herself she had wanted to see what happened to Angela. For the Harveys to go was like having a book she was interested in taken away before she had read half.

Suddenly her face changed.

'The Lockwoods won't like it, will they?' she said, cheered by this aspect of the situation.

Oliver recovered from his own preoccupation to answer her. He always had to be quick to do that; to be ordinary in spite of his love, to humour her.

'They won't,' he said.

'It'll make an enormous difference to Mrs Lockwood,' she said with satisfaction. 'She doubled her own importance by having Lady Harvey as a friend. She and the twins will be quite diminished now. And I should think it will make a difference to Mr Lockwood, too, won't it?' she said hopefully.

'It certainly will,' Oliver allowed with indulgence. 'Lockwood plus Sir Robert was a power in the town. Lockwood minus

Sir Robert must be less of one. Besides, he's losing his most important client. Oh, yes, Lockwood's bound to feel the draught.'

'Good!' said Thea.

'You do hate those Lockwoods, don't you?' he said.

'Wouldn't you?' she challenged.

'I not only would, I do. I hate them for the way they've treated you and I hate them because you hate them.'

She smiled warmly at him for his championship, and he thought grimly: 'Funny if she likes me because I hate the Lockwoods.'

He got up and reached for his hat.

'Well, I suppose I'd better be off,' he said. 'You've got enough to be going on with, I suppose.'

'Oh, yes, I think so.'

She was rummaging, as if he'd gone already, in the high desk he had bought second-hand from an architect's office. He looked at her dark hair curling up from her little neck, at her long slender legs. She wore a dark blue dress with a round white collar; very trim. Better go, he said to himself, sighing; better get away and think of something else.

When he was a boy, he had a cat, a princely young creature, short-haired and shining like black lead. It threw itself down in such beautiful attitudes that the boy Oliver had to plunge across the room to dote on it. But if he touched it, it got up and stalked out of the house. If he tried to pick it up, it slid from his arms. To keep the cat where he could look at it, he couldn't go near it. His eyes he could feast, but never his hands. And one day the cat walked out and never came back.

He knew that if he didn't keep his distance, it would be the same with Thea.

'Well,' he said, with rather a grim smile. 'Goodbye for the present.'

'Goodbye,' she said, smiling kindly.

She turned to her work; such as there was. There seemed to be very little these days.

The packing of the powders had been transferred to the warehouse. Thea should have been transferred, too, but Oliver kept her where she was. It was near home for her, and for him, too. When he had time, he could drop in and be sure of finding her alone. At the warehouse, there would be no chance of spending any time with her. It wouldn't do, either, he decided. Business was business, and must be run as such. His enterprise was growing. He had brought his pastes and powders under one name and put the advertising of Guerison Products Ltd in the hands of a first-class London firm. At a cost that ought to have frightened him, he told himself; but didn't. It was a gamble, but he was sure it would come off. The name of 'Guerison' was beginning to appear on hoardings, on railway stations, in magazines and daily papers, on the screens of theatres and cinemas; and results were coming in. He had struck the match and a little flame was beginning to crackle through the length and breadth of the country. His white-overalled girls were kept busy in the warehouse, but he wasn't going to have Thea among them. He kept on the room over the shop and directed enough work into it to keep Thea occupied, and no more.

Thea didn't know enough about office work or business of

any kind to suspect this. She only felt the lack of incentive. She no longer felt that the success of 'Guerison' depended upon her. She couldn't see the enterprise as a whole now. The division of labour made it much less interesting, but she tried to feel devoted to 'Guerison'. She did the work that came her way to the best of her ability, because she was grateful to Oliver for making it possible for her to work at all. If he hadn't provided her with this work, what other would she have done, she asked herself?

It was entirely due to Oliver too, that a new era was beginning for the Hunter household. Money was beginning to plump out its long-starved sinews. Most of the money was provided by Molly. The shop showed immediate and quite startling profits. Mrs Hunter often remarked nowadays that she couldn't understand why anyone should look down on trade. If she had done so herself, she said, it was simply from ignorance.

Molly seemed to want little for herself. She used her money for the benefit of the household. A woman was engaged to come in every morning to relieve Mrs Hunter of the housework. One by one rooms of the house were painted and papered, for the first time since the Hunters had moved in. There was a discussion about putting a new fire-grate into the front room, but they decided against it, because Molly said it would be better to move into a better house than to spend too much on the present one. New prospects were certainly opening out before the Hunters.

Thea had her salary, now increased to two pounds ten shillings a week, and finally Mrs Hunter herself, to her extreme astonishment, received a wholly unexpected percentage from 'Guerison'.

'But I can't take this, Mr Reade,' she protested. 'When I gave you the prescription, I didn't think anything would come of it. It's ridiculous that you should pay me anything.'

'That was our agreement,' said Oliver firmly. 'And we stick to it. I hope there'll be a steady increase in the money I pay you for the rest of your life, Mrs Hunter.'

'For the rest of my life?' she repeated incredulously.

'Why not? I think I've found my line at last. I think this is what I'm going to stick to. I intend to make my fortune, Mrs Hunter, and if I do, I might easily make yours, too.'

Mrs Hunter laughed.

'I suppose all young men dream of making a fortune,' she said. 'But most of them come to be content to make a living.'

'All right,' said Oliver good-humouredly. 'We'll see.'

III

The cold day was coming to a bitter, blustery end. As he went along Wells Road, the dust stung Oliver's face as if it were made of ground ice. Things were being blown over; noticeboards, dustbin lids. Shadows of bare trees darted like witches over the lamp-lit pavements; hedges shuddered round small front gardens.

Oliver reached the side door of the shop with relief and let himself into the yeasty warmth. Making for the stairs, he saw Molly behind the counter, serving hot pies to a little boy. She was beaming so benevolently that Oliver smiled. The shop certainly had been the making of her, and to give her her due, she had been the making of the shop. He wanted to branch out now, but she was obstinate. She wanted to keep it as it was; manageable, she said, a personal business. When Edie got married, as she would very soon, he would probably let Molly buy him out, he reflected. He liked businesses that grew; it was the expansion of business that really interested him. The shop could pass to Molly; it could be all hers. She would like that, he thought, going up the stairs two at a time.

From the relief with which Thea greeted his entrance, he gauged the extent of her boredom and his heart smote him. She ought not to be cooped up here all day. She ought to be out, enjoying life. He had noticed how she had flagged lately and wondered if she was still fretting for the Frenchman. She had a controlled look that made her extraordinarily like her brother sometimes.

He felt he wasn't doing enough for her. If only he could give her all she wanted. He longed to pour the riches of the world into her lap and all he could do was to fiddle about with a few pastes and powders. Not that he didn't believe in them. He did, and in himself, too. But it was all so slow.

And another thing, he thought, hanging up his hat and coat, he hadn't done as much as he intended, to make himself acceptable to her. It wasn't enough to read books and go to classes. It was polish he needed now.

He sat down at his desk and she came to sit beside him, with her notebook, as she had seen secretaries do in films. He began to take papers from his many pockets. His hands travelled from pocket to pocket, her eyes following them to see what he would bring out. He noticed with misgiving that his hands were not altogether clean, though what could you expect when he had been going about with them all afternoon in this dusty wintry weather?

He hardly ever saw himself unless he saw himself through her eyes. Now that she looked at his hands, he looked too and saw that they were rather dirty and not really, he said to himself, the hands of a gentleman. Too big. Too red; though she must remember that it was cold, he put forward mutely.

With the letters, he took out a printed card, looked at it and put it back in his waistcoat pocket.

He sighed.

'Well, let's write to Palmers first,' he said. '"Dear Sir, your letter to hand." No, you don't like me to say that. Put what you like. You know.'

They went through the letters.

He sat humped at the desk, his cheek on his fist, his dark hair rough and streaked over his brow. She wondered why he was so preoccupied, and if something had gone wrong with Guerison. She waited.

Turning, he said as if he had suddenly made up his mind:

'I'm going to take lessons on how to speak properly.'

It was so unexpected that she gaped at him. She didn't know how to take such an announcement. She blushed.

'Oh – why?' she said.

'So I can speak better, of course.'

'But I like the way you speak,' she stammered with sincerity. 'It's full of energy.'

'You're used to it now,' he said. 'But it gave you a shock at the beginning, I bet. And quite right, too. It's too rough. I'm too rough. I must put some polish on myself. I've been meaning to a long time and now I'll make a start.'

He brought the card from his pocket and handed it to her.

'Mrs Maynard,' she read. 'Lessons in deportment, public speaking, elocution.'

'In Manchester?' she said.

'Aye, Manchester. I wouldn't go to anybody in this town. Everybody'd get to hear of it. They'd chaff my life out. I shall feel a fool as it is.' He looked oppressed at the thought of Mrs Maynard. 'If you notice me trying to speak different and all that, don't laugh, will you?'

She blushed again. 'Oh, *no!*' she said, shocked that he should think she ever would.

His face cleared. She had given his plan her approval. More, she understood. And because she understood and approved, he knew that he darn well would improve now, and before long too. He began to deal briskly with the remaining letters.

But Thea was uncertain whether she should say more or not. She was touched by his wistful aspirations, but they seemed unnecessary. It didn't matter how he spoke or what he did. Somehow you knew at once that he was a person who mattered. She hoped this Mrs Maynard wouldn't try to overlay his native vigour with gentility. But she couldn't say this, she decided. He must please himself. He must try Mrs Maynard if he wanted to.

Watching him as he paused to think over what he wanted to say in the letter, she felt that, in his way, he was very engaging. But she daren't show him that she thought so. She didn't want him to think she was in love with him. Or ever going to be. Because she wasn't. There wasn't a spark of that sort of thing left in her. All that was dead; or left behind in Villeneuve. No good twanging that string again. There was no response.

'Well,' he said, coming in a few days later at the end of the afternoon, 'I've had my first lesson. She's nice, is Mrs Maynard. I'm going to get on with her. And everything's wrong with me that possibly could be wrong. Wrong from head to foot,' he said with satisfaction. 'To begin with I've not to wear brown shoes with a blue suit. Not with this blue anyway. Why didn't you tell me? I bet you knew,' he charged her.

She blinked at the attack. 'Well – ' she hedged.

'Never mind, you won't find me doing it again,' he said. 'I'm getting a new suit, too. I've been to the best tailor in Manchester.'

He gave the three syllables the same stress, then corrected himself and threw it on the first.

'I shall have to keep doing that,' he explained. 'But I'll get into it. I'm glad I like Mrs Maynard. I don't feel a bit embarrassed with her.'

He stressed the first syllable, but corrected himself and stressed the second.

'Isn't it confusing?' he said. 'You have to say "*Man*-chester", but you haven't to say "*em*barrassed". Mrs Maynard says you want to listen to good speech as much as you can. I said I was with a young woman who spoke beautifully, so she said I must cultivate you.' He glanced slyly at her. 'I must cultivate you so that you can cultivate me,' he said. 'So if you notice me running after you, if you've not noticed it before, you'll know why.'

Thea laughed. She threw her head back and laughed, showing her lovely teeth, and his heart filled with pleasure. That was the way, perhaps. Make a joke of his love.

He worked to acquire polish as he worked at everything else. He took his coat off to it.

'That woman's good at her job,' he said, coming in some weeks later. 'She made me take her out to lunch today and made me order. I'll take you out if you like and show you how I'm getting on.'

Thea smiled, but she hedged. She murmured, and went on going through the card-index. His face clouded. Not time yet? She still wouldn't? The patience it took. He didn't know where he got the patience from. He marvelled at himself; he wouldn't have thought he had it in him.

CHAPTER THIRTY-ONE

I

But another young man had finished with patience. Martin told Clare that he'd had enough of dodging the twins and deceiving her parents. The moments they snatched in the dark dusty honeycombs of Assembly Rooms and Halls, on the back stairs of private houses, in back streets in remote parts of the town, wonderful though they had once seemed, were now nothing but a source of exasperation and misery to Martin. They were not half enough.

It was time to come out into the open, he said. He must make his position clear. If her parents were trusting him not to fall in love with Clare, as Clare said they were, it was time to tell them that he *was* in love with her. Though why they should trust or expect him not to fall in love with her, he couldn't understand.

'But they do, they do,' insisted Clare. 'They've no idea that we love each other.'

'But why should they reckon on my being so safe as all that?' said Martin. 'They couldn't. They don't, either. You're wrong, darling.'

'I'm not.' Clare shook her head. 'They think of me as a child, their youngest child. They think I won't fall in love for years yet. In fact, I'm afraid they don't want me to fall in love or marry at all.'

'But that's nonsense,' said Martin. 'If it wasn't me, it would be somebody else. That's one reason why I want to make sure of you quickly.'

He kissed her, and Clare smiled, but anxiously.

'I don't think it's safe to tell Daddy anything yet,' she said again. 'Let's wait a bit longer, Martin.'

'I can't wait any longer, Clare. I haven't your patience. You're too patient. You're too patient with Bee and Muriel. You let them monopolise me so easily I sometimes feel you can't love me. You don't put in any claim to me at all, you simply hand me over to them.'

'I do it because it's safer.'

'I'm sick of safety,' said Martin. 'I can't keep on dancing about with Bee and Muriel any longer and seeing other men go off with you. To have to stand by and watch that Cooper fellow pawing you the other night nearly drove me mad. I just had to stand there as if it was nothing to me. I can't do that sort of thing any longer.'

Clare put her hand to his cheek and he turned his lips inwards and pressed them to her palm.

'Besides, I'll be giving myself away one of these days,' he said. 'And it'll be much worse if the twins go to your father than if I go to him myself. No, Clare, I've thought about it for weeks. Our best chance, I'm convinced, is to do the straight thing and go to your father. He loves you and he always behaves as if he likes me. The only thing he can possibly have against me is my miserable lack of money. We know the bank won't allow me to marry for about four years . . .'

'So what's the use of telling anybody?' said Clare. 'We can be secretly engaged, can't we?'

'But I'm hoping your father will help me to get a better job. He knows all about jobs and making money and I'm hoping, when he knows about us, he'll help me to a better job so that we can marry sooner. Even at once, perhaps,' said Martin, bringing out his bright absurd dreams. 'Without your father's help, darling, we're doomed to a four years' engagement. But if he would only help us . . .'

'Ah – if,' echoed Clare. 'But I'm so afraid of ruining everything by asking.'

She feared an adult struggle with her father. This was not a thing she could sit on his knee and weep into his neck about. She must meet him on strange, dark ground and she felt his possessive love rising in its formidable power, even before it was challenged.

'I know Daddy better than you do,' she said to Martin.

'Of course, darling, but my argument is that your father would never have let me come to the house and be with you so much, if he hadn't at least envisaged the chance of my falling in love with you and your falling in love with me. The thing's absurd. He must have thought of it.'

Clare looked into his face to see if he knew best, to see if her fears were groundless. He looked so strong and sure that she began to be infected with his confidence. His urgency thrilled her, too. She wouldn't have liked it, she told herself, if he had been so lukewarm about her that he would wait indefinitely and put up with anything.

She let herself be persuaded. She agreed that he should try.

II

In the passage leading to the library there was not much likelihood of being caught by the twins, so the young lovers were able to cling to each other's hands and whisper briefly before Martin cast the die and knocked at the door.

'Come in,' said an irritated voice, and Martin, with a reassuring glance at Clare behind him, went into the room and closed the door.

Mr Lockwood was at his desk, the fire behind him, a single strong light shining closely down on his papers. He lifted his head above the lamp to see who was making the interruption.

'I'm very busy tonight, Martin. What is it?'

Martin came up to the desk.

'May I speak to you, sir?'

'You are speaking to me, aren't you?' Mr Lockwood tried to keep his testiness good-humoured in tone.

'Sit down then,' he said. 'I can't see you when you tower over me like that. But for God's sake be quick and say what you have to say. I've a lot of work to do tonight.'

He looked down at his papers again. Mrs Kirkby had startled him by calling at the office that afternoon, a thing she hadn't done for years.

'I hadn't any money in the Moreton Development Scheme, had I?' she asked, and he assured her she had not.

'What made you think of that just now?' he said.

'Well, a long time ago you asked me if I wanted to put some money into it and I couldn't remember whether I'd said yes or no. But now the scheme's failed, I thought I'd better find out. I'm so glad to hear I'd nothing in it, because my son will be home from India this year and he would have been cross with me.'

'He won't have any reason to be cross with you,' Mr Lockwood assured her, thankful to have been warned of John Kirkby's impending arrival.

He brought his mind back to the library and was almost startled to find Martin sitting on the other side of the desk, apparently not having yet uttered a word.

'Come on, my boy. Out with it.'

'I want to tell you . . .' began Martin.

Mr Lockwood gave him his attention. He leaned a little forward under the lamp. He imagined the boy was going to ask him to lend him some money.

'I want to tell you,' Martin brought it all out with a rush, 'that I love Clare and she loves me. I want to ask you if we can be engaged, sir.'

Mr Lockwood leaned farther across the desk. His face went dark.

'What? What is it you say?'

Martin swallowed with difficulty and began to repeat the words he had so often rehearsed.

'Didn't I make it clear when you first started to come to this house,' said Mr Lockwood, speaking with deliberation, 'that I wouldn't tolerate anything of this kind? I told my wife that you came here on that condition – that there was to be no nonsense about falling in love with any of the girls.'

Martin stared at him, his face gone drawn and anxious.

'Mrs Lockwood didn't say anything about that to me, sir,' he said.

'Didn't say anything!' William Lockwood struck the desk with his fist. 'There was no need to say anything. You should have known that we would never allow it. Good God, are you crazy? What are you making? What's your salary?'

'A hundred and forty-five pounds a year,' faltered Martin.

'And you propose to marry Clare, brought up as she has been, on a hundred and forty-five pounds a year? D'you realise she spends as much as that on her clothes alone?'

Martin, his eyes fixed on Mr Lockwood, swallowed again on a dry throat.

'The bank won't allow you to marry,' said the lawyer. 'Haven't you to reach a certain salary before you can do so?'

'Two hundred and fifty, sir.'

'And how long before you reach that?'

'About four years.'

Mr Lockwood sat back, his dark hands spread on the desk.

'You amaze me,' he said in a quieter, more dangerous voice. How you have the cheek to come asking for Clare in your circumstances amazes me.'

'But I'm asking for Clare as well as for myself,' pleaded Martin. 'Clare loves me. She'll tell you so. You'll hurt her as well as me if you don't help us.'

'I care too much for my daughter ever to help her to you,' said Mr Lockwood. 'You're not going to drag Clare down to your level. I haven't worked as hard as I have for Clare to live somewhere like Byron Place on two hundred and fifty a year.'

'But we – we hoped you might be able to find me something better to do, sir. Some job I could make more money at, so that we could get married sooner.'

'Oh, you were looking to me to provide for you, were you?' Mr Lockwood's lip curled. The presumption of this boy with no prospects thinking he could take Clare away, and the damned cheek of him thinking that he, he, her father would help him to do it. 'You thought you were on to a good thing, did you?' he went on brutally. 'You were having a nice time going about with the girls, spending my money, having the best of everything provided for you, so you thought you'd like to go on like that for the rest of your life, did you?'

Martin's nostrils sharpened.

'That's not true. I've hated taking your money. I only did it so that I could be with Clare. I've always loved her and she's always loved me. I've put up with anything so that I could be with her. What I'm asking now is that you should find me some work where I can earn enough money to marry her. I want to work for the money,' he said vehemently, his brows down. 'I don't want you to give us a penny.'

'Work,' said Mr Lockwood contemptuously. 'What can you work at? You've no training, no experience, for all I know, no brains. You shouldn't have gone into a bank if you wanted to make a fortune.'

'It was you who put me into a bank,' said Martin.

Mr Lockwood was taken aback. He had forgotten. It was a

long time ago and much had happened since. But his flushed face darkened further.

'Circumstances put you into a bank,' he said levelly. 'But of all the damned cheek,' he went on through his teeth. 'To throw it into my face that I tried to help you. What claim had you on me? What claim had your mother on me? Yet her idea, and yours too, evidently, is that I should do for you what I do for my own family. But why the hell should I?'

He glared at Martin.

'We've put up with altogether too much from your family,' he went on. 'Your mother used to pester my life out with her niggling affairs. Then your sister pushes in and goes to France with my girls and disgraces them. Then she insults my wife. And now you come trying to tie a girl like Clare to a four years' engagement, if you can't cadge enough from her father to get married on sooner. Now get this clear' – Mr Lockwood leaned far over the desk – ' when Clare marries, she'll marry a man who can keep her in the way she's used to. Clare's worth the best and she's going to have it. You mustn't come to this house again.'

Martin, white to the lips, got up from the chair.

'Clare . . .' he began.

'You leave Clare to me,' said Mr Lockwood, a great vein swelling ominously on his forehead. 'And get out. You've ruined my work for tonight, coming here with your silly talk. I needed all my wits tonight, and you've scattered them. Go on. Get out.' He struck the desk again. 'Didn't you hear me?'

Martin stood, dazed by the quick ruin of his hopes, staring desperately at Mr Lockwood. But when the furious voice shouted again, he made for the door. He went through it, leaving it wide, and Clare came running round the corner of the passage.

'Oh, Martin, Daddy's angry. I knew he would be. I knew . . .'

She clasped his arm, but he strained away, shaking away angry tears.

'Clare!'

At the thick anger of the voice from the library, the young lovers froze. Clasping Martin's arm, Clare looked to the open door. Martin felt her response to her father. He twisted round to search her face. His own, when she looked up at him, was so convulsed and strange, that she shrank from it.

'Clare!' William Lockwood got up in a fury from his desk.

That he should call and she shouldn't come. . . He made a rush for the door. But suddenly, he fell headlong.

'Clare!' he shouted in outraged astonishment as he went down. He wasn't used to falling. He had never fallen in his adult life. By the time he was scrambling to his feet, Clare, with Martin behind her, was beside him.

'Oh, Daddy, are you hurt?' she was asking, her arms round him. 'Are you hurt, Daddy?'

'Yes, I am,' said William Lockwood angrily, his coat worked up under his arms, a line of white shirt showing round his thick middle. 'That blasted boy. Upsetting me. I nearly knocked myself out. I'm too heavy to fall like that,' he complained, breathing heavily. He stood, leaning on Clare. 'I'm quite winded,' he said.

The disturbance had communicated itself to the hive. Mrs Lockwood came hurrying from the drawing room, the twins flew down the stairs. In a flash, they had grouped themselves about him, all questions and concern.

'William! What happened?'

'Daddy, are you hurt? Daddy, what is it?'

'Have you been fighting him?' said Bee, whipping round on Martin.

They had closed in, all eyes upon Martin. In a few moments he had become a complete outsider. Their faces showed him how absurd it had been to think he was one of them. He looked back at them, at Clare. She was one of them, she was on her father's side. Although her father had the others, she clung too; she wouldn't come out and stand beside her lover. The appalling conviction strengthened in him; she hadn't enough of love or courage to make a breach with her family. Not for his sake, anyway.

'Get him out of the house,' said William Lockwood, his heavy arms on his daughters' shoulders. 'I've told him to go. It's coming to something if we can't have our house to ourselves.'

'You must go,' said Mrs Lockwood coldly.

They didn't even ask what he'd done, why he should be ordered out. They were united to thrust him out, even she, even Clare. Although she said soundlessly over her shoulder: 'I'll write,' she wanted him to go. She didn't want him to upset her father. Father came first, that was plain.

Tightening his accusing lip, Martin turned and went down the passage. Behind him with murmurs of concern and support, his family helped William Lockwood to a chair. Effie kept her arm about him, the girls knelt on the floor looking anxiously into his face.

'Bee, I think you'd better telephone for Dr Gray,' said her mother.

William shook his head in protest.

'Yes, dear, just to be on the safe side,' said Effie, and Bee ran.

William Lockwood, his eyes closed, kept his hand over Clare's. His quick brain saw the advantage he could draw from the situation.

He would sham illness and take Gray into his confidence. Gray had a girl of his own and would have been no more willing than he was for her to marry a bank clerk. Gray would order him a holiday. They would all go away for several weeks and get Clare out of that young fool's neighbourhood. Clare would do anything for her Daddy if she thought he was ill.

He looked through his apparently closed lids and the sight of her face at his elbow smote him with compunction. It was a shame to make her so anxious. But it had to be done. Far better that she should suffer a little anxiety now than get herself tied up for life to that impoverished young whipper-snapper.

And it would be easy to detach her from him, because see how concern for her father had driven out all thought of the lover already. The choice she had obviously made warmed William Lockwood's heart. Bless her, she loved her Daddy best after all.

With a sigh, he let his limp hand slip from hers. She gathered it back in both her own and held it lovingly.

But she strained her ears for the sound of the front door

closing on Martin. She couldn't go after him, she couldn't leave her father. That was unthinkable, but her eyes wandered piteously over the faces of her mother, her sisters, her father – the ones who kept her there.

CHAPTER THIRTY-TWO

When he came in at the end of the day at the bank, and saw a letter from Clare on the hall table, Martin let it lie. He knew there was no hope in it. She had chosen her father, as he ought to have known from the beginning she would. He hung his hat on the pegs and stood in the hall for a blank moment.

But when his mother called from the kitchen: 'Is that you, Martin?' he seized the letter and went swiftly upstairs without answering.

Closing the door of his room, he threw the letter onto his table. He told himself he wasn't going to read it. What was the good? But in the end, he opened it.

It was short, no more than a few lines. Her father was ill, Clare wrote. The fall had upset him very badly. He needed her and she was with him all the time. That was why she couldn't write properly yet. She was very, very sorry, she wrote, about it all.

'But I told you it wasn't the time to say anything to Daddy, didn't I?'

She ended, as usual, with all her love; but it seemed a mere phrase to Martin. Just something to end up with, something shallow, girlish and meaningless. All her love, he thought bitterly. It looked like it, didn't it?

He threw the letter into the mean iron grate they put into bedrooms in Byron Place and struck a match. It was the first letter of hers he had ever destroyed. Then he went down to tea.

In the bosom of a family, nothing can be hidden. One might wish, when things are bad, to suffer unobserved, but in a family there is no chance of that. Martin's mother and sisters knew at once that something had gone wrong.

'What can have happened?' said Mrs Hunter, looking to Thea for explanation. At some point in the family history, parents begin to look to children for explanation, instead of children to parents.

'What is it?' said poor Mrs Hunter.

'They've found out he's in love with Clare and got rid of him,' said Thea.

'Oh, Thea, do you think so?'

'Yes, I do.'

Mrs Hunter was silent for a time.

'I'm afraid I've managed very badly for you all,' she said wistfully at length.

'Don't think like that, darling. You didn't manage at all,' said Thea, unconscious of irony. 'It just happened. But I think even you will agree that our association with the Lockwoods has done us a lot of harm.'

'Yet I don't know why, dear,' said Mrs Hunter in a bewildered way.

'I'm not sure that I do either,' admitted Thea. 'But it's turned out like that, hasn't it?'

Mrs Hunter sighed.

They sat in silence by the fire in the front room. Now that there was no need to be so careful they had a fire there every day. But tonight they couldn't enjoy it while Martin moved about so restlessly overhead. Sometimes it sounded as if he threw himself on his bed in despair, thought Thea.

She knew what he suffered. No one knew better, she thought bitterly. She had been through all this herself.

But underneath the compassion she felt for her brother ran a strong undercurrent of satisfaction. *Now* Martin knew what the Lockwoods were. Martin had joined her now. They had injured him too now.

Staring at the familiar cracked yellow tiles of the fireplace before her, she was alarmed to realise that she was glad this had happened. She seemed to be glad, she thought in amazement, that Clare had proved so weak and Mr Lockwood such a villain, and glad that she and Martin had suffered so at their hands. It was very strange to feel like this, and not at all estimable. Her expression, for once, was rather like her mother's in its bewilderment.

Upstairs, Martin's door opened and closed.

'He's coming down,' said Mrs Hunter, and made room for him at the fire.

But he went through the passage and out of the house.

He had decided, suddenly, to go to Oakfield and try to attract Clare's attention somehow, to get her to come out to him and put an end to his misery by making a decision one way or another. He told himself he could bear anything if only he knew what she was going to do. Would she stick to him, or would she give him up to please her family? That was what he must know, he told himself, hurrying up the main road, deserted on this wild wet night and lit by the unearthly radiance of the high arc lamps.

There was no light at the gates of Oakfield. No one was expected. He walked up the drive on the grass verge, noiseless as a thief. The dark bulk of the house loomed up, cracked by a chink of light at Mr Lockwood's curtains. They must all be up there with him, he thought, imagining them clustered round the bed, solicitous, concerned. Just because he'd fallen, he thought with scorn. She'd give him up because her father had tripped over a rug.

He circled the house, impotent, despairing. How could he get her down? How could he let her know he was there?

One occupant of the house knew. Boz, her dog, whimpered on the other side of the front door. He always came joyfully to meet Martin and he came now.

Martin, tonight, was slightly crazy in all he did. He went up to the door and crouching low to the dog's level, spoke through the crack.

'Boz, old chap, fetch her. Fetch Clare. Bring her down Boz. Good dog.'

But when the dog broke into excited barking and it was likely someone would come to the door, Martin plunged away and ran down the drive as if pursued.

What was the good of bringing a maid out and asking to see Clare? Mr Lockwood was out of the way, but how could he get past Mrs Lockwood and the twins? He couldn't get past her family, but Clare could, and if she really wanted to, she would.

He hurried home to write again to beg, to implore her to want to. That was what he had to do; to rouse her to a passion of love and longing equal to his own; and if he couldn't do it, it was all no good.

But while he was writing to her, she was writing to him. The next morning, before he had posted his letter, hers came to say they were going to Switzerland at once. She had promised not to see him before she went, or write to him while she was away. She had promised, for this short time, to devote herself entirely to her father.

'I had to promise, Martin,' she wrote. 'After the doctor had gone today, Daddy told me, though he asked me not to tell the others so that they shouldn't be frightened, he told me his heart is bad and that if he is to recover, he mustn't be agitated in any way. It is a shock about his heart. I shall always be frightened of anything happening to him now. He has been so good to us and worked so hard to give us everything we could possibly want. I must do as he asks, at least until he is well enough to stand the shock of my going against him. When this will be, I don't know. I feel very hopeless about us today, Martin, but I have no choice but to do as Daddy asks. You do see that, don't you?'

With an expression of bitter disillusionment, almost of contempt, Martin tore up the letter and went to the bank as usual.

Mrs Lockwood put it about that they were going to take a family holiday in Switzerland because William had been working too hard, but the twins let it out to their friends, and the friends to the town in general, that Clare was being got away from Martin Hunter, who had actually dared to think he could be engaged to her on three pounds a week. Three pounds a week, reiterated the twins, demanding that their hearers should be as indignant as they were. Wasn't it incredible, they said, working off their own chagrin in this way.

They had looked upon Martin as something to be shared by the three of them, rather in the nature of a second car. To find that, while they had been using him for their ends, he had been using them for his, was a shock to the twins. Unforgivable, they said, so dreadfully underhand.

'But we can't blame Clare too much, Bee,' defended Muriel. 'You know what she is. So sweet she could never keep anybody in their place. But, really, Bee, it is the most frightful presumption on his part, isn't it?'

'Awful,' agreed Bee, her mouth full of chocolate creams. 'Simply awful.'

It was nearly six o'clock, nearly time to close the office and go home. Oliver stood at the long desk, going through a letter book. Thea was tidying things away.

The days were lengthening. A wet primrose light lay over Wells Road. The lamps were like jewels, pale but piercingly bright. The air that came in at the top of the windows was fresh and mild.

Thea came to a stand at Oliver's elbow. She waited, careful, as usual, not to interrupt. He always felt rather guilty, sustaining the part of a busy man, whereas the truth was he hardly did any work in this office. He only came to be with her. But he kept her waiting for a few moments for the sheer pleasure of it. She waited with simplicity, like a good child.

'Well?' he said at length.

She looked into his face.

'Oliver, I wish we could do something about Martin.'

'Martin? I thought he looked pretty sick. What's wrong?'

'Clare Lockwood must have turned him down. I suppose they made her. Anyway they've taken her to Switzerland to get her away from him.'

'That's it, is it? I knew Lockwood was out of town.'

'Martin hardly eats anything and he doesn't sleep either. I hear him moving about in the night. He is so wretched and it's all hopeless. They'll never let her marry him.'

'Well, I don't suppose he'd let any of us say anything to him about it,' said Oliver.

'Not one of the family, no. We never do butt in and I daren't now. Specially not about one of the Lockwoods. He would only think I was trying to turn him against Clare to get my own back. But perhaps you could say something, Oliver? Perhaps you could make him see that it's no good hoping. It's better when you give up hope, I think.'

She was referring to herself, he knew, and was stung.

'What d'you want me to do?' he said roughly. 'I can't call and pen him in the front room while I tell him love's nothing, really. Just something he'll get over by and by. It's so true, isn't it?'

Her eyes fell. She turned away. He was smitten with compunction.

'What is it you want me to do?' he said.

She turned back eagerly.

'I thought you might talk to him somehow. You know, there's some sort of tremendous common sense, or uncommon sense, about you, Oliver. I don't quite know what it is, but it has a bolstering-up effect.'

She smiled up at him and he felt a glow of pleasure. Fancy her saying this to me, he thought. He was too pleased to make any modest disclaimer. He looked like a boy given an unexpected piece of cake.

'Martin tramps about the streets half the night now,' she said. 'Could you follow him and come up with him by accident, sort of?'

'I can try it,' he said.

At once, that very night, he set about trying. To be asked by her to do something filled him with pleasurable strength, as if she called all his powers into play. He felt able to move heaven and earth, he said to himself. She was his enthusiasm. When she asked him to do anything, he was like a runner ready to shoot away from the mark. But he had to disguise it. It wouldn't do to let her see how eager he was. He must keep up a bit of dignity.

All the same he couldn't help clapping on his hat and going out that very night to stalk Martin.

Though it was dark, he recognised him by his walk. Both Thea and Martin walked noticeably well, and even with his shoulders hunched in depression, Martin walked with easy grace. Coming up with him, Oliver said: 'Hullo. Where are you going?'

'I'm not going anywhere,' said Martin, pulling up like a difficult horse, his very stance implying that if Oliver was going that way, he wasn't.

'Pity. It's a nice night and I feel like a walk.' Oliver brought out a packet of cigarettes, took one himself and offered them to Martin, who hesitated to take one, but did. Oliver lit it for him and the flare of the match showed the other's face.

'Thea's right,' thought Oliver. 'He's badly hit.'

'Come on, come with me,' he said. 'I'm worried and I want to walk it off. Let's walk round by Firbank and home again. It's only half-past nine. Come on.'

'I can't,' said Martin. 'I don't want to.'

'I don't want to go by myself,' said Oliver. 'Be a good chap and keep me company.'

Martin stood for a moment, then with an expression of annoyance, he turned and began to walk up the main road.

No matter how you resent other people's company, when you have it, you can't concentrate so fiercely upon your misery as you would without it. The enduring of the company acts as a counter-irritant.

Martin walked for some time in savage silence, but the night was fine. Aldworth might be ugly, but the air was good. It came straight from the sea. The main road was almost empty, the street lamps shone into the budding trees making them miraculous in beauty. In spite of himself, unaware that Oliver was speeding up the pace, Martin walked more briskly.

The two tall young men, one broader, solider than the other, left the last lamp behind and entered the soft country dark. The ring of the pavement gave way to the scrunch of the stony lanes. Over the fields and woods the stars were bright. They passed by Firbank Hall, the bulk of the house dark. No one had taken it. And no one would, said Oliver. The day of big houses was over. Martin snorted briefly. He thought Oliver didn't know what he was talking about, but couldn't be bothered to say so. The Lockwoods and all their friends were firmly established in their big houses, weren't they? And what could shake them?

'I'm very interested in stars,' said Oliver, lifting his face. 'I've got a book. . . . See,' he said, taking Martin by the shoulder. 'I'll show you Orion. See there, and there. And there. See him striding the sky. The Mighty Hunter, he's called. See his belt and hunting-knife? The first time I found Orion, I let out a shout. To think he's been there since the beginning of the world and I've only just found him.'

'Mmmm,' mumbled Martin.

They walked through the little wood where Thea had first seen Angela Harvey years ago. How they came to halt and lean on the railings and begin to talk, Oliver didn't quite know, but he managed it somehow. Clare's name was not mentioned. He made the bank the scapegoat.

'I think you ought to get out of that bank,' he said. 'You've never liked it.'

Martin said nothing. There was the sound of running water; the branches of the young trees reached up without stirring, and the stars shone.

'If you don't mind my saying so,' said Oliver carefully. He didn't know whether it was best to sting Martin into action or whether to sympathise and comfort. Whether to be soft or hard, he didn't know.

'If you don't mind my saying so, I think, as a family, you're inclined to give up. Give you a blow, you don't rally. You shrink and nurse your pride. Look at Thea and that French affair. I admire you all, you've got things our family hasn't and never will have, but by George, I don't think you go the right way about living. Look at your mother, sweet though she is. I think it's resentment,' said Oliver, puzzling them out. 'But you'd better remember that if you fall out of life, you fall out. No one bothers. Those nearest to you fall out with you, perhaps, but your neighbours don't care, the town doesn't care, the world doesn't care.

'I think you've got to get rid of all idea that you've had a bad deal,' he said, lighting another cigarette. 'Ten to one, you've not had half such a bad deal as the next man.

'I'm talking to myself as well as you,' he said, suddenly gloomy. 'If I could take my own advice, I'd be all right.'

'You?' Martin was pricked out of self-preoccupation with surprise. 'Why you? You get everything you want. Everything you touch does well.'

'Huh,' said Oliver shortly, and was silent.

'Well, never mind me,' he said by and by. 'I can look after myself. It's you we're dealing with at the moment. I tell you what,' he said, suddenly turning to the other, 'it's just struck me. By George, I think it might be the very thing. Leave the bank and come into Guerison. I can put you in London. Waterworth's just gone there, but I'd like him in Manchester really. He's more the type. I can do with you in London when you're trained.'

'But I don't know anything about your work,' began Martin. He was as alarmed as if his happiness were threatened, instead of his misery.

'You can learn, can't you?' said Oliver.

'But London . . .' said Martin.

'Aye, London. That's what you need. To get away.'

'But how can I leave Mother and the girls?'

'Why not? You're not doing much for them here, are you?'

Martin was silent for a moment, hanging over the railings.

'You're right,' he said bitterly. 'I'm not. Molly does ten times more and Thea does as much.'

'Give your notice at the bank, that's the first thing. Give it tomorrow. I'll see the manager, too. I'll say I need you. After all, I've got a pretty big overdraft there now. I'm important.'

'London . . .' said Martin heavily.

'Oh, you'll be miserable all right, but you'll be miserable in a different way. It's quite a benefit, a change of misery,' said Oliver wryly.

'I tell you Guerison's going to be good,' he said, straightening from the unaccommodating railings and beginning to walk home. 'You'd better come in when I ask you. If you don't, you'll be sorry later.'

'It's very good of you, Oliver,' said Martin. 'But I never thought . . .'

'Well think now, by way of a change,' said Oliver. 'Lockwood put you into that bank and there you've stuck ever since, resenting it all the time and doing nothing about it. I should think the manager'll be dam' glad to get rid of you. You're keeping better men back. Come on now. Walk up and let's work things out.'

On the way home, Martin was subjected to a battery of persuasion and argument.

'Take one step, that's all that's necessary at first. If you can't really stick London, you can come back. But make the move out of here. You know,' said Oliver sheepishly, 'c'est le premier pas qui coûte.'

He paused expectantly; but Martin made no comment. He was disappointed, until it struck him that it was a greater compliment that his French should be taken for granted. He applied himself again to the task of persuading Martin to leave the place of his torment.

'You want to get away, don't you?' he said, when they reached the Hunters' gate. 'Before she comes back, you want to get out, don't you?'

'Yes,' said Martin. 'To tell the truth, I had thought of going to Canada.'

'Don't be an ass,' said Oliver roughly. Rough treatment had been fairly successful. 'What could *you* do in Canada? It takes men like me to succeed in Canada.' Then he hoped Thea hadn't heard through some open window. But for her, he thought suddenly, I'd have been a great braggart.

'Well, let me know in the morning,' he said. 'Good night.'

He was at his own gate before Martin caught him.

'Here – Oliver – you're a good chap! First Molly, now me. I may not be able to take your offer, but thanks all the same . . .'

'Oh, go to bed,' said Oliver. 'And let me. See you in the morning. I'll walk down with you.'

He went into his own house. Easy enough, he thought, to arrange other people's lives, or at least see how they could be arranged, but a different thing to deal with your own. If anyone advised him to cut adrift from Thea for his own good, would he? Not he, he thought grimly, going into the house and shutting the door on the stars.

Martin emerged haggardly to join Oliver at the gate next morning.

'All right, I'll go,' he said.

'Good lad,' said Oliver warmly. It took guts to come to that decision, he knew, and he was glad the boy had them. 'Now, I'd like you to put in some time with me before you leave,' he said, and plunged into an exposition of his plans.

But if he had hoped to inspire Martin with immediate enthusiasm, he was disappointed. Frowning with the effort of concentration after a sleepless night, Martin listened. It all seemed pointless in the extreme, but he tried to pin his mind to what Oliver was saying.

He felt, not better, but worse for his decision. The operation was severe, nothing less than amputation, but he knew that if he shirked it, he would waste in sickly expectation. The strain of being where he might come across Clare at any moment would keep him on the rack. The only thing to do was to go.

He gave notice at the bank. Oliver followed it up and arranged that he should be released at the end of the week. The manager, he reported, was very decent about it. The truth was, as he knew, that the manager was relieved to let Martin go.

'You are good. I knew you'd find some way of helping. You always do,' said Thea, coming to stand at the desk, so close that when Oliver turned, her hair brushed his cheek and made him slightly dizzy.

'He had to make the decision himself,' he disclaimed. 'And I'm glad he made it, though, mind you, he'll be just as miserable there as here.'

'Yes, but here, he'd get worse and worse. There, he may get better. There's a chance anyway, isn't there?'

Unobtrusively, careful never to refer to the reason for his going, Martin's mother and sisters got his things together. There was a tacit agreement that he should go off so quietly as to seem not to be going at all.

Thea was restive. She wanted to discuss the Lockwoods with her fellow victim, she wanted to know what had happened, to compare notes, to burn with mutual indignation. But to look at Martin's closed, almost expressionless face was to be silenced. She didn't know that she had looked the same when she came home from France.

The family barriers were kept up all the time, even to the last moment of departure.

Oliver went with them to see Martin off. As he stood waiting for the train, it struck him suddenly that, although it often seemed as if he made no headway with her, things had entirely changed since he was last on this platform with Thea. He looked at her to see if she remembered, but she seemed to take it as a matter of course that he should be there, one of them, included. Yet at the last time she had repudiated and snubbed him; and from that had sprung his determination to make himself unsnubbable, by her or anyone else.

With apparent nonchalance, he walked away down the platform to pass a looking-glass set in an advertisement panel. He glanced sideways and felt a modest satisfaction at the job he had made of himself. He fancied he looked like any other 'Manchester man' now in his well-cut suit, with his bowler hat at the correct angle. He almost blushed to think what a bounder he must have looked when she went off to France. She was right to snub him; he needed it. He was too cocky by half in those days; but she had fairly knocked the stuffing out of him. She had been the one to teach him that work, money, determination couldn't get everything. What he wanted most, he couldn't have and because of that, the rest seemed almost worthless. He went back to stand beside her, humble again.

Far down the line, the train appeared, its chest out, its plume of black smoke rolling. People moved to the edge of the platform.

'Goodbye, dear,' said poor Mrs Hunter. She daren't weep; by sheer force of repression, Martin wouldn't let her.

With his singularly sweet smile, he bent to kiss them. He picked up his cases and got into the nearest carriage. He sat down in the corner near the window. His mother and sisters stood watching him, wistfully, but he did not look at them until the train started. Then with another of his smiles and a lift of the hand he was borne away.

Thea walked quickly off, blinking tears back. If only Martin were different; if only he would say something, show something, he wouldn't wring their hearts so much.

Oliver stalked behind her, thinking she must want to be left to herself. But in the subway, she turned and took him by the arm.

'It's too bad,' she said. 'Those Lockwoods driving him away . . .'

Oliver walked on, holding his arm very carefully under her hand. He daren't press it in sympathy; he daren't even look down to see if it was really there. But it certainly had been for a moment, because there was such a difference when it was not.

As she came out at the front of the station, Mrs Hunter came to a halt.

'Oh, dear,' she said.

'What is it? What's the matter?' they asked.

'I meant to ask Martin to go through those papers before he went and I forgot.'

'What papers?'

'My papers. The ones Mr Lockwood sent back, the ones in the hat-box. There might be something Martin ought to have looked at. I don't know,' she said helplessly.

'He's not gone for ever,' said Oliver indulgently. 'He'll get a summer holiday like anybody else. Is there anything urgent in the papers?'

'No, I don't think there's ever been anything urgent. It's only because he's gone and can't look at them that I remembered perhaps he ought to,' admitted Mrs Hunter characteristically.

'Well, come along,' said Oliver, smiling. 'I can look at them any time you like.'

Mrs Hunter's face cleared.

'That would be kind of you, Oliver. My mind would be quite at rest then because I know you know all about that sort of thing.'

CHAPTER THIRTY-THREE

The Lockwoods were having what for them was an unusual holiday. They had never been enterprising in the matter of holidays, but went to places principally because other people had been to them. In their social circle names of resorts and hotels were handed about like chain-prayers and the Lockwoods received and passed them on in their turn, gratified to be able to add their personal recommendation.

This year several people from Aldworth had been to Switzerland for winter sports and when a holiday of several weeks suddenly opened before them, the Lockwoods decided to go to Switzerland too. The sports were over, the snow was gone, but when the Watsons and the Bensons talked about Switzerland, the Lockwoods, that is, Mrs Lockwood and the twins, wanted to be able to talk about it too; and you can't really do that unless you have been there.

But the people who go to Switzerland for winter sports are not the same sort of people who go for spring flowers. When the Lockwoods put themselves into the hands of a young man at the Travel Bureau, he took it for granted that they were going for the flowers and placed them accordingly.

The Lockwoods were taken aback by the simplicity of the little hotel, midway between the lake and the mountains, at which they in due course arrived. As with the girls at Villeneuve, it was not what they had expected. Shown to their rooms, they were inclined to be affronted by pitchpine and whitewash. Mrs Lockwood wasn't at all sure it would do, and spoke at once of moving down to one of the great hotels below.

'But what a view!' cried William, going out to their balcony. 'What sunshine! And what air!'

Mrs Lockwood, though doubtful still, conceded these.

'You know, Mummy, it *is* rather nice really,' said Bee, as they met in the passage to go downstairs.

In hotels, the Lockwoods always went up and downstairs in a body.

'I'm going up now, dears,' Mrs Lockwood would call, and the girls would rally to her side to go up too.

'I'll be ready in a moment,' a twin would announce from her door and the others would linger on the landing until she joined them.

They assembled now, the twins from their room, Clare from hers. She was glad she was not a twin. It would have been unbearable to share a room with anyone, however dear, in her present misery.

In the first flush of self-sacrifice, in her fear for her father's health, for his very life as she had thought, she had cut herself off from Martin. But already she was appalled by what she had done. What did Martin think of her? What would she have thought of him, if he had given her up for Mrs Hunter, she asked herself.

At the time, it had seemed she was doing a noble thing, and that Martin ought to recognise it and have no difficulty, or not much anyway, in agreeing to it. But already she felt that she wasn't going to be able to keep the nobility up. But what if he took her at her word and expected her to? She alarmed and bewildered herself by these questions.

She was discovering that self-sacrifice is a most unrewarding thing; you seemed to get nothing in return. In giving up Martin for her father and her family, she had lost them too. She didn't feel right with them any more. Her mother and sisters now seemed to talk far too much and hardly ever about anything that interested her.

As for her father, she was beginning to doubt whether, even though gravely ill, he ought to have asked her to sacrifice Martin. Worse still, she was beginning to doubt if he were really as ill as he made out. To doubt the one she had always implicitly trusted was torment. At night, unable to sleep, she took herself to task for it. She wept and prayed about it. But the doubts persisted; they grew.

No such snake as family criticism had ever reared its head among the Lockwoods before. She was careful that they should not suspect it now. She kept her thoughts hidden and made a smile as she joined the others to go downstairs.

'It is nice, really. It has its own charm, hasn't it?' said Bee, looking about her at the sunlit passage with its white walls and arched doorways.

'You're right, dear,' said Mrs Lockwood, walking firmly down the strip of coco-matting. 'Although we wouldn't put servants into rooms furnished like these at home, it's quite attractive here in its way. I suppose it's because everything is so spotlessly clean. Be careful, girls, this matting is quite slippery on the stairs.'

Switzerland was just the place for the Lockwoods. In Venice, one whiff from a canal, the sight of one dead rat floating by as they breakfasted on a terrace, in Florence, one flea on a warm marble floor, and all the art and beauty of Italy would have been as nothing. The Lockwoods would have condemned Italy. When the twins talked of Villeneuve, the first thing they told everybody was that there were no tablecloths. But Switzerland was so clean, tidy and beautiful. Near and far, everything was perfect. Mrs Lockwood was as delighted with the purity of the muslin curtains at her windows as with the mountains she saw through them.

The food was exactly what they liked best. So wholesome, Mrs Lockwood kept saying with satisfaction at the butter, the cream, the chocolate and, above all, the cakes. Every afternoon the Lockwoods went down to Montreux and ate cakes until they could eat no more. Except Clare, who said they were too rich.

And the flowers, exclaimed the Lockwoods. The flowers, they cried, walking among them like children, even William. The fields and fields of wild narcissi filling the pure air with their lovely scent. 'But why do they pull them up in such hundreds and tie them to their bicycles?' lamented Muriel. The fritillaries and higher up the soldanellas and the gentians. The Lockwoods bought a book to identify them.

'The flowers alone are worth coming for,' said Mrs Lockwood.

'I'm so glad we didn't come in the snow,' said Bee.

Everything delighted them. The neat arrangement of logs at the little sawmills. The little graveyards, with no foolish outlay on memorials, Mrs Lockwood pointed out. Only tiny tombstones no bigger than a plate with 'Alphonse Petit. Au revoir' on them.

'And what do you need more than that?' asked Mrs Lockwood, holding her husband's arm and unaffected by death.

The edge of tiny white beads sewn to the bus-conductor's jacket collar took her fancy tremendously. 'Think of the washing it saves!' she said. 'And it looks just as good as linen.'

All the arrangements of the thrifty and practical people pleased her. A good housekeeper herself, she felt a warm affinity with this good-housekeeping nation. She had never thought to be at home in a foreign country, but, she frequently remarked, she did here.

They did only one thing that didn't suit them. They went to the top of a mountain. Carelessly, ignorantly, Mrs Lockwood and the girls in their thin frocks, Mr Lockwood in his thin suit, they boarded a little train. Smiling, they were carried higher and higher. Looking round, they marvelled at the view.

But it began to be chilly. William closed the windows but it didn't seem any warmer.

To the Lockwoods' amazement, their fellow passengers produced hitherto unsuspected fur coats, fur bonnets, fur gloves. The Lockwoods watched them put them on, their own cheeks blue, their bare arms turning to goose-flesh. They eyed with alarm the changing scene. No flowers now. No grass. But snow: actually snow. When the train ran into a cutting twenty feet deep in the snow, Mr Lockwood tore off his jacket and clasped it about the protesting Clare.

'When she's had a warm, Effie,' he said, 'you must have it.'

The other passengers didn't look at the Lockwoods in case they should have to lend them something.

The train reached the top. The Lockwoods got out. To make things worse, the sun for the first time was not shining. It was bitterly cold. The mountain top was terrible in desolation. The soul of Mrs Lockwood began to mew like a kitten up a tree. She was terrified.

The other passengers ran about in the wet snow exclaiming at the crocuses springing up at the edges. Mercifully, there was a bleak little building into which the Lockwoods were able to hurry. They had hot chocolate until the train was ready to start down again. It just saved them all from pneumonia, said Mrs Lockwood. They were very silent. Not only were they cold, but they had committed a solecism and they didn't like that. They hoped no one in Aldworth would hear of it.

The train started at last and the Lockwoods were gradually lowered to warmth and inconspicuousness.

They did not get over it as quickly as might have been expected. Strangely, no one made a joke of it. For some time there was, in Mrs Lockwood's pleasure in Switzerland, a gap torn by the icy wind from the top of the mountain. It was not only the cold up there, it was the awful loneliness, the changed aspect of the world as seen from that height. Somehow Mrs Lockwood had never thought the world could look like that.

Since the day he set up in practice for himself, William Lockwood had not been absent from his office for more than a week at a time. In his headlong career he had hardly ever paused. The very length, as well as the nature, of this holiday was having a curious effect upon him.

He had undertaken the holiday for the sole purpose of saving his daughter. His one idea had been to get away with Clare and keep her for himself, or at any rate from young Hunter. Snatching her up, he fled without much forethought, which was, for him, unusual. He had spent a few days in furious arrangement, hiding things, getting them out of the clerks' way, battening down the hatches until he could get back. Then he sped out of England, across France, and fetched up with his family in Switzerland with the sense of having brought something off.

All he meant to get out of the holiday was Clare. But the place put a spell on him. He found to his astonishment that he, the town-dweller, the harsh, hard-pressed man of affairs, was capable of quite simple happiness. He enjoyed sitting by the lake, taking placid excursions upon it, walking through the flowers, listening to the sound of the waterfalls and cow-bells. All this was very new to him. So far in his life, his happiness had mostly consisted of seeing his wife and his children happy. He had snatched and grabbed pleasure for them, passing it on to them and snatching incessantly at more, making himself very unpleasant in the process.

The bird that plucks its breast to line the nest for its young may be very disagreeable with other birds. And the fact that its young don't need more than a minimum of down, or that something else less hardly come by would do just as well, probably doesn't stop the bird from plucking. Mr Lockwood went on snatching and grabbing wealth, often other people's, long after his wife and daughters had more than enough.

Where he differed from the bird was that he had enjoyed snatching and grabbing for his family; whereas the bird can hardly, one imagines, enjoy plucking till the blood flows.

William Lockwood had enjoyed it; but in this long absence from the office, in this change of scene, in the companionship of Effie and the girls, cheerful, chattering, unexacting and therefore suiting him and resting him as no other could, he began to wonder if he would enjoy it so much in the future. He began to wonder if he wasn't rather tired of juggling, of keeping so many things on the go, of taking a bit here and putting a bit there, keeping his eyes open on all sides and his fingers in every pie in his office.

During this holiday, William Lockwood came to the conclusion that honesty is the best policy, if only because it is the easiest. And having come to this conclusion, having glimpsed the blessing of a quiet mind, it was ironical that some of his new-found peace should at once desert him.

It was chiefly in the night that he began to be a prey to apprehension. Lying in the pitch pine bed, with Effie asleep in hers beside him, the windows wide open to the vast, high sky, so much higher, so much vaster, it seemed, than the sky over Aldworth, William Lockwood would break into a sweat of fear. Suppose something should go wrong in his absence? In all the years it never had, but suppose it should now? Suppose Croft should take it into his head to go to Bolton and *look* at the property, on which he had taken out mortgages? And found it worth half what he thought? Suppose Besson should want to see . . . ? Suppose . . . ?

'I can't stop here,' thought William, tossing and turning in his bed, as, on the other side of the wall, Clare tossed in hers. 'I must tell Effie and the girls in the morning. We must all go back.'

He was mad ever to have left the office, he told himself. Let him go home, straighten everything out and *then* they could all come back and have a real holiday here.

But in the morning, he wondered what had possessed him. Breakfasting on the balcony in the glorious sunshine, the girls breakfasting next door on theirs, he returned to what he considered normal. Of course nothing could go wrong. It was all too minutely complicated, too well 'spread.' Nothing could happen to him unless every client he had came down upon him at once, and that, of course, was ridiculous.

All the same, as soon as he got back, he would begin to put things straight. He could do it now without making too much difference to Effie and the girls.

Mr Lockwood was still unregenerate enough to be glad he had had the use of his clients' money until it was convenient to him to do without it. All he wanted was not to be found out. The combination of majestic beauty and peaceful simplicity that is Switzerland had not brought about a complete reformation in the sojourner.

During the first part of the holiday, Mr Lockwood had remembered that, in Clare's eyes at least, he was supposed to be in poor health. He had remembered to stop now and again on the slope of a hill and spread a hand over the left side of his waistcoat. He was gratified by Clare's instant reaction.

'Are you all right, Daddy?' she asked anxiously.

'Yes, pet, thanks to you, I am,' he would say and with a little picturesque panting would walk on, supported by her arm.

But now in his preoccupation with his affairs, he forgot to play the invalid, and Clare, watching him, felt the time was coming when he would be strong enough for her to fight him openly about Martin.

CHAPTER THIRTY-FOUR

Edith Reade was to be married on the fifteenth of the month, and walking about the room to evade his sister's sharp eye, Oliver said he thought it would be a kindness to ask Mrs Hunter and Thea in on the day of the wedding.

Edie looked at him.

'Molly's coming, of course, but what d'you want with the other two?'

Edie kept up a smouldering hostility to Thea. She resented the fact that Oliver was in love with her, but she resented it still more that Thea hadn't jumped at him. If she had, Edie would have said: 'Trust her to get on to a good thing when she had the chance.' But as she hadn't, Edie was affronted.

The truth was that no one, in Edie's opinion, was good enough for Oliver. He had been her hero from childhood. All her life she would remember Saturday nights in Gas Street, when he, a boy of twelve, thirteen, fourteen, came in towards midnight from the market. She used to jump out of bed and run down, a little girl in her nightdress, to see what he had brought home. And from his old bag, he would bring out black puddings, bits of cold pork, damaged apples and oranges, over-ripe bananas, fish, tripe, vegetables, all sorts of things he had picked up or had had given to him by the stall-holders he had helped to pack up. The Reades could sometimes live for a week on the things Oliver brought home from the market. When he had emptied his bag, he brought his hard-earned money from his pockets and put that on the table too, banging down a bigger heap of silver and copper every week. 'Not bad, is it?' he would say, with a wag of his head at his mother and sister.

He had always been full of resource and cheerful strength. He had brought them, little by little, from poverty to plenty. He'd brought them from Gas Street to Mill Lane, to Byron Place, and would go right on to the top. There was no one like him, thought Edie indignantly, yet that girl wouldn't have him. She kept him dangling after her and made him suffer. She was changing him, too. He was trying to live up to her. Before long he would be too grand for his own folks. Not that there was any sign of that yet, but Edie felt it was bound to come. That girl would take him from them before she'd finished. And Edie didn't want her at the wedding.

'She and her mother'll cramp everybody's style, including yours,' she said to Oliver. 'Leave them alone, Noll. They're not our sort.'

'I'd like them to come, though,' said Oliver mildly. 'They're pretty down about Martin. It would be a change for them.'

'Oh, go on,' said Edie caustically, implying that she knew very well why he wanted them.

'We won't ask them to the church, of course,' said Oliver, as if that was quite out of the question, 'but we'll have a glass of champagne just before you go and ask them in to drink it with us. You won't see much of them then.'

'Champagne!' said Edie.

Fancy me having a wedding with champagne, she thought. As well as all those lovely clothes and linen and furniture. Champagne was the finishing touch to all Oliver had given her, and at that thought she relented.

'Oh, ask them if you're so set on it,' she said.

Complacency at getting his own way overlaid his face. She could have slapped him. There never was anybody so obstinate. Let him set his mind on a thing, he'd get it. That girl had better look out; he'd get her yet.

She watched him as he prowled up and down the room, setting his mind on getting the girl into the house, and she shook with hidden laughter. He was funny. He didn't know how funny he was, but men never did. You could see through most men as easily as glass. And those you couldn't see through, you'd better beware of. Thank goodness, Joe was as transparent as Noll.

She dealt her brother a fond clout as he prowled past her, and left him.

When Oliver gave the invitation, Thea and Mrs Hunter looked cornered.

'You're very kind, Oliver,' said Mrs Hunter. 'But we never go into society.'

'Society!' Oliver was astonished. 'You don't call us society, do you?'

'We never go out then!' amended Mrs Hunter.

'But why not?' asked Oliver.

Mrs Hunter could find no reply.

'Surely, you won't refuse to drink Edie's health?' he persisted. 'Molly will be there already. What's to stop you walking three doors down the street?'

Put like that, it was impossible to refuse.

So towards half-past one on the day of the wedding, Mrs Hunter and Thea, with the shrinking of nuns compelled to leave the cloister, emerged from the gate of number twenty-one and turned towards number fifteen.

They saw at once that the bay-window was full of faces, hats, hands holding glasses. Talk and laughter poured through the open front door like fumes from the exhaust of a fast-running car.

'Oh, dear,' murmured Mrs Hunter, recoiling.

'Mother, we can't . . .' began Thea.

But Oliver was on the look-out for them.

'Do come in,' he said, appearing in the discreet splendour of a new suit, a flower on the lapel, a cigar in his hand. 'It's so kind of you to come, Mrs Hunter. My mother will be delighted.'

Thea looked at him; she almost gaped. He was 'doing Mrs Maynard' and doing it so well that you couldn't have told. She looked into his face in amused congratulation. But his expression remained good-humoured, urbane, and he led the Hunters through the wedding guests, who obligingly flattened themselves against the walls of the passage.

The bride was in the front room.

'I shall do the thing properly,' she had said to Molly, and that was what she had done. She was in white satin and cotton orange-blossom. Her veil thrown back now, she stood under the chandelier with the guests packed around her, a hot, hilarious crowd. She darted an unwelcoming look at Thea, but gave her hand graciously to Mrs Hunter and introduced her groom, a stocky young man, compounded, it seemed, of sense and good humour.

Oliver settled Mrs Hunter in a chair in a corner and Thea stood beside her.

'Excuse me for a moment,' he said, and struggled out to the kitchen to open the champagne.

Thea felt self-conscious not to know anyone. She wished she could get to Molly at the other side of the room, but that meant pushing through the guests again and she couldn't face it.

Molly was bending happily over the table where her masterpiece, the white and silver cake, towered above her lesser achievements in the shape of patties, canapés, rolls, sandwiches, cakes and biscuits. A current of goodwill flowed from Molly through the food to the people who ate it and back again the same way. Her good cooking made the connection; she seemed to need no other.

She was quietly and with satisfaction seeing Edie off. She would now have the shop to herself. She would pay Oliver out by easy stages arranged by him. She had Mrs Haines to help her and a girl she had known at the cookery classes. She was enjoying today and looking forward to tomorrow. Smiling, she handed her plates about.

Weaving unobtrusively among the lively guests came old Mrs Reade, a little Noah's Ark figure in a black dress, her hair white and flat with a pink parting, her face worn and quiet. She had reached a place in life where the battles are over.

She came peering round the elbows, a plate of bread-and-butter in her hand. Although good things abounded on the table, it didn't look right to old Mrs Reade without a plate of bread-and-butter. She had just been to the kitchen to make some and now she put it on the table in case anyone fancied something plain.

She stood beside it, looking smilingly from one face to another. Although she took no part in it, she enjoyed the noise. It would be quiet enough tonight when Edie had gone.

Thea pressed forward and touched her arm.

'Mrs Reade, I'm Thea Hunter. And here is my mother.'

'I'm so glad to meet Oliver's mother at last,' said Mrs Hunter. 'How do you do, Mrs Reade?'

'Nicely, thank you,' said old Mrs Reade. 'Are you all right?'

'Thank you, I'm quite well,' said Mrs Hunter, who, from anxiety about Martin and consequent sleeplessness, didn't look it. 'We've been neighbours for a long time, Mrs Reade, but this is the first time we have met. It's dreadful, isn't it? I ought to have called, but I so rarely go out, you know.'

'I'm not one for going out much myself,' said Mrs Reade acceptingly.

'This is a sad day for you, I'm afraid,' said Mrs Hunter, whose code of manners made her keep on talking. 'You will miss your daughter.'

'Yes,' said Mrs Reade.

In spite of Mrs Hunter, there was a pause.

'I'm glad she's had it fine,' said Mrs Reade, looking up into Thea's face.

They smiled at each other. Thea was touched and charmed by the old woman's simplicity. She wished she had known her sooner.

Oliver and the best man came in with trays of glasses, and silence fell out of respect for the champagne. The guests took their glasses.

'Thank you very much, I'm sure,' said Oliver's Uncle Ned.

'Thank you, Noll,' said another with feeling.

'The bride and bridegroom. May happiness and long life attend them,' said Oliver, raising his glass.

He did just glance at Thea there to see if it met with her approval, and over the rim of her glass she smiled at him. Mrs Maynard must be a very good coach, she thought. He had no elocutionary airs and no affectation. He had deliberately acquired polish without spoiling his native grain; in fact, the polish brought that out. He had an ease now he hadn't had before; and ease had been all that was necessary.

He came to stand beside her. He saw at once that his mother and his love had taken to each other, and his heart filled with happiness. His mother might have been too plain for most girls, but Thea understood her worth. He stood beside them, not joining in their conversation, but being comfortable with them.

'Eh, Edie,' said Uncle Ned, warmed by the champagne, 'you've been a grand girl. Your mother will miss you.'

A look of affection passed between the bride and her mother.

'I shall miss her,' said Edie. 'She must stay and look after Noll for the time being, I know, but when Noll gets married, and I dare say somebody'll nab him before long,' said Edie, with a black look at Thea, 'then Mother'll come to live with us in Manchester, won't she, Joe?'

'She will,' said Joe heartily, 'and be very welcome.'

'Ten past two, Edie,' said Oliver.

'My goodness!' said Edie, plunging to the door.

When she had come down and had been waved off, the Hunters took their leave.

'Upsetting things, weddings,' said Oliver, accompanying them to their gate. 'I feel I don't know what to do with myself for the rest of this day. I must keep Mother company till she goes to bed, but she'll go early, she has had a hard day. I tell you what, Mrs Hunter, if it's all the same to you, I'll come in about nine o'clock and go through your papers. They've got to be gone through, so it may as well be now. I might be able to lay out something to better advantage for you. You never know.'

'It's very good of you, Oliver,' said Mrs Hunter. 'I'll get the hatbox down.'

CHAPTER THIRTY-FIVE

Although it was May, the evening was cool and Mrs Hunter was glad of an excuse for a fire in the front room. She had always found the long light evenings melancholy. A fire made them less so. She knelt at the hearth now, tidying it up, passing the brush over the cracked yellow tiles, chasing the ash round the side out of sight. The state of the tiles and the fact that the fire was always falling through the grate, no longer filled her with despair. They could afford to leave both grate and house now and probably would before long. Indeed, if only Martin hadn't fallen in love with Clare Lockwood and had to go away, they could all have been quite comfortable now, she reflected, sighing.

Molly had gone back to the shop to clear up after her wedding preparations. Thea was making coffee in the kitchen. In the yard, on the topmost twig of the ash-sapling, a thrush was singing with rapture. Looking at him over the short curtain, Thea wondered why he didn't go and live in the country. How could he be so happy as he was, among the backyards?

A door banged down the street, an energetic step rang on the pavement, Oliver tapped on the door and came in.

'Ah, Oliver,' said Mrs Hunter, rising from the hearth with a smile. She was glad to see him. Men do make a difference, coming in, she thought suddenly.

When Mr Lockwood removed his support, Mrs Hunter was left wavering helplessly in mid-air. But for some time she had been turning gradually, inexorably, to Oliver Reade. In the old days, when Thea said indignantly that Mr Lockwood never did anything for them, her mother used to close the subject by saying with finality:

'Well, dear, however that may be, I have the satisfaction of knowing that he is always there.'

Now she drew comfort from the fact that Oliver was 'there'. Happily there was justification this time for her confidence.

Oliver came to the fire.

'Heard from Martin again?'

'Yes, this morning. He's found quite a nice boarding-house in Endsleigh Street.'

'Good,' said Oliver.

Thea came in with her tray, making his heart beat faster, and he took the coffee from her hand.

'I know these little cups are the thing,' he said, looming large on the rug. 'But dashed if I can drink out of them. I can't get at the coffee. I never know whether to sup it up or chuck it down my throat.'

Thea laughed aloud, but Mrs Hunter murmured that next time he must have a bigger cup.

'Not I,' he said. 'I must manage like other people. Now where are these papers?'

Thea picked up the hatbox and poured the papers on to the table. Oliver sat down to them. Mrs Hunter and Thea drew up their chairs; they prepared to give him, for what it was worth, their full attention.

'There aren't many,' said Oliver, pushing them to the left and beginning to go through them.

'No,' said Mrs Hunter.

'This is the probate? Yes,' said Oliver, laying it to the right. 'And the life insurance. What's this?'

This was an envelope labelled in Richard Hunter's hand: 'Ancient History'.

'Only his mother's letters,' said Mrs Hunter. She pressed the old wound, but there was no pain now; only a deadness.

'And here are the particulars of your annuity, I suppose. Mmm. Well there's nothing to be done about that now, but I don't mind telling you that it was a rotten arrangement, even for a lawyer to have made.'

'Was it?' said Thea.

'Rotten. Lockwood did it to save himself trouble, I suppose.'

'His sole object, when he had to do anything for us, was to save himself trouble,' said Thea.

'Thea!' protested Mrs Hunter.

'More coffee, Oliver?'

'Thank you. You make good coffee.'

She smiled at him and put his cup carefully to his hand.

'Let's see what this is,' he said, picking up an envelope.

'Just particulars of War Savings Certificates my husband had bought for the children,' said Mrs Hunter.

Oliver laid it down. He drank his coffee.

A little roll of tracing cloth was conspicuous among the papers on the table. He took it up.

'That,' said Mrs Hunter, leaning forward, 'is the plan of the paddock adjoining Hill House. At least it's the plan of what my husband was going to do with it.'

'That was yours, was it? Isn't it the Lockwoods' now? You sold it to him apart from the house, did you? Rather a mistake, wasn't it?'

'I didn't sell it to him.' said Mrs Hunter. 'He took it over in discharge of a – of a debt.' Even after this length of time she didn't like to remember that Richard ever had a debt. 'My husband owed Mr Lockwood some money. He owed him three hundred pounds. In fact, he borrowed the money from Mr Lockwood to buy the paddock. I didn't know anything about it. Mr Lockwood told me the day he came to do Richard's papers. My husband had given him a note or something. That should be here, too. Yes, here it is.'

She handed a small piece of paper to Oliver and Thea craned over his arm to read it with him.

> I promise to pay William Lockwood, or order, on demand, the sum of three hundred pounds for value received.

'Mr Lockwood took the paddock in payment of the debt,' said Mrs Hunter. 'You see, he receipted it. It was very good of him.'

'Good of him?' said Oliver. 'How do you know that? Did you have the paddock valued? It might have been worth more than three hundred. Besides, it would have added to the value of your house. You seem to have made a bad deal, Mrs Hunter.'

'I left it to him,' she said. 'He was very good in seeing to my affairs after my husband's death. If I did lose a few pounds, it doesn't matter. He did so much for us.'

'Mother,' said Thea, who had been puzzling over the promissory note. 'Why did Father borrow the same sum twice from Mr Lockwood? Why did he borrow three hundred pounds both times?'

Mrs Hunter looked at her.

'He didn't, dear. He only borrowed once. I asked Mr Lockwood and he said that was the only time your father had borrowed money from him, and, as far as he knew, the only time he had ever borrowed from anyone.'

'But there's another receipt for three hundred pounds borrowed from Mr Lockwood,' said Thea. 'It's in the little bag I took to France. I think it's there still. I always meant to ask you about it.'

'But that bag was empty, dear. Quite empty. I remember that.'

'Well, this bit of paper was under the lining. I found it there, and it was such a safe hiding-place that I – I put something of mine in while I was at the pensionnat.'

From the tone of her voice, Oliver knew that it had been a love letter or love token of some kind.

'And you say it's still there?' said Mrs Hunter, bewildered.

'I think so. I'll go and see.'

'She must be mistaken,' said Mrs Hunter tranquilly to Oliver.

Thea ran upstairs and took the bag from the cupboard. The Cook's folder was inside, the receipt was inside that, but she would take the bag down to show them how successfully it had been hidden under the lining.

First, though, she must take out Jacques's note. On the little piece of paper, worn and soft from the constant handling it had once been subjected to, the tiny script was still clear: 'Have you been to the wood yet?' Dear Jacques, she thought. But all the magic had gone out of this note now. Yes, incredible though it was, there was no magic left. She looked at it for the last time, then rubbed it in her fingers and dropped it into the waste-paper basket. Bag and folder in hand, she ran down again to the front room, where Oliver and her mother waited comfortably, with no impatience.

'Here you are,' she said, laying the receipt on the table before them.

They bent over it.

'But I don't understand,' said Mrs Hunter after a long scrutiny. 'Thea, can you find my spectacles, dear?'

Thea found them on the bookcase and Mrs Hunter put them on. She bent again over the receipts now laid side by side by Oliver.

'You see,' said Mrs Hunter. 'You see, this one, the one Mr Lockwood gave me when he took over the paddock, is dated a fortnight after my husband's death, but the other one, the one Thea found in the bag is dated *before* . . .'

'I must have a cigarette on this,' said Oliver. He proffered his case absently to Thea. 'Oh, I forgot, you don't smoke . . .'

He lit a cigarette and stared at the two small pieces of

paper. Mrs Hunter and Thea looked from him to them, waiting.

The fire fell softly together, pouring a little shower of red cinders through the grate. Thea got up and shovelled them back again. She put more coal on and returned to lean on the table, her eyes intently on Oliver's face.

'Can you remember exactly what happened when Mr Lockwood took over your husband's papers, Mrs Hunter?' he said.

Mrs Hunter brightened, like a pupil who knows the answer to that question, if to no other. She had a good memory, too good, perhaps, since it held her imprisoned in the past.

'I remember very well,' she said. 'He came one morning and went through the papers, just as they are here, except for these few connected with the annuity and things. He went through them at this very table. He found this plan for the paddock and was very angry, because he'd tried to buy the paddock himself, you see. So had several other people, but Richard got it because old Sir Thomas had once been a patient of my father's. Mr Lockwood went away at lunchtime and when he came back in the afternoon he told me Richard had borrowed three hundred pounds from him, evidently to pay for the paddock. Mr Lockwood said he would accept the paddock in payment of the debt, and promised not to let anybody know that Richard had borrowed money from him. I was very relieved not to have to find three hundred pounds. And that's all.'

Oliver was thoughtful.

Excitement began to invade Thea. She shook with it, so

that she had to steady her attention like a burning-glass on the point at issue.

'Oliver, d'you think he cheated? D'you think Father had already repaid the money and he let Mother think he hadn't, so that he could take the paddock before anybody else could get it?'

'Well,' said Oliver cautiously. 'It looks rather like it.'

Thea jumped to her feet.

'That's what he's done,' she cried. 'He's cheated.'

Her face blazed with something more like exultation than anger.

'Here, wait a minute,' said Oliver. 'Don't leap to the worst conclusion too soon. We must look into this. Keep calm.'

'I can't,' said Thea breathlessly. 'He's cheated. It's obvious.'

'But why should a clever man like Lockwood take such a risk? He knew he'd given your father a receipt. Did he never look for it, Mrs Hunter?'

'I don't know,' said Mrs Hunter faintly. 'How do I know? All the papers were in this little bag. I remember he searched it very well and so did I. He asked over and over again if all the papers were there. But I can't believe he would cheat us . . .'

'He *has* cheated us.' Thea was angry it should be suggested that Mr Lockwood wasn't as bad as she was certain he was. 'He looked for the receipt, Mother, but it was under the lining and he didn't find it. He banked on its never turning up. He either made another promissory note, or he had the other already. I don't know which, but he cheated. Because he wanted the paddock and didn't want the person who bought our house to know he'd cut the paddock off first.'

'I can't think why such a man should take such a risk,' said Oliver thoughtfully.

'Because he didn't think there was one. He had such a contempt for Mother's brains. Oh, yes, he had, Mother. He always treated you as if you were a congenital idiot. That's why I hated him so when I was little. He thought she'd never find out, Oliver. Besides, he had all the papers. Who else was going to see them? All the same . . .' she faltered suddenly. 'Why did he send them back with the promissory note among them? Why didn't he destroy it?'

'Well,' said Oliver, 'he'd either forgotten all about it . . . You can't keep your eye on everything, specially if you're doing a lot of tricky business – or he came to the conclusion he was safe after – how many years – eighteen? Oh, he'd think he was safe. But the probability is that he'd forgotten all about it.'

'Wait, wait,' said Mrs Hunter, who had been looking from one to the other in bewilderment. 'You mustn't suspect Mr Lockwood like this. He would never cheat me, Thea. When your father had been dead only a few days? He would never cheat me.'

'Wouldn't he?' Thea was like a young fury, her hair swept back from her white face, her eyes blazing. 'Well, he did. He swindled us. And the insults we've suffered from them, the pride of those wretched twins. And the way Mrs Lockwood used to come round here patronising us and the way Mr Lockwood treated you when you went to his office. And I travelled to France,' she cried. 'I made that horrible journey, humiliated all the way by the Lockwoods, while I was carrying in my hand the evidence of their precious father's swindling.

And when I left the pensionnat that morning, when they stood by and sneered at me, I carried that bag past them, with the receipt in it. Then they came home and told everybody and people cut me all over the town and thought the worst of me. And Martin!' she flashed at her mother. 'What about Martin? He need never have gone. We had the Lockwoods in the palm of our hands. We *have* them in the palm of our hands, because *now*,' she said vehemently, 'now I'll get my own back.'

She stopped, breathless.

'Thea,' faltered her mother. 'After all, it was a long time ago.'

'Mother!' cried Thea in furious impatience. 'First you say he couldn't have done it, and then you say it was a long time ago. You don't mean to say you'd let him get away with it?'

'No, dear,' said Mrs Hunter timidly. 'But I would point it out quietly and ask for the money.'

'Oliver, have you ever met anyone like her? I'll point it out, Mother, but not quietly. I'll blaze it all over the town. Oh, if I could only get at him tonight. If they were at home now, I'd run all the way to Oakfield to charge them with it. Oliver, what can we do? How can we begin? You know. You'll help me, won't you?'

'I certainly don't think he ought to get away with it,' said Oliver.

She clasped his hand in both hers.

'I knew you'd be with me, I knew, Oliver. Oh – here's Molly coming in. Molly! Molly!' she called. 'Come here. Come quickly and hear the most staggering news you've ever heard in your life.'

Molly appeared in the doorway in her hat and coat, her eyes enquiring.

'D'you know,' said Thea, speaking very deliberately, 'that we've just found out, this very minute, that Mr Lockwood – eighteen years ago, a few days after Father died, swindled Mother out of the paddock by pretending Father owed him money, when he knew Father had paid him back.'

She waited, breathless again.

'What?' Molly was completely at a loss.

'Mr Lockwood swindled Mother when Father had been dead no more than a few days . . .'

She said it all over again, she hammered it home, but Molly caught no fire from her. She still looked puzzled.

'There must be some mistake,' she said. 'Nobody would do a thing like that.'

'But he has done it,' said Thea, flaring up again. Never had her mother and sister appeared so spineless as now. 'It's perfectly obvious he's done it. Look at the receipts for yourself. You can see the one I found refers to the promissory note. It's as plain as a pikestaff. If you can't see it, it's because you don't want to.'

'Why shouldn't I want to,' asked Molly, who was tired after her long day and not so ready as usual to be mild.

'Because you don't want to disturb anything,' said Thea. 'You don't want to bother. Have you forgotten,' she said ringingly, 'how miserable you were at the Watsons?'

'I don't particularly want to remember,' said Molly. 'Besides, if I hadn't been miserable then, perhaps I shouldn't be so happy now.'

'Bah,' said Thea. 'You've no guts.'

'Thea!' protested Mrs Hunter distressfully.

'She hasn't,' said Thea. 'I suppose you'd let him get away with this?' She turned on Molly again. 'You're so sunk in dough and sausage-meat. I suppose three hundred pounds is nothing to you now?'

'I'd certainly make him pay for the paddock,' said Molly. 'But it seems as if you mean to expose him publicly.'

'Of course I do.'

'But, Thea, it will be so dreadful for them. And for us,' said her mother. 'Such dreadful publicity.'

'He should have thought of that before he did it,' said Thea.

'You've always been obsessed with the Lockwoods,' murmured Molly, hardly daring to say it.

'And if I have,' cried Thea, 'you should have been too. I'm the only one, except Martin when it was too late, to see what they've done to us from the beginning. What's the matter with you? Why do you defend them? They injured you too, didn't they?'

'Once I'd shaken them off, I thought no more about them,' said Molly. 'And I've come through all right, haven't I?'

'But have I? Has Martin?' challenged Thea.

'You can't tell yet,' said Molly. 'It may be a good thing that Martin has gone to London.'

'What about me? You can't think it made no difference to me to have the Lockwoods coming home from France and spreading lies about me, can you?'

'It may turn out not to matter,' murmured Molly obstinately.

'Oh, just because it wasn't *you* who suffered,' said Thea bitterly.

She turned away from them.

'Oliver, let's go out. Let's go and walk up and down or something. I shall quarrel if I stay here. You keep these receipts, will you?' she said, gathering them up. 'Put them in your pocket-book. Put them in. That's right. Now come on.'

She was out of the front door before he had left his chair.

'She's right,' he said to the others. 'He ought to have it brought home to him. It's one of the dirtiest tricks I've ever heard of.'

'But we are such old friends. I can't think he would deliberately defraud us,' said Mrs Hunter distressfully.

'Well, that's what he's done,' said Oliver.

'Aren't you going to put a coat on?' he called to Thea from the door. 'You'll be cold.'

'Cold?' she cried from the street. 'I've never been so hot in my life.'

'All the same, you're going to have a coat.' He took one from the pegs in the passage and held it for her to put on. 'Which way?' he said.

'Oh, any way, any way, so long as we walk,' said Thea, and took his arm.

He almost hung back. He didn't think this arm-taking was a good sign. It might mean that it didn't mean anything. He glanced sideways. She was pressing forward like the figurehead of a ship, her dark hair blown back from her face, white and lovely in the moonlight. She was certainly not thinking of him.

'You see, Oliver,' she began, trying to explain to herself as well as to him. 'It's not only that he defrauded Mother in such a particularly mean way, it's – well, it's *if I had only known*. That's what I feel so dreadfully: if only I'd known. It would have saved me so much. I dare say it sounds crazy to you, but I've been at the mercy of those Lockwoods ever since I can remember.'

'Mmm,' said Oliver.

'Doesn't it seem hard, Oliver, that as children, when we'll take any mould, we should be formed for the rest of our lives by small things that don't really matter in themselves at all? My grievance is that the Lockwoods were silly, selfish, snobbish, creatures with no single saving grace – except, perhaps, Clare – and yet I minded about them.

'I minded about them,' she repeated. 'I don't know why. Too young to know I shouldn't. And I feel such terrible resentment now because, if I'd only known about Mr Lockwood, I needn't have minded at all.'

'Yes, well,' said Oliver, moved that she should have been hurt by anyone or anything, 'life's often hard on children.'

'But now,' her voice changing. 'Now, I'm going to get my own back. No matter what Mother says – or Molly – I'm going to bring Mr Lockwood to book.'

'Your mind's made up, is it?' said Oliver. 'You're really bent on it?'

She stopped in amazement and faced him.

'Of course I am. Aren't you going to help me?'

'I'm going to help you all right, so long as you know what it means. You'll probably ruin him, you know.'

'He deserves it, doesn't he? Surely you don't think he doesn't deserve it?'

'Probably, yes. In fact, he probably deserves it even more than we think. He's been so crooked in such a comparatively small thing that I'd be willing to bet he's crooked all through. Your mother's not the only one he's swindled. You may be pretty sure of that.'

'Oh, Oliver, do you think so?' She hoped so. She hoped Mr Lockwood would turn out to be the biggest villain the town had ever known.

'How are we going to begin?' she said.

'First of all, of course, we must be absolutely sure. I'll take these receipts to Gardiner tomorrow morning and put it all before him. By George, but he'll be interested! Everybody'll be enormously interested. Lockwood – who's been such a lion! There's a fable, isn't there, about a mouse who helped a lion? There'll have to be a new one about a mouse who ruined a lion.'

'Are you likening me to a mouse?'

'From Lockwood's point of view, you were no more. This will make a terrific sensation, you know. You're prepared for that, are you?'

'The bigger the better. What will you do when you've seen Gardiner? What's the next step?'

'I've only to mention it in a first-class carriage, going to Manchester and rumour will do the rest,' said Oliver.

'Ah – rumour! No one knows better than I do what rumour will do,' she said grimly.

They walked on. Byron Place was like a woodcut in the moonlight. The slate roofs were glistening tents, the iron railings ranks of dark spears. They walked up one side of the street and down the other, through the dark tunnel of the 'back' and out into the moonlight again.

'I don't know why,' she said. 'But a spell's broken.'

Everything would be different now. Martin avenged, the Villeneuve affair cleared up. When people knew what Mr Lockwood really was, she would be vindicated. But it wasn't only that.

'I feel released,' she said.

When they neared the house again, the front room was dark.

'They've gone to bed,' she said. 'I can go in now.'

He opened the gate for her, but going through, she paused and took a long look at him as he stood in the full light of the moon.

Puzzled, but his heart beating fast with sudden hope, he looked back at her. She was conscious of not wanting to leave him, of being deeply attracted to him, but she didn't understand why. He was surely just the same as before? Yes, of course he was the same, she thought. It was only the excitement about the Lockwoods getting into everything.

'Good night, Oliver,' she said and went into the house.

She went to bed but not to sleep. She was too excited even to lie down properly. She lay on her face, both arms clasping her pillow. In the darkness of the night, she waited for rumour to spread, she willed it to spread. Let but a spark reach such people as Mrs Barrett and Miss Wood and it would go like wildfire through the town. She had always despised Mrs Barrett and Miss Wood.

'But they have their uses,' she said wryly.

CHAPTER THIRTY-SIX

In the narrow old house with keystones over the square windows, converted long ago into lawyers' offices and now occupied entirely by William Lockwood's, Bromley, the managing clerk, was speaking on the telephone.

'Well, sir, we expect Mr Lockwood any day now. Is it anything I can do for you? Well, no, sir, Mr Lockwood always deals with your affairs himself. I have the keys of the strongroom, of course, but I don't really know how things stand, sir. I'm sure Mr Lockwood will be home at the end of this week. Very good, sir. I'll tell him to expect you. Good morning.'

He replaced the receiver and sat without moving at his desk. Something was up. That was the fifth enquiry this morning. Why did everybody suddenly want to see Mr Lockwood? And why had Bolton, Mr Gardiner's clerk, given him such a funny look in the bus yesterday?

Mr Bromley's skin suddenly crept with apprehension. Was it what he had said to Tom? Had it got about already? Had Tom . . .?

There would be the devil to pay, as it was, when Mr Lockwood came home and found rumours going about. But at the thought that Mr Lockwood might trace the rumours to him, Bromley felt almost suicidal.

Bromley had been Mr Lockwood's managing clerk for years, but he was still afraid of him. Mr Lockwood was too clever for him. It is both tiring and depleting to work with someone who always knows better and more than you do. Bromley had found years ago that if ever he did anything on his own initiative, it was sure to be wrong. The only way he had been able to keep going at all, in the confusion caused in him by Mr Lockwood's phenomenal sharpness, was to make his own mind a blank, and do and think exactly what Mr Lockwood told him to. For years Mr Lockwood had dominated Bromley.

But for the last five weeks Mr Lockwood had been absent. The pressure had eased and Bromley had begun to think for himself, and not only to think, but to talk. Only a little, though, and only to Tom, his wife's brother. But if he had betrayed him, if Tom had talked . . .

Unable to bear the thought any longer, Mr Bromley sprang up from the desk and seized his hat. He must go down to the brush-works, middle of the morning though it was, and see Tom at once.

But before he could reach the door, the intercommunicating telephone clicked again and he had to come back.

'Mrs Johnson wants to see you, sir,' said the office boy.

Bromley's first impulse was to say he couldn't see her and to slip out by the back way, often used by Mr Lockwood to avoid clients. But he changed his mind. Perhaps the old woman could tell him something.

'Send her in,' he said, and put his hat back on the peg.

Old Mrs Johnson's face was piteously crumpled with anxiety.

'Oh, Mr Bromley,' she began before the door was closed upon her. 'Is this dreadful story true?'

'What story, Mrs Johnson?' He waited with apprehension.

'Why, I've just heard that Mr Lockwood absconded weeks ago with everybody's money.'

In his relief, Bromley shouted with laughter. This was no tale of his. Nothing he had said to Tom could have turned itself into this. Watching him laugh, the old woman's face cleared.

'Then it isn't true?' she said.

'True? I've never heard anything so fantastic in my life,' said the clerk. 'I've had a letter from Mr Lockwood this morning. They'll all be home at the end of the week. I've just been on the telephone to Oakfield to tell the maids to make ready for them.'

Mrs Johnson sat down; relief was so sudden that it made her tremble.

'Oh, Mr Bromley, thank God it isn't true,' she said, pressing her handkerchief to her damp cheek. 'Thank God. I felt so ill about it, I thought I'd never get here.'

'Now, tell me, Mrs Johnson,' said Bromley, sitting beside her. 'Where on earth did you hear such a silly tale?'

'It was Mrs Barrett and Miss Wood just now in Queen Street. They said they'd heard from Mrs Dennison that her husband had heard that Mr Lockwood had been detected in a fraud. Something he'd done years ago to a widow and it had only just come out. And Mrs Barrett said wasn't it funny that he'd gone away five weeks ago and she wouldn't be surprised, she said, if he never came back. And I felt so frightened, Mr Bromley, because I'm a widow, aren't I? And I wondered if it was me he'd done something to and I didn't know about it. Because the money Mr Lockwood manages for me is all that stands between me and one of those Homes I'm so frightened of ending up in before I die.'

Mr Bromley stifled a sigh. Really, women ... especially old ones. Still, they had to be soothed. Also he was grateful to her for setting his fears at rest.

'Now, Mrs Johnson,' he said, even pressing her hand in its baggy glove. 'You have nothing whatever to worry about. There's not a word of truth in this tale. Mr Lockwood will be back at the end of the week, and you will be able to see him for yourself on Monday at the latest.'

'My money's safe, isn't it, Mr Bromley?'

'Your money, Mrs Johnson, is as safe as ever it was,' said Bromley with ambiguity. 'And if I were you, I'd go and have a nice cup of coffee to pull myself together.'

'That's just what I'll do, Mr Bromley,' said Mrs Johnson, assembling bag, parcels and umbrella. 'And probably I shall find Mrs Barrett and Miss Wood at the café and be able to tell them what I think of them for giving me such a fright.'

Mr Bromley returned, humming, to his desk. No need to go and see Tom now. This rumour was so crazy it could be ignored. Besides, it would so easily be disproved by Mr Lockwood's return on Friday. He picked up his pen.

The telephone rang.

'Is that you, Bromley? This is Major Croft speaking. Mr Lockwood isn't back, I suppose. Friday? Will he be in the office on Saturday morning? Well, ask him to make a point of being in the office on Saturday morning, will you? In the meantime, these are my instructions, Bromley. The money from the sale of my property in Achurch Street is not to be invested. It is to be paid direct to me. At once. Not invested, you understand.'

When Major Croft had finished, Bromley put down the telephone and reached for his hat. He must go and see Tom after all.

But Tom, coming out from the brush-works to speak to him, was indignant.

'Of course, I haven't breathed a word. I should have thought you knew me better than that, Sid. I said I wouldn't, didn't I? Well, I haven't and I won't, so you can rest easy.'

Bromley believed him; it was impossible not to. He went away very thoughtfully. If rumours had started from some other source, then something really was up.

CHAPTER THIRTY-SEVEN

A NIGHT in Paris, another in London; it took so long to get home, thought Clare, sighing carefully in case the others should notice. But her father, who sat opposite, was preoccupied with his own thoughts. From time to time, he, in his turn, suppressed a movement of impatience. The length of the journey irked him as much as it did Clare. But with the consideration they all showed within the family, if nowhere else, both were careful to hide it. The nights in Paris and London were part of the holiday, part of the treat, and mustn't be spoiled. Mr Lockwood and Clare smiled, though absently, whenever the others chanced to look at them.

Across the Pullman, Mrs Lockwood and the twins were engaged in a running comparison between Switzerland and England. It was to the disadvantage of England, but they were surprised and sorry that it should be so.

'It looks so tame . . .'

'Aren't the towns terrible? I never noticed before, but all the houses are the *same*,' said Bee in a shocked voice. 'And all these dreadful back bedrooms, Mother.'

'I know, dear,' said Mrs Lockwood with feeling. 'And doesn't the washing look grey on the lines?'

'After the utter cleanliness of Switzerland,' said Muriel.

Their fellow travellers heard them with amusement or irritation according to their kind. One middle-aged woman, returning from Italy, was annoyed by this indiscriminate praise of Switzerland, the picture-postcard place, the tourists' dream, she thought scornfully. As the train drew into London, she caught sight of the Italian flag over some building. 'Viva Italia!' she cried, and with a final glare at the mystified twins, collected her odd-looking luggage and departed.

Next morning, there were some hours before train time and the Lockwoods spent them in walking in Regent Street. The twins were on each side of their mother, the three of them seeming almost to bounce with happy well-being. Mr Lockwood walked a little behind them on the outside, Clare a little behind on the inside. Both stopped patiently to let the others look in a shop window whenever they wanted to.

They say that you can, in time, meet every friend you have walking down Regent Street in London. The Lockwoods had been walking for some time behind a thin girl with her hands thrust in the pockets of a camel-hair coat, before Bee darted forward and caught her by the arm.

'Angela!'

Angela Harvey confronted the Lockwoods with amused pleasure.

'Oh, hello,' she said, her eyes disappearing behind their dark lashes in the old way.

The Lockwoods' faces registered shock; for a moment, they couldn't even smile. Angela's coat was old, the collar of her blouse was creased and not quite clean. That a Harvey, once so cared-for, so waited-upon, should present this shabby appearance dumbfounded the Lockwoods.

'Angela, you're far too thin,' Bee burst out in her old possessive way.

'What're you doing? Did you get on the stage? Could we have seen you in a play last night? What a pity if we've missed you,' said Muriel.

'Yes, I'm on the stage, sometimes,' said Angela. 'But you won't see me yet.'

'How's Mother, dear?' asked Mrs Lockwood.

'And Sir Robert all right? Do they like Tunbridge?'

'I think they're both well,' said Angela. 'But we don't correspond at present. They won't give me an allowance so long as I stay on the stage and I won't leave it, so we're rather at a deadlock. I think they think they'll starve me off.'

'Oh, Angela, not really?' said Bee in alarm.

'No, of course not, silly,' said Angela, flashing her smile. 'I'm doing quite well. I'll get there in the end. I'm learning at present – as I must, of course. But how are you all? Any news of any kind?'

The Lockwoods couldn't think of any in particular.

'How's what's-her-name – how's Thea Hunter?'

'We don't know. We don't have anything to do with the family,' said Bee stiffly, while a look of reserve passed over the others and Clare turned away.

'Will you come and have lunch with us, Angela dear? We have time if we go now,' said Mrs Lockwood.

'Thank you so much, Mrs Lockwood, I'd have loved it, but I have an appointment. I'm rather late as it is, so I must really go. So nice to have seen you, all looking so well, too. I may join the Liverpool Rep. in September, so you'll come over and see me then, won't you? Goodbye, Bee. Goodbye, everybody.' Her brilliant smile passed over them and she turned down the side street.

The Lockwoods watched her go. Then Bee broke from her family and ran after her.

'Angela,' she panted, opening her bag and thrusting her notecase into the other's hand. 'To please me, take this. To please me,' she pleaded.

'Bee, don't be such an ass,' said Angela furiously. 'You Lockwoods! You're so literal. Don't be so *clumsy!*'

But seeing that Bee's eyes were actually full of tears, she laughed mitigatingly.

'Dear Bee, you're very sweet, but I simply don't need your money. D'you know I'm earning three pounds a week?'

Bee's practical mind grasped in a flash what it had taken Angela months to learn, namely, that when you'd been brought up as Angela had, you can't live in London on three pounds a week.

'*You're* the ass,' she said, keeping the note-case in Angela's hand by sheer force. 'Three pounds a week! And you only get that sometimes when you're playing a part or whatever it is. Take it, take it!'

In the struggle, the note-case fell to the pavement and Bee

rushed off and left it there. Angela had no alternative but to pick it up, which she did. She stood with it in her hand, looking in exasperation after Bee.

But Bee did not look round. She thrust her arm through her mother's and glared ahead up Regent Street with tears still in her eyes. She was angry with a life that could deprive Angela of anything whatever and make her struggle for a success she had always been so confident of.

Mrs Lockwood pressed her daughter's arm against her comfortable side.

'I'll give it you back, love,' she said.

Bee shook her head.

'No, don't. I wouldn't have given her anything then.'

Passing Galeries Lafayette, Bee sounded her first mature note. This was not the childish, self-indulgent pipe her mother loved and was used to, and Mrs Lockwood glanced at her daughter with anxiety. She had always made things easy for her girls, and why shouldn't she, she asked herself. But if they weren't going to let her, half her pleasure in life would be over.

She sounded a note of her own.

'Angela's simply gone to pieces now she's left her mother's care,' she said. 'I don't know what Lady Harvey would say to that blouse.'

They continued their journey. Bee had fallen out of the comparison game. She was composing letters in her head to Lady Harvey. She must get Angela's allowance restored. Even if it meant going to Tunbridge Wells and pleading in person, she must get some money for Angela.

Mrs Lockwood and Muriel kept up comparisons until they were appalled into silence by the industrial north. The sun was put out by a dull haze, through which the giant chimneys stood sentinel to – what? This hideousness was nowadays mostly for nothing. The cotton trade was almost non-existent.

Yet when the train drew into Aldworth, Mrs Lockwood and the twins recognised that there were advantages after all in coming back to it. They resumed at once something they had left behind when they went away: they resumed their importance. Only here did people know who they were and how they mattered.

Everybody looked at them, Bee noticed complacently, leading the way out to the front of the station, where Siddle waited with the car, the outporter's lorry in attendance for the vast amount of luggage.

'Well, Siddle,' she called out in her old lordly way. 'Here we are. How are you?'

Without noticing his reply – for what should one's chauffeur be but well? – she looked round the square. As if in welcome, Queen Victoria had had a clean-up, and was now unnaturally pallid and quite featureless. Bee took her usual place beside the driver, and occupied herself in arranging the pleats of her skirt over her plump knees while her family bestowed themselves behind her.

'Ah, well,' sighed Mrs Lockwood comfortably, as Siddle shut them in. 'We're home again.'

A look of vivid life had come into Clare's face. Now she was in the same place as Martin. She might even see him on the way home. He might just chance to be coming out of Byron

Place on his way to tennis. Though probably he hadn't had the heart to play tennis much since she went away. But soon, with the letter she would write as soon as she got in, she would put that right. Tomorrow, at the latest, she would see him, she thought, with delicious shootings of excitement through all her veins.

As the car approached Havelock Street, Mr Lockwood leaned forward. There was his office, and tomorrow morning, because he couldn't wait till Monday, he would be back. After all his nightmares, it was good to find the office still there, and his opportunity of putting things right still there as well. He threw himself back in his corner with a great sigh of relief.

'What is it, dear?' said Effie. 'Are you worried by the thought of all the work waiting for you?'

'No, no,' said William. 'On the contrary.'

He felt ready for anything. A sense of power, engendered by the sight of his office standing there just as usual, had driven out apprehension. He had managed pretty well for his family, he thought, looking round on them, and he would manage still. Bless them. He had given them a splendid holiday and saved Clare. She seemed to have been successfully broken of young Hunter. Her mother and sisters said she never mentioned him. There had been no running off to Postes Restantes, they reported, or scribbling in the bedroom. Clare had given her word and he knew she had kept it. At the thought of his daughter's faithful dealing, his eyes watered.

He watched her as she looked through the window of the car. She looked much better than she had done when she went away. She was all right, she was happy enough, and nothing but a child. He would make it up to her now. She should have everything she wanted. Not, of course, young Hunter, but everything else.

The car turned into the gates of Oakfield. The drive was freshly raked, Mrs Lockwood noted, and here was the house, here was home. All the Lockwoods smiled upon it. Clare, too. She hadn't seen Martin, but tomorrow she would. She jumped out of the car to Boz, who was barking in wild excitement.

'Oh, Boz, Boz, Bozzy.' She lifted the awkward loving lump into her arms. 'I've missed you too, darling. But I'm back and now we'll be happy, won't we? Come on – race you to the summer-house.'

They rushed from the scene.

'A real home-girl,' said her mother, smiling after her. 'I don't think she's really happy anywhere else. Well, Parsons, we're glad to be back,' she said, handing over her dressing-case and walking into the house. 'How nice everything looks.'

She made a mental reservation about the flowers. You can always tell by the flowers when the mistress is away, she thought. The prospect of getting to the flowers and everything else filled her with sudden happiness. It was good to be home.

For a time there was all the bustle of settling in; the unpacking, the rustle of tissue paper, the opening and shutting of drawers and cupboards, the calling out from room to room. Clare thought she was never going to get her letter written. But at last the twins had finished and had gone, at their mother's bidding, to the greenhouses to see what there was in the way of flowers for tomorrow. Mrs Lockwood herself went down to the kitchen to talk further with Cook and the maids.

Clare closed her door and sat down to the gilt desk.

Martin, it has been terrible to be away from you and not to be able to write. But my promise is up now and Daddy is better. He seems quite well. I am so sorry for making you unhappy, darling, but I made myself unhappy, too. Please ring up as soon as you leave the bank tomorrow lunchtime and say you forgive me. And say we can meet in the afternoon in the spinney by Firbank. At three, shall we? Thank goodness it is Saturday tomorrow. I long to see you. I shall be counting the minutes until you ring up at lunchtime tomorrow. I love you so much.
    Your own
    Clare.

With Boz at her heels, she stole from the house. She skirted the paddock and ran down the hill. As the letter fell into the box at the corner, such relief came over her that she stood trembling for a moment. At last it was going to be all right. At last he would know.

She turned and sped back up the hill, her hair flying.

The gong went. Cook was on the point of sending in the soup when the telephone rang. Mr Lockwood answered it.

'Bromley here, sir.'

'Ah, good evening, Bromley. You're pretty prompt, I must say. We've only just got in.'

'Yes, I'm sorry to worry you so soon, sir,' said Bromley awkwardly. 'But I just wanted to know. . . Are you thinking of being at the office in the morning, Mr Lockwood?'

'Yes, I shall be down. Why? Anything urgent?'
'Well – er.'
'What?'
'Er . . .'
'Come on, man, out with it. My dinner's waiting.'
'Well, Mr Lockwood, I don't know how to put it, sir, but a lot of people want to see you tomorrow morning. I had to let them make appointments; they were so determined. There's Mr Gray and Major Croft, and Miss Entwistle and the Reverend Foster and several more . . .'
'You don't mean to say you've arranged for me to see all those people tomorrow morning?'
'They arranged it, sir. They insisted.'
'Insisted? No one insists with me, Bromley. What d'you mean by booking me up like this on my first day back?'
'It's been very awkward for me, Mr Lockwood.' Bromley suddenly adopted a firmer tone. 'I've been asked a lot of questions these last few days that I haven't been able to answer.'

There was an almost imperceptible pause.

'Questions?' said Mr Lockwood. 'What sort of questions?'
'I'd rather not say. I'd rather you found out for yourself, Mr Lockwood. I've stemmed the rush as best I could, but you can deal with it yourself now, sir. That's why I think you'd better be in the office tomorrow morning.'
'I don't know what the devil you're talking about, Bromley. But you never could make yourself clear. I'll see you in the morning.'

He rang off and went to stand in the library, so deep in

conjecture that he didn't hear the second gong and Muriel had to come in search of him.

'Put through a call to the stables, Muriel, and tell Siddle to bring the car round in half an hour.'

'I must go to the office,' he said, sitting down heavily to table.

'Oh, William,' protested his wife. 'Our first evening at home. It's too bad.'

'I must go,' said William shortly. 'Did you get Siddle, Muriel?'

'Yes. He didn't sound too pleased.'

'Lazy blighter,' said her father savagely. 'He's had five weeks of complete idleness, hasn't he?'

His face was dark, and his family looked at him with surprise. The change was very sudden. All the care-free geniality of the holiday was gone. Business, they supposed. They fell back subdued before the mysteries of business and were very attentive in passing the pepper and salt, which was all there was for them to pass, since Parsons saw to the rest.

In half an hour, having swallowed three cups of black coffee, William went out to the waiting car and was driven away.

CHAPTER THIRTY-EIGHT

All night, awake and asleep, though mostly awake, Thea had been waiting for morning. Now it was here, and though it was Molly's turn to get breakfast, she went down early to get it herself, to help the time to go.

As she came down the dark stairs, she saw the white square of Clare's letter on the hall floor. When she picked it up and saw a Lockwood hand, a queer thrill ran through her. They were back. The clerk had said they would come and here they were. Mr Lockwood was within striking distance at last.

She took the letter into the front room and propped it against the cigar cabinet no one had used since the day, long ago, when Mr Lockwood had helped himself to cigars. She wished the letter hadn't to be sent on to Martin. What good could Clare do now? All commerce between Hunters and Lockwoods ended today. Today the breach was final. The Hunters would strike their only, but their knockout, blow. What a turning of the tables, she exulted. What tricks life could play!

She started to go to the kitchen, but changed her mind and darted out of the front door. She must tell Oliver. She knew he would be up early; he always was.

Oliver was standing in the window of his own front room with the *Manchester Guardian*.

'Thea!' He came out to meet her, his face as bright as a boy's at the sight of her.

'The Lockwoods are back,' she said.

His face changed. Irrationally, he had hoped for something else.

'Well, yes,' he said. 'They were expected, weren't they?'

'Yes, but they're actually here,' said Thea.

'Ten o'clock then,' she reminded him.

He was to call for her at the office in the hired car he used for getting about in nowadays.

'Right you are,' he said, and she darted away.

He went back to the *Manchester Guardian*. It was absurd to hope she would run in first thing in the morning just for the pleasure of seeing him, though that was what he would have done every day if he dared. He might have known it was something to do with the Lockwood business that brought her. And naturally, too, because if he himself found it exciting, how much more so must it be for her?

His eyes scanned 'Miscellany', but his thoughts were busy with the prospect of running Lockwood to ground today. A good many others were on his track now. People soon got nervous about their money. Nothing could cause a panic so quickly as a hint that it might be in danger. The first rumour had been lost sight of in a host of others now.

At the Club, the latest story was that Major Croft had been to Bolton to look at some property on which Lockwood had taken out mortgages for him. Not only was the property worthless, but it appeared that it was actually owned by Lockwood himself. There was much silent whistling, lip-pursing and eyebrow-raising among members at this. They were certainly enjoying the situation at the Club. Excitement and suspicion mounted daily. Everybody waited tensely for Lockwood to come back.

Oliver's interest was not spoiled by any concern for William Lockwood himself. He didn't like him, and he was ready to do whatever Thea wanted, even if he didn't quite understand the intense feeling behind her determination to get her own back.

'Noll,' called his mother. 'Your porridge is getting cold.'

At number twenty-one, Thea was taking up her mother's tray. Mrs Hunter's eyes followed her anxiously about the room, but Thea wouldn't meet them. She kept her own averted, her lips set. She wouldn't give any opening. She wasn't going to let herself be diverted from her purpose.

For the same reason, she didn't breakfast with Molly, but fiddled about in her room until her sister left the house. Then she swallowed her cold coffee, ate a piece of toast leathery from standing and hurried to the office to go through the motions of working until Oliver should call for her.

She was waiting at the kerb when Oliver arrived, prompt as always, at ten o'clock. All he had to do was to open the door and let her in. She was pale. She wasn't used to being the Hand of Fate and was finding it a nervous experience.

They spoke little because of the driver, and when they did, it had nothing to do with what they had in hand. Thea sat on the edge of the seat. Oliver kept far back in his corner so that he could watch her unhindered. She looked as if she might take flight from fright at any moment, and he was struck by her youth. She was, after all, so young. Not yet twenty.

The car seemed to Thea to reach Havelock Street in a trice. She gulped apprehensively and got out.

'Don't wait,' said Oliver, banging the door. 'I don't know how long I shall be, but pick me up at the warehouse at half-past twelve, will you?'

'Very good, sir,' said the man, and drove away.

The office looked as it had looked all the years Thea had visited it. Just as respectable, as secretive, the door-brasses as bright, the step as freshly stoned, though from the footmarks it looked as if many people had been in and out already that morning.

Oliver opened the door; the long-familiar flight of stairs covered in brown linoleum with brass treads met her eye.

'Straight up to his room,' said Oliver. 'No "Enquiries" for us.'

Bromley darted out of the back office, but only in time to see their heels disappear round the bend of the stairs. He was outraged. The practice might be on the point of dissolution, the very office doomed, but people needn't think they could behave like this. Tramping upstairs without as much as by your leave.

'Will you come down, please?' he called out. 'Not up there, I say.'

The heels did not pause, so he pelted after them. The intruders had already reached the landing.

'I must ask you,' puffed Bromley, pushing between them and the door of Mr Lockwood's room, 'to go down to the general office and wait in the ordinary way, until I can ascertain if it is convenient for Mr Lockwood to see you.'

But at that moment the door opened and Major Croft came out, obviously a very angry man. He came out; then went back to stand in the doorway.

'I suppose you know what this means, Lockwood?' he said.

He came towards the stairs again. Bromley's whole attention was absorbed. Oliver, his hand on Thea's arm, walked past him as he gaped, into the room beyond and closed the door.

Mr Lockwood, standing at the desk with papers in his hand, peered across at him. He had been at work for many hours already.

'What is it?' he said. 'You must go away. I'm too busy to see strangers.'

He put a hand to the bell on his desk.

'Don't ring,' said Oliver, 'we're not going. And Miss Hunter is no stranger to you.'

'Hunter?'

Mr Lockwood looked at Thea. He hadn't recognised her. He hadn't seen her for years.

'What are you doing here? Who's this man you've brought with you?'

'We haven't come to be questioned,' said Oliver, 'but to question you.'

'I've no time for your questions.'

'You'll have to make time.' Oliver took out his pocket-book.

'Will you kindly leave my office?' said the lawyer furiously. 'I have clients waiting to see me.'

'This interview will do for all. We're the root of the matter, so you'd better take us first.'

'What the devil d'you mean?' Mr Lockwood put his papers down. He leaned on his fists, pushing his heavy shoulders up to his ears. His aggressive lower lip was thrust out like a spout.

'When Thea's father died,' said Oliver in a level voice. 'You took possession of a paddock, didn't you?'

Mr Lockwood stared at him.

'You said it was in payment of a debt of three hundred pounds,' Oliver went on, Thea mute and white at his shoulder. 'But you knew no such debt existed.'

In the silence, Mr Lockwood's breathing was loud.

'He'd repaid the money. Here's a copy of the receipt in proof of that,' said Oliver, laying a small piece of paper on the desk. 'And here's a copy of the promissory note you surrendered to Mrs Hunter.' He laid the second piece of paper beside the first.

'Explain those away if you can,' he said.

Mr Lockwood dropped his eyes to the papers. A vein appeared like a swollen worm in the middle of his forehead.

Motionless, he hung over the papers. Then he raised his eyes and fixed them on Thea.

Although she was in the right, she reminded herself wildly, she shrank from that look. Involuntarily, she closed her eyes against it. When she opened them, he was looking at her still.

'So it's you,' he said slowly.

Why should he look as if she had betrayed him? He was a bad man, he had cheated . . .

'This is the widow I'm supposed to have defrauded, is it?'

Mr Lockwood struck the receipts with the back of his hand. 'After all this time, you bring up a thing like this and set it about the town? After all I've done for your family? I've repaid your mother in work I've done for her a dozen times over . . .'

'So you admit it, do you?' said Oliver.

The look he turned on Oliver was not the one he had fixed on Thea. He looked cornered now; dreadfully and pitiably cornered. Thea moved behind Oliver. She didn't want to see.

'No court will care if you've repaid it a hundred times,' said Oliver. 'You committed a fraud and a particularly repulsive one. You cheated the widow and the fatherless and now you're going to pay for it. Everybody's going to know, if everybody doesn't know already. And it serves you dam' well right, Mr Lockwood.'

Holding to the sides of his desk, William Lockwood lowered himself like an old man into his chair. He leaned forward and rubbed his face with his hands. While they stared at him, he rubbed at his forehead and his eyes, at his mouth, like one distraught.

It struck Oliver uncomfortably that he was putting up very little fight. He didn't know that a great deal had already happened to Mr Lockwood since the night before.

'Leave me, will you?' said Mr Lockwood, dropping his hands and looking indescribably weary.

'Have you nothing to say for yourself?' said Oliver.

'Not to you.'

'You'll have to say it somewhere,' said Oliver. 'I suppose you know what all this means?'

Mr Lockwood nodded.

'I shall be obliged if you will go now,' he said.

'Certainly,' said Oliver. He almost said 'Good morning.' He and Thea covered the distance to the door, which seemed a long way. They closed it behind them and stole down the stairs.

'Oh, Oliver,' said Thea with distress in the street. 'It was awful.'

He laughed ruefully.

'Aye, it wasn't so good, was it? I didn't think he'd take it like that. I thought he'd put up a bit of a fight. It's not much fun baiting a chap who doesn't show some fight, I must say.'

'I hated it,' said Thea. 'I wish I'd never done it.'

'We mustn't be soft,' said Oliver. 'He did wrong; he's got to pay. It's only just.'

They walked up and down the street.

'I should never have tried to harm them,' said Thea. 'I know them too well.'

A car drew up, a man got out and hurried into Mr Lockwood's office.

'Another of them,' said Oliver. 'The news fairly got round, didn't it?'

'Oh, Oliver, can nothing be done?' asked Thea.

'Not now, no.'

Thea stood on the pavement, looking frightened. Where had all the exhilarating heat gone to? She had expected a triumphant satisfaction, but what she felt was remorse and an overpowering sense of dread for the Lockwoods. What would happen to them now?

'And I dare say, if we'd given him time, he'd have put it all right,' she said to Oliver.

'Probably. They all mean to put it right. Jabez Balfour was going to put it right, I believe, and that other chap – Wright or White. But you can't get away from the fact that these men are dishonest. Downright dishonest, Thea. Don't lose sight of that.'

She looked hopefully at him. She wanted him to keep on like this, she wanted him to let her feel that she hadn't done anything so dreadful after all.

'Now look,' said Oliver. He took her hand and she clasped her fingers round his, waiting for reassurance. 'Don't think any more about this. Don't bother about it. Leave him to – well, funnily enough, leave him to the Law. The Law will deal with him.'

'It sounds so awful,' she said.

'Yes, it's awful all right. But he should have thought of that before he put himself within its reach. He knows better than anybody what penalty there is to pay. Now look, darling.' The word slipped out and seemed natural to both of them. 'You go home. Don't go back to the office this morning.'

He was always trying to keep her from shutting herself up in the office and she was always determined to earn the money he paid her, as far as she was able.

'I must go back,' she said. 'There's still something to do there. Besides, I don't want to go home. Mother might ask . . .'

'Very well. Go to the office. I must go to the warehouse now. Burgess is coming from Manchester this morning to see me, you know.'

'Yes, I know you must go,' she said, but her fingers tightened. She didn't want him to leave her. Without his reiterations that what she had done was right, she would have to face the conviction that, for her, it had been deadly wrong. She hardly knew why, but it had turned out to be disastrous for her as well as for the Lockwoods. She was involved in their catastrophe; if they would never forget it, neither would she.

She loosed Oliver's hand suddenly. No use clinging to him or to anybody. With a sick look she turned away.

'You must go. You're going to be late,' she said. 'Goodbye, Oliver.'

'You're sure you'll be all right?' he said anxiously.

'Yes, yes,' she said, making a smile. 'I'm going to catch this bus. Goodbye.'

'Shall I see you this afternoon?' he called after her.

She shook her head as she ran.

She was borne up through the town in an empty bus: most people were going down at this time in the morning. She hurried along Wells Road, and swiftly and silently, two steps at a time, she went up to the room over the shop. She closed the door, hung up her summer straw hat and sat down to the desk with relief.

But in a few minutes the sense of relief deserted her.

There was something within, some other self that knew what you could do and what you couldn't. This self mostly slept or was easy; it let you go on without bothering much. But now it was awake and was inexorable. She didn't know how to escape from it.

'What's the good of regretting it now?' she said. 'I can't undo it. It's too late.'

Yet she was driven from the desk to the window, from one window to another and back to the desk.

'I should never have done it,' she kept saying. 'What will happen to them now?'

'I didn't like them, but I was close to them,' she thought miserably. 'And now they're going to be hurt, I don't want them to be.'

There was no work to do. No telephone rang, nobody called. There was no distraction for her of any sort, and yet she shrank from going home.

She thought of going down to Molly and got as far as the head of the stairs. There was the usual Saturday morning smell of toffee. Molly always made toffee on Saturday morning and all Saturday afternoon the shop bell tinkled continuously, while she smilingly dispensed it to the children who came from far and wide.

Thea leaned disconsolately over the banisters. She could hear Molly talking to Mrs Haines. It was no good going down unless she could find her alone. Besides, she had cut herself off from sisterly comfort. Molly was already coldly disapproving of what she thought Thea intended to do: what would she be when she knew it was done?

Thea went back into her room and closed the door again.

Time dragged on. It came to half-past twelve at last. Thea put on her hat, locked everything up and stole to the stairs again. But she was not to go unnoticed this time. Molly was waiting with a basket.

'I've made a pie for lunch.' She spoke with reserve, as she had spoken since their quarrel. 'It's quite hot, but you'd better put it into the oven for ten minutes or so.'

'Oh, thank you,' said Thea shamefacedly, and taking the basket, went out, leaving Molly to look after her in conjecture.

By dint of continually jumping up from table on one pretext or another, Thea managed to get through lunch. She didn't deceive her mother, but she kept her from asking questions. It was with relief, merely temporary again, that she saw her mother go slowly up the stairs for her afternoon rest. Thea's eyes followed her with anxiety. Her gentle, oversensitive mother would suffer with the Lockwoods and suffer doubly because it was through her own family that disaster had fallen upon them.

'I should never have done it,' thought Thea for the hundredth time, running the water for the washing-up. 'It needed someone ruthless to do a thing like this. But what can I do now? It's too late.'

Had Mr Lockwood gone home yet? Did they know? Even if he said nothing, they must see that something terrible had happened. He looked so awful, so tired and old. To think that he, so powerful, irascible, confident, could look so broken.

'Oh, well, it's no good thinking about it,' she said desperately. And continued to think about it.

When she had cleared away, she went up to her room. She stood at her window and looked at the empty street. Saturday afternoon, when you have nothing to do, is the most melancholy time of the week. The feeling that you should be enjoying it, like everybody else, and aren't, makes it worse than any other afternoon. Except Sunday.

'I hate weekends,' thought Thea. 'For a long time, I've hated weekends and this is going to be the worst of them all.

It's strange that because of the Lockwoods I hated weekends once, and now it's because of them again that I hate this one.

'If only I could undo it. If only I could do something to stop it all.'

She decided suddenly to go and see if Oliver was in yet. He would reassure her; he would bolster her up. But he wasn't in. Old Mrs Reade said no, he hadn't come yet and she wished he would, because everything was getting dried up in the oven.

Thea went back to her room again, back to her window.

Two. Half-past two. Three. Half-past three, and she was still standing at windows, first upstairs, then down, drawing curtains aside, letting them fall back again. She was looking out as if help might come from the street. She realised suddenly that she was looking for Oliver to come and rescue her. And that was ridiculous, because he couldn't. She had put herself where she was and there she would have to stay. For ever.

She took *Emma* from the shelves and sat down with determination at the table, thrusting her hands through her hair to assist concentration. But Jane Austen, who rarely failed to charm, had no power now. She put the book aside and stared before her.

She was being slowly, but inexorably, pushed to a decision. She resisted it with all her might, because it was senseless. And not only senseless, but profoundly humiliating.

'No,' she said, setting her lips and going upstairs again. 'I won't do it.'

Nothing for her to do now but to keep out of the way. Never to be seen by any Lockwood again, because she couldn't bear any of them to look at her as Mr Lockwood had looked that morning when he said 'So it's you'.

'I ought to have said "No, it's you". That's what I ought to have said. Why turn the blame on me?'

She found some relief in that thought for a time. But before long she was back in the window.

'Well, I'll go if Oliver will come with me. To the gate, that is. I'll have to go in by myself, but I'll go if he'll come with me to the gate.'

She went to his door again. But he hadn't come home, said old Mrs Reade. He had telephoned to say that he was taking the man from Manchester to see the site for the new factory.

Thea turned away and went back to the house. She needn't go to Oakfield now, because she had only said that she would go if he came with her.

But in a few minutes she was putting her hat on. She didn't know what she would say or do when she got there. But she had to go. She must avoid saying she was sorry, it would sound so inadequate and childish. But she must go. She must go because she was sorry; terribly, unbearably sorry, she said to herself, tears filling her eyes as she went out.

Making her way through the half-holiday crowds in the main road, she hurried, nervously rehearsing what she was going to say when she got there. She must see Mr Lockwood first, she said to herself. He was the one she had to see, because she had to ask him if there was anything, anything that could be done. She had to know.

When she reached the gates of Oakfield, she daren't go up to the house. She turned down the path to the stables until she should find enough courage. She walked with head bent, her hands clasping and unclasping each other in agitation. She started violently to hear her name called.

'Thea.'

It was Clare, her voice ringing with hope and welcome. Thea shrank back against the laurels. How could a Lockwood greet her like this?

'Thea, you've brought a message, haven't you?'

Thea stared and Clare's face changed.

'It's not bad news, is it? Is it bad news?'

There was nothing but bad news. What did Clare mean? Didn't she know?

Thea's throat contracted at the thought of being the one to tell her.

'Is it bad? What's happened to him? Tell me!' Clare grasped Thea's arm.

'What d'you mean?' Thea was suddenly terrified. 'Has anything happened to him? Since this morning? What is it, what is it?'

The two girls stared in fear at each other.

'I thought you'd come to tell me something about him. Why didn't he telephone? Why didn't he meet me at three?' asked Clare.

'Who?'

'Martin, of course. Martin.'

'Oh, Martin.' Thea fell back with relief. 'Oh, yes, your letter. Yes, it came. But Martin's in London. He's been gone a fortnight. He works there now. He's got a job there, you know.'

'Isn't he here?' said Clare incredulously. 'He's in London?'

She looked about her as if the whole scene had gone quite dead, as if it had drained of life, because he was not in it.

'Oh, did he go because of me?' she asked piteously.

'Yes, he did,' said Thea in the simplicity of her own distress. 'Yes, he went to get away before you came home.'

Clare's lip trembled.

'Won't he come back? Do you mean he won't forgive me and come back?'

'Yes, I think he will,' said Thea, seeing suddenly that something could be done for Clare, at least. 'I think he'll come, now you need him so much. You must write to him again. Don't say why, but tell him to come at once. No – you must telephone. I've got his telephone number here. He's in a boarding house in Endsleigh Street. Go and ring him up now. Tell him to come home, if it's only for one night.'

She took Martin's last letter from her bag and gave it into Clare's hands.

In her eagerness, Clare did not wonder why Thea should be so urgent. She clasped his letter ecstatically.

'I'll ring up at once. Perhaps he'll be out, because it's Saturday afternoon, but I'll keep on ringing until he comes in. Oh, thank you, Thea, it's so good of you, because it must seem to you that I treated Martin so badly, but I'll explain it all soon.'

She leaned forward and kissed Thea and darted away up the path. Then she turned and ran back.

'If you didn't come with a message, what did you come for?'

'I came – to see your father,' said Thea.

'He isn't here,' said Clare. 'He's still at the office. Mummy keeps ringing up, but last time he told her not to ring again.

Mummy's getting worried, but he doesn't want to be disturbed. Will you come in and wait?'

'No,' said Thea, drawing a long breath. 'No, I must go.'

'Goodbye then,' said Clare. 'I'll go and ring up Martin. Oh, Thea, thank you for coming. It was bad enough this afternoon, waiting, but it would have got worse and worse. Goodbye, Thea dear. We're friends now, aren't we? I always wanted to be, but you would never let me. You will now, won't you?'

She smiled warmly and sped up the drive to the house.

CHAPTER THIRTY-NINE

Thea went slowly out of the gates and stood looking about. She was being drawn deeper into the desperate situation. In the house behind they didn't know yet. Was there time, was there any chance of lessening the blow that must fall upon them? Of herself, she could do nothing. But inaction was unbearable, the pressure of self-reproach was unbearable. She must go and see Mr Lockwood. She was afraid to go and it seemed as if it could do no good at all, but still she must go. She had a sense of absolute compulsion. She turned and went down the hill to the bus.

She must go, because, for one thing, she must ask him not to tell the others that it was she who had brought this upon them. Not only could she not bear them to know, but if he told them they wouldn't allow her mother to do what she could for Mr Lockwood and they wouldn't accept help from Oliver. She was so used to looking to Oliver for help that she was sure he would find some way of helping now.

At the thought of Oliver, her heart filled with love. She knew suddenly, beyond all doubt, that she loved him. But to know brought no more comfort at this time than to look over a dark landscape with a patch of sunlight showing far away. The sun wasn't shining where she was; not yet.

The bus carried her down into the town. It was about five o'clock and the Saturday crowds were thick in the streets, thickest round the shops and market stalls. But Havelock Street was deserted. The offices were closed. There was no one about.

Cautiously she tried the outer door of Mr Lockwood's offices. She expected it to be locked, but it opened under her hand. She closed it again very carefully. She was afraid, if he heard, he would come from his room above and order her out before she had said what she had come to say.

She stood in the narrow passage, looking up through the well of the old house. There was no sound, except, in her own ears, the thudding of her heart.

She laid her hand to the banister rail and in her light summer slippers went up without a sound. As she came to the top of the stairs she halted. The door of Mr Lockwood's room was open and there was no sound. Wasn't he there?

As she stood, listening fearfully, someone began to speak in the room ahead. Startled, she turned to go down the stairs again. There must be somebody with him. But she paused again. There was only one voice speaking and it was his. Her hand on the rail, her foot poised to go down, she realised that it was Mr Lockwood talking to himself.

Her throat dry, her eyes dilated, she listened. The low anguished mutter came again.

'I can't do it. No. . . I can't, I can't.'

There was a long silence. Then he began again.

'But I must. I can't face them.'

He gave a great sigh.

'Effie . . .'

'Oh, God,' he said. 'God, give me courage. There's no other way.'

With terror, she realised that he was trying to find courage to kill himself. She was rooted to the spot. She wanted to run down the stairs and out into the street, but she couldn't move. She wanted to call out, but she was voiceless.

She held on to the banisters, steadying herself. What must she do? It was vital that she should do the right thing. If she ran for help he might kill himself while she was away.

She must go into the room. No matter what she would see, she must go in.

Noiselessly, she crept back to the door. She pushed it wider and went in.

Mr Lockwood, in his shirtsleeves, was lying half across his desk, his hand on a revolver. His eyes were closed, his face glistened with sweat. Around him and all over the room was a great confusion of papers and boxes.

She stood. She passed her tongue over her dry teeth to be able to speak.

'Mr Lockwood.'

'Who's there?' he shouted, springing up, his eyes bolting, the revolver shaking in his hand.

But the sight of her, the unexpected sight of a girl steadied him. After a long stare, he came round the desk, gun in hand, and walked towards her.

'You?' he said incredulously. 'You again?'

She couldn't speak, her eyes were fixed on him.

'What have you come for again? Who's with you?'

He threw the door back and looked out on the empty landing. He walked to the head of the stairs and looked down. He listened. Not a sound, except, to Thea, still the loud knocking of her heart.

'God damn you,' he said savagely, going back to her. 'I'd have done it in another minute.'

He gave a terrible loud cry that chilled Thea's blood.

'Now I won't be able to. I won't be able to find the courage again,' he cried in despair. 'Oh, damn you, damn you.'

He burst into tears. He flung himself down at his desk and cried, and she stood and watched him, helpless, terrified.

He got up suddenly and went towards her, with blotched cheeks and distorted mouth.

'Get out!' he shouted.

She raised an arm like a child warding off a blow.

'I can't,' she said, finding her voice. 'I must stay, Mr Lockwood.'

'Get out.'

'No, I can't. I can't. I must stay, so that you don't shoot yourself.'

She darted away from him and got behind the old mahogany armchair her mother used to sit in when they came to the office long ago.

Mr Lockwood wiped his face with his handkerchief. She noticed, with fear, that one moment he seemed out of his senses and the next quite normal. He laughed grimly now.

'You won't stop me from shooting myself by being here,' he said. 'In fact, that's what I'll do. I'll shoot myself while you're here and then you'll be involved in this nice little scandal. How's that? Eh?'

He looked at her as she stood behind the chair, her fingers white on the mahogany rose on the back.

'You thought you'd get your own back, did you, by spreading that tale about the paddock? Well, I'll get mine back now. I'll have the last move after all.'

He went back to the desk and sat down. He put the revolver before him.

'I'll shoot myself in a minute. No particular hurry. In a minute. One moment more,' he said with a great sigh.

Cold sweat broke out along the line of Thea's hair and under her eyes.

He sat in silence at his desk. His face was quite composed now. He looked as if he had found the courage he had prayed for.

Thea moved. She came from behind the chair and took a step or two towards him. She had to distract his attention.

'Mr Lockwood,' she said.

He didn't answer. He seemed to have forgotten she was there.

She stood for what seemed a long time in silence.

'Mr Lockwood, why should you shoot yourself?' she faltered.

'Why should you?' she said timidly again. She felt she must make him talk. It would be safer if he talked.

'How would dying help? Why should you die?' she insisted.

'Because I've no choice,' he said in a curiously normal voice.

She saw, with a leap of hope, that he didn't want to kill himself. She had an ally in his will to live.

'I've no choice,' he said again. 'You brought all these people down on me at once. I could have put things right. I came home to put things right. And now I haven't the time. It's time I need, and I haven't got it. No more time for me.'

He picked up the revolver and looked it over carefully.

'Think of them,' said Thea desperately. 'Think of your family. You'll kill them, too. They love you. Think of Clare.'

'D'you think I haven't thought of everything? I've been thinking all night and all day. I have thought,' he said. 'It's because of them I must do it. I can't face them.'

Thea prayed she would find the right thing to say. Every word mattered. God help me to say the right thing, she prayed.

Tears were running down Mr Lockwood's face again. Her tears ran with his. Timidly she put out a hand and touched him.

'Get off, you!' he said roughly, snatching his arm out of her reach.

She shrank back. There was silence.

Her mind darted this way and that like a trapped animal.

'Will you get out?' said Mr Lockwood, suddenly turning and looking her straight in the eyes. 'I've told you to go. You don't want me to shoot myself in front of you, do you? It won't be a pretty sight, I warn you.'

White to the lips, she stood her ground. They looked at each other, these enemies of long standing. Girl though she was, she was the one to be with him in his extremity, and it seemed to her that his eyes, desperate though they were, appealed to her for help.

'I came to ask if nothing could be done,' she said. 'I came to say I was sorry . . .'

'*Sorry!*' said Mr Lockwood bitterly. 'Don't be so childish. You little fool.'

'Yes, I am,' said Thea with a sob.

'Don't begin that. As if I haven't enough . . .'

Thea wiped her eyes on the back of her hand. She daren't divert her attention sufficiently to get her handkerchief out of her pocket.

'I saw Clare this afternoon,' she said, on another tack.

He turned sharply.

'Why? Why did you see Clare?'

'I went to the house to see you, and I saw her and she said you hadn't come home and they were worried.'

He groaned.

'They'll be more than worried soon. And I've always tried to keep them happy.'

'They have been happy. You've been the happiest family I've ever known.'

He stared at his desk.

'Don't break their hearts,' pleaded Thea.

'I've broken them, you fool. I've broken them.'

'No, their hearts won't break so long as you are with them. If you're there, they can bear anything. I've never – got on – with the twins, but I know they're strong and can stand up to trouble. And you know what Mrs Lockwood is. So practical and good at managing. And Clare will have Martin . . .'

She paused, fearfully, in case that set him off again. But he said nothing. He was staring at his desk, lost in conjecture.

God help him, she prayed.

She was watching him. She never moved her eyes from him and it seemed to her that a new look was coming into his face. He was beginning to look as if he were considering the possibility of living. She waited.

Through the windows, open at the top, came the sounds of Saturday afternoon: shouts from the market stalls, rumblings of buses, children's cries and laughter, the hooting of car horns, the walking and talking of crowds of people, all the mingled, muffled sounds of vigorous life.

'You don't know what you've let me in for,' said Mr Lockwood in his normal voice again. 'I shall be struck off the Roll. I shall have to realise everything I have to pay up. I shall go to jail, and when I come out, I shan't be able to earn a living. No one will employ me, even as a clerk. And you ask me to face that.'

'Yes,' she said eagerly. 'Because you can. You've always been strong and clever. You'll find a way. If you shoot yourself, it'll not only break their hearts, they'll have to hear people saying you were a coward. People will say you got out and left them to face everything alone.'

He laughed grimly again.

'They little know. I find it hard to die.'

'You must live, Mr Lockwood. They need you.'

She was so close, she could have picked up the gun and thrown it through the window. But though she thought of that in her desperation, she dismissed it. It would have been a betrayal. It would have brought somebody up. He must make his own decision.

'You must live,' she said. 'You've got them into this situation. I am to blame, too, I know. But only you can get them out of it. Not comfortably, not with what they've got now, but you can bring them out of it. And you know you must.'

He remained slumped over his desk in silence. She didn't know if he even heard.

Her heart beat in great thudding beats. Every nerve was strained to bring him to consent. She trembled with standing so long, but she daren't make any move to sit down.

Suddenly, startling her so that her whole skin prickled, the telephone on the desk rang shrilly. Mr Lockwood looked at it.

'It's from home,' he said, but did not touch it.

It rang on and on; ring and pause, ring and pause. On and on.

Thea waited.

With a sigh, Mr Lockwood moved at the desk. He sat up and looked long and gravely before him. Thea swayed on her feet.

Then he put out a hand and took up the receiver. He put it to his ear.

'Yes, Effie. Yes, I know. I know, dear.'

He spoke heavily, but he spoke like a man concerned, not with death, but with life.

'I'm sorry, Effie. It couldn't be helped. But you can send Siddle down with the car now. I'll come home.'

If you have enjoyed this Persephone book why not telephone or write to us for a copy of the Persephone Catalogue and the current Persephone Biannually? All Persephone books ordered from us cost £13 or three for £33 plus £2.50 postage per book.

PERSEPHONE BOOKS LTD
59 Lamb's Conduit Street
London WC1N 3NB

Telephone: 020 7242 9292
sales@persephonebooks.co.uk
www.persephonebooks.co.uk